WRECKED

DIRTY AIR SERIES BOOK THREE

LAUREN ASHER

WRECKED

Editing: Erica Russikoff

Proofreading: Gem's Precise Proofreads

Cover Designer: Books and Moods

Interior Formatting: Books and Moods

Trigger warning:
Reader's discretion is advised.

To my anxious people out there—this one's for you.
Don't let your worries win.

PLAYLIST

WRECKED - LAUREN ASHER

Lonely – Noah Cyrus	2:24	+
My Stress – NF	4:13	+
Me, Myself, & I – G-Eazy & Bebe Rexha	4:11	+
Slow Grenade – Ellie Goulding ft. Lauv	3:37	+
Tongue Tied – Marshmello, YUNGBLUD, & blackbear	3:06	+
Strange (Piano Version) – Gabrielle Aplin	2:50	+
Love Like That – Lauv	3:05	+
Rainbow – Kacey Musgraves	3:34	+
Catching Feelings – Drax Project	3:39	+
Graveyard – Halsey	3:02	+
Bad Things – Machine Gun Kelly & Camila Cabello	3:59	+
Somebody – Dagny	3:10	+
Conversations in the Dark – John Legend	3:57	+
Put Me Back Together – Caitlyn Smith	3:30	+
Unsteady – X Ambassadors	3:14	+
What We Had – Sody	3:03	+
Let Her Go (Acoustic) – Passenger	4:27	+
You Should Be Sad (Acoustic) – Halsey	3:18	+
Happiest Year – Jaymes Young	3:48	+
This Love – Taylor Swift	4:10	+
The One – Kodaline	3:53	+
Thinking Out Loud – Ed Sheeran	4:42	+

PROLOGUE

THIRTEEN YEARS AGO

Elena

"If you're not ready in five minutes then you don't get a story. You may be twelve years old now, but your bedtime is still at eight." My dad's voice booms through the halls of our second-story house.

I rush toward my bathroom. I'm a girl on a mission, hurrying through my bedtime routine since my homework took extra long today. After brushing my teeth, I rapidly pull my wavy hair into a braid and swap out my contacts for glasses.

I make it to my bed with thirty seconds to spare, jumping onto the soft mattress with a loud thud. *Papi's* footsteps echo through the hall as he pops his head in to check on me. I shoot him a large grin as I cross my legs and clasp my hands.

He opens the door wider, his brown eyes staring me

down. "Should I check if you flossed?"

I shake my head from side to side while fighting a giggle.

"The payment for your next dentist visit should come out of your piggy bank."

"I promise to do it tomorrow. I'm dying to read with you, and homework took forever. Why can't I go to school with all my friends? They're done with their work in an hour."

Ever since my dad became an ambassador for Mexico a few years ago, our lives have changed. I was enrolled in a private school, we moved to a better neighborhood, and now we have money to go on a few vacations. Mami stays home while *Papi* travels to and from the United States, working on important things with the government.

"Because one day you'll thank me for forcing you to attend an American school. All those hours I spend putting away bad people and fixing Mexico are paying off."

"But they make me speak English all day," I whine.

He taps my scrunched nose. "And what a great accent you have now. I'm glad the tuition is worth it. I look forward to the day you'll walk across the graduation stage at an American university."

He sits next to me, my bed dipping under his weight as he presses against me. He opens my copy of *The Hunger Games* to the last chapter we left off on, ready to start our nightly tradition. With his position, comes a lot of responsibilities, including missing our reading nights.

"Are you ready to get started?" My dad flashes me the chapter page.

"Yes, yes, yes!"

"You know the deal." He brushes aside a loose wave,

which escaped my braid.

I fight the urge to roll my eyes into the back of my head. "Yup. You start, I finish. Woo. Let's get this going." I swirl my finger in a motion telling him *less talking, more reading.*

His rough voice picks up right where we left off two weeks ago. I sit against my ruffled pillows, hanging on to every word, excited about Katniss surviving the cornucopia.

He passes me the book halfway through the chapter. My dad corrects me as I read, with my accent becoming heavier as my enthusiasm grows. The chapter flies by and leaves me desperate for more after a cliffhanger.

"One more chapter? *Please?*" I bat my dark lashes at him. They're long enough to brush against my glasses, an annoying issue usually prevented with contacts.

He shakes his head at me. "I wish I could, *chiquita. Mami* wants me to help her with the dishes before bed."

I cling to his side, pulling out all my stops. "But you've been gone *forever* so you owe me at least ten chapters."

"*Diez? No mames.*" He chuckles as he hugs me. "How about tomorrow? I'm willing to bargain with three chapters."

I pull away and cross my arms against my chest. "Fine. If you must." I wave him off, sighing as I fall against my pillow dramatically.

"I knew the new school was good for you. Look at you, acting like a proper lady. Your reading has improved a ton this year. I'm very proud of you." My dad plants a soft kiss on my forehead before he closes my bedroom door.

I turn off my lamp. My eyes shut and my mind drifts, thinking about the book and how the chapter ended. Curiosity about what will happen next eats away at my patience. Unable to fall asleep, I pull out a small flashlight from my nightstand I keep for nights like this.

I grab the book and enter my closet. If my parents found me reading this late on a school night, they'd give me a whole speech. To save us all, I hide in my usual spot behind my clothes and a couple of cardboard boxes. The flashlight casts away shadows as I open the book to the next chapter.

My finger guides me, holding my place as I practice reading. Katniss runs away from others while avoiding getting killed. She's brave and cool.

A scream sounds from somewhere downstairs. The hairs on my arms raise from how scary it sounds. My dad's shouting startles me, and my shaky fingers release the hardcover. It falls to the floor beside my feet with a heavy thud.

I hold my breath as I try to make sense of what I heard. Glass shattering in the distance and my mother's faraway pleading makes me panic. My heart beats faster in my chest as my father switches from English to Spanish, begging for mercy. Strange voices shout back before something else smashes.

Papi warned me about things like this. He taught me to stay in my room and wait for one of them to come get me.

Another scream from my mother takes my breath away. I stay stuck to the carpet, my fingers fumbling to grab the flashlight.

My dad shouts, his begging carrying through my closed bedroom door. I struggle to control my body's shaking.

The loudest popping sound echoes through my house like someone set off a firework downstairs. My dad stops shouting as my mom lets out a pained shriek.

My fingers tremble as I shut off my flashlight. The clicking noise sounds too loud, breaking the silence as darkness hides me. More pops happen, cutting off my mom's cries, sending a chill up my back.

One. Two. Three.

My eyes water as I struggle to breathe, the whooshing sound of my heart messing up my hearing. Deep down, I know something is wrong, with my parents not crying anymore. I shake my head as if the movement can erase the worry from my brain. The thought of something bad happening to them is too much for me.

I suck in a sharp breath as my door creaks open.

This is it. They're going to find me.

The closet door muffles the sound of footsteps. I pull my body into myself in an effort to disappear into the smallest corner of the closet. Boxes and racks of clothes hide me.

I'm no Katniss Everdeen. I'm a faker, hiding away, fear making me curl into a small heap of nothing. My closet doors open, and acid crawls up my throat at the noise. I don't dare swallow in fear of the stranger hearing me.

Some hangers rattle and my shoes are pushed around. I hold back the urge to breathe as something thuds against the box in front of me. As quickly as the unknown person came, they close the closet door.

"His daughter isn't here. Maybe she's with another family member? Or should we check all the rooms?"

I cover my mouth to prevent any sounds from escaping. Tears splash against my fingers, but I stay silent.

"*Olvídalo.* We got the job done. *El jefe* will be proud of us and he'll have to promote us after this. Eduardo has been a pain in his ass for years."

I fight with everything in me to not get sick and give myself away. Katniss wouldn't be crying. She would have marched out of the closet and done something. Anything.

I'm a weak, pathetic coward who barely catches my breath as I fight back the need to throw up.

A door slams somewhere downstairs.

Mami *and Papi will come for me. They're okay. Maybe a little hurt, but they will come.*

Minutes pass yet I don't hear any sounds in my house. More tears run down my face as I pray for *Papi* to come find me and carry me to bed.

I don't move for hours, afraid to step outside. My eyes adjust to the dark as I rock myself back and forth to calm down.

Eventually, I crawl out of my hiding place, my stomach dropping as I push the closet door open. I stop, listening for anyone who might know I'm here. Minutes pass before I think it's safe to move again.

Taking a deep breath, I open my bedroom door. It groans like one of those Scooby-Doo episodes. My heartbeat speeds up as I let out a shaky breath.

I hate the dark. My house feels creepy, with the lights all shut off and shadows lingering in the blackest of corners. The skin on the back of my neck tingles. My feet carry me down the stairs as I clutch my flashlight in my hands, desperation giving me the strength to keep moving.

"Mami? Papi?"

Silence. Pure silence and darkness make the vein in my neck pulse. I fight back the craving to run up the stairs and hide beneath my covers. Katniss would be brave in the dark—

strong and unafraid.

I trip over something blocking my path into the kitchen. My head drops on its own. "No! No no no no no."

The flashlight drops with a thump by my feet before rolling away. My legs give out as my knees hit the floor, my fingers clutching onto my mother's hand, cold in mine and feeling all wrong.

Tears flood my eyes, running down my cheeks before landing on her. I crawl over her body and tug her into me. "*¡Mami! ¡Despiértate!*" My trembling fingers brush her hair out of her face, my heart squeezing at her empty eyes staring back at me.

Cold, lifeless eyes without any sign of her warmth.

"*Mami, ¿qué pasa? Regresa a mi.*" My hands become slick as I lose my grip on her. I check out my fingers, but the lack of light makes it difficult to see what made them wet. Tears mess up my vision as I move toward my flashlight. The light lands on my dad, lying next to my mother, a trail of blood following him.

A sob breaks free as I crawl over to *Papi*, hugging him as I press my ear against his chest, hoping he's still alive. I can call a doctor or *Abuela* to help me.

"*Por favor, Papi, no me abandones.*"

Silence.

No heartbeat. No breathing. Nothing.

"No, no, no." Pained sounds escape me. I cry into his chest, losing control of myself. He smells all wrong. My fingers grip his suit, shaking him as if he can come back to life.

To come back to me.

"Don't leave me." My broken voice croaks.

No one responds. No one hears my cries. No one can save my parents. They are gone.

Dead.

Murdered.

My hands shine in the poor lighting, bloodied and slick. A wave of nausea hits. I barely make it a few feet before my dinner makes its way back up my throat, my body heaving until there is nothing left.

I place my shaky hands on the hardwood floor. A shard of glass impales my finger, the sharp pain pulling a hiss from me. Blood pours out of me as I rip the thick piece from my middle finger.

Tears run down my face before landing on the floor, disappearing into the blood trail my father left behind.

I lay on the slick tile, pulling my knees into my chest, wishing the killers had taken me too. My body shakes as I rock myself back and forth. I shut the flashlight off and allow the shadows to creep in, surrounding me, the silence tearing at my last bit of calm.

CHAPTER ONE

PRESENT DAY

Jax

"**J**ax, your breakfast is getting cold! What do you do all morning in your room? We threw out all your *Playboy* magazines years ago!" My mum's voice buzzes through the intercom in my old room.

This is what happens when I visit my family during the winter break. Nothing says vacation quite like early morning wake-up calls and accusations about jerking off before my morning tea.

I groan as I get out of bed and press the button on the speaker. "I'm disappointed in you. The last thing I want to hear when I'm on the brink of orgasm is my mum's voice."

Her laugh makes the tiny speaker in my room crackle. "You're disgusting. God forgive me for raising someone with such a naughty mouth. Get down here—your dad left for a meeting and I hate eating by myself."

We're that type of family, with intercoms and a full-time staff because Dad was a hotshot boxer back in the day who built a lavish life with nothing but his fists. He doesn't fight anymore, but his investments speak for themselves.

We fall into the same upper-crust financial bracket as the wankers who used to laugh at Dad because he came from poverty. Welcome to the dark side; we have trust funds and more investments than the goddamn stock market.

"I'll be there in a few." I step away from the wall and enter my bathroom, wanting to wash away my morning grogginess.

I hadn't planned on visiting before the start of the F1 season, but Mum begged me. It's hard to say no to her, especially when she says I won't be home for Easter. Plus, it's not like I had many fun activities planned, seeing as Liam's busy with Sophie, and Noah spends all his spare time with Maya. Our original trio is down to me.

God help us all.

I grab my medicine bottle from my toiletries bag. A pretty white pill stands out against my bronzed skin, tempting me to take the edge off. With a short half-life, an American doctor's clearance, and F1's mental-health clause, I'm able to take a Xanax whenever the mood strikes. And as of lately, it seems to be a fuck ton.

Me—a Formula 1 driver and arsehole extraordinaire—suffers from clinical anxiety. If people got wind of it, they might laugh their arse off before I kick theirs, showing them exactly what happens when I feel a different type of edgy. From the outside, I don't look anxious, but on the inside, I'm a motherfucking mess.

Ever since I was a kid, my brain's like a hamster on a wheel, focusing on the same issues over and over again. With anxiety comes panic attack symptoms. They hit me, with my knees nearly buckling, my chest feeling tight, and my fingers shaking to the point of uselessness.

The panic attacks started a couple of years ago, putting a damper on my mood and productivity. They usually hit when I'm stressed to my maximum like when I'm dealing with my parents or if I become overwhelmed with the future. They've progressively gotten worse over the past year. After one discreet attack last year in the middle of a race that McCoy labeled a "technical malfunction," I decided pills were my only solution. I didn't want to go to therapy, so I found an American doctor who would fix my problem without sharing my feelings. Now, Xanax keeps me sane enough to ensure my race car doesn't end up in the nearest wall during every race.

I count the panicky feelings as my penance for living my life to the fullest while my mum suffers. The shit happening to me is a constant reminder of Mum's similar symptoms. Huntington's Disease is a bitch like that, stealing moments from her year by year. It makes her weak and feeble. My role model and light of my life experiences the worst kind of medical prognosis, yet here I am living a lavish life with F1. Panic attacks and anxiety seem small in comparison.

But you know what the professionals say: a couple of Xannies a day make the worries go away.

I swallow back the pill before exiting my room, no longer in the mood to hang around with my shitty thoughts. My footsteps echo off the marble floors as I walk through our luxurious home. The bright walls match the light tones Mum chose, creating a welcoming space I find hard to leave at times. Hotel rooms I live out of each week fail to compare.

My mum smiles at me as I enter the kitchen built for a chef. "If it isn't my favorite son."

"I'm your only child, which means I'm automatically the favorite." I walk over and place a kiss on the top of her head before taking a seat across from her.

"You've always been a cheeky little thing who can never take a compliment." Her shaky fingers pull at her blonde, straight strands.

I'm the loving result of my mum's Swedish heritage and my dad's Black Londoner genes. Kids used to call me a mutt. Although it used to bother me, I've since learned women dig the pouty lips from my dad and the fused hazel eyes from both my parents. Not to mention the soft curls I currently have cropped at the sides while unruly at the top.

"I apologize. Where are my manners?"

"Probably lost somewhere between here and Monaco. Jackie brings up your casino night every year like clockwork."

"That story has outlived Prince Harry's Las Vegas trip. I'd like to say I'm possibly the rowdier Brit after all." I lift my brows up and down.

Our family maid, Jackie, places my breakfast and tea in front of me. "Even though your mother treats you like her little prince, you're anything but a royal."

"Ouch. You'll be kissing my boots once I'm knighted." I wink.

"By who? The bottle server at your VIP table doesn't count." Jackie crosses her arms as she leans against the kitchen island.

My mum lets out a loud laugh. "Do you have to leave in a week?"

"You're the only one I'd ever consider quitting F1 for, even if it was for a whole two seconds." I shake my head at her.

"That's one second better than yesterday. Imagine if I keep you here for months, then I'll probably get my way eventually." My mum lifts her teacup to her lips. Her trembling fingers cause the liquid to slosh before half the contents spill onto her hand and dress.

"Shit. Let me help you." I grab my cloth napkin and mop up the spilled tea, swiping away droplets from her pale skin.

"How embarrassing." She sighs.

My heart aches at the resigned look on her face. I sense a wave of panic building in my chest, the burn making my lungs hurt with each breath. *Xan, please feel free to kick in any time now.*

I exude a calmness that doesn't match my accelerated heart rate. "What did the doctor say yesterday?"

She sends me the smallest smile. "You don't need to fuss over me."

"Mum…"

She gives me the sassiest eye roll, replacing her distress. "Okay, fine. He said we can monitor the recent issues I've had with my mood and movement. But overall, I'm doing pretty well. They have high hopes."

"Is that good news then? Maybe it's not as bad as they think."

Her trembling hand cups my cheek. "Well, they say I can potentially live a few years longer than expected."

"So, you're talking another fifteen years with us, give or

take?" I resent how uncertain my voice sounds.

"It's not a sure thing. I wish I could give you more information, but that's all I have." Her smile wobbles.

I push my plate aside, no longer in the mood for food. "And what did he say could fix the tremors?"

"The only thing we can do is monitor how bad they get. Oh, and he said to help with stress, my son should stop being stubborn and get—"

"Nope."

"But—"

"The answer is no." I sigh. "I'm sorry. I hate to disappoint you, truly, but there's no point." My hands shake beneath the table.

"I can't help trying. Whenever I go to the doctor, I worry about you. I think of how anxious you get and the pills you started taking last year. Benzos aren't even good for you, so don't try to downplay it. I wonder if the shaking is because of—"

"Mum, please stop worrying about me." My voice comes out in a whisper. Shit, I hate how she can get to me like no other, but I need to stay firm. "Can we please drop this conversation? Let's enjoy the last week before I have to go. I don't know how soon I can make it back with Liam gone and everything changing at McCoy." My voice reeks of desperation, rasping and cracking as I look at her with wide eyes.

"I will, for now, but only because I fall for your puppy eyes every time. That's how you ended up with four cavities by five years old."

"I've always been a charmer." I shoot her my most dazzling smile, hoping to ward off all her worries about the topic.

"Trust me, I'm quite aware of your *Daily Mail* headlines. You've tempted me to bleach my eyes one too many times."

I cringe. "Sorry, Mum."

"I look forward to the day you meet the right kind of woman and put those club days to rest."

I laugh. "Meeting and committing are two very different things."

"With that smart mouth, who could resist you?"

Jackie grabs my unfinished plate. "Any woman who thinks with her brain rather than her clit."

Mum stifles her laugh. "Jackie, you're awful."

"I say it like I see it." Jackie shrugs before heading toward the sink.

"Now after ruining my appetite, the least you can do is make your mum happy. You know what I love more than anything."

"Dad?"

She snorts. "Good one. It looks like you got your jokes from me after all. Kind sir, please take me away to our spot."

"Only for you." I stand and offer her my tattooed hand.

She leans on me as I lead us through the house into the main living room. The grand piano gleams in the center of the space. I set her down on a comfortable chair before I sit on the piano bench, turning to look at her.

She claps her hands together and smiles. "The best decision I made as a parent was forcing you to take those lessons."

"Really? Of all the options of things you've done, that's the best?"

"Oh, yes. Your father can't carry a tune to save his life, so you're the next best thing."

I smile as I turn my back. My fingers lightly run across the ivory keys before I begin playing the *Jurassic Park* theme song.

My mum's voice carries over the music. "I can't even say I'm mad about how you rejected learning the classics for this kind of music."

"Once a rebel, always a rebel."

"Don't I know it. Who do you think you got it from? You grew up listening to bedtime stories of me ditching my family without a second glance back."

"You were a rebel with a cause. That's the best kind."

"And don't you forget it." She winks at me. "Play me *Clocks* next. I know you love it, too."

I lose myself in the music. Like a valve, I shut off my thoughts, letting the worries of my life float away with the melody.

The tune is hauntingly beautiful, echoing off the high ceilings. My mum smiles the entire time. She makes my whole visit worth it despite the ache in my chest every time she struggles.

Life resumes once I cover the piano keys and help Mum up the stairs to my parents' room. Her shaky legs and cane rip my good mood away from me, replacing happiness with despair.

That night, after Mum becomes tearful after dropping her fork three times during dinner, I text some old party friends about hitting up a club. And like nothing, my foul mood gets washed away with alcohol and bad decisions.

CHAPTER TWO

Elena

"With the care your grandmother requires, I'm not sure her needs are being met here. She should be put in a more permanent home meant for long-term patients. And with your funds, I'm not sure it's possible." The doctor looks up from his clipboard.

Everything always comes down to money.

Want to know how much I have? If you grabbed a euro, lit it on fire, and threw it in the trash can, that would summarize my bank account.

Every last euro I've made has either gone toward paying for my grandma's care or bills. Adulting is hard, but adulting with debt is the hardest.

Abuela warned me about getting a degree from an American university, but I didn't listen. I wanted to follow my father's wish of me attending a school in the US, only to learn how dreams look better on paper. What should have been the American dream has turned out to become my recurring nightmare of high-interest rates and excessive loans. Hell, the loan I took out for my degree could feed a small country for a month.

The ache in my chest builds as I look over at my grandmother—the only connection I have left to my dad. I'd do anything to keep her happy and healthy for as long as she will live.

Her glassy eyes find mine. "*¿Marisol?*"

"*Sí. Estoy aquí.*" I shove the bitter feeling of resentment toward *Abuela* down. Having a relative with Alzheimer's Disease has a funny way of making you crave simple things like not being called by your mother's name. The notion makes a dark cloud take up a spot over my head, but I fight the sadness at the reminder of my parents.

While I despise the bitterness about my *abuela* confusing me for my mom, I love looking like her. People say I'm a spitting image, with curves, dark hair with a natural wave, and average height. The only reminder of my father I'm left with is my brown eyes and long lashes. *Abuela* used to say it was the best of both of them.

I face the doctor. "How much more do those facilities usually cost?"

"Right now, you're looking at an estimated 4,000 euros per month, give or take."

The room spins as I process his words. That's an extra 48,000 euros a year I don't have. I'm barely making ends meet with my small Monaco flat the size of a child's shoebox.

"We can have her stay here for another month while you sort everything out, but you'll need to find other arrangements. Her condition has deteriorated rather quickly, I'm afraid, and our staff isn't equipped for her. The trial didn't work."

I fight the battle to keep the tears at bay. "There's nothing else you can do? No other medicine you can try?"

"In these cases, no. I'm so sorry, Ms. Gonzalez. I recommend enjoying the time you have left and getting her settled somewhere that can take care of her until..."

"Right." I bite my tongue to prevent myself from saying something I'll regret.

"If you wanted to consider moving back to Mexico, the services there are much cheaper. You could find a nice facility with your limited funds."

"I'll keep it in mind."

Nothing says a good plan quite like quitting my job and moving back to the same country my parents were murdered in. Sounds like a future as bright as the apocalypse.

The doctor leaves the room with a tense goodbye, giving me privacy with *Abuela*.

"*Nena*, how is Eduardito?" *Abuela* grabs onto my arm with a frail hand. Her words feel like she took a razor blade to my heart.

"Good. He's busy working." He hasn't worked since thirteen years ago, but who's counting.

Stop being bitter, Elena.

"Why do you look sad? Tell him to stay home more with you and baby Elena. I told him to work less but he doesn't listen. He's stubborn like his father."

I let out a deep breath, continuing on as if I'm my mother. There's no reason to remind *Abuela* how I'm not her daughter-in-law and her son is dead. The last time I mentioned it, she cried before threatening to kill the murderers herself. It took two nurses and a shot of something powerful to put her down. I realized that day how I was truly alone in my pain. *Abuela* can't handle the truth, and in the end, there's no point. The two thugs who wanted to earn the respect of a low-life gang leader by killing an ambassador died before ever seeing a court of law. That's how Mexico works. Seeking retribution is pointless, with its broken system filled with corruption and death.

For another painstaking hour, I spend time watching TV and eating lunch with her. I give *Abuela* a kiss on the cheek before saying goodbye. Once I step outside the facility, worried thoughts of how I'll afford the costs of her living arrangements consume me. I don't know how I'll go about helping her while staying afloat.

Option 1: Move *Abuela* into my apartment and become her full-time nurse while working from my office-slash-bedroom.

Option 2: Move back to Mexico AKA the seventh circle of hell.

Option 3: Become a stripper even though I was born with two left feet and a nasty case of stage fright.

I throw out the idea of moving back to Mexico. That option is both terrible for my mental health and my job, thus solidifying my reasoning against it. *Abuela* needs my help, which means keeping my job on this side of the hemisphere. I've spent years making European connections in the F1 world, and I refuse to give them up. With Elías's help and relationships with teams, I built a small business representing athletes.

Are there bigger firms that can do my job? Of course.

Are there firms willing to bend over backward to help their clients, no matter the time and situation? Definitely.

But those firms can't offer the kind of care I do. I only take on a few clients at a time, building up their social presence and putting them in the best light with an individualized plan. With Elías's referrals, I've built a steady base of loyal clients. It's nothing compared to a large PR company, but it's all mine. I built it from the ground up, and I'm not willing to part ways by moving back to Mexico. That feels like giving up, and *Papi* taught me to never give up, no matter how hard everything gets.

I walk back to my pathetic flat that's one year away from being condemned for structural instability. Self-pity doesn't suit me, but I deserve one night of drowning in my sorrows.

I consider calling Elías, but choose against it because he is busy with F1's pre-season checks. Even my best friend can't help me out of this mess. Dishing my financial woes to Elías always results in him offering me money. Even though I refuse, he does what he can, connecting me with other F1 companies to work on their PR. His referrals then recommend me to others, which has helped me build my brand as a reputation fixer.

Last year I had my biggest break yet after one of my newer client's recommended me to McCoy, a legendary F1 team. I was hired to help one of the top racers, Liam Zander, with his reputation. While that job was a highlight for me, it had an expiration date once Liam switched teams.

The walk back to my flat ends too quickly. I walk up the rickety steps and enter my studio apartment. My wallowing continues as I skip dinner, take a shower, and flop onto my bed. Done with putting off the inevitable, I pull out my phone and reassess my bank account.

It takes less than one minute to understand how screwed I am. I throw my phone toward the end of my bed as hopelessness destroys my positivity. "God, I know we've been on bad terms lately, but I'd be eternally grateful for a lifeline right about now. I'll take anything. And let's be real, I could use a miracle or three. I think I've paid my dues," I whisper up to the ceiling.

My head pounds as I come to terms with my situation. I mourn my *abuela* and the loss of her memory. Another year, another failed trial. The last connection to my old life is slipping through my fingers and there's nothing I can do to stop it. *Abuela* will never meet my kids, let alone remember me anymore. Grief wraps around me like a cloak.

I hate when the sadness comes in, like a dark fog stealing away my happiness. The feeling grips onto me with invisible talons and holds me hostage. It doesn't happen often, but when it does, my whole life turns upside down.

My phone buzzing interrupts my thoughts. I move to grab it from the corner of my bed. An unknown number flashes across the screen, and I answer without hesitation. "Hello?"

"Hi, is this Elena Gonzalez?" A male's voice greets me.

"This is she." My voice cracks.

"Great. My name is Connor McCoy. I was given your contact information because you worked for Peter McCoy last year. I'm not sure if you're up to speed with everything, but he had to take a permanent leave of absence, so I took over his position. I know the season is about to begin, but I need your help with a PR project."

"What type of project?" It takes everything in me to control my voice, not wanting it to reek of desperation.

McCoy only has two racers. Elías, who is new to the team

after Liam left last season, and the other…well…I know enough.

"We want to hire you for a private job. It requires a lot of your time, including an exclusivity contract and a non-disclosure agreement."

"What are the stipulations?" I remain nonchalant despite my body buzzing with anticipation. At this point, if it doesn't involve removing my clothes, I'm all for it.

Hell—even that sounds tempting after checking my funds.

"We would be paying you eight thousand euros per month for ten months, starting this March. Plus, a bonus of twenty-thousand euros if you can make it until the final Prix the first week of December." He makes the second sentence sound like a prayer. "We want you to work solely with Jax Kingston. The job would include keeping an eye on him and helping positively boost his presence in the media."

One-hundred thousand euros? For that kind of money, I'd do just about anything.

"I have a few clients I would need to check in with. If that's okay, then I can absolutely help with whatever you need."

Connor breaks down the main parts of my contract, listing everything I need to do throughout the race season. His plan is smart and well-thought-out. I say yes with little trepidation, knowing I can't resist the answer to my prayers.

Not all heroes wear capes. Turns out some rock badass tattoos and a McCoy race suit.

CHAPTER THREE

Jax

When I was seven years old, my dad thrust me in front of a punching bag after I took a whack at a kid on a kart race podium. I was mad at the young wanker who made fun of my parents' relationship. That day, my dad looked me in the eyes and told me I needed to chase away my demons. Unfortunately, after all my dad's efforts, it looks like I decided to run beside them.

Demons come in all shapes and sizes. Anger. Anxiety. An aversion to the future. Mine tempt me to submit to Xanax in order to have some peace of mind. I'm not a drug addict. I swear it. But I'm addicted to the temporary relief a Xan provides.

I imagine heaven is a lot like my head after the pill kicks in—silent, calm, and a hell of a lot less dark.

I didn't mean for my life to take such a drastic turn this year. As Mum's condition becomes more pervasive and Dad grows desperate to help her, I toy with instability. I give in to my vices when the going gets tough. But with avoidance comes anxiety, like a freight train hitting me when I least expect it.

Racing keeps me sane. Some people say they don't believe in love at first sight, but to me, that was it. I fell in love with adrenaline—a nasty lover who leaves me as quickly as she came. I chase after her in any way I can have her. Drinking, driving, fucking—all adrenaline-inducing activities to keep the edginess inside of me at bay.

"You sure made a mess of things." Connor McCoy faces me in all his glory. Instead of having fun in Melbourne before the season starts, I get to park my arse inside of a conference room.

"I fucked up. You know it, I know it, even Elías, my new fucking teammate, knows it."

"What you did is concerning. Fuck—" Connor closes his blue eyes and pinches the bridge of his nose "—don't blow my trust and force me to find a different solution to manage your anxiety." His British accent has an edge to it.

"It won't happen again because I've learned my lesson. Those pills don't pair well with alcohol, no matter what the rap songs say." I didn't consider the side effects of mixing the two, seeing as Xanax only recently became my newest crutch to ease my anxiety.

Connor's jaw ticks. "Quit fucking around. There were videos of you dancing on tables, acting like a wild man, before blacking out next to a urinal."

I withhold the urge to cringe. "I hate to say I'm not a man of class and honor in the wee morning hours."

"Your dumbassery can compete with a Bravo reality show."

I drop my mouth open in faux shock. "I'm almost insulted. Unlike those shows, my life has a captivating storyline."

His grim expression sets me straight. "Be serious. I understand your reason for being upset. I'm sorry about your mum. Mine visited yours last week, and she told me it wasn't a good one."

"Don't. We do *not* bring her up here," I snap.

Fuck Connor's mum for gossiping about mine. You'd think with London being a huge city, the rich would stay in their own mansions far away from one another. But nope, Connor's mum happens to attend a weekly smutty novel club with mine.

"Fine. How about you evaluate your public image? Kids look up to you for fuck's sake. What you're doing isn't doing wonders for your career, with sponsors and fans questioning your stability."

"I guess you're lucky that I only have one more year on my contract before it gets renewed."

Connor tugs on his blonde hair. "No. *You're* lucky I like you, despite how much of a dick you are. At least I like you enough to defend your position to the board of sponsors who dislike me as it is. I refuse to give those lazy twats what they want, so pull your shit together. With Liam gone, you're the company's only hope of landing on podiums."

"I'll try my best to be better." I swallow back the regret. Connor didn't need to stand up to the board, but he did so as a favor to me. And for that, I'm grateful.

"I want to make sure I've made my point clear." Connor's teddy bear stare doesn't pack the same punch as his predecessor, Peter. But at least he's a positive guy who sneers less, plus he puts up with my shit.

"Trust me, I got your point. Last week was a lapse in judgment." Guilt sits heavy inside of my goddamn chest, tightening around my lungs like a boa constrictor.

"More like last week was a tough week for your family that you happened to experience firsthand. But with your mum's condition and your unpredictability, I can't take the risk of this happening again during the season. The press is saying you're in a downward spiral, and we can't have that."

"I'll be better and won't make mistakes again. Call me a whiskey bottle half full kind of guy."

Last week was rough, to put it lightly. I used alcohol to dull the torture of sitting by while Mum battles her own hell. Tremors. Mood swings. The whole fucking spectrum of symptoms put a damper on our week together.

Connor glares at me. "I'm being serious. You know there are better options out there to maintain anxiety symptoms, right?"

"Tell me, how does one say they don't give a fuck because there's no point?"

"Well, I see a point, so I've taken your problem into my own hands. Think of me as your fairy godfather."

"I prefer Al Pacino's version over a Disney fairy tale."

"Well, be prepared for my offer you—quite literally—can't refuse."

I slowly clap my hands together a few times in the most sarcastic way possible. "Well done. Can't wait to hear what your grand plan is."

"Since I'm busy with all the crap Peter left behind, I hired someone special. I thought it would do you some good to have a little one-on-one PR help."

I curse to myself as I lean my head against the back of the chair. PR teams are the worst, contributing nothing but headaches and judgments.

Connor's perceptive eyes find mine. "I won't share what's going on with your mum to the PR rep because my mum would kill me. But your alcohol issues and party ways are up for grabs. Whenever you feel like being an arsehole, think of the team and your chance at a World Championship this year. Do you really want to blow it?"

"No, I don't." I take a deep breath as someone opens the door.

Whiskey-colored eyes stare at me, framed by thick lashes. Her thin nose tips at the end before my eyes land on her plump lips. Bee-stung doesn't cover it. More like she ran straight into a wasp nest and her lips lost the battle, both upper and bottom about the same size. Wavy, dark hair falls around her, sitting above her breasts, swaying against her silk blouse. Her outfit emphasizes her figure, the curves of her on display, begging me to kneel in front of her like a fucking shrine.

Elena checks all my boxes. Hips I want to grip, an arse I want to watch while I fuck her from behind, and tits I wouldn't mind kissing my way around. But with her, I don't have the ability to think with my dick.

I somehow withhold a groan as my head lifts from the back of the chair. "Elena, fancy seeing you here."

"Jax, can't say I'm sorry to be back." She takes a seat across from me and puts her small hand out. I grab onto it with one tattooed hand, black and white fake bones engulfing hers as I give her fingers a squeeze. A hum of recognition buzzes through me. Hot, burning desire makes my hand squeeze hers harder as my dick registers her presence. I frown, hating the way one touch from her throws me off.

Last time I saw Elena, Liam announced he was leaving

McCoy after placing runner-up in the Championship. With his departure, I thought I was free of her. But like the moron I've been lately, I was oh-so wrong.

I don't like being around Elena more than I have to. Elena has this way of looking at me like she knows there's something off about me. Like she wants to see *me*. Not the guy who lands on podiums each week. Not the man with hundreds of tattoos, looking like a badass yet falling short because of poor decisions. And definitely not the guy who sleeps around to cover up the emptiness he feels each day of his life.

And if there is anything I've learned over the past few years while watching my mum struggle, it's that I can't allow myself the luxury of someone learning my secrets. To be honest, Elena couldn't afford a piece of my mind even if she won the lottery three years in a row.

Connor claps his hands together. "I called Elena after I heard she worked with Liam and you last year. I thought it would be better to hire someone you know."

More like someone I know I want to fuck, but A for effort. "Long time no see. Vacation over in hell?"

"Lucifer asked for you to stop by sometime soon. Says he's got a special place ready for you." Her accent lulls on the words, a melodic rhythm capturing my attention.

"Only if I get to drag you down there with me. After all, hell is only fun when I'm paired with the best tour guide."

Connor claps his hands together and smiles at us. "Well, glad you two get along well, seeing as Elena will be your favorite fan this season."

My eyes dart from Connor to Elena. "I really hope that doesn't mean what you're insinuating."

Elena laughs at my gruffness, her eyes shining bright under the lights.

Connor hands Elena an F1 exclusive access pass. "Elena is going to assist you in fixing up your image. She'll be staying with you throughout the Prix schedule to keep you in line."

My jaw tightens to the point of popping. "And what the fuck does that entail?"

"Elena signed a contract where she'll live with you, making sure you have McCoy's best interests at heart. We'll cover all her expenses because we want her to concentrate on helping you. Also, she'll be joining you for summer break wherever you decide to stay. Seeing as last week didn't go so well, I think it's best to make sure someone watches you all season, break included."

Not only do I have to hang out with this vixen but now I have to live with her? Bloody hell. If there is one thing I'm sure about, it's how I don't deserve this kind of karma.

"This has to be a joke. I didn't sign up for a ball and chain." My words come out in a half-growl.

"And I didn't sign up for a driver with enough loose marbles to ruin a game of Mancala." Connor throws me an agitated look.

"And what do you expect us to do? Braid each other's hair and watch movies together?"

Connor's eyes slide from me to Elena, shooting her a warm smile. "Ignore his temper tantrum. He'll get used to having you around." *Fat fucking chance that happens.* "I expect we're good from here, but you can text me if you have any questions." He looks over at me and silently mouths *behave* before exiting the room.

"Well, you reacted like I expected." She crosses her legs,

pulling my attention toward them. Her jeans cling to her body and emphasize everything I need to avoid.

"Looks like you got upgraded from PR rep to glorified babysitter. I've always wanted to live out that fantasy. Care to roleplay?"

She taps her manicured hand on her knee. "Only if you promise to go to sleep by ten o'clock."

"It can be arranged after a good fucking."

A healthy blush creeps into her cheeks as her eyes roam over my upper body. I sit taller, enjoying the buzz from her perusal. Similarly, the blood in my head rushes to another place. The more fun kind that wouldn't mind making Elena blush under different circumstances.

Her eyes narrow. "Can't you fall asleep to a Netflix show like the rest of us?"

"Where's the fun in that?"

"Speaking of fun, I have some rules since we will be living together." She flips her hair over her shoulder, evading my gaze.

"I expect nothing less from you."

She pulls out an iPad from her purse, unaware of my attraction toward her. The very one making my jeans uncomfortably tight and my breathing heavy. "You lasted three months without my help. I checked out your social media presence and it looks like we have our work cut out for us. Since your image has hit an all-time low, there's no way but up."

"And what exactly does that entail? Will you be my fake girlfriend? I love that type of story."

She rolls her eyes. "Not even a girlfriend can save you from your reputation. I've been planning different outings and experiences to make your persona so clean, you'll rival a Disney

Channel star."

I raise a brow. "Before the drugs and alcohol?"

Elena laughs. I hate the way it sounds—soft, carefree, untainted by anguish. While I struggle with hidden jadedness and pessimism, she radiates hopefulness and warmth. I'm tempted to test how long it takes to pop her bubble of positivity.

"Sure. But before we get started, I need you to tell me about what happened during your one-night stand with a club urinal."

A throaty laugh escapes my mouth. The sound is foreign, especially after my week from hell. "Well, when a man and a woman love each other very much..."

She throws a pen at me. It bounces off my chest before rolling back toward her.

I rub my chest. "Violence is never the answer."

"Says the guy who recently broke a paparazzo's camera worth two thousand euros."

"Okay, violence is *usually* not the answer, but the reporter's racist undertones set me off. Hey, from a PR perspective, at least I paid for a new one."

"Throwing a thousand euros in his face doesn't count."

"Yet he bent over quicker than my last fuck to grab the bills."

She scowls at me. "So, the club story?"

If she isn't letting me off easy today, I can't wait to see how the rest of the season will go. "Over break, I made a stupid decision when I drank and took an anti-anxiety med in the same night. Honest truth. So, it's safe to say the night didn't turn out like I wanted it to."

Her eyes soften, losing the hardness she had moments before. "I didn't know you needed medication to control your anxiety."

I shrug. "Not many people do."

"Have you tried to talk with a psychologist to help manage your anxiety symptoms? Or have you reconsidered your current medication?"

"No because that would involve talking, and I absolutely, under no circumstances, like talking about my feelings. Fuck that, so don't bother trying. I have a US medical doctor on retainer who does the job just fine." I tap my fingers against the table.

She stares at me. It's unsettling how much I pay attention to the gold flecks in her brown eyes. Absolutely positively un-fucking-settling.

"You need to be honest with me. Is there anything else I need to be on the lookout for besides bouts of anxiety?"

Her words activate the ominous timer in my head. I push away the swell of anxiety building up inside of me, not keen on freaking out in front of her. "Nope. Just my usual stint with a bottle of Jack. We're mutually exclusive, so please don't get any ideas."

She gives me a half-assed eye roll and a shake of her head, diverting her attention back to her iPad. "Speaking of alcohol... I may not be part of the babysitter's club, but I still have some rules."

"My favorite part of rules is finding a way to break them."

"Jax..."

The sound of my name leaving her lips sends a rush of energy through me. Her eyes burn, tempting me to push for more of a reaction from her.

Stop being a total wanker. "Okay, fine. Let me hear how you want to suck the fun out of this season." A small smile tugs at the corners of my lips as she nervously twirls her Apple pencil. At least I make her as uneasy as she makes me.

"First, you need to lay off the alcohol. I'm not telling you to stop completely, but practice self-control. I can't pull you out of a random bathroom, let alone help you walk back to our hotel room."

Why does my dick throb in my jeans at the thought of us sharing a hotel room? That's rather...unusual. The idea of sharing a space with a woman in the past would've had me laughing to the point of tears. But with Elena, I find it enticing, the forbiddance of our situation like an aphrodisiac of the worst kind.

Gritting my teeth together, I nod. "Fair enough. I don't want to drink like I did over break either." Sometimes I can't help it, and alcohol clouds my brain enough to offer me a temporary reprieve. But for my chance at the Championship, I'll try to battle my problems in a different way during this season.

Try being the keyword.

"Second, you need to be honest with me. If something goes wrong, I want to know so I can help you. If I find out the next day in the papers, then it's too late and I'll be pissed."

"Fine." I nod my head at her second rule because a raging Elena sounds almost as fun as crashing my car during the first lap of a Prix.

"Next—"

"Fuck me. How many rules do you have typed up?" I cross my arms against my chest. Her eyes linger on my forearms before snapping back to my face, catching my devious smile.

She blushes as she tucks a loose wave of hair behind her ear. "Only a few more. If we both go back to the suite at night, that's it. No leaving. I want to trust you, which means you can't go sneaking off to do God knows what."

"God may not know but the Devil sure approves." My smile grows wider as her fidgety hands return to nervously twirling her pencil.

"Right…well either way, no sneaking off. This job means a ton to me and I need to be able to trust you. They're paying me a lot of money to help you." Her eyes dart off to the side.

"Well, love, at least the paycheck at the end of all this will keep you around. Don't pretend you don't get off on helping out wankers like me who are more fucked up than Donald Trump's White House."

"No. I get off on helping people reach their fullest potential. And I see what you can be if you move past this terrible public persona."

"Don't strain your eyes too hard. You may not like what you find after all."

"I don't need to like you to do my job."

Well shit, she has me there.

Elena taps away on her tablet. "Last thing. I'm going to be following you pretty much everywhere. It's a part of my contract." She bites her lip, revealing the edge of her white teeth.

It's concerning how she gives me a semi with a glance and a bite of her lip. My cock doesn't understand why Elena is bad news. The worst fucking news, like worse than Prince Harry leaving the royal family, and that shit was catastrophic.

Dear cock, please meet the rock and the hard place you'll be stuck between this season.

"Does that mean we share a bedroom? I've always wanted a human pillow to cuddle with."

She lets out a mock gasp. "Would you look at that? Bedrooms are not included. Really, I plan on keeping it PG-13 between us so..."

"I hear PG-13 movies have sexy scenes now..." I let out a low whistle.

"Oh my God. Nothing like that will happen between us."

The way her eyes light up as she laughs worries me because I'm tempted to make her do it again. I remain silent, trying to wrap my head around having to spend months with someone like her.

Google, how does one say I'm fucked *in Spanish?*

She shuts her iPad case closed. "Seriously, Connor didn't include an interoffice relationship clause, but it's kind of a given why we're not pursuing that option."

Of course, Connor didn't include something like that. He wants to stake his claim on a hot piece of ass. F1 has few and far females working in the industry because women avoid our hostile workplace cloaked in sexism and manipulation.

Despite Connor not including a clause, I need to remember to keep my distance from her. No matter what, she and I can't happen. It's the reason I resent being around her more than necessary. She causes reactions I'm not accustomed to, ones I don't want to explore no matter how much I like her brand of attitude.

I don't get that kind of story.

While my friends are fit for an ending straight out of the latest cheesy rom-com, I'm better suited for the *Game of Thrones'* Night's Watch—isolated until the day I die.

CHAPTER FOUR

Elena

Welcome to hell. Population: Two.

Last week when Connor called and gave me a rundown about my job this year, he told me how I needed to live with Jax. It marks my weirdest contract deal to date, but I couldn't say no to the thousands of euros he offered. With everything at stake, I'm willing to do just about anything to revive Jax's reputation.

Connor explained the surface-level issues with Jax and why McCoy needs him to be the best this season. With Liam switching teams this year after a falling out with McCoy's ex-CEO, Peter, Jax is the new face of the company. This season is Jax's best chance at winning a second World Championship.

With all the new stress, Connor's worried Jax might crack. I'm here to make sure he handles the pressure with the added bonus of me fixing up his image.

Jax and I walk into our extravagant hotel suite. If I want to approach life more positively, I can highlight the two-thousand-square-foot space with its own dining area, sectional couch, and separate rooms. Except one look at the hulking figure next to me throws my positivity out the window of our penthouse.

No area seems large enough when I have to spend time with Jax day in, day out. I barely made it out unscathed last season working around him. Jax prevented me from getting anywhere in his vicinity besides the forced PR sessions with Liam. Any time we were in the same room, Jax avoided any conversation with me. I'd take it personally if it weren't for the fact that most athletes hate working with PR reps.

At first when I started working with racers, I thought it was my personality. But a few years in this line of work has taught me no one likes being told what to do, especially cocky athletes who have listening skills similar to a toddler. My job helped me build a tolerance for assholes whose egos are so large, they could apply for their own zip code.

Elías asks me every year why I choose to work PR for the biggest douchebags in Europe. The answer is simple: I don't like perfect people. The most challenging jobs are the best ones, so give me all the broken individuals who desperately need someone to help them. Those are the clients I like. The ones who are unapologetically themselves, time and time again. They're my favorite kind because I find the journey to help them reach the top all the more exciting.

Despite my resilience and experience, Jax triggers me like no other, with his aversion toward me. I can't understand why it bothers me, let alone understand him. But I'm not an idiot. I see how he treats others, and—newsflash—it isn't as standoffish as he acts with me.

Does it affect my self-esteem? No.

Does it affect my patience? Hell-freaking-yes.

I don't know what to make of him, but I'm on a mission to learn everything there is to know about him. Jax wears angst like an accessory. Black tends to be his aesthetic unless he needs to wear McCoy's white branding. His daily wardrobe includes Doc Martens, T-shirts, and ripped jeans. He rocks jackets with slogans and decorates his tattooed fingers with rings. To put it lightly, he's bad to the last British bone in his body.

No matter how attractive he is, his guarded hazel eyes scream to stay the hell out of his way. Not to mention his attitude toward me is about as friendly as walking down a dark alley at midnight.

"Welcome to the land of the lavish. Enjoy it while it lasts." He waves his hand around the suite like a half-assed episode of *MTV Cribs*.

"Wow, way to set the bar with your warm welcome. Thank you so much." I stare at him, trying not to linger on how his shirt highlights bulging muscles and arms covered with tattoos.

Jax coughs, getting my attention again. His eyes have a rare lightness about them. "If you want to see my tattoos up close, all you have to do is ask."

"Not interested, but thanks for the offer."

"Some women would beg for a chance to see them in all their glory."

I wrinkle my nose. "If that's what women beg for, they should reassess their priorities."

His laugh pulls a smile from me. "Don't knock others' priorities. Not everyone is a masochist, volunteering to work with me."

"That's rich coming from the guy who enjoys blowing his career to shit as a pastime."

He runs a hand across his stubble. "There is one thing I like blown, and I can assure you it isn't my career."

I hold back the laugh I desperately want to let out. "Let's play a game: you keep quiet and not speak anymore. Your mouth is going to get you into trouble."

"You'd be surprised by the kinds of trouble I can get into silently." He shoots me a wicked smile.

"Surprised? Probably. Interested? Definitely not."

"I'm going to appreciate having you around. There's nothing that gets me going quite like someone hell-bent on resisting me."

"Resisting you insinuates I'm interested in anything more than helping you."

"I vote helping me orgasm is right up there with fixing my reputation. What do you say?"

I hit him with my best *get over yourself* look. I grab onto my luggage and move toward my room. "I'm going to take a nap and shower before the press conference."

"Sleeping on the job already?"

I let out a deep sigh, not in the mood for his teasing anymore. "Connor emailed you the questions and answers I came up with yesterday. Think you can manage reading them?"

"Already done."

I freeze, caught off guard. "Really?"

"Yes, contrary to your opinion of me, I can read. Rather quickly too, if I do say so myself. Now, since I've been a good boy, can you set up the telly with my favorite cartoon to make sure I don't get bored?" He throws himself onto the living room couch.

My brow arches. "Telly?" I need to google British slang because some of the things he says make no sense without context clues. Who started calling a car trunk a *boot* anyway?

"*Televisión.*" His fake Spanish accent rolls off his tongue as he points at the remote on the TV stand next to me.

I attempt with everything in me not to smile. "I'll see you in a couple of hours." Choosing to ignore his request, I enter my room and shut the door behind me.

"I can do this. Think of it like any other job. A job with a man whose voice sets off every nerve ending in my body, but a job nonetheless," I whisper to myself as I unpack my clothes.

A warm shower sets me up for success, ridding me of the jet lag I felt earlier. I lie down and shut my eyes, willing myself to find the patience to deal with Jax.

After my hour-long nap, I get dressed. A silk blouse and high-waisted paper bag pants are my usual outfit—simple, basic, and professional. My accessories include heels and my iPad.

I leave my room to find Jax lounging on the couch, tapping a booted foot against the coffee table as he lazily switches channels. His eyes rake over me. As if my body tracks the movement, my skin warms.

Wow. If this is the feeling I have from a simple look, I'm screwed for the season. Maybe the roommate idea wasn't the best after all. He manages to cause a fluttering sensation in my stomach from one gaze and a simple tug of his lips.

"I'm impressed. You made it out with two minutes to spare." He taps at his expensive watch. "Usually ladies are always running late."

"Unlike the lovely company you've had before, I tend to be on time. Especially for schedules I create."

"Well, I rushed so hopefully my hair looks okay." He runs a finger through his curls, cropped to his skull on the sides, while looking wild on the top. My fingers itch to check if they're as silky as they look. His defined facial bones appear etched from bronzed metal, perfectly balanced with soft, kissable lips.

"Your hair is fine, but your smile looks like a nightmare." I fiddle with the strap of my tote bag.

His smile makes my skin feel like someone cranked up the thermostat in the room. "We're going to have fun together. Nothing I like more than a girl who gives as much as she can take."

"Somehow you make things sound more perverted than necessary."

"It's a talent."

"A talent to make every sane woman run in the opposite direction of you."

He shakes his head. "I don't want the sane ones. Where's the fun in that?"

"For someone like you, I can imagine it's a bit of a bore to be with someone stable."

"I don't know. You look stable yet I bet you're wild in bed. Kind of like the look you get in your eye as you check me out when you think I'm not looking."

I choke on my sudden intake of breath. "What?"

"It's okay, love. Your secret's safe with me."

"About as safe as fucking a one-night stand without a condom."

Jax lets out a loud laugh. "Maybe having you around won't

be a total nightmare after all."

Wait, what?

He picks up his buzzing phone. "The car is here."

I walk to the hotel door. "Let's not be late for your first conference because that's not a good look after everything."

"Being good is boring, and I loathe being boring." Jax follows me into the hall.

I hide my smile behind my hair as we walk toward the elevator. "You couldn't be boring if you tried."

"Careful now. You're going to make me think you're flirting with me." Specks of gold and green swirl around his eyes.

"Flirting with you means I have to like you first. And well, that's a no from me, *burro*."

"Liar, liar, Elena's cheeks are on fire." He taps his with emphasis. A pair of snake eyes stare back at me, slithering through the fake skeleton bones inked on his hand. "You're testing my self-esteem, but your sexy Spanish talk makes up for it."

We enter the waiting elevator. Jax keeps his eyes focused on the elevator's buttons as I spend the short trip explaining today's obligations and expectations. He nods his head, easing my growing nervousness about his first publicity event since his last PR disaster.

We exit the hotel and step into the back of a waiting McCoy SUV, evidence of the lavish life Jax lives as an F1 driver. The fresh scent of lemons and leather invades my nose.

I look over at Jax, attempting to get a read on him. Last year, although I focused mainly on Liam, I was intrigued by the man sitting next to me. The little time I spent with him was enough to pique my interest and made me want to learn what weaknesses he disguises as strengths.

Jax met his match. I'm not one to back down from a challenge, especially with my future on the line. He might be a beast on the track, but I can hold my own in the PR scene.

The silence doesn't last long between us, with Jax breaking it first.

"Why did you agree to this dumb challenge?" Jax taps his fingers against his knee to an unknown tempo.

"Because you're a nuclear bomb waiting to deploy at the push of a red button."

"What a fascinating visual. Have you been planning to say that one all day?" His eyes harden.

"You caught me. I spend hours thinking of my rebuttals."

"I'd prefer for you to think of me in a different circumstance, but it's only a matter of time."

I tilt my head at him. "You think rather highly of yourself."

"Quite the opposite. But I understand women find me rather irresistible."

My scoff sounds more like a laugh. "I find you irresistibly annoying. Does that count?"

"It's a start."

I ignore him, not interested in flirting. He continues to move his fingers against his knee to the beat of something I can't put my finger on.

"I never wanted this," he mumbles while looking out the window.

"What?"

"To become this kind of guy." His eyes meet mine as he turns his head toward me.

"And what kind of guy is that?"

"The kind who ruins things before they ever have a chance at becoming something good. The kind who needs a babysitter because they can't be trusted."

"It's your choice to teeter on the edge of too much drinking and partying, functioning yet barely living. No one is forcing you to mess up your career."

"Right. My career." His resigned voice hints at more.

"Do you even want to win a Championship?"

His spine straightens. "If you're asking that question, then I guess you lack the intelligence to help me. What a pity to support the old stereotype of beauty over brains."

I grind my teeth together, fighting with everything in me to not snap at him. How does someone go from somber to full-blown asshole in a few seconds? "Well then, you have to start acting like a winner. You've lived in Liam's glory for years, taking a backseat on succeeding. So, instead of pretending to be a badass, why don't you become one?"

He turns in his seat, giving me a full-frontal vision of him I can't ignore. The sight of him alone makes my lungs constrict. Everything physically about him appeals to me. From his straining muscles to the way his jeans cling to his body.

Jax's eyes brighten as if our back-and-forth gives him energy. "I like your form of bluntness. Vicious words from seductive lips, my favorite kind of torture."

"I could say the same thing about you except I'm not a glutton for punishment."

"For someone who looks all uppity and perfect, you sure have a naughty mouth. I've yet to meet someone quite like you."

My heart beats faster at his look of appreciation. "Someone

who can put up with your attitude? Must be a bit jarring, I'm sure."

"You have no idea." He surprises me when his thumb runs over the thin bones of my hand, tracing the divots of my knuckles. I take a deep breath, inhaling Jax's woodsy soap scent, wondering if he even bothers putting cologne on.

Damn, he smells intoxicatingly good.

"What are you doing?" I rasp. Something electric happens wherever his thumb lingers, leaving behind a path of warmth. *¿Qué pasa conmigo?*

"Seeing if your skin is as soft as it looks." His eyes capture mine, the swirl of colors darkening.

"Well, can you not? New rule: no touching." I pull away from him despite the urge I have to keep my hand on the leather seat.

Ugh. I'm such a cliché, physically attracted to a guy who I should stay far away from.

He chuckles, the rough sound rumbling against his chest. "So many rules. I think a small part of you wants to be let free."

"And let me guess: you want to be the one to offer that kind of help?"

"Nope. You don't want someone like me. I'm not what you're looking for."

That's not what I expected to come out of his mouth. "Why's that?"

"I'd be the kind to break you rather than set you free. Like a caged bird, pretty to look at, clipped wings and all."

How the hell does anyone respond to that? I didn't think Jax would be as gloomy as he is. He comes off more jaded than last year, calling out to the dark, little twisted part of me.

We stay quiet for the rest of the car ride. I ignore the way Jax stares at me, although my body remains hyperaware of him.

Excitement replaces annoyance as we near the F1 paddock area. Our driver drops us off along the main street, the equivalent of F1's fraternity row. Each team has a motorhome where crew members and racers kick back and relax before and after races. Jax and I stroll past the shiny buildings of all different colors and styles, oozing energy and ostentatiousness.

We walk up to the press conference suite, a plain gray building where reporters, camera crews, and racers meet for pre- and post-race conferences. Jax opens the door to the press room, which is stirring with activity. Cameramen rush around setting up tripods while reporters gather their microphones and notepads for questions.

Two tables are centered on a stage with name cards. Jax's best friend, Liam, sits beside Noah and Santiago, two Bandini racers. My first F1 client and Jax's new teammate, Elías Cruz, sits behind Jax's assigned seat.

"Remember to play nice with the other kids," I say low enough for only Jax to hear.

"But what if they don't like me?" He hits me with puppy-dog eyes that should be banned for people like him. No one with tens, if not hundreds, of tattoos should be able to look as innocent as he does.

I give him a soft shove, my hands embarrassingly lingering on his firm chest. He shoots me a smile over his shoulder before stepping onto the stage. I chalk up his happiness to being surrounded by his friends for the first race of the season.

Elías abandons his chair to come over to me. "When you told me about your private project, I didn't think it was working solely with Jax. Forgetting the little people already? I thought we were best friends."

I laugh as I look up at him. Elías has a preppy handsomeness to him with a perfect smile, light skin, and a head of dark hair. Brown eyes meet mine before he pulls me in for a hug and gives me a kiss on my cheek.

"It's only for the season."

"What if I need something? Like what if I do something stupid, or I punch someone in the face by accident."

"If you punch someone in the face by accident, seek legal counsel, not me. Anyway, I'll be working around you all the time. Don't be dramatic."

"I almost thought you were too good for me now. I was your first client after all." His lower lip juts out.

I tap my chin with my index finger. "When you put it like that…maybe."

He softly elbows me in the ribs. "One month with him and you'll be begging to work with me again."

"Two hours with him and I'm already tempted."

Elías laughs. "Well, at least he's pretty to look at. Could be worse."

That's Elías. He's my daily dose of positivity.

"Cruz, get your ass over here. You're holding everyone up." Jax's rough voice reverberates off the walls of the press room.

Heads snap in our direction, drawing unwanted attention.

"See? Catch you later. Looks like my new teammate is in a mood today." He waves before jogging over to his seat.

My body turns toward the stage, finding Jax scowling at me.

Balled fists rest in front of him. I shoot him my fakest smile. His eyes flash with annoyance before he focuses on Noah, tuning me out again.

Noah's blue eyes assess me before turning his attention back to Jax and Liam.

Jax, Liam, and Noah are close. They're a group of guys with enough issues to compete with *Abuela*'s old *telenovelas*. They could have a show based on Noah dating Santiago's sister, Maya, while Liam dates Maya's best friend, Sophie, the daughter of Noah's team principal. I wish I were making this up. It's like if *Romeo and Juliet* met *The Fast & The Furious* minus the crime and Shakespeare's tragic ending.

I can't get the image out of my head of Jax's clenched jaw as he stared at Elías. He can't be bothered by me talking to Elías, right? There's no reason for Jax to be that way since Elías has been secretly cheering for the other team since he was born. Jax has even less of a reason since he doesn't care about anyone but himself. The problem with selfish people is that they want everything they can't have.

Sorry, Jax, I'm not an option because I'm too busy being your solution.

CHAPTER FIVE

Jax

"It's about damn time you showed up. I was beginning to worry you didn't want to hang around me anymore now that you're a hotshot racer." Liam welcomes me to his private Vitus suite.

"Exclusive reports say you're too busy with Miss Sophie Mitchell. Care to comment?" I hold an invisible microphone to his face.

"Ah, fuck off. The same insider told me McCoy got you a human ankle monitor. How's it going?" He throws himself on a leather couch.

"As bothersome as the real deal."

"And you know how an ankle monitor feels, how…?"

"Got in trouble back in the day. Imagine that."

"I'd almost believe you, except I know your mom would kick your ass. Since she's busy in London, you'll have Elena to do the job for her."

I pretend the mention of my mum doesn't cause me discomfort. All my best mates think she lives her happy life in London, away from the media and race drama. I keep that part of myself locked up from everyone in the hopes of hiding my family's issues. "Don't remind me. I don't know how I got stuck with Elena."

"I told you to lay off the alcohol, but you didn't listen. Elena was probably the only one crazy enough to accept a deal following your ass all year. I, for one, wouldn't want to."

"I regret what I did." I settle into the couch across from him.

Liam places a pillow under his head. "Good. Use it as a reason to kick ass. By the way, nice job with your third-place qualifier. You actually have a chance to beat Noah on Sunday."

Like a little brother, I feel a sense of pride at Liam's praise. "Thanks. I couldn't have done it without you. Quite literally, by the way. Now with you gone, the attention is all on me, so thanks."

"You may pretend not to give a fuck, but you seek the approval of those around you. How cute." Liam presses a palm to his heart and bats his lashes at me.

I throw a pillow at his face. "Arsehole. We all have goals: you being the best of the rest, and me being *the* best."

"Oh, how the tables have turned."

"After placing fifth today, do you regret your choice?"

He shakes his head. "Not at all."

I tap my fingers against my bouncing knee. "Why not?"

"Because I got to hook up with Sophie after and she did this thing with my—"

I throw another pillow at his face. "I prefer chugging champagne on podiums."

"Spoken like someone who is one drink away from his first AA meeting."

I flip him off. "Do you know how much I hate you?"

"If by *hate* you mean *love*, then I already know." Liam flashes me a shit-eating grin.

"How do you know?"

"It's a feeling I get inside, all warm and tingly. Kind of like heartburn after spicy Mexican food. And speaking of Mexican…"

I run my hand across my face. "Oh, no."

"Oh, yes. You may have diverted me earlier, but I see through you." Liam makes a ridiculous *I'm watching you* motion with his fingers.

"There's not much to share except I'm now under house arrest."

He snaps his fingers together. "Like Ant-Man?"

"More like *Disturbia.*"

"Your common knowledge of Shia LeBeouf movies is a red flag. Actually, I take that back. *You're* a red flag. A big, walking, talking, red flag."

I smile at him. "And I'm going to wave it loud and proud."

My phone rings twenty minutes later, interrupting my round of catch-up with Liam. I excuse myself, telling him I'll meet up with him before the race tomorrow.

"Hey, Dad. How's it going?" I exit Liam's suite.

"Better than expected."

"And Mum?"

"Hanging in there after everything. But also important, how are you doing?" My dad's serious voice pulls a smile from me. He intimidates everyone but Mum and me, seeing as he treats us like his most cherished belongings.

If people think my crappy attitude is because of bad parents, they're sadly mistaken. The Kingstons are all about the feels and shit, with me having weekly movie days while growing up and family pizza nights after my kart races.

I exit Vitus's motorhome. The sun beams down on me as I lean against the side of the temporary structure, away from prying eyes. "Everything is fine and dandy."

He chuckles. "Wow, no wonder you're such a pro in front of the cameras. Now tell me how you really feel, minus the bullshit, please."

I let out a loud breath. "It sucks arse being away from home. I feel guilty about competing while you're both in London, dealing with doctors and checkups."

"We all need to act normal for your mum's sake. She couldn't bear thinking you're changing your life for her. I only ask that you keep her in mind when you think about doing stupid shit like what happened over break. It affects her the most, especially when she knows you're hurting because of her."

How is it possible to feel his disappointment from thousands of miles away? My hands begin to shake, and I clench them to stop the movement. "I have someone to help keep me in line, so I don't think this issue will happen again. At least not to the level of what happened before."

"And you think you can keep yourself together for the foreseeable future? Your mum has enough going on, and I love you, but her health is the priority right now. I can't worry about the two of you at the same time." My dad sighs. I imagine him squirreled away in his gym, hiding this conversation from Mum.

The sharp pain in my chest grows stronger. "Yes. I can be

better. For you and her."

"I didn't call to give you a hard time about your mistake because I know the team will do it for me. I wanted to let you know that maybe you should give your mum a call. She's been having a rough day and it would mean a lot to her."

My hands tremble more as I fight to get air in my lungs. "What happened?"

"You know some days are harder than others. Your phone calls bring a smile to her face, so if you can make time in your busy schedule, I'd appreciate it."

"Of course. I'll give her a call as soon as I can."

"Thanks. And congratulations on your great qualifier. We love you lots and are proud. This is going to be your year. We know it."

"Thanks, Dad. Love you too."

"I've got another call coming in. I'll talk to you tomorrow." He hangs up.

I can't wait for my usual Sucky Sunday Special of feeling like shit after talking to my parents. The moment I hang up, I book it back to my private McCoy suite, needing a little help in the form of a pill before I call my mum.

The last person I want to see at a moment of weakness has her arse planted on one of my couches.

God, Elena can't go, I don't know, fix a PR crisis? I run an agitated palm through my curls.

"Hey, that was fast. I expected Liam to babysit you for at least an hour longer. I almost beat my highest score." Elena flashes me a hesitant smile as she shows me some interior design creation from a game on her iPad. She created a huge living room with beachy decor, similar to my parents' mansion back in

London. The memory of what I'm missing out on causes a pain of something strong to shoot straight through my heart.

I hate Elena's stupid, timid smile. I hate how I want to see more of it to ease the rush of emotions inside of me. My uncontrollable reaction toward her results in anger replacing anxiety. Like a tsunami, I'm on an irreversible path of destruction. "McCoy doesn't pay Liam to take care of me, they pay *you*. Maybe you should concentrate on your job instead of messing around with a stupid game. If this is what you do during your free time, maybe you're not worth the extra pay after all."

"You don't need to act like an asshole." Her left eye twitches. It's rather endearing, which adds to my frustration.

"Acting insinuates this isn't my normal behavior. That's where you're wrong. This is me, and maybe you need to start wrapping your pretty little head around that. I'm not here to be your friend, love." Something about fighting with Elena invigorates me. It's fucked up, but the rage toward her feels better than the anxiety threatening my control.

Her left eye wages a war to remain open. "If you're having a shitty day, don't take it out on me. I'm only here to help you."

"You're only here to make money. The sacrificial martyr routine is a bit stale, especially for someone walking away with a padded bank account after all this."

Something like guilt flashes in her eyes before she recovers. "Not everything is about money."

"Yet you'll be the first one to collect a monthly check from my struggles."

She lets out a resigned sigh. "I don't know what made you this angry. There's nothing wrong with being anxious and irritable, but you need to get a hold of yourself. I can help you if you let me."

"You can't fix everything."

"I'm not going away. So, if I can't fix it, I'll find someone who can."

That's my worry. I can't have her getting close to me, trying to make me better. To make me *want* to be better.

Hope is for idiots with their futures ahead of them.

Hope is for those who wish under stars, or in a church, or in a desperate moment of need.

The hopeless don't get those types of moments. We get a biological clock ticking above our heads, reminding us how shitty the world is.

Spoiler warning: we all die in the end. Except some of us end up there quicker than others.

I enter my room without looking back at her. The thud of the door closing fills me with dread. Alone again with my thoughts, self-hate, and never-ending worries. A dream team of the worst kind.

My breathing grows erratic as I consider the consequences of my actions. Fighting with Elena adds to my emptiness, black and endless. Sucking up her happiness fucks me up even more. I pace the small space, attempting to ease my racing heart, but failing.

My thoughts race in my head, my brain switching from one issue to the other with no reprieve. Thoughts of disappointing my dad, worrying my mum, and forcing Elena away push my mind past its breaking point. Forced breaths leave my lips as I attempt some deep breathing. All my strategies to relax fail me. The cold gray walls feel as though they're closing in, giving me little space to breathe. Anxiety is a nasty wanker like that. It rips away my sense of an escape, growing larger by the day.

I grab my trusty pill bottle from my gym bag with shaky hands. Nothing can chase away my fears quite like my medicine. I've tried to take them less. I really have. Moments like these test my mental strength, and I can't call Mum when I'm two seconds away from flipping my shit.

Relief floods my bloodstream twenty minutes later, easing my regret as I dial my mum.

I crave the numbness a Xan provides. My coping skills are shit, but name something about me that isn't. I won't hold my breath because they'll be listing my flaws for a long-arse time.

CHAPTER SIX

Jax

Music blasts through the hotel suite, waking me up. I growl as I throw off my covers and check the time on my phone. *Five fucking a.m.* A solid half hour before I need to wake up for the race.

I exit my room, forgoing a shirt in favor of finding out what the fuck is going on. My feet stop as my eyes land on the object of my frustrations.

And I mean *all* my frustrations.

The mental kind. The physical kind. The kind making my dick twitch to life in my shorts.

Elena wears a tiny scrap of clothing better suited for a Victoria's Secret runway. Her silky nightgown hugs her curves with the hem hitting her mid-thigh. The globes of her ass call to me, begging me to check out what's underneath her tiny dress.

"Good morning." She speaks in a singsong voice that doesn't suit her. The way she speaks and the look she sends me over her shoulder scream mischievous.

Either I'm experiencing the best fucking dream or a living nightmare. The smell of eggs and bacon tells me this is all very real. My dick throbs in my shorts as I assess Elena's legs and arse. That fucking arse.

Shit. This is actual torture.

"Do you want breakfast?"

Well, fuck. Who am I to say no? With Elena looking like a wet dream, I'll take anything she has to offer.

I sit at the dining table, hoping to hide my growing erection. My eyes track her every move. From the way she grabs the coffee mug on the top shelf to her bending over to check on the bacon in the oven.

Every fucking move she makes teases me. I honestly can't wrap my head around her nice behavior, especially after me being a dick to her yesterday.

Her shining eyes fail to match the fake frown plastered on her face. "Are you okay? Your face looks a bit pained."

That's not the only thing in pain.

She walks over, holding a full plate of food in front of her. I could absolutely get used to this kind of treatment. Maybe having a babysitter isn't the worst thing after all.

She leans in close, hitting me with the scent of strawberry shampoo. "This situation can go two ways. Either we can treat each other with respect, or you can act like a dick to me. But if you choose the second option, be aware that I don't take shit lying down. There's more than one way to torture someone." Her eyes move from my face to my crotch, eyeing my erection.

Shit. This is both hot yet so fucking wrong. "And I'm being tortured how? Seems like I'm getting the better end of the deal with breakfast and a show."

"Oh? You thought this was for your benefit? More like I scheduled you two back-to-back interviews after your race because everyone knows you love the spotlight. Although the added blue balls to your morning is a plus." She smiles wide.

The way she plotted for me to have the worst day impresses me more than it annoys me.

"You played me."

Elena shakes her head. "Think of this as an enlightenment." She walks toward her room with the plate of what should have been *my* breakfast. "P.S. If you want breakfast, call room service for yourself. I'm not your maid." Her smirk is the last thing I see before she shuts the door to her room.

Elena motherfucking Gonzalez proved herself a worthy opponent.

Game on.

The crew runs around the garage, running last-minute checks before the Australian Grand Prix. The Xanax I took after breakfast has worked its way into my system, turning my anxiety into a temporary issue of the past. I take the right amount to dull the worries while staying alert because the last thing I need while driving a car at three hundred kilometers is a panic attack.

Elena smiles at me from a corner of the garage, gloating about her move earlier.

I take advantage of a busy Elías to talk to her. "So, that's how it's going to be between us? I push, you pull?"

"That depends. Are you going to be an ass to me for the entire season?"

"I don't know." I genuinely don't. It's not like I can predict when shit will hit the fan for me.

"How reassuring."

I let out a low laugh. "Some call me unpredictable."

"Are those the same people who left you passed out next to a urinal? Because they're not wrong."

Damn. She does not hold back. Somehow, I find it... refreshing.

Woe is me. A rich boy who has everyone and their mother kiss my arse for fifteen minutes in the limelight. Hanging around someone like Elena reminds me of how very human I am. It's humbling while also scaring the hell out of me.

"Speaking of unpredictable, I could say the same about you. This morning's show was something else... Did you pack all those nighties for me?"

Her cheeks turn the best shade of pink. "It's what you deserved."

"Do people know about this side of you?"

"The one that doesn't go down without kicking and screaming? Oh, yeah."

"I'd rather have you screaming than kicking, but I'm game if that's your kink."

Her cheeks go from pink to blood red. "You can't—"

"Talk to you that way? I can't tell you how, after your little show, I jacked off to the image of you bent over my bed while I fucked you? It sure was one way to get me high before a race."

Elena's eyes roam around the garage, landing everywhere but where I want them.

I snap my fingers in front of her face. "You can play your little games, but I can play mine. And I assure you I'll get the better deal out of this."

A crew member calls me over to prepare for the race.

"I better get going. Enjoy the Prix." I love getting under her skin. Elena's smooth, tan, *wouldn't mind kissing every inch* skin.

Yup. I'm so fucked.

"Good luck," Elena mumbles under her breath.

I throw her a smile over my shoulder before hopping into my car.

The crew pulls me up to my third-place qualifying spot. My P3 location lands me behind Noah and Santiago, the Bandini boys who battle with McCoy during every Prix.

Flame retardant gear protects me from head to toe, ensuring my safety if anything were to go awry. My arse shakes from the rumbling of the engine.

Lights above me illuminate before going black. My trainer presses against the pedal, and my car accelerates. I race down the first straight of the Prix. The wheels grind against the rough pavement as I recreate yesterday's practice drive I completed in McCoy's simulator machine.

"Welcome back to the grid. Liam, Elías, and a fuck ton of others are behind you, so keep up the good work." Chris, the team principal, speaks into the team radio. He's a man of choice words and a no-nonsense attitude.

"Tires feel good. Engine is hot as hell."

"Sounds like it's working then. I'll check in soon."

My car rips up pavement, lap after lap. I pit, giving the crew two seconds to change my four tires. Rubber meets the road, propelling me down the pit lane before I reenter the race. After pitting, I need to work my way back up the rankings.

"Liam's in front of you. On the next turn, go on the outside instead of the inside. Cut him off before you hit the straight road." Chris's voice reverberates through the tiny earpiece.

My car creeps up behind Liam's navy one. Everything in this sport is down to a millisecond, which means every turn—every goddamn tire rotation—matters. I pull up to the side of Liam's car before I brake. He takes the inside like Chris thought, and I keep on the outside.

My car surges past Liam's, his engine no match against mine. I rush down the straight at over three hundred kilometers.

"Now beat Elías back into his rightful place," Chris snorts into the mic.

"So, to the back of the grid?" I muster between pants, my breathing growing heavier as the engine warms behind me.

Chris and my main engineer laugh as I cut in front of Elías at the next turn.

"You only have Santiago and Noah ahead of you. Show them who's their daddy."

I bark out a laugh. Bandini's red cars shine, looking glossy as fuck under the hot sun. My car pulls up next to Santi's at one of the turns, but he pushes me down again into third place. His car takes up the center of the road, but I inch up behind him, my front wing creeping up. At the next turn, I drive up to the side of his car before I push in front. His tires squeal at his sudden braking.

"Nice work. Your move will be an interesting topic at my press conference. James Mitchell will have a fucking field day if you beat his boys."

Last but not least, Noah Slade. F1's four-time World Champion and newly elected President of the Pussy-whipped Squad. He brake-checks me before the next turn.

I fucking want this win. For myself, for the team, for my damn sanity. Winning means pushing past my self-doubts. Placing first means I'm worthy of the fans who care enough about me to wear my race-car number. A podium finish sets a bar and makes my time away from my mum worth it.

Noah doesn't make it easy for me. He meets my moves with resistance, giving me limited opportunities to push him out of first place.

"Bloody hell," I mumble under my breath.

Chris unmutes himself. "Please show this man what McCoy cars can do."

Noah has won enough Championships to last a lifetime. It's time for someone else to beat him down a peg…or ten. I don't know how Maya deals with his ego.

Tires rotate, car gears change, and my heart races to the thrum of the engine. I make it around Noah's car at one of the last turns, pulling in front of him when it matters most. The crowd goes wild when I pass the checkered line. A shit-eating smile tugs at my lips because I fucking did it.

CHAPTER SEVEN

Elena

I exit my room to find Jax sitting on the couch, bouncing his knee in agitation. He looks handsome and ready for the Shanghai gala in his black button-down shirt and pants. As if dressing up means conforming to society's expectations, he ditched the bowtie. His muscles bulge against the expensive material of his shirt.

Basically, Jax is the worst kind of temptation. For my job. For my mental health. For the insane, lusty feeling inside of me that wouldn't mind taking him up on his offer to hook up. But good thing I value my job more than a quick fuck with Britain's baddest bachelor.

"Well, you don't look half bad." His lip twitches at the corner before settling on a scowl instead.

I snort. "Your compliments suck."

"I'm the last person you want to compliment you."

"Because you lack any tact?"

"Tact isn't our issue." His British accent enunciates his words.

"It's *my* issue with you." I tap my pointer finger to my chest.

"What would you like me to do about it?"

"Would it kill you to be nicer to me? Hell, how about less moody?"

He runs a hand across his stubbled chin. "You want the honest answer?"

"Sure?" Except my voice sounds anything but sure.

"We aren't cut out for sweet moments and special words." His eyes scan my body again as he closes the distance between us.

I ignore the rush of energy coursing through me at his perusal. "Okay then. What kind of moments are we meant for?"

His hand brushes across my face, eliciting the slightest shiver from me. He grabs a strand of my hair and rubs it between his fingers, analyzing it as if it holds all the answers. "The kind that only end in disappointment."

"I'm proud of you. Not all men can own up to their faults in the bedroom." I tap his chest, hiding how much my heart races at his proximity. My hand warms as it trails down the buttons of his shirt to flatten a wrinkle.

"*Disappointing* is the last word you'd use to describe me in the bedroom." His voice drops low with a rasp.

"Oh really?"

His hand flexes as if he wants to touch me again before he places it in his pocket. "I've always been better at showing, not telling."

"Fitting since you have the emotional range of a five-year-old. They follow the same concept."

He throws his head back and laughs. "I can assure you in

all the years I've been with women, I can safely say they haven't complained."

"Probably because you're the one leaving before they have a chance to speak."

"Ahh, learning my tricks already?"

"Tricks insinuates they're sneaky. You're forgetting it's my job to learn everything about you."

His eyes darken. "Even the bad parts?"

"Especially those. It makes this job more interesting." I push my palms together and wiggle my fingers, giving off my best evil genius impression.

"Not the fact that I'm devilishly handsome and have a killer accent?"

I roll my eyes. "Nope. I would label that a con."

Lies. His accent and looks are very much a pro in this situation.

"Because you find it hard to resist me?"

"Ehh. I'm not into guys who act like you do."

"And that is?"

"Like they're above me."

His mask of disinterest slips for a moment. "That's not how I feel."

"That's how you come across, which is all the same. It's okay. I'm a big girl and can handle men like you. You're not the first client who has treated me this way." I walk toward the main door to exit the suite. My silk champagne dress clings to my body, making it difficult to make long strides.

Jax catches up to me easily. He grabs onto my elbow softly, turning me toward him. "I can't speak for other men, but I don't think I'm better than you. Quite the opposite, actually. You're too—" he bites down on his lip as he scans my body once more before lingering on my face "—good for someone like me."

"Someone like you?" I stare at his hand, trying to understand why my skin pebbles at his touch.

His thumb lazily brushes across my skin. "I'm better suited to destroy someone's happiness than be their reason for it."

I let out a deep sigh. "Are you always going to speak in statements shrouded in confusion?"

"I'm like Jim Carrey's Riddler."

"Out of all the movies you could reference, you choose George Clooney's Batman franchise? I'm losing all my respect for you."

"The fact that you have a little respect for me at all is concerning."

"Don't worry, it's dwindling by the second."

He shakes his head, fighting his smile before settling for a scowl. "Let's go. Time to get this shit show over with."

"Why do you hate sponsor events?"

"I hate everything that isn't racing my car. I'd much rather drop off the face of the planet than deal with a new crowd of people every week who ask me too many questions."

We both walk into the hall and toward the elevator. "I think you chose the wrong career path then. Racing and celebrity status are synonymous with one another."

Jax presses the button. "Trust me, I wasn't thinking of the consequences when I was younger."

"Because you're more likely to get anxious around others?"

"Part of it."

Vague, but I let him keep his secret. The elevator doors open, and we enter.

I press the button for the lobby. "How long have you been anxious?"

"Since forever."

"And it's gotten worse?"

"You're not a therapist. Stop poking around my brain searching for answers."

I laugh as I lean against the railing. "It's called having a conversation. You should try it sometime with the opposite gender. You'd be surprised what women can talk about when you're not fucking them into silence."

"You're cute, goading me into more dirty talk. Does it get you hot and heavy thinking about me with other women, wishing it was you?"

Oh, shit. Nice going, Elena. Enjoy talking yourself out of the mess you created.

I roll my eyes. "Nope."

"Yet you like to bring it up. Why is that?" His smirk annoys me.

My eyes narrow at his lips. "It's called a joke."

"I can assure you sex with me is anything but."

I scrunch my nose in distaste. "Yuck. You're like a five-star review from the owner of a sketchy Chinese buffet restaurant."

"What the fuck does that mean?"

"No one should trust your glowing recommendation until they try it themselves."

A burst of laughter escapes him. "How the bloody hell do you come up with half the shit you say?"

"I have a quick tongue. It's a talent."

His eyebrow lifts as my words sink in. *Well, shit, stupid tongue is more like it at the moment.*

I attempt to recover. "Let's ignore that. And we're going to be spending a lot of time together so maybe you can learn to speak about things other than sex."

"Are you always this bossy?"

"I prefer the term *assertive*. *Bossy* tends to carry a negative connotation, especially for women."

His eyebrows raise. "You've gotten a lot of shit for being a woman working in F1, haven't you?"

"What gave it away? How there are barely any women around the racing paddock or how all the men ignore me in the press room?"

He shakes his head. "Another reason to hate people."

"I don't see it that way. I think of it as another reason to prove people wrong."

Jax and I walk into the Shanghai gala thirty minutes later. Crystal lights hang from the ceiling, casting us in a golden glow as Jax navigates us through the crowd. Luxurious doesn't begin to cover it, with waiters walking around offering hundred-dollar glasses of champagne and food straight out of Gordon Ramsey's kitchen.

Jax's attitude takes a nosedive once he's forced to speak to strangers for longer than five minutes. I chalk up his irritability to unwillingly having to play nice for hours on end.

"Ah, Elena. I thought it was you. I've been trying to find you for an hour, hoping you'd save one dance for me." Elías's voice gains my attention.

"Elena needs to stay by my side this evening. Maybe you

can try again—I don't know—never?" Jax shoos him with his hand, conveniently extending his middle finger.

"He's joking. Ignore him." My eyes narrow at Jax.

"Good. I'm going to ask the DJ to play one of your favorites. I'll be back." Elías shoots me a secretive smile.

"Stop leading him on." Jax's growl of a voice makes my blood run hot in my veins.

"It's one dance with a friend. Stop making such a big deal of things."

Jax's jaw clenches, the shadows lingering where the chandeliers don't shine. "Friend?"

"It might seem like a foreign concept to you, but men and women can be friends without having sex."

"That's bullshit. Liam and Sophie are a perfect example of what happens between two *friends.*"

I roll my eyes. "Elías and I have known each other for years. It's not like that between us."

"I didn't ask for an explanation. Do whatever you want." He walks away, dismissing me.

I ignore my budding annoyance as I search for my friend. Elías is easy to spot near the DJ booth, striking up a conversation with the man working the turntables. He shyly smiles at the DJ as he walks away.

He pulls me out onto the dance floor, spinning me in a circle to *"La Bicicleta."*

"So, you and the DJ?" I waggle my brows.

He shakes his head. "You know how it is."

"I can't even begin to imagine how you feel."

"It's hard in a sport like this. I don't want to be the first... you know."

No time will ever feel right for Elías to come out to the

world. With his career, he remains secretive about his sexuality despite how much it pains him to hide a major part of himself.

"I'm sure that's scary, but times have changed."

Elías's voice drops to a whisper I struggle to hear over the music. "I don't know about that. I hate when guys assume I'm going to hit on them because they have a dick and a good ass."

"I would hope in today's day and age, people would be more accepting."

"I don't want to be the one to test it out. At least not yet. Definitely not now after scoring a contract with a top team."

"Whenever you're ready, you let me know, and I'll help you."

Elías smiles. "What would Jax and I do without you?"

"While you may forget your answers to questions during a press conference, Jax might end up as the next trending Twitter hashtag. And not for a good reason."

"You've got to admit, hashtag JaxAttack is pretty damn catchy."

"Almost as catchy as the STD he's bound to get from whatever woman he hooks up with at the club."

Elías's chest shakes as he laughs. "Say what you will, but he brings out a fire in you I haven't seen in a while. I was getting worried, you know, but I didn't want to say anything last year. You looked tired and sad, and I wasn't sure if you were stressed or if it was because of other stuff with your grandma…"

"I don't want you worrying about me. Especially not about the other stuff." My eyes scan our surroundings.

"Someone has to. How's her new facility working out?"

"It's expensive but worth it. They even send me pictures of her every day, and she calls me once a week. Supposedly she's become friends with her roommate."

"I'm glad to hear she's happy. She could have been there years ago if you had only accepted my help."

"I'm not a charity case."

"And yet you help everyone else who is one." He offers me a small smile.

"I can afford the place now because of this job. With the monthly payments to help Jax, I'm able to pay for her place and my loans, plus my apartment. I'm even looking at a slightly bigger place now."

"That's good. I don't like where you live."

I roll my eyes, ignoring him.

His frown doesn't let up. "Are you still getting those nightmares?"

"Elías... No quiero hablar de eso."

Call me superstitious, but I haven't had a nightmare since the start of this season.

"I think you and Jax have more in common than you think. You both avoid talking about shit bothering you. At least with you, I know what happened. But with him, obviously, he screams bad boy with a sad past. What do you think?"

"What sad past? His parents are alive, they support his race career, and he has access to anything money can buy. He's the poster child for what happens when mommies and daddies give their kids everything. What more could he possibly want?"

Elías turns me in a circle. "Maybe you're not asking the right questions."

The crowd eerily parts, revealing Jax, brooding in a corner with Liam and Noah.

As if he senses me, his eyes meet mine. Every nerve in my body lights up. His smirk screams trouble and unspoken promises, and my body's response to his attention worries me. My attraction to Jax threatens the carefully laid plan I made to help him. But I shove those thoughts aside because I'm here to learn exactly what makes Jax Kingston tick.

Turns out I get to work with the biggest challenge of my career thus far. While some might be intimidated by Jax's poor attitude and brooding, I can't wait to start repairing him from the ground up.

I flash him a broad smile that has his eyebrows pinching together and his frown deepening.

Bring it on.

CHAPTER EIGHT

Elena

Somehow Jax doesn't hear me when I enter his room. I tiptoe to his window, grab onto the curtains, and open them with a dramatic flair. "Rise and shine!"

A strange snarl escapes him as he turns away from the light. "What the fuck?"

"Time to get up. We have a busy day planned."

"Can you come back in a few hours? Better yet, don't come back at all." He grabs a pillow and covers his head. His voice has a rough tone to it, hoarse from waking up.

I take the opportunity to gaze at his naked back, covered with tattoos, barely an inch of space available. Smooth muscles strain, creating ridges across his body.

My fingers itch to touch him. I nearly give in, but somehow catch myself. "That's a tempting offer."

"Not as tempting as a morning blowjob. So, unless that's on the table, you need to go." The pillow over his face muffles his voice.

"Who knew you were such a charmer in the morning?"

"What can I say? You bring out the best in me," he says dryly.

My eyes strain as I attempt to make out the tattoos spread across his defined arms. I lick my lips, fighting with everything in me to not step closer.

Jax suddenly lifts himself up against the headboard. I rush to look away, but the smile on his face tells me how busted I am.

"Elena Gonzalez, were you checking me out? I'm flattered."

"Please." I roll my eyes. "I was questioning how quickly I could suffocate you with the pillow."

"If someone told me I'd die in bed with you, that wouldn't have been my first guess."

My eyes drop to the hotel carpet as heat floods my cheeks. "I can't believe you kiss your mom with that mouth."

"She doesn't mind me. It's not my fault you have your Apple pencil permanently implanted up your arse," Jax snaps.

I try to ignore the way his muscles tense and ripple from the quick movement, but I only have so much self-control around him. "Moving on… I have your first activity planned to help repair your image. Get ready because we have to be there in an hour. And be sure to wear workout clothes." I exit his room without a backward glance. Let's be real, I don't have the kind of self-restraint needed to watch him get out of bed.

Jax meets me in the living room twenty minutes later. Adidas pants cling to his muscular legs and his black T-shirt emphasizes his toned form.

I'm tempted to hit myself for planning an event where I get to see him in all his fine glory.

"You're going dressed like that?" Jax's eyes start at my boxer braids a la *Million Dollar Baby* before roaming over my top and leggings.

"Yes. We're going to be getting physical." I do a little fist pump that should've stayed in an eighties' workout video.

"Fuck my life," he grumbles under his breath as we leave the hotel room.

His reaction fills me with pride I shouldn't feel. No matter how much I desire his hidden glances and taunting, I resist for his sake and mine.

A quick car ride later, we arrive at the location of Jax's first event.

"Shit. A boxing gym?" He looks at the lobby with wide eyes and an open mouth.

I smile at him. "Surprise! I've heard you like to box as part of your workout routine, so I thought it would be a good idea. At least it's something you're interested in besides your usual extracurricular activities."

"Are you hinting at my sex life again?" he tsks.

"What sex life? The one with your right hand?"

Fans stare at us from all directions as Jax curls over, laughing. Even I'm caught up in his reaction—happy and carefree.

I regain my composure and pull him toward the welcome table.

"*Fighting Back Against Domestic Violence.* Nice choice." He shoots me a genuine smile. One making him look youthful and unplagued with the worries bothering him more than he cares to admit.

"I thought it was an amazing cause to donate to. I invited a bunch of people from F1, plus local businessmen. All the proceeds are going to a UK-based charity helping support women once they leave their abusers."

It took some additional planning, but I love the cause. I watch lots of documentaries, and one about a woman who described the grueling process of escaping her abuser stuck with me. I vowed to give back, so here I am, with Jax's money funding the cause. Plus, I thought it would be the perfect first event to warm Jax up to my help while keeping his interest.

Fans and guests walk around us, chatting and participating in a silent auction. Mass amounts of people registered earlier, including F1 fans who are willing to donate a hundred euros for a few minutes in the sparring ring with Jax, Liam, Santiago, or Noah.

I turn to find Jax's eyes on me. A weird sensation takes up a spot in my stomach, similar to the one I have when a plane is about to land. "I told you I'd help you with your reputation. But I didn't mention how I plan on helping lots of people along the way with the help of your plush bank account and celebrity connections."

"Only you would use my fame to help raise money for philanthropies. Bloody hell."

"Your compliment got lost somewhere within your comment."

"I don't even mean it as a jab. It's… This is incredible." He looks around with bright eyes and a large smile. Almost as if he feels at home in the gym, surrounded by sneakers squeaking and swinging punching bags.

Before I have a chance to comment, the main person I hired

to help set up the event interrupts us. She explains the goals for the day while Jax intently listens. His willingness to participate surprises me, especially when he messages other racers to make sure they're coming.

Over the next few hours, I try to tear my eyes away from Jax in the ring, but I find it hard. Like *harder than his muscles flexing under the bright gym lights* hard. His skin glistens from sweat and he has a permanent smile on his face all morning. It's so breathtaking, I find it hard to stare for an extended period of time. Kind of like looking at the sun too long with my eyes burning and my skin growing hot.

"Want me to take a picture of him for you? They usually last longer." A tan woman I instantly recognize as Noah's girlfriend, Maya, shows up by my side. Maya is a bit shorter than me. She dresses in similar workout gear to mine, with her brunette ponytail bobbing behind her. "Awesome event, by the way."

"So great and I love the cause. Maya, take a photo of me while you're at it. I'm going to send it to Liam's nieces." Sophie, with blonde space buns and a matching fluorescent sports bra and leggings, waves at Maya as she walks toward the ring. She looks small compared to the raised sparring octagon.

"She loves a good photo moment." Santiago Alatorre throws an arm around his sister's shoulders as his brown eyes glance over at me. His dark hair drips with sweat after his round of sparring with a fan.

"Sunshine, I told you to stay five feet away." Liam leans against the cables as he smacks a kiss on top of Sophie's head.

Sophie makes a gagging noise. "I told you to stop calling me that months ago."

"Not my fault when you're dressed up like that." Liam

flashes her a cheerful smile as he shakes his head, and a tiny sense of jealousy floods through me. Not at them in particular. God, no, I don't like Liam like that. It's more because I find it difficult to ignore my sense of loneliness at seeing a couple truly happy and in love.

The last relationship I had was ages ago, before *Abuela* got sick and I started working the F1 circuit. That coupled with my inability to imagine a future with them set me up for failure. I didn't think I'd miss having a romantic connection with someone but seeing a happy couple hits me hard.

"Why do you want her to stay away? I'd donate a thousand euros to see Sophie kick your ass in there." Noah takes a sip of water from Maya's bottle.

"I'd like to watch her try. Jax taught me how to spar years ago." Liam lowers himself onto the gym floor.

"And you're still terrible! I'd have better luck teaching Santiago to fight." Jax throws his hands in the air as he follows Liam out of the ring.

Liam cranks his middle finger like a jack in the box. A soft laugh escapes my lips, bringing Jax's attention back to me. His narrowed eyes fail to have the effect he wants, instead causing goosebumps to run down my skin.

Note to self: stop planning events that require Jax to take his shirt off. His abs are distracting for the onlookers.

Me. I'm the onlooker.

"I don't know about that. I've seen Santi's right hook." Noah walks up to his friends.

"And don't you forget it. One wrong move toward Maya and you're done." Santi throws a couple of punches in the air.

"Hey, it's Elena, right? Do you mind taking our photo,

please?" Maya offers me her camera.

Ignoring the increasing sense of loneliness, I snap a few pictures and return the camera to Maya. The group laughs as Santiago drags Noah into the octagon, claiming he needs to remind him what happens if he breaks his sister's heart.

For the rest of the day, I feel Jax's eyes on me, even when I pretend to busy myself with other tasks.

I shouldn't notice it. Shouldn't want it. But most of all, I shouldn't wish for more of it.

CHAPTER NINE

Jax

Surviving the first two races included a Xan a night and a shit ton of deep breathing.

Race three is going strong, with me acting more like a dick than usual because I hate how Elena is unavoidable. The more time I spend around her, the harder I find it to resist the urge to learn all about her.

I could blame the stress from the Bahrain Grand Prix for my recent irritability, but it's a cop-out for how I truly feel. Conflicted. Frustrated. So damn scared of having someone like Elena around me day and night.

I push my thoughts aside because it's a bloody qualifying day. A buzz trickles down my spine before the third Prix of the World Championship schedule.

My car gleams under the pit lights, sleek silver paint shining, the wheels smooth and fresh. McCoy's cars are some of the best and the team works their asses off to produce podium-finishing race cars. Liam and I smashed it for a couple of seasons together before he left, moving onto another team after he fell in love with Sophie.

For the first time in years, I have confidence in the garage. When Liam was here, McCoy focused on giving him the best strategies. He could handle the pressure while I've been a loose cannon one moment away from misfiring.

But now, with him gone and my new partner fresh off a sucky lower team, I have a chance at winning the whole World Championship. All I need to do is handle my anxiety and my growing irritation toward my unwelcome roommate.

Elías hangs around his car with Elena. I didn't find him annoying before, but now I'm not too sure. He openly flirts with Elena right in front of me. I'd rather introduce a drill bit to my eye than watch them get together.

My distaste toward the idea isn't because I'm jealous. Pretty boy Elías looks like he can offer Elena everything someone like her deserves in the first place. An easygoing life with laughs, positivity, and a shit ton of other happy words I can't begin to name, let alone experience myself.

Okay, I sound slightly jealous. But so fucking be it.

I try to ignore Elena the best I can, but I steal glances every now and then. The push and pull between us is damn near intoxicating. My dick pulses to life in my race suit as I stare at her from across the garage, becoming distracted by the dress she wore today. It looks like it was made for her, hugging her in all the places I want to touch.

Elena walks up to me, ruining my idea of evading her. "Hey, you. How do you feel about today's race?"

"Excited to ruin the competition." My lips lift at the corners as I picture Elías watching me from the podium's sidelines.

"The smile on your face should worry me."

"This one isn't the one *you* need to worry about. That's a whole different look altogether."

She rolls her eyes. "You don't scare me."

"Then what scares you?" *What the fuck are you doing? Stop trying to get to know her, you stupid fucker.*

"A couple of things. But most of all is regret." She clutches onto her iPad tightly.

How does one word sit heavy against my chest? I cross my arms and she startles, the cloudiness in her eyes dissipating. "Deep shit, Gonzalez. Meanwhile, I'm afraid of spiders. Nasty little fuckers with beady eyes and the potential to jump." My answer pulls an awkward laugh from her.

She brushes her dark hair aside, hitting me with the smell I've come to know as distinctively hers. "I don't know if I would've ever pegged you as someone who's afraid of spiders."

I tap my chin pensively. "Probably because your assumptions of me couldn't be further from the truth."

"Are you saying you're better than my idea of you?"

"No. I'm so much worse."

Her head tilts back, hitting me with soft eyes and a small smile. "All you're missing is the dark sky, a lightning strike, and ominous thunder to complete your villain montage."

I clap my hands together. "Now you're getting it. I've always been one for making a hell of an entrance."

"And now I'm here so you don't make one hell of an exit."

I let out a whistle. "I'm impressed by your level of clap back."

Elena beams. "Thanks. My *abuela* taught me well."

I definitely should be apprehensive about the way my dick

twitches when Elena switches from English to Spanish. "She sounds like someone I'm afraid to meet. If she's the queen, what does that make you?"

"The pawn."

"I think you need to brush up on those chess references, love. No one wants to be the pawn. But I guess it fits. You look weak and untouched by true adversity, not strong enough to play with the big boys on the board."

"Comments like yours are *exactly* why I like the pawn. It's the most underestimated piece." She looks up at me, goading me with her smile.

Screw her and her sparkling eyes, specks of brown and gold reflecting the lights above us, entrancing me. "Then why do you want to be one?"

"Because in real life, we don't start out as the strongest. It's about surviving the little battles. Once the pawn makes it to the other side, it can turn into a queen. That's who I want to be. The person who comes out stronger than when they started."

Her words hit deeper than intended. I can't fight the temptation to learn more about her. "And what happens when you become the queen?"

She lets out a soft laugh. "What happens when anyone becomes a queen? They rule the world. Well...my world that is."

I look away, growing uncomfortable at the idea of enjoying her company more than I should. "You've proven yourself a worthy opponent."

She tilts her head at me, her brows pinching together. "Why am I afraid to ask what you mean by that?"

"Because evolution embedded a fight-or-flight response in each of us."

"Are you suggesting I should run away?"

"Nope. You're all fight. And that's what makes you dangerous." I play it cool despite my own instinct to run in the opposite direction of her. It's a feeling starting from deep within me, whispering how nothing good can come from this. A feeling I need to hold on to, for the sake of my dwindling sanity.

I don't want to like her. Bloody hell, I don't want to crave her like a lovesick twat who can't keep his dick in check. And I sure as fuck don't want to let her in.

Some people have defense mechanisms while I have weapons of mass destruction.

And like a detonated bomb, I can't take them back.

"We're so proud of you. You've been having such a splendid performance this year." My dad's pride carries through the phone.

"Who knew I had it in me this season?" I hang around the garage, checking in with mechanics after my earlier qualifier round.

"We did. We always knew you'd be a front-runner once Liam left. We love him, but we can't help being happy for you. I mean, what an amazing qually today! You're a powerhouse this season." My mum's voice gets louder as my dad hands the phone to her.

"Don't keep boosting my ego, Mum. Elena won't be able to keep me in check if you keep it up."

"Who is this Elena girl you've mentioned a couple times?" my dad grumbles into the phone.

"He talked to her last week when you went to the bathroom. I think Jax likes her." My mum attempts to whisper except the phone's microphone picks up everything.

"Should we run a background check on her?" My dad's voice drops low.

I picture my dad rubbing his eyebrow as he thinks about contacting a private investigator. Might as well nip this concern in the bud before they get carried away. "I hope you both know I can hear you. Let's not overreact. I don't have a crush, and I wouldn't exactly appreciate someone snooping into my past, so let's leave hers alone."

"Oh, yeah. He's definitely interested in her." My dad laughs.

"Are you two for real? What has gotten into you? I barely know her, let alone like her. It's the opposite actually of what you think. Can't stand her presence."

Mum giggles. "Oh, enemies-to-lovers. Nice. That's a great story to tell people when they ask how you fell in love."

I exhale a wheezy breath. "Who the hell said anything about love? She's my PR rep for fuck's sake. I've been around her for all of three weeks."

Three weeks of heated conversations and disgruntled reactions. Days filled with palpable tension neither one of us tries to alleviate, which leads to more awkward moments. Mornings of her puckered nipples taunting me as she pours herself a cup of coffee. Evenings of her lounging on the couch with her toned legs on display, begging me to grip onto them and explore her body. And worst of all, there's no escape from her laughs and daily challenges. I look forward to hearing the shit coming out of her mouth, which adds to the level of concern growing in my chest with each passing day.

Basically, living with Elena is like treading water by myself in the middle of an ocean—deadly, useless, and one wrong move away from going under.

"Mums get these types of feelings about things."

My clammy fingers grip my phone. "Dad, please control your wife. She's delirious."

Dad's laugh sounds like thunder rumbling. "Why would I want to control what makes her special? That's like asking the sun to stop shining."

Their romance makes acid crawl up my throat. Not because I dislike how they love each other, but for how bitterness takes up a spot in my heart knowing my mum will be robbed of these moments. My dad will wither away with her once she gets worse, losing a part of himself too.

Their random call to congratulate me means everything to them, but it destroys me bit by bit. It's sickening to pretend I'm okay despite the mentally exhausting war I'm losing week by week.

Instead of voicing my concerns, I keep them hidden. "I'm going to hang up before you both ruin my appetite. When I call you tomorrow, please keep the flirting to a minimum. It's rather gross."

Mum snorts. "Maybe if you flirted with the right kind of woman, then you wouldn't be disgusted by us. Imagine going on a real date. And I'm not talking about the rubbish you do with random women."

My dad takes over. "Ignore her. She's only having fun with you."

I let out a laugh. "All right. I need to get going before Elena reams me about being late to a press event. Talk to you both tomorrow."

I hang up once my parents say their goodbyes. Despite the sad feeling lingering after our chats, I answer their random calls because I'm a sucker for my parents. I love them, and I want to make my mum the happiest, despite her one wish I won't fulfill.

I arrive at the press area with a few minutes to spare. My feet freeze as my eyes land on Elena and Elías talking, causing a grumbling reporter to slam into my back.

An irritated groan seeps past my lips. My teammate clearly hasn't learned Elena is mine for the season. She should be concentrating on me instead of him. Without thinking, I eliminate the space between us, pulling up to Elena's side. Her scent calms me, centering me enough to not make a fool of myself.

"Oh goody, if it isn't my favorite person." My words come out as a snarl as I stare Elías down.

"And what does that make me?" Elena smirks and crosses her arms across her chest.

My eyes lazily flick over her in feigned disinterest despite the craving to scan her body from head to toe. "Hell reincarnate."

"At least I'm hot." She shrugs.

Elías laughs to the point of bending over.

My fists curl on their own accord. "Can't you do your job instead of flirting with my teammate?"

"Ay, Dios." Elías sighs.

"Weird, you know jealousy has a way of making people do dumb things. Kind of like marking your territory for no reason since there isn't a threat." She purses her lips.

"I'm not marking my territory. I'm simply stating facts." I tap her scrunched-up nose.

"Careful, Kingston. With how you keep acting, I'd think you care about someone else besides yourself."

Her words do little to ease the growing agitation inside of me. Of course, I care about others, including my friends and family. Who is she to cast shitty judgments? I keep my comeback to myself, choosing to brush past Elías to take my seat next to Noah.

"Hey, man. I thought you were about to bitch out Elena and Elías there." Noah's eyes assess me before returning to Elías and Elena whispering in a corner.

If looks could kill, Elías would've been eviscerated. Instead, I return my gaze back to Noah, catching his poorly hidden smirk.

"Elías can't take a hint. They hired Elena to help me, not spend time with him." I flick a piece of lint off my black jeans.

"Why does it bother you if he talks to her?"

"Because we tend to argue, yet whenever Elías is around, she's all happy and shit."

"You sound envious of their relationship."

"Their *friendship*."

Noah's head drops back as he laughs. "Right. Friendship. Tough luck with Elena. But what do you expect? I doubt she wants to risk her job for a one-time fling with you."

"What am I supposed to do? I can't exactly turn my dick off and act like I'm not interested in fucking her."

Noah crosses his arms. "If you're only interested in fucking her then you don't need to act on your impulse. I think you've made enough mistakes to last you a lifetime. So that means you keep your dick in your pants. Let her do her job and leave her alone."

Screw Liam and him for cocking up our routine of fucking around and having fun during the season. Now I'm stuck avoiding PR disasters and a seductive roommate, all while my friends are too busy snogging with their girlfriends.

I'm on a lonely path of destructiveness with no end in sight. Turns out misery loves company, and I found her in a bottle of Jack and a refill of Xans.

CHAPTER TEN

Elena

I walk into the hotel's elevator with my takeout bag. Jax told me he'd stay in the suite while I went out and grabbed dinner for myself. When the elevator stops onto the floor of our room, I can tell something is not right by the music thumping through the hallway.

My frustration increases as I approach the door, awareness running through me at how Jax decided to take advantage of my thirty minutes of freedom.

I enter the suite, finding it dark and packed with bodies. Music pours from speakers, which weren't present before I left.

Lovely. Droves of people partying like rock stars. Lots of bodies dance, swaying to the music violating the hotel's policy. I move around them as I look for the man behind this.

It doesn't take me long to find Jax, sitting on a couch with a bottle of Jack in one hand while a woman tries to speak to him. She leans into him, whispering in his ear as she strokes her hand across his bicep.

I roll my eyes at the sight of her. Fury replaces irritation as Jax remains oblivious as I rip away the bottle of whiskey from his hand.

Jax looks up at me, bored and distant. "Look who it is."

"Get everyone out now." My voice remains eerily calm despite the anger threatening to burst out of me.

"Love, you're killing my buzz. If you don't mind, please go to your room."

Instead of fighting with him, I turn around and go to my bedroom in a rush to collect myself before I explode. I enter my bathroom and go to the sink, dumping the amber liquid down the drain.

"You will not kill him. You will *not* kill hi—"

Someone shouts in the distance about shots.

"Okay, you're totally going to kill him." I grip the bottle tighter as I shake the last few droplets out of it.

"Why are you pouring out good liquor?" Jax's husky voice surprises me.

"Because tonight's fun is over. I don't care if you landed on the podium earlier, this isn't how you're supposed to celebrate." I leave the empty bottle on the counter.

Jax gives me room to walk around him. "Your eye is twitching."

"Yeah, I've heard when that happens, people better run. You included." I grab my phone and look up the top clubs in Bahrain.

After I find the perfect one, I give them a call. I repeat Jax's Amex information to the hostess because he needs to learn his lesson. At the start of the season, he gave me the approval to use it in cases to help his reputation, and well, this calls for it. I'm saving him from himself.

Jax's lips form an O as I hang up the phone. I exit my room, not waiting to check if the object of my frustrations follows behind me. With little effort, I find the speaker cords and tug hard, basking the room in silence.

"Sweet, sweet quiet." I cross the living room and hit the lights, resulting in groans from suite-crashers.

I make my way to the wooden coffee table in the center of the room and stand on it. "I'd like to invite everyone to Club XS in honor of Jax's epic race this morning. First twenty people there get free bottle service on Jax!"

The room clears in a matter of minutes, with people nearly tripping over one another as they rush out the door. Not even groupies can resist access to one of the most exclusive clubs on someone else's dime. I would laugh if I wasn't pissed.

I check out the hotel room. Plastic cups litter the floor, along with counters covered with half-filled alcohol bottles and some white powdery substance I have no interest in cleaning. A rolled-up euro next to it screams the debauchery expected of the rich and shameless; meanwhile, Jax hangs around, looming in a corner, gauging my reaction.

Jax's eyes bounce between me and the counter. "I didn't do drugs. I only drank to the point of feeling a little tipsy. I'm not even drunk, sadly because I couldn't go through with it."

Instead of yelling at him, I grab a trash bin and start cleaning up the mess. It takes ten deep, cleansing breaths for me to gather a few words to express myself. "I shouldn't speak when I'm this pissed."

"To be fair, you told me I couldn't go out. You never said people couldn't come in."

The extra breaths I take do nothing to calm my escalating

heart rate. "Are you seriously trying to justify this?" I gesture toward the mess around us. "Week after week I try to help you boost your image and make you look like you have it all together. Clearly, it's a lie, based on the way you keep trying to ruin everything good I've done."

I clean up the room in silence, ignoring Jax who helps. He even cleans up the drugs on the counter.

"I thought it would make me feel better." Jax places a discarded cup in the bin I'm holding.

"And how did it work out for you?"

"I felt nothing. All these people here, and I stared at the front door, waiting."

I freeze, unsure of his confession. "Why?"

"Why do I feel nothing?"

"No. Why did you stare at the door?"

His eyes flash with a rare vulnerability I'm unaccustomed to seeing from him. "I was waiting for you. Because when you're around, I feel something."

"And what's that?" My hoarse whisper fills the quiet. Based on how he acts lately, I can't tell whether he has the good or bad kind toward me.

"I don't know. And I really don't want to find out."

My chest squeezes to the point of discomfort. I can't ask Jax what he means because he retreats to his room, shutting me out, leaving me to clean up his mess yet again.

My eyes open to the sun peeking through the curtains. I shut off my bedside lamp before stretching out in my bed. Like every morning, I grab my picture frame of my parents and say a quick prayer. I place it back on my nightstand and go through my morning routine of shutting off all the lights in my room.

I'm slightly ashamed to admit I still don't sleep in the dark. I can't stand the shadows creeping in at night, reminding me of memories I struggle to let go of. One day, I'll sleep like a normal twenty-five-year-old. Until then, I'll continue to sleep with the lights on because it keeps the nightmares away.

Opening the door to my room, I pummel straight into Jax's body. I let out a squeak as I lose my footing. My hands grab onto his chest to steady myself from falling over. A very strong, tattooed, shirtless chest I wouldn't mind exploring. The same chest belonging to a male who makes me angrier than a scorned woman on *Jerry Springer*.

"Oh, I was about to go check if you were still alive. What a shame. I almost thought you suffocated in your sleep, but I realize I'm not that fortunate."

Somehow the two functioning brain cells working before my morning coffee assemble some words together as I remove my hands from his chest. "Good God. Do you take asshole pills every morning instead of vitamins?" My eyes run up and down his body before settling on his face.

Why was he waiting outside my door? Why is he shirtless? And why the hell does he have to look so damn good? No one should look like him at 7 a.m. It's a disgrace.

His lip twitches. "Nope. This kind of attitude doesn't require a supplement. I was about to wake you up because I don't want us to be late for our flight." He sucks in an audible breath as I reach out and brush my fingers across a tattoo of an unfamiliar constellation.

"Hmm." I trace the individual stars, trying to make sense of the way my body responds to him. It's a mystery I've yet to fully comprehend. I never liked confrontational assholes before, but here I am, intimately touching him. A lover's caress when we're anything but.

"I'm a Gemini." He lets out a soft sigh, his skin pebbling where my fingers linger.

Interesting. Joy rushes through me at the idea of me having the same effect on him that he has on me. At least my attraction isn't one-sided.

"That explains so much."

"Do tell." His voice has a humorous tone to it.

"You're hot and cold. Up and down. Kind of like that Katy Perry song." My fingers impulsively run down a set of butterflies near his rib cage. His muscles contract at my touch. He may be all sharp edges with his words and attitude, but the delicate butterflies trailing his side tell a different story. A story I might never get to know, seeing as he resists any semblance of a friendship with me.

"And what's your sign then? My turn to judge, especially when you're feeling me up for free."

I rush to remove my hands from his body, too embarrassed to pay attention to the way my fingers buzz from touching him. "Virgo. AKA the best one."

"Spoken like someone who's biased." He grabs his phone from the pocket of his shorts and taps away. "Oh, look. Analytical, observant, sarcastic, judgmental. Ah, and they even mention Virgos in the bedroom. It says you like a heavy dose of petting before getting, and you might be one for many fetishes. I wonder what weird shit you enjoy?"

"Besides guys who actually treat me with respect? The

horror." I mockingly gasp.

He laughs, the sound soft and unlike his abrasive personality. "My guess is porcelain dolls watching you while you have mundane sex. You scream creepy doll addiction since they kind of look like you: vacant and small."

I laugh to the point of wheezing. Unfortunately for me, I find him funny when he says something so ridiculous with a seriousness I admire. "Oh, God. You caught me. I thought my secret was safe, but here you go figuring me out in a few weeks. I keep a doll in my carry-on for those types of nights."

"Hmm. I knew you were weird." He continues scrolling. "Oh, see they say Virgos tend to suffer in silence."

"So, we have something in common then?"

The glare he sends my way makes me feel as if someone dragged an ice cube across the base of my spine. "Suffering means I feel guilty. And if you're trying to get me to admit I feel bad pissing you off, try again. Just because McCoy hired you doesn't mean I need to make your time here any easier."

"I don't back down from challenges." I hold my chin up high. He thinks he can instill fear in me, but I've already seen the worst of people. "By all means, good luck trying to make my life hell. I don't mind the heat."

Jax steps out of my way so I can walk toward the kitchen. I fiddle with the hotel's coffee maker, desperate for something to kick my butt into gear. I'll need all the help I can get with Jax in an irritable mood first thing in the morning.

He frowns as he leans against the counter. "Every time I think I've said or done something to make you quit, you surprise me by staying. Why is that?"

"If I quit because you make fun of something I do, then I

need to reassess my job. Get over yourself. I'm here for the long game."

"That's my fear with you. Short game, long game, endgame." His eyes flash with uncharacteristic vulnerability before it disappears as quickly as it came. "I'll leave you to it then. I need to get ready for our flight."

I'm left staring at Jax's retreating body. Why is he afraid of me?

Truly, I'm afraid of him. I have no idea how to cope with my attraction toward the one person I can't and shouldn't want.

"Where have you been hiding this for the past few weeks? When you mentioned us going on a private jet, I didn't expect *this*." I stare at Jax's sleek plane, the black paint gleaming under the morning sun.

"My dad had to borrow it for work stuff, but we get it for the rest of the season. Don't get used to it though. One season will fly by and then you'll be back on commercial airlines with cheap pretzels and screaming kids." Jax struts the carpet like a catwalk, his Doc Martens thumping against the ground as he twirls.

"Did you say a bad pun? I'm shocked." My eyes linger on his butt. I can't even remember the last time I was this focused on every part of a man. From Jax's long legs to his muscular thighs, to his corded arms straining from dragging his luggage behind him.

"My eyes are up here." Jax snaps his fingers.

My eyes lift, meeting his hazel ones. "I know. I was checking out the carpet. Black just like your soul, I'm guessing?"

"Now you're getting it."

Seeing as Jax is the human equivalent of a Rubik's cube, I was—under absolutely no circumstance—getting it. "My bad. Insinuating you have a soul means you're redeemable. You're like my dolls: vacant and cold."

He taps his chest with one tattooed finger. "Emphasis on the cold, especially around my heart. You're lucky I give a shit about my career because if not, you'd be fucked out of a job."

I let out a shrill laugh. "No, I wouldn't. I'd end up working for people who actually want my help instead of an entitled prick who acts like he's God's gift to Earth."

Okay, maybe I would be out of a job paying double what I usually make. But at least I wouldn't be a few months from finding my first gray hair.

"Elena, dear, stop showing your true colors. I'd almost think you have a thing for our back-and-forth. I won't lie to you though, that type of self-inflicted torture would make for an interesting personality trait."

"My personality is begging me to shove a heel up your ass, but I keep it in check. I deal with greater douchebags behind the scenes at press conferences."

"Who knew you had such naughty kinks?" Jax laughs at my growl of frustration.

We walk up the stairs of the plane and greet the pilot. The interior of the plane is creepy. I'm surrounded by black—from the leather chairs to the carpet to the walls. "This is yours?"

"That's what my accountant tells me. Why?" Jax deposits himself into one of the captain's chairs.

"It's so…"

"Depressing?"

I nod my head. "You'd think something this expensive would be more welcoming."

"I like the color."

"It's the equivalent of a flying coffin."

Jax scowls at me. "Fitting, seeing as I'm mourning the loss of your career."

"A little premature, don't you think?"

He shrugs, grabs his headphones from his backpack, and messes around on his phone. I sit on the opposite side of the aisle. Jax remains engrossed in whatever he does, ignoring my presence.

I pull out a puzzle box from my bag and place it on the glossy tabletop in front of me. The moment Jax mentioned a private jet, I asked if I could purchase a few things to keep myself entertained over the weeks of flying. He looked at me weird and said to have at it.

I sort the pieces in groups based on edges versus normal pieces. The task is calming, with me getting lost in the arranging process.

My body prickles with awareness. I turn to find Jax staring at me, his usual scowl replaced by a small smile. On command, my cheeks flush at his appraisal. He holds my gaze when our eyes meet, trapping me in a temporary hypnosis. It feels like he wants to let me in for a moment, showing me someone different than the one I've seen over the past three weeks.

Something about the way he looks at me entices me to invite him. "Want to join?" I smile as I flash him a puzzle piece.

He shakes his head, replacing his smile with a frown. "No."

My smile flattens. "Okay." I turn back toward the table, resuming my task.

"Maybe next week." He speaks low, making me think I misheard him.

I say nothing. Maybe next week he gives me a chance, even if it's in silence while working together. Jax's mind is nothing like the thousand-piece jigsaw puzzle in front of me. He's one I'll have the hardest time putting together, wondering if it's worth even trying.

I spend what feels like hours organizing the pieces by color groups. The stunning photo of hot-air balloons mock me, all happy colors and a bright day. My chest burns at the sight of the breathtaking festival.

I envy the kind of freedom hot-air balloons have. They're not bogged down by responsibilities and extra baggage like me.

I don't know what pushed me to choose this puzzle. By the end of the flight, I promise myself I'll go to a hot-air balloon festival. Not because of the beauty or the rarity of it, but because I want it to represent me moving on.

From my past. From my pain. And from the creeping emptiness threatening my future.

CHAPTER ELEVEN

Elena

"I'm going out." Jax walks toward the main door of our Sochi hotel room.

"Uh, with whom? I thought we were staying in." I lift from the couch. We agreed to not go out while adjusting to the jet lag after flying from Bahrain to Sochi.

"You're staying in. I'm going to hang out with my friends."

My eyes scan his face to gauge his seriousness. "You can't leave without me. We have a deal."

He pinches the bridge of his nose and shuts his eyes. "For fuck's sake. I want to hang out with my friends, knock back a beer or two, and catch up before our practice rounds tomorrow. It's not exactly a rager."

"What friends?"

"I can't believe I have to explain myself like this." He lets out a deep breath. "Noah, Liam, and Santiago. We plan on staying in this very hotel. If you're so damn worried about me ruining the image you've been working on, don't be."

I sigh. "It's part of my job to make sure you stay out of trouble."

"Well, seeing as my friends all have squeaky clean reps now, I doubt I can muster up too much bad press."

"Are you asking for me to trust you?"

"To want your trust means I'd have to care. And honestly, with you, I could care less."

"*Couldn't* care less. If you're going to insult me, make sure you're being grammatically correct. It tends to pack a bigger punch."

Jax turns and grips the handle of the door. His back rises to match his ragged breaths. "You can trust me to not go off to a club or get drunk tonight. I only want a night with my friends. No stress, no girlfriends around them. Just a normal night to forget."

"Forget what?" I whisper the words.

"To forget what it feels like to worry every damn day of my bloody life."

This feels like the progress I've wanted since our first weekend together. It took a month longer than I expected, but the small victory feels worth celebrating.

"You can always talk to me."

Jax looks over his shoulder, hitting me with a withdrawn gaze. "Opening up to you is the last thing I need this season. Be back later." He opens the door and takes off, the thud of the door matching the throb in my chest.

I call Elías thirty minutes later because I don't want to spend my night alone. He comes without any questions, proving time and time again why he's the best person in this whole organization.

Two hours and one batch of popcorn later, Elías has erased any worries I had about Jax.

"Why did you have to pick a chick flick? I may be gay, but I still have manly preferences."

"Last week you picked. I didn't ask to watch the newest Marvel movie, but it's not like you gave me an option."

"You can't compare Marvel to whatever this is. No self-respecting woman should take back a man who hooks up with her sister. She should have some class. Listen to a Taylor Swift song, meet a new man, and move on." Elías dramatically lays his head on my lap.

"Easier said than done."

"If I could, I'd be on the next dating app, no questions asked. No one would dare swipe left on me. Have you seen my cheekbones? Those suckers could make a straight man want me."

We both laugh as he shows off said bone structure I'm slightly jealous of.

He taps his chin. "What if I quit F1, become an influencer, and then we travel the world together? Let's be honest, I'd probably get a ton of views and you could manage me like Kris Jenner. Be my momager, please?"

I laugh obnoxiously.

"Now you two are fucking out in the open? Can I ever catch a break from you both?" Jax's irritated voice surprises me.

My head snaps toward him, flashing a bright smile to combat his mood. "You missed the best part! Elías does this magical thing with his tongue despite me having literally all my clothes on."

"She's joking. We were watching a movie. Relax." Elías puts a healthy space of distance between us.

"Whatever. You guys are weird as fuck." Jax enters his room and shuts the door.

Elías cringes. "Whoops. Looks like Mr. Grumpy is back at it again."

I tuck my legs under me. "You'd think after a couple of beers he'd relax a bit. I don't get why he keeps thinking we're hooking up."

"There's no use denying you're a babe and I'm hot. It's not a shock he'd jump to conclusions about us."

I laugh. "He doesn't need to be a jerk about it. It's one thing to be annoyed, but it's another to voice his dislike every time he sees us."

"The reasoning is simple."

"What do you mean?" I whisper in case Jax can hear us.

"He's got the hots for you."

"If by hots, you mean a burning desire to have me disappear, then yes he does."

"Nope. Have you not noticed how he checks you out across the garage? JaxAttack may say one thing, but his dick doesn't agree. I think it makes him even grumpier because he wants what he can't have."

My eyebrows raise. "And you know this how?"

"I recognize someone walking with a boner when I see them. It's a rather awkward experience, with him wobbling away when you bend over to check out my car."

I cover my mouth to muffle my laugh. "You can't be serious."

"I know it's a shock, but Britain's Most Ineligible Bachelor has a thing for you."

"It's a shock because he acts like an asshole too often for me to find him endearing."

"But the real question is do you find him sexy? Now that's something I wouldn't mind exploring." Elías waggles his brows.

"I think nice guys are sexy."

"Snore. Boring." He pretends to nod off.

I shove his shoulders. "Who said they were boring?"

"Me! I had to sit next to them for multiple dinners."

"Really, what was wrong with them?" I cross my arms.

"Juan was sweet but a sucky lay based on all your stories. Poor guy didn't stand a chance against you in the bedroom. Your alpha needs couldn't be met, let alone satisfied. And Pablo needed to get his head out of his ass and move out of his parents' house. Even flowers and chocolate lose their appeal when it comes out of a twenty-five-year-old's allowance from his parents. Miguel—sweet Americanized Miguel—was amazing at the time; I'll give you that. Except he was a momma's boy who dumped you because she didn't approve of a woman from Mexico City. She treated you like you snorted cocaine to make it through the day."

"To be fair, Miguel's family was sheltered."

"From what? Common sense?"

A hysterical laugh erupts out of me. "Okay, thanks for a reminder as to why you didn't approve of any of my boyfriends."

"I'm only trying to tell you that Jax might like you, so he probably struggles with that. Maybe that's why he's extra mean to you."

"Well, that's not a good enough reason to be a jerk. At least not for me. I'm not into the *grumpy guy is mean to the girl he really likes* plot. It's a bit overused and dated for my taste."

"But think of how fun it would be if you gave in. I'm sweating here thinking about it."

I roll my eyes, getting up from the couch. "You need to go. I've had enough of this intervention."

Elías walks to the door and steps out into the empty hallway. He flashes me a lopsided grin. "Face it. Maybe you need to try one round with a naughty boy to realize what you've been missing."

"Says the guy who is sweeter than a bottle of *ponche*. Good night and sweet dreams."

"A true friend would wish for me to have naughty dreams. The naughtier the better."

I giggle as I shut the door. Naughty dreams might be good for orgasms, but bad for the heart. Hate to break it to Elías, but Jax Kingston is not what the doctor ordered.

Based on Jax's recent history on the track, I didn't expect him to land on the podium every race this season. My eyes stay glued to him as he exits his race car after placing second for the Sochi Grand Prix.

The cocky man did it. He got between Noah and Santiago, which alone is a huge accomplishment compared to his laid-back approach last year.

"Damn, why can't he suck this year? I order you to stop helping him. Honestly, I can't handle this level of betrayal from my best friend." Elías tugs me into a hug. His sweaty race suit presses against me.

"Ay Dios, ¡para! You smell disgusting." I wrinkle my nose and gag.

"This is the smell of labor and love. You wouldn't understand with your recent plush lifestyle of private jets and fancy hotel rooms."

"You caught me. There's absolutely no work required when dealing with your teammate all day, every day." I stick out my tongue at him.

"Elena, I need you to help me with something." Jax's prickly voice catches our attention.

"Duty calls." I throw my hands to the side and do a twirl in my heels before walking away from Elías.

"You needed me?" I stop in front of Jax.

"Follow me. I've got shit to do before we fly out tonight and I don't have time to sit around while you flirt with Cruz."

"Alllll right." I drag out the words. One would think after placing on a podium, Jax would be in better spirits.

I was wrong. So very wrong.

I follow Jax through the empty McCoy halls to his private suite. Somehow, a month around him helped me build resilience to his attitude. My days include a morning reminder of how I'm not here to play nice, followed by wishing my coffee was something of the alcoholic variety.

"If you plan on sleeping with him, at least give me a warning. I want to stay away from you both when shit hits the fan."

I stop in my tracks and laugh up to the ceiling. "Why are you jealous? It's not like you try to hang out with me."

He grimaces. "This has nothing to do with jealousy."

"Weird because for some odd reason your words sound an awful lot like it."

His race sneakers squeak against the tile floor as he eats up the space between us. Everything about him draws me in despite our contrasting personalities. We're like two magnets. With a flip, we're polar opposites, but if he stopped being an ass, I have a feeling we'd click into place.

"Jealousy means I have to like you, or at the very least want you." His darkening eyes trail down my body, failing to match his words.

He intoxicates my brain with a simple glance and a curl of his lip. Some wires in my brain must be crossed if I'm attracted to his level of assholery.

"Could've fooled me."

"How so?"

I lean in closer, giving him a good look down my blouse. How can I give a damn about modesty when I'm trying to prove a point? I'm done dealing with his attitude for the week. "You may dislike having me around, but I have a theory it has more to do with you wanting me than you hating my help. You can't help craving something more and it scares you."

Okay, my last sentence is a hunch influenced by Elías, but a plausible hunch, nonetheless.

"Cravings are for weak people." His eyes remain on my chest.

The heat of his gaze acts like invisible fingers tracing across my skin. I ignore the goosebumps left behind. "You're right. Cravings are for the weak who don't have the balls to chase after what they want."

Flirting with disaster has a look, and this is it. The flash in his eyes should warn me away. Instead, I stay rooted to the floor, unmoving as he leans in. Everything stops around me as his lips lightly trail the curve of my neck. Hot air escapes his mouth, causing me to shiver at our nearness.

I didn't expect him to get this close. Hell, I didn't expect his lips to feel amazing on my skin. His tongue darts out, running down the column of my neck. My legs threaten to buckle.

"Oh, I chase after what I want. Hate to break it to you, but you're not it, love." He steps away and enters his suite, leaving me confused and slightly embarrassed as he shuts the door.

Jax does want me. He's a liar, attempting to convince himself more than me about his disinterest.

After taking a few deep breaths to calm my racing heart, I enter his suite. My eyes scan the empty room before landing on the closed bathroom door. I stop myself from knocking once Jax speaks.

"Cut this shit out. You can't keep going on like this, shaking and ruminating and shit when you're supposed to be celebrating. No wonder it's been years since you won a World Championship. You're a pathetic wanker who can't win because you're too busy doubting yourself."

Oh, no. Everything spins around me as I try to wrap my head around how much contempt Jax saves for himself. A small kernel of guilt shoots through me at eavesdropping, but I need all the help I can get to understand him better. Even if it comes at the expense of something I'm not exactly proud of.

"She's right. You're a weak piece of shit. Anyone who got a look at you right now would agree." His voice cracks.

I cringe at him referencing what I said. I don't really think he's weak. Maybe slightly delusional and frustratingly oppositional, but not weak in the slightest. It's hard to ignore the sharp pain shooting through my chest as he continues on with his self-hate speech.

"You're going to go to the cool-down room and act like you usually do. Then you're going to call Mum and Dad later and suck it up like a man. No more anxiety shit after talking to them. Grow the fuck up."

My heart aches to the point of bursting. I step away from the door, knowing he deserves a semblance of privacy.

I sit on a couch and turn my back away from the bathroom, mulling over everything he said. My stomach clenches at the notion of listening in on him clearly having a moment of distress. I'm not proud of snooping, even if I learned about a crucial part of Jax he keeps hidden from the world. Who knew the dislike he has for me is equal to what he saves for himself?

The door creaks open a few minutes later. My spine straightens as Jax's eyes burn a hole into my back. "Do you still need my help with whatever you mentioned in the garage?"

Okay, I didn't sound half as guilty as I feel.

He lets out a deep sigh. "Not anymore. I handled it. We better go celebrate the win before Connor loses his shit. Can't be late to my own podium."

I ignore the desire to console him. He moves toward the main door, silently prompting me to follow. His eyes remain hidden behind a pair of dark glasses as we walk toward the podium, pretending as if nothing happened.

As if I didn't find a breaking point in his rough exterior.

As if I don't want to like him more than I dislike him.

As if I don't want to help him for more than a paycheck at the end of the season.

And the last one is the most concerning thought of all.

"If it isn't my favorite fixer?" Connor motions for me to take a seat across from his desk. His office is bare, with no personal mementos to decorate the place. I find it unwelcoming and sterile.

"I can tell by your face you think this place is boring. I won't lie to you—I'm still waiting for the other shoe to drop, wondering when the board will revoke me of my job." His eyes find mine, flashing with an openness I find refreshing compared to Jax.

"Not if I can help it on my end." I raise my chin with confidence.

"That's the spirit. You've been doing a great job thus far. Well done keeping Jax under control. And according to my sources, your first fundraiser went amazing. You should be proud of raising thousands of euros for such a great cause."

"I'm glad you think so. I actually have something to ask you that could help improve things around here a little more."

"Say it, and it's yours." Connor flashes me a sweet smile.

Wariness sets me on edge, unsure if Connor means to flirt. He must notice the shift in me based on the way he coughs before laughing.

"Oh, no. Please don't take my willingness as anything but an extension of good faith. I truly want Jax to perform his best, and I have a feeling you're one of the few people who could help him. I'm willing to give you anything you need to keep him at the top of his game."

"Well, this is something I think can be useful for both teammates, actually." *Sorry, Elías. Please forgive me, but you need someone to talk to as well.*

"Spit it out. Your obvious hesitation is choking me here."

"Okay, well, I did some research about athletes and performing under stress. I think the guys could benefit from speaking to a psychologist who specializes in sports. I found a few and compiled a list of those willing to travel with McCoy's team."

"Why do they need a psychologist?"

"We both know Jax struggles with anxiety, and with Elías being new to the team, it wouldn't hurt for him to talk to someone too."

Connor rubs his chin. "And anything said in these sessions remains confidential?"

"That's the psychologist's job. I think it could help both guys and make a difference with managing stress and performance fears."

Jax needs all the help he can get, and as confident as I am with my skills, I can't compare to a mental health professional. Something in my chest tightens at the reminder of his conversation in the bathroom. There is something seriously getting in the way of him achieving what he's capable of, and maybe talking to someone can help.

I'm willing to try anything to help him manage his anxiety.

"Done. Whatever you need is yours." Connor looks at me and smiles.

"I'm going to need you to somehow convince Jax it's a part of his contract. I doubt he'd go to these sessions willingly."

"He'll do what I say. Give me a week to get the contract with the psychologist settled. I assume you'll email me the list of potential ones," Connor says with an authority I haven't seen in him yet.

"Yes, sure." I lick my lips. "I have one last favor."

Connor sighs. "Why do I feel like this is one I'm going to regret?"

"Sorry." I cringe. "Can you please pretend you're the one who came up with this? Jax will hate me if he found out I forced a psychologist on him."

"He won't hate you."

Seeing as Jax has vocalized time and time again how much he hates talking about his feelings, I have a hard time believing Connor.

I tuck a lock of hair behind my ear. "Trust me, he would."

"Jax can't hate anyone. He hates the world and the shitty cards dealt to people, but he can't hate you. Trust me—I've known him for a while."

I have no idea what to make of his comment.

Connor doesn't give me a chance to ask what he means. "I know he's been difficult, but he's a good guy. A loyal family man who has some issues that can get in his way. He's been a bit lost, but I know he'll get out of this. I like your idea of the psychologist. And don't worry, I'll pretend it's my doing."

"Thank you." Relief washes away my previous anxiousness.

I count today as a win for Team Elena.

CHAPTER TWELVE

Jax

'm an idiot. Based on the way Elena stares at me, I should've never planned a stupid dinner on our flight from Sochi to Barcelona. Now she looks at me with hope and shit. Hope I need to extinguish since there's no use for it. At least not toward me.

"Whoa." Her eyes move from me to the plated tacos and wine.

This totally looks like a date. Shit. "I was craving Mexican tonight."

She eyes the food, ignoring the flight attendant ushering her to sit across from me.

"Stop acting weird. Your food is getting cold." I grab a cloth napkin and place it on my lap.

She settles into the seat across from me. "Tacos?"

"Yes. Tacos. You know more words than this, come on. Did I literally stun you? I know I look good but…"

She lifts her eyes from her plate. "I'm surprised. I guess your Prix win put you in a good mood."

Fuck. I really am a total arsehole. If this is a sweet gesture, I'm doing my job fucking everything up with us too well. The only reason I set up this dinner was because I wanted to thank her for her help thus far.

Instead of expressing my thoughts, I keep my thanks to myself. "Now I know the way to get you to stop talking."

The flight attendant asks us if we need anything, but I send her away with a thank you.

"So, we have almost eight hours together. Any bets on how long it will take before one of us says something nasty?" I sip my wine to calm my nerves.

"Based on your history, I give it two minutes."

"That's the only time I want to hear you referring to me and two minutes in the same sentence."

Blood rushes to her cheeks. "I walked right into that one."

"I couldn't resist." I brush a finger across her pink cheek without thinking, enjoying the way her eyes cloud and her lips part.

She pulls away from my touch. A smile graces her lips as she grabs a taco and takes a bite of her food. "So...you kept it together for a month already—minus your failed attempt at a suite party. How do you feel?"

I smirk. "The music sounds better on the podium than standing on the sidelines."

"I'm sure there are more of those wins to come."

Why does she always believe in me? No matter how many times I brush her off, she keeps up her positive shit with a smile. "Tell me, does McCoy pay you extra to be my personal cheerleader?"

"I should've included that in my contract. Probably could've gotten a couple extra thousand euros for being your motivational coach."

"Your loss is my gain."

She shrugs, choosing to eat quietly.

I hate sitting in silence. For some masochistic reason I can't comprehend, I want Elena to pay attention to me. To see me as something more than an irritable arsehole, even if it's for an hour. "So, tell me something no one knows about you."

Who the fuck opens up with a question like that?

Me, a motherfucking idiot, that's who.

She chokes on her drink in the most unladylike display I've seen of her. "What?"

"Come on, let's play a game."

"Pick a different game. I don't like this one." She crosses her arms.

My eyes drop straight to her cleavage because I have the self-control of a teen. *Hello, brain, meet the gutter you're permanently moving into.* "No. So, tell me what's something no one knows about you."

"You're a jerk 99% of the time so I don't want to share secrets with you."

"But think about the 1% of me you actually enjoy. That's worth it."

She blinks at me without responding.

I roll my eyes. "Fine. A secret for a secret. I'll start to give you a little faith in me. I love One Direction."

She laughs before stopping, probably because of my scowl. "I'm sorry. I thought you were messing with me."

"I assure you I'm not, seeing as I was a VIP at their last

concert. Their breakup made half of the UK cry."

"How do you have a Coldplay tattoo yet love One Direction?" She points to the tattoo of Coldplay's *Parachute* album cover on my arm.

"The same way you love watching *Real Housewives* reruns and *Downton Abbey*. I won't answer honestly if you're going to judge me."

She puts her palms up in submission. "All right. I'll be better."

"Fine. You can make it up to me by telling me something no one knows about you." I grin at her.

"I collect snow globes."

I scoff. "Bullshit. For sure someone knows about your collection."

"Well, no one knows *why* I collect them. They only know that I do."

I lean in closer, intrigued. "Okay, fine. Tell me why."

I regret taking a deep inhale because her fruity scent assaults my nose. My lungs constrict and blood rushes to my dick. She smells good. Really, really fucking good.

Which is really, really fucking bad.

"Snow globes are special, especially the ones that play music. Those are my favorites. I love them because I feel like they're a moment in time, captured and remembered. I have some from different cities, one from university, and a couple of others that are important to me." Her smile drops as if she remembered something unpleasant.

I don't like the sad look on her face. "Where's your collection now?"

"I have a small apartment in Monaco where I used to work

before all this F1 traveling with you."

"Have you collected any during this trip?"

She blinks at me. "Nope. Why?"

"I'm wondering what's your next memory worth saving."
Well, fuck, that sounded dreamier than intended.

Based on the way her eyebrows raise, I can tell she has the same surprised reaction. Instead of waiting for her to answer, I keep the conversation going. Solely out of kindness. Not because I'm interested in getting to know her more.

Bullshit. Fuck me sideways with a ten-inch dildo please because I'm actually enjoying Elena's company.

"What's your favorite thing to do in your spare time? Obviously besides babysitting me."

She smiles. "I like to watch YouTube videos of people doing makeup."

"Let me get this straight: you like to watch people put makeup on themselves?"

"That's what they usually do. But they also do challenges like putting makeup on their boyfriends, getting ready with no hands, and doing makeup while getting drunk."

"Those are some committed wankers, doing that for their girlfriends. I could totally see Liam doing that shit for Sophie. I won't lie though, I'm surprised you like watching people do makeup instead of doing it yourself."

"The most talented YouTubers make it look like art. It's my guilty pleasure."

I shake my head. "If that's the kind of pleasure you like, men are fucked. I love foreplay as much as the next guy, but I draw the line at makeup brushes."

A rush of laughter escapes her.

I don't think before I speak. "I like it when you laugh like that."

She eyes me like I admitted I have a secret collection of sex toys. "What?"

"Nothing," I blurt out.

She lets my comment go. Somehow, we last a whole dinner without arguing. An hour of us getting to know each other more than we ever have. I hate to admit talking to Elena was calming and fun—the exact opposite of what we should be doing together.

Once we're done, she settles into the chair across the aisle to work on her puzzle. She shoots me a timid smile in a silent invitation.

I shake my head, denying her request. Not because I don't want to. My rejection is because I crave more time with her. More attention, more of her laughs, more of her goddamn twinkling eyes.

Her shoulders drop as she returns her attention back toward the puzzle. It's obvious she hoped I'd join. But doing something like that together could give her the wrong idea.

A relationship, even something as platonic as a friendship, wouldn't work between us. It can't work. If I've learned anything from Liam and Sophie, friendships only end one way, with *I love yous* and dreams of forever.

Someone like me will always disappoint someone like her. It's written in my DNA, intertwined with an arsehole gene and other shit that can't be overridden.

"Hope you're ready for the next reputation-builder event!" Elena's singsong voice wakes me from my nap on the couch. I didn't bother making it to my room because of how knackered I was after our flight to Barcelona.

I lift into a sitting position, prompting her to move away from me. "You have way too much serotonin to be considered human. How the fuck do you have so much happy energy all the time?"

"Says the guy who works out a lot yet lacks the endorphins to match."

"And let me guess. 'Endorphins make you happy and happy people don't shoot their husbands.'" I attempt my best Reese Witherspoon Southern drawl.

"You did not quote *Legally Blonde*." Her eyes bulging makes a grin spread across my face.

I bend and snap for some goddamn unknown reason. The giggle pouring out of Elena's mouth makes the stupid idea worth it.

"You love movies, don't you?" Her eyes light up.

"Absolutely. I reckon I would've been a movie critic or some shit if I wasn't racing."

"Really?"

"Oh yeah. IMDB is my bible and *Lord of the Rings* is the best book-adapted-to-film series. I'm a cinephile."

"Oh my God. Ew. Don't say it like that." She purses her lips in the most adorable way.

Adorable. God help me because I think my balls have been permanently detached from my body.

I cross my arms. "There's nothing wrong with being a cinephile."

"Please, just say you like movies. That's my PR advice for you. The last thing I need is someone posting how you're another kind of 'phile.'"

I drop my head back and laugh. "Fuck no."

She shakes her head and laughs with me. "Seriously, you need to start getting ready. I don't want to be late."

"Can we reschedule for never?"

"Sorry, I'm booked out an eternity from now, so this is my only free slot." She taps her watchless wrist.

"Of course, you are. Wouldn't you say that's rather convenient?"

"Anything related to you is anything but convenient." She rises from the other side of the sectional. "Are you ready for what I have planned?"

"Not in the slightest."

"Perfect! Get dressed in the suit I placed in your room while you were sleeping." She covers her mouth with her hand, but her eyes betray her amusement.

I eye her skeptically as I enter my room. An Easter bunny suit scares the shit out of me, with huge eyes and a neon green vest covered in fluorescent eggs.

"Surprise! An Easter egg hunt!" She claps her hands together exaggeratedly.

"You've got to be fucking kidding me. A suit? Seriously?"

"I know. Isn't it cool? You have no idea how hard it was to find one of those on such short notice." She leans against my dresser.

"Why can't I dress like a normal person?"

"Because you're hosting the event and kids want a real Easter bunny."

"Bunnies don't even lay eggs. This is stupid as fuck."

She shrugs, ignoring my turmoil. "Stupid but effective. We're raising money to fund local playgrounds in Barcelona's most underserved areas."

Damn, I nearly give into her stupid bunny suit request based on the way her eyes light up at the idea of donating money to children in need.

Nearly being the essential word.

"I'm not wearing that. I refuse." I shake my head.

She wobbles her lip on command and clasps her hands together in mock prayer. "Please? Think of the little kids. They'll want to take pictures with a real bunny and have fun. Plus, the parents are donating lots of money to find eggs on the racetrack with you."

"What do I get out of this?"

"Besides fundraising for kids from impoverished neighborhoods who deserve new, safe playground equipment?"

When she puts it that way, I sound like the biggest dick. But the bunny suit is horrendous, and one whiff in its direction tells me it smells offensive. "I get to cash in on one favor from you."

"What kind of favor?" Elena's eyes widen.

"Not the sexual kind based on the look of horror in your eyes. Anything is on the table, as long as it isn't illegal."

"Fine. Nothing illegal, nothing sexual, and nothing that can make me lose my job." She holds her hand out to me.

I grasp it, enjoying the feel of her hand in mine. "Deal."

"I'll be damned. This is the best shit I've seen in…well… forever…" Liam flicks one of the eggs on my hideous vest.

"Don't tell Sophie that." Noah punches Liam's shoulder.

"Not another word about this from you guys." I glare at them despite the lack of visibility from the large headpiece.

"I'll be sure to hire you for my kid's birthday one day. How much do you charge an hour?" Noah tugs on one of my ears.

"I'm retiring after this. If you want to book me, I hope you're okay with your kiddos learning every foul word in the dictionary."

"If my kid learns bad words from you, I didn't do my job as a father." Noah smiles at me.

"Look at you, having a steady girlfriend and talking about kids. Does Maya hold your balls hostage for collateral?"

"Asshole." Noah scowls at me.

"Oh look, Elena's bringing over another kid. Check out that little sucker holding on to her hand. I think he's in love." Liam bats his lashes in a dramatic way that makes me want to smack the back of his head.

Elena looks down at the kid with the most genuine smile. I'm stuck staring like a creep, enjoying how she beams at the kid before offering him a full-size candy bar. The way my chest clenches as she brushes away a tear from his face stirs up a mix of emotions nearly knocking me back a foot. Yearning sticks out to me most.

Elena walks up to us, stopping my inner dilemma. "Hi, everyone. This is my new friend Rafael. Some kids took all his eggs when he dropped his basket by accident, so I told him he could meet the best racers instead of collecting candy."

Jesus Christ. Kids can be brutal.

Liam kneels down in front of Rafael. "Who's your favorite racer? If it's me, I have extra candy for you."

Rafael shakes his head, making all of us laugh as he points at Noah.

"Of course. Everyone loves the famous Noah Slade," I grumble low, the suit muffling my voice.

"Don't be jealous. With the way you're driving this season, who knows what will happen next." Noah squats in front of Rafael. He grabs his own hat off his head and signs it before placing it on Rafael's tiny head.

Elena points at my headpiece. "You can take that off already. I honestly only expected you to wear it for the photo op."

"And you planned on telling me this *when*?"

She lets out the loudest laugh. "As soon as the egg hunt started. But once you kept it on without complaining, I couldn't resist. I meant it when I said it was nearly impossible for me to find one of those at the last moment."

"Damn, she got you good." Liam gives Elena a high five.

"Payback for weeks of attitude." She shrugs her shoulders.

"You're such a—" I start.

"Kid!" Noah interrupts us.

Liam eyes me as he signs Rafael's shirt. "You can only blame yourself for being such a temperamental jerk."

"That's fine. I got a favor out of this one." I smile wickedly at Elena once I tug off the bunny head.

Her mouth falls open as she gazes at my friends. "It's nothing bad or anything!"

Rafael smiles at me and gives my leg a hug. I awkwardly pat his head, unsure how to act around kids.

Liam shakes his head at Elena. "We're not the type to judge."

"Yeah, and to be honest, we're more afraid of Jax corrupting you." Noah's eyes slide from me to Elena.

Elena throws her head back and laughs. I can't take my eyes off her, no matter how much I want to. Though I want to hang around her more, I can't. Even something like today has pushed me closer than I should be with her.

When push comes to shove, I'm the first one to hit the road running. And I'm the type who doesn't look back.

CHAPTER THIRTEEN

Jax

"I'm not talking to a shrink." I shut the door to Connor's office and take a seat across from him.

"Yes, you are. It's in your contract."

"Where? Please show me because the last time I checked, psych sessions weren't in the fine print."

"It's under the clause saying you'll do whatever the fuck I want, whenever the fuck I want it. Section 3B if you want to get specific." He turns his laptop toward me, showing me the highlighted section.

"You've got to be kidding me. I don't want to talk to anyone."

"It's a new company policy. Athletes speak to a psychologist once a week for an hour. Anything said between the two of you remains confidential."

I clench my fists. "Why are you doing this to me?"

"It's not a personal attack. It's healthy, and I hope other teams copy us. You guys deal with high speeds, collisions, stress, and a ton of other things. I'd rather have mentally sound athletes driving our cars. And don't pretend you haven't had other shit eating away at you."

"That's different. It has nothing to do with my driving skills."

Connor scoffs. "Oh, sod off. Of course, it does. You taking a Xanax the day of a race says otherwise."

"That's not because of racing and you know that. It's tough to be around tons of people. I feel like I'm constantly on, exhausting myself by trying not to say the wrong thing or act the wrong way."

He shuts his laptop, giving me his full attention. "Exactly my point. Everyone can use someone to talk to, including you. I want my drivers to be in top condition this season."

"So Elías has to do this too?"

"I can't say who sees a psychologist, but I'm saying *you* will be doing it."

"What if I don't say anything during the session?"

He lifts one shoulder. "Then don't. It's your hour to waste however you want it. If you're done, I need to make a call. And don't be late for your first session." He dismisses me with a nod toward his door.

I grumble a goodbye as I make my way toward the office of Dr. Schwartz, McCoy's newest addition to my personal hell.

I knock on his door. He opens it, letting me into his office with a couch, low lighting, and a candle smelling like I walked onto the set of *The Great British Baking Show*. How fucking Zen of him.

"Welcome, Jax. It's nice to meet you." Dr. Schwartz takes a seat across from me. His brown eyes scream calm and welcoming while mine say I'd rather be fucked up the arse with a chainsaw than be here.

Graphic yet oddly imaginative.

"Well, Dr. Schwartz, I hear I'm stuck visiting you every week for the rest of the season."

He runs a hand through his brown hair before he adjusts his thick glasses. "Please call me Tom. And yes, I've been told we will meet once a week, but I'll be on call if you need me for more sessions." His words carry a Southern drawl.

"Doubtful."

He chuckles. "Most athletes are resistant to work with a psychologist in the beginning. At first, it can be intimidating opening up to someone, especially for those who are in the spotlight all the time. It's understandable how you want to keep your private life private."

"What would you know about athletes?"

"I'm a sports psychologist, which means I specialize in high-profile clients who deal with stressors not typical of a normal person. I've worked with the NFL and NBA. Although I'm new to F1, I can assure you I'll be tuning in on Sundays now."

Well, it seems like Tom has some credentials to his name. "Fabulous."

"So, why do you think you're here?" He clasps his hands together.

"Because Connor is in the mood to get his arse kicked."

Tom raises a brow.

I continue. "And in case you aren't aware, I don't want to be here. This is the biggest waste of an hour when I have limited time as it is."

"Noted. I only hope with time, you grow to enjoy our sessions together. My job is to help make your time with F1 easier rather than harder." His smile reaches his eyes.

"My life would be easier if I didn't have to be forced to do this every week."

Tom leans forward in his chair, his gaze easing my discomfort. "I understand it's not exactly what you want. No one likes to be forced into anything, especially something requiring you to express private thoughts with a stranger. If you don't mind me asking, what about this process feels forced to you?"

"Connor made me come. Literally. It's in my contract." I tug on my hair.

"Although it's a part of your contract, whatever you want to talk about is up to you. Is there anything at all that you would want to get out of coming to these weekly sessions?"

"Besides surviving an hour under your microscope?"

Tom chuckles. "I'm here for whatever you need. My job isn't to assess you, but rather assist you through the process of coping with major stressors—both on the track and in your life."

"Sounds dandy." Sounds like a nightmare, but Tom isn't on a *need to know* basis.

"If it's okay with you, I'd like to set some goals for treatment. It's something I do with all my clients."

"Easy. Goal 1: survive this season. Goal 2: kick everyone else's arse. Goal 3: win another World Championship."

He tilts his head. "Are all of your goals related to F1?"

"Is there something wrong with that?"

"No, it's typical of athletes. You might find yourself having your goals change once you attend more sessions and grow more comfortable with me."

"Swell." I lean my head against the couch as I begin to count ceiling tiles.

"This is your hour to do whatever you want and say whatever

you feel, Jax. Take advantage or stay silent."

"You won't force me to talk?" I cross my arms.

"I'll probably ask you some questions, but you have the right to refuse them. Like I said, this is your hour to make of it what you may."

"Then, I prefer silence, thank you very much."

"Very well." Tom keeps to his word, staying quiet for the remainder of our time.

Somehow an hour goes by faster than expected, with me counting ceiling tiles to pass the time.

"Same time next week?" Tom offers me his palm as I exit the room.

I take it and give it a good shake. "Sure. Not like I have a choice."

"We all have choices in life. You made a choice not to speak, like I made a choice to stay quiet. The mistake people make is thinking they don't have any other options. There are always alternatives, they're just not always the easiest."

I try to keep myself busy the night before the Spanish GP's practice rounds. The attempts include working out, cooking dinner in a small kitchen unfit for anything not straight out of the freezer section, and watching an episode of a TV show my mum recommended. Clearly the last attempt was a stupid decision, seeing as Elena parked herself on the small couch next to me, claiming she loves the show. There goes my attempt to stay away from her.

I see what you did there, Mum.

Throughout the night, I attempt to ignore Elena's glances my way. The way she bites on her lower lip tells me she tries equally as hard as me to focus on the show. My hope for her to not speak fades away as she opens her mouth, releasing the bottom lip she bit raw.

"Can I ask you a question?" Her melodic voice pulls for my attention.

"No. I want to see what happens next." Netflix betrays me, asking if I want to continue watching.

The universe truly hates me. It's official.

"Come on. What's the harm in one question?" She turns toward me.

"Coming from the person who makes a living off asking hard questions? Everything. Plus, I want to know if they find another clue to the treasure."

"Are you scared?" she teases.

I let out a forced laugh. "Of?"

"Answering a question or two."

I lift a brow. "So now it's two questions?"

She shoots me a beaming smile. "I'm bargaining."

"I haven't even agreed to one, let alone two."

"What would make you agree?"

"If you get to ask questions, then I do too." *Yup. There goes my plan to avoid Elena at all costs.*

"You always make everything so complicated." She shakes her head. "But okay."

"All right. Hit me with your first question."

She tucks her legs under her. Her attempt at getting comfortable only means trouble. "What's your biggest regret?"

Her question sparks my curiosity but not enough to make me answer that question right away.

"Can't you hit me with easier questions to get to know me? Like what's my favorite color?"

Her eyes narrow. "That's easy. Green."

My face must scream *what the fuck* because she lets out a breathy laugh. Elena gives me a look that would make other men kneel before her and beg for her time. But I'm not anything like other men. Too jaded, too disheartened, too damn self-deprecating.

"Aw, you expected me to guess black. I'm insulted how little you think of my skills. Your toothbrush and your water bottle are green. You may only wear black, but I'm onto you."

I hide my smile behind my hand. "Lucky guess. Name one of my favorite movies."

"Jurassic Park."

Well, shit. Either she stole my phone or she knows her stuff.

"How did you guess that one?" I choke on the words.

"People say the best way to know the enemy is by conducting thorough observations."

"You're absolutely crazy." And I absolutely like it.

She makes a funny face I end up laughing at. "I'm obviously joking. Your only shirt with color is a black T-shirt with the park's logo. And if you're ever going to wear color besides your uniform, it's bound to be something you love." She bites her bottom lip—a nasty habit I wish I could do to her instead.

"Now a hard one before I answer your original question. You must prove yourself worthy of deep ones." I lean in close and eliminate the space between us on the small couch. My lips linger near the shell of her ear, whispering words, not caring for the repercussions of my actions. "What's my favorite sex position?" My lips brush against the soft skin, my teeth grazing her before I pull away.

She trembles on command. I love it. I hate it. But most of all, I want more of it.

"I think you like doggy style because you don't have to face the person. Mindless, tight, and gets you off just fine." Her eyes darken as they land on my lips.

Fuck. She keeps me on my toes.

I fake indifference, scooting away despite craving her closeness. "No comment."

She lets out another laugh. Damn her for looking fucking endearing. "I'll take that as a yes. So, once again, what's your biggest regret?" Her bright eyes fill me with some sense of warmth I can't pin down.

"Being a dick to my mum when I was a teenager."

She tilts her head at me. "I didn't expect that one at all. Why?"

"Because she didn't deserve my attitude. I wish I enjoyed the time we had more, instead of acting like an arsehole."

"I'm a little scared to know how a younger Jax behaved if this is how you act now."

"I was a brat. Now, it's different. I only want to make my parents happy." I sigh. "My turn. Tell me why you like playing that interior design game on your iPad?"

"I'm saving up money to buy a decent apartment, so I want to practice my designing skills. I know you think it's silly, but I'm not too bad. Plus, who doesn't like working with fake money?"

"Where do you plan on moving?"

"I have a flat in Monaco, but I'm searching for a better one there. When I moved to Europe two years ago to start my job, I was low on funds, so my apartment isn't the best. That and supporting my grandma has put a damper on the kind of apartment I could afford." She looks away, tucking her hair behind her ear.

"Does your grandma live with you?"

She shakes her head. "No. She lives in a facility for patients with Alzheimer's Disease. I recently had her moved to a new one that's meant for long-term patients." She looks away. "It's the reason I accepted this job. Her care, my school loans, and affording to actually live adds up."

"Those places aren't cheap. What about your parents helping her?"

Elena slips on an unreadable mask which I recognize all too well. "It's my job."

"You're kind of young to shoulder that kind of responsibility."

"Not everyone can grow up with the Kingston name, getting everything they want with a snap of their fingers." She lets out a resigned sigh.

Elena would've been better off shoving an icicle through my heart. Her judgment irritates me, bringing my biggest concern back to the surface.

"Contrary to your opinion of my family, being a Kingston can't get you everything," I lash out, thinking of my mum. Money will never buy back the years of her life she's bound to lose, no matter how much my dad wishes. He'd give away all his money to have more time with her, minus the pain.

Thinking of my mum taints my mood, pushing me to end this exchange. "I think I've had enough talking for today." I rise from the couch.

"Jax, I'm sorry. I shouldn't have said that. It was rude and judgmental." She jumps from her spot on the couch and walks up to me, placing her palm on my chest. Her touch soothes the anger she helped bring about in the first place.

I attempt to step away, but she moves toward me again. "Fine. Whatever."

Fuck this shit. I don't need Elena bringing me the same level of calm as a Xan.

"I didn't mean to upset you. You have the world at your feet, yet you throw it away with poor decisions. I wasn't thinking."

"That's how it is between us. A couple of conversations without us bickering won't change that."

"If that's what you want."

"What I want is for you to get a fucking hint and leave me alone."

Her shoulders drop. I shouldn't be such a dick, but I can't stop it. There's no point to us getting close. She's working while I'm surviving the season. I almost forgot for a moment, but she brought me back to reality.

"You know, you spend way more energy pushing people away than trying to get to know them. One day you'll realize what a mistake you've made, and I'll be there for you once you do." Her lips tug into a wobbly smile. One I hate to see in the first place, not because it isn't beautiful, but because it's too fucking perfect.

Like everything about her. Too focused, too put-together, too damn unattainable. I hate her for it. I hate her for barreling into my life and showing me what it's like to want something different for once.

But most of all, I hate her for coming into my space, for making me pathetic, for simply believing me.

And hate makes me angry.

So fucking angry.

CHAPTER FOURTEEN

Elena

I n the past six weeks I've worked with Jax, he never openly expressed disliking me. I thought part of his witty comments were because I could take his shit before handing it back with a smile. But tonight, as he does the exact opposite of what I asked of him yet again, maybe I need to accept how he dislikes me after all.

Jax somehow had me agree to go to some club with him to celebrate his second-place win for the Barcelona GP. To be fair, he told me he would stay calm because he was there to hang out with Liam and Sophie. My mistake was believing him in the first place. Clearly, I'm an idiot because he did exactly what I should've expected.

For the first hour, he was relatively normal. That is until he disappeared for a solid ten minutes claiming he had a phone call to answer. After he returned from whomever he spoke to, he knocked back multiple rounds of whiskey despite my protests. When I told him Liam would carry his drunk ass home, he laughed in my face. Safe to say that conversation sucked.

Liam has been shoving glasses of water at him whenever possible, but Jax is too far gone. Now, a few women dance around him, groping him while he gets lost in the music.

The whole thing is disgusting. But also, it's beyond heartbreaking. His pain is obvious to the point that I feel it deep within my chest as if it were my own. It's hard not to miss the hurt he tries to hide. In his eyes, in his attitude, in his need to close himself off from everyone.

I don't know what pushed him over. And I don't know how to help, let alone how to talk to him.

"I haven't seen him this drunk…well, I think ever." Sophie stares at Jax with her eyes wide open.

"That's because he didn't do it in front of you. This season he's been different though, with him being less collected than usual." Liam's eyes track his friend's movements. "I'll make sure he doesn't do anything to hurt all the work Elena's done to help him."

"Do you know why he acts out like this? He won't tell me anything," I probe, hoping Liam has some answers.

"Sometimes he gets pissed. It's random so it's not like I can pin down the cause of it. But when he gets in this mood, it's better to leave him be so he clears his head."

"Which head, because the way those women grab onto him makes me think we are talking about two different types." My stomach twists in knots at the thought of some woman coming to our suite tonight. I don't know what to make of my tiny surge of jealousy. There's no place for it in my line of work, yet I can't ignore it.

Turns out Jax isn't the only one slipping up tonight.

Liam grimaces. "Emotionally he's off. But he's been better this season—at least in the media. Of course, that's all thanks to you. Thank God you put an end to the public blowjobs and trashy women exiting his suite at all hours of the day."

I fail to hide the way my body cringes. "Great. Glad to know I'm doing something right." I look away as I roll my eyes. I'm tempted to go back to the hotel and leave Liam to take care of him. Instead, I stay because of my job, and because Jax looks lost even though groupies surround him like he's a homing beacon.

"Ugh. Don't bring up his bed-fellow behavior. It's disgusting." Sophie elbows Liam in the ribs.

"I'm going to go check on him." I stand, not wanting to sit through another minute of this torture. No one is having fun tonight but Jax, who looks drunk and depressed as he sways to the music. It's about time I call an end to all of this because it's my job, whether I like it or not.

I sidestep sweaty dancers and men with grabby hands as I move through the crowd of club-goers. Jax is easy to spot, with his tall frame and the small hoard of women pawing at him. I push through them and stand in front of him.

"Love, is that you?" He smiles at me, all goofy with glazed eyes.

"Who's she?" A woman clutches onto his arm, pointing at me with a red-tipped finger.

"The best part of my day," Jax answers with another smile.

Well, that's unexpected. My heart thumps in my chest faster than before.

"She can go now. I promise to be the best part of your night." She turns her back on me, inching closer to Jax.

Gross. I roll my eyes before yelling over the music. "Are you sure about that? I should warn you both then. Jax, the doctor called and said the rash on your penis is herpes. Make sure to wrap it up tonight if you plan on sleeping together." My voice carries loud and clear.

The woman purses her lips in disgust and abandons Jax, leaving a drunken mess for me to deal with.

"Now that's not nice." He pouts his lips.

"I'm not here to be nice."

"I know that. You're here to ruin my life." He lets out a soft sigh.

"What do you mean? Half the time you say things I don't understand."

"Dance with me?" He ignores me.

"Are you out of your mind? You're so drunk you can't even stand straight."

He grunts. "Okay, forget dancing. How about fucking? It can be done lying down."

"I'd be impressed if your dick even worked after the amount of alcohol you've consumed."

"Let's test it out." He has the audacity to act all smug at his idea.

I close my eyes as I count to ten, willing myself to be patient with him. Ten seconds too long, giving Jax the opportunity to close the gap between us.

My eyes open to find his half-lidded gaze inches away. Jax's body presses against mine, the hard edges of him meeting my softer curves. It feels like my body comes alive, bursting with energy, pulsing like the speakers in the club. His scent of spice and whiskey wraps around me as sweaty bodies push us closer together.

He holds my chin between his index finger and thumb. "Why you? Why couldn't it be anyone but you?" The loud music can't conceal the pain in his voice.

"For the job? I was available. It's nothing against you, *por el amor de Dios.*"

"That's not the question I'm asking," he slurs.

"Estás tan borracho, it's not even funny. We need to get you home."

Jax has another idea as he tugs me into him. One of his arms wraps around my body as his lips find mine. His kiss is anything but gentle. It demands, stealing my breath and rationality away in one go. The taste of whiskey floods my mouth as his tongue dominates mine, testing my resistance.

My fingers clutch onto his shirt, desperate for something to stabilize me. To connect me to the ground before my mind drifts away.

And damn I'm tempted to let every worry about him fly away as his tongue strokes my bottom lip.

Oh. My. God. What is he doing? And more importantly, why am I not pushing him away? His kiss heats up my body. It's a feeling I've never had before—one addicting despite the wrongness of the situation.

He's drunk.

I have a job to do.

He has too many mood swings to be deemed stable.

The list could go on and on.

"Jax." I rip my lips away from him, unclenching my fingers from his shirt and placing my hands against his chest with every intention of pushing him away. Except I'm stuck in place, not moving, because his touch is electric. Toxic. Addictive.

It's everything I should avoid while being everything I desire.

His mouth moves onto my neck, his tongue darting out to run down the column. A shiver works its way down my spine when he sucks on the sensitive skin.

I lean into him, needing support, both emotionally and physically. "We need to stop this before we do something we'll regret." I sound as breathless as I feel.

His tongue traces a mindless pattern down my neck. "I live every day with regrets. What's one more?" His sad voice hits me right in the chest.

He nips at sensitive flesh, eliciting the smallest moan from me. One I hope he can't hear over the music.

I shove at his chest, finally getting the distance I need. "And whose fault is that?"

"Mine. Always has been. Always will be." He sighs as he stares at my lips with clouded eyes.

My heart beats in unison with the thump of the speakers—fast, irregular, and loud enough to hear in my ears. With little protest from Jax, I lead him back to the VIP table.

Liam and Sophie's attention snaps to us. Sophie struggles to hide her smile while Liam shakes his head, rubbing his temple.

Mierda. I'd rather go back into the crowd and hide for the rest of the night than face these two.

"Well, you got him under control in under fifteen minutes. I'm impressed. I usually have to drag him out of the crowd." Liam stands and grabs his friend, letting him lean against him. At least he has enough sympathy to save me from my embarrassment.

I'm grateful for the low lighting hiding how my face

resembles the color of a brake light.

"Your secret is safe with me." Sophie pinches her fingers together and makes an invisible zipper symbol across her lips before throwing the fake key behind her shoulder.

I let out a nervous laugh as Liam eyes me with pinched brows. He doesn't say anything, choosing to focus his attention on Jax. Both of them remain normal as we make our way through the club. We exit through the back entrance to escape paparazzi. A rental car driver greets us, opening the rear door for us. Liam pushes Jax into the back seat.

Sophie looks at Liam. "You should talk to him. It's not only about him anymore, you know, because Elena's job depends on him, too." She frowns at Jax as she shimmies into the center seat next to him, forcing me to sit on the other side of her. Probably best, seeing as Jax already mauled me by accident.

Right. Because his lips fell on mine. Who am I fooling?

This is fantastic. Really, my confidence in my work is at an all-time high.

Not.

I close the car door. "It's fine, please don't speak to him. I'll handle it and talk to him about this not happening again."

"Of course, she can talk to me. She *always* wants to talk to me. She won't run away no matter how many times I tell her to go," Jax mumbles.

"Ignore him. He says stupid shit when he's wasted." Liam enters the passenger seat, shooting Jax a look that tells me he wishes his friend would shut up and go to sleep.

"Sober words, honest thoughts." Jax laughs to himself.

"No, asshole. Drunken words, sober thoughts," Sophie corrects him.

"Oh, got it. So, does that mean it's okay for me to tell Elena I think she's pretty?"

Sophie throws her head back against the headrest and laughs. "Sure, go right ahead. Finally, the night is getting interesting. Why don't you tell us how you truly feel?"

"Don't encourage him," Liam grumbles.

"Elena is so pretty it hurts to look at her." Jax's words cause a steady buzz to take up residence in my stomach like I chugged a two-liter bottle of soda in under two minutes. I'm seriously messed up.

"Then why are you a moody jerk around her?" Sophie taunts him.

"Because I can be."

Liam groans. "That's a bad reason."

"Fine. Because I don't have a choice." He snarls.

"That's an even worse reason. You're not getting the point." Sophie taps Jax's temple.

Liam twists his body around the seat and smiles at Sophie. "Probably because he drank enough to kill off a majority of his brain cells."

Sophie clasps her hands together. "He's supposed to compliment her and then apologize."

"You can't make Jax do anything he doesn't want to do. That's what makes him…well…so Jax." Liam looks over at his friend.

And that right there is my biggest dilemma. I want to know what makes Jax feel like he doesn't deserve anything good in his life.

I want to know about the man who hides behind trashy news articles and mindless sex. The man who whispers to himself about not being good enough.

I want to know more about him, and I'm not sure if I have enough control to hold myself back from trying.

The moment Jax wakes up, I'm in his space. He looks about as fresh as one would expect after drinking their mind into a stupor the night before. I wouldn't be surprised if his skin tasted like his precious bottle of Jack. The image of me doing that to him has me swallowing back my groan. I shove the thought into the darkest corner of my mind, hoping it never sees the light of day.

I rise from the couch and follow him into our small kitchen. "We need to talk about last night."

"I ask for very few things in life. The first is that no one bothers me before my morning tea. And the second is that no one bothers me *after* my morning tea."

"Jax…" I warn.

"Fine. There's not much to say. My head aches to the point of wanting to hurl, so please save your speech for when I feel like I can stand straight without the world spinning."

"How about I help you. Start with the words 'I'm sorry, Elena,' and go from there."

He eyes me as he starts his electric water kettle. "Are you mad because I drank?"

"Yes." The words come out in a hiss. "What if Liam wasn't there to help me? What if a random person took a video and posted it online? I've spent the better half of this morning scouring the internet to make sure no one reported anything bad about you. You told me you would try to be better, and I want to believe you, but then you do stuff like this, making me question how serious you are about your own career!" My accent grows heavier as I become more frustrated.

His bloodshot eyes slide from the tea kettle to my face. "Would you believe me if I said I didn't mean to get that pissed?"

"Why are you able to be pissed? You're the one who kissed me! And got drunk! *I* should be pissed."

He shakes his head before wincing. "*Pissed* means drunk. Jesus, I drank too much."

"And what about the kiss? You can't do that anymore."

"Kiss?" His eyebrows scrunch together.

My heart takes a dive somewhere into my stomach. I didn't expect him to not remember. For some reason, his amnesia feels like another form of rejection.

Allow me to introduce another layer of fucked up between us.

"Did we kiss?" He says the words in a hoarse whisper. His eyes land on my face before they close.

I stare at him, attempting to keep my cool. It takes everything in me to not go to my room and lick my wounds in private. Some things take precedence, like teaching him a lesson. "Everything that happened last night won't happen again."

He runs a hand through his hair. "Shit. I'm sorry for kissing you. I shouldn't have done that."

"I'm not talking about that anymore. I'm going to pretend it never happened since you already have." *Okay, I sounded slightly bitter.* "I'm talking about you getting drunk and out of control."

He abandons fixing his tea to give me his undivided attention. "Fuck. I'm sorry. I haven't drunk like that since the break, and clearly my system didn't agree."

My anger returns like a wave, uncontrollable as it sweeps through me. "That apology would suffice if I hadn't asked you over and over to stop drinking. I thought the suite party was your last hurrah, but clearly I was wrong. I can't help someone who is hell-bent on ruining their own damn life. And not that you care, but it's not only your career on the line—it's mine too. Did you ever take a second to think about how your reputation affects mine? It's not fair for you to go dragging me down with you because you have a superiority complex and a will to kill off all your functioning brain cells before the age of thirty."

Jax strides over to me, standing toe to toe. Our proximity reminds me of last night. Of his lips on my skin, kissing me, licking me, nipping me. I suppress a shiver at the memory. I'd rather feel anger than attraction.

He stares into my eyes before he closes his. "I'm honestly sorry I did exactly what I said I would avoid doing. I'm sorry for putting my reputation at risk, therefore risking yours too. Even if I don't want your help, I don't want to ruin the effort you've put into building your business. And most of all, I'm sorry for kissing you when I was drunk." He winces.

"Yeah, well, sorry won't cut it anymore. Words are empty. They don't mean anything unless you back them up."

He fists his hands by his side. "That's exactly my problem. I can't back up the words I want to say, so all I do is get angry."

"Why?" The question bouncing around in my head for the past few months escapes me. Why is he the way he is? Why can't he do what he wants? Why does he choose to make destructive decisions?

"I'm not getting into this with you."

"If you won't talk to me, then learn how to control yourself."

He lets out an exasperated sigh. "Don't you get it? That's all I've tried to do."

I step away and throw my hands in the air. "What do you mean? You're beyond frustrating! Honestly, you give me a serious case of emotional whiplash."

"Controlling myself includes staying the fuck away from you. Looking at you annoys me because it reminds me of everything going wrong in my life," he blurts out.

I eliminate the last bit of space between us, placing my hand on his bicep. "What's going wrong?"

He looks at my hand, the fire in his gaze fading as his eyes shut. "It's not about what's *going* wrong because everything *is* wrong. Including having you around."

What does someone say to that?

I don't have a chance to think of a response because Jax strolls into his room, closing me off once again.

CHAPTER FIFTEEN

Jax

"**H**ey, *Mr. Second Place in the Entire World Championship.* Way to represent the Kingston name." My mum's voice echoes through the speakerphone.

I place my luggage in my closet, ready for Baku's race week. "Oh stop. Your fanfare is too much for me."

"Get used to it. She's your biggest supporter," Dad says. "So, what's your plan for today?"

"Not much. I have a sponsor event and some interviews today," I grumble.

"What a chore, living the high life." Dad laughs.

"And how are all your friends?" Mum loves to hear about them.

"Liam and Sophie are good. She couldn't come to this race because of uni. She's been trying to travel with us some weekends between her school schedule. And Noah and Maya are all hot and heavy—lots of snogging involved. I bet they'll get married within a year or two."

"Young love." Mum sighs.

"And is that Elena girl still following you around?" Dad can't help but probe about her.

"Yup. Still here keeping my image squeaky clean." Not that I've been much of a help. I've done everything in my power to keep to myself since last week's supposed kiss with Elena that I can't remember for the life of me. I don't know whether to be grateful for the amnesia or hate myself for forgetting.

"Thank God. It was hard defending your actions in front of my book club. They keep labeling you as some bad boy and I can't bear my son matching the antics of some of our characters. Absolute arseholes, some of them." Mum laughs.

"How dare your friends objectify me that way!" I let out a mock gasp of horror.

"You have no idea what they say about some men. Not that you need to worry, honey," she whispers to my dad.

I cough once the speaker picks up their kissing. "I'm still here."

"Sorry. Oh, no! Look at the time. I need to run. Gwen asked me to grab some type of wine for our movie night. Take care, love bug!"

We all know Mum won't run anywhere. The thought alone makes my stomach roll.

"Bye, Mum and Dad." I hover over the red button.

Dad's voice stops me. "Jax. Wait."

Like a sixth sense for bad news, my spine straightens as a chill rushes through my body. "Yeah?"

My dad's footsteps carry through the phone, followed by the sound of a door closing. "I've been meaning to talk to you.

I didn't want to bother you while you were celebrating last weekend and all."

"Why do I have a feeling this isn't good news?"

"It's not terrible, but it's not great. Mum's been having a lot of mood issues lately."

"She didn't sound like it." *Way to go making assumptions, Jax. This is ironic coming from a guy who doesn't look like an anxious piece of shit all the time either.*

"The tremors have been getting worse, so the doctor switched her medicine. She's having difficulty adjusting. They're heavy-duty stuff, and she'd benefit from some of your attention. If you have the time, of course. I don't want to burden you."

I take a deep breath. Guilt surges through me at Dad thinking I'm too busy to help Mum. "I'd do anything to help her. I can call her more and check in."

The thought alone makes me panic. More phone calls means more anxiety. Seeing as I've done a crappy job controlling that so far, I can only imagine what will happen to me with more calls.

If I was brave, I'd open up to my parents and express my concerns. Instead of voicing my feelings, I bottle them up. I can handle this. I *need* to handle this. "You know family always comes first."

"That's what makes you a Kingston."

How fitting. The same thing that makes me family has the power to destroy me.

My irritability hit a new high after I spoke to my parents earlier. I spent my lunch thinking about skipping this week's session with Tom, but I decided to attend in all my arsehole glory.

Tom sits across from me in his usual leather chair. "Anything you want to talk about today?"

"Not really." I stare up at the ceiling and count tiles. Every time I think of my mum, I restart.

After twenty minutes, I still haven't made it past ten tiles.

I let out an agitated breath. "My mum is sick." I don't look at him. Shit must be hitting the fan today because for the life of me, I can't fathom a good reason why I decided to open up to Tom.

"I'm so sorry to hear that, Jax. From what you've shared in the past about her, I can tell she means a lot to you. Her being ill must be extremely difficult for you."

"It's the absolute fucking worst. I hate hearing about it. Hate knowing she's struggling, or that my dad is home helping her while I'm here racing and having fun."

"It's completely normal to feel upset about everything you've said. And it can't be easy for you to battle these feelings every week by yourself."

I let out a deep sigh, hoping to expel some of the negative energy stewing inside of me. "Is it normal to feel upset every single day?"

I don't know what I'm looking for by opening up to Tom. But I need to vent to someone because I despise the man I've become to avoid all the feelings I have about Mum's illness.

"Of course, it's normal. I wouldn't expect anything less from someone who talks about your mom like you do. It shows how much you care."

"Yeah well, I hate the constant guilty feeling in the pit of my stomach every time they text or call me. And then I hate myself for feeling that way in the first place. I should be grateful to talk to Mum as it is."

"You can be grateful and still be upset about her being sick. It's okay to feel like that. If you don't mind me asking, what illness does your mom have?"

"Does it matter?" I don't need Tom's pity about her disease. Those who know about Huntington's Disease always give us the same look. One that's a mix of horror and sympathy, as if that does us any good.

"It would help me have a better grasp of the kind of situation you're dealing with, but I understand if you're not ready for that."

"I'm not."

Tom nods. "That's fine. I'm wondering what you find is the hardest part about talking to your parents?"

"Every time I do it, I feel worse. It adds to my anxiety, knowing she keeps deteriorating while I'm thousands of miles away. Now my dad asked me to talk to her more because she's down, and it stresses me out."

"What about phone calls stresses you out the most?"

"She pretends nothing bothers her. I'm well aware of her private suffering, so I hate when she puts on a brave face. And then after, my dad informs me about her progress and it's not the best news lately, which adds to my anxiety."

"It seems like you want to speak to her, but it's difficult to manage the anxiety that comes with those conversations."

"Of course, but I take Xanax, and that helps."

"Are you aware of the pros and cons associated with the long-term use of Benzodiazepines?"

"Yes. I wanted something fast-acting and starting

something like Zoloft wasn't going to do the trick. Now I'm not sure if Xanax was the right call. It's addicting as fuck to have my problems disappear with the swallow of one pill."

"Benzos are known for those instantaneous effects. If you ever want to consider changing meds or having a second opinion on the matter, there are plenty of psychiatrists I know for referrals."

We stay silent for another five minutes until the second case of the warm fuzzies hits me. "This is the first year I find my guilt choking me. I don't know why, but F1 hasn't been as fun knowing she's getting sicker while I'm away. I feel like I'm losing precious time with her because I'm selfish."

"Have you thought of taking a break from F1 to be with her?"

Yes, but I'm not going to admit that to him. "It doesn't matter. It won't make her better."

"It might not. The real question is if it will make *you* feel better."

Dammit, Tom, stop making so much sense. I return to counting the ceiling tiles, closing myself off from the one person I've opened up to the most.

I sit in my usual seat of the private jet. The nine-hour flight from Baku to Monaco allows me to stew in my emotions. For the first thirty minutes, I ignore Elena and her stupid puzzle.

My eyes drift back to her every five minutes. She proves a worthy distraction from my shitty thoughts. She stares angrily at a piece, attempting to jam it where it clearly doesn't belong.

"Maybe if you bend the piece hard enough, it will finally fit how you want it."

Her head snaps in my direction. "Those who don't help can't offer opinions." She switched her usual prim clothes for leggings and a hoodie looking three sizes too big. The site of her in something so casual has me craving her like a damn wanker. I shouldn't want her like this—shouldn't desire her at all. But here I am with a semi because of a Mexican Billie Eilish wannabe.

"Just observing." I put my hands up.

After another couple of minutes with her attempting to try a different piece, I get up and sit across from her.

I don't know why I bother, but I want to check out her progress. "Wow, you've done what? A solid hundred pieces in a few weeks?"

To be fair, the puzzle looks hard as fuck. It beats me why she chose a one-thousand-piece puzzle reminding me of someone's brain while tripping on ecstasy.

"Are you going to keep running your mouth or are you going to help me?" she taunts with a smirk.

I grab at the puzzle box, wanting to keep my hands busy. "You had to pick the most colorful, complicated puzzle?" There's a shit ton of hot-air balloons with the most detailed patterns. Looking at it for a couple of seconds has my eyes straining.

"Would you believe me if I said it looked easier on the website?"

I laugh. "Did you read the reviews?"

"Do people even review puzzles? I didn't think that was a thing." Her mouth drops open. "But now that you mention it, maybe I should've because I'm convinced half the pieces are wrong. This is what I get for ordering off some sketchy website."

"Or maybe you suck at solving things."

"Spoken from the second-hardest puzzle I've ever encountered."

I tilt my head at her. "I'm competing with a set of hot-air balloons? I'm slightly insulted. Maybe I need to up my game."

"I've yet to decide what's harder. I'll keep you posted." She tries to hide her smile behind her hair as she looks down at the puzzle, but I catch it.

For once, I don't avoid her. I can't decide whether it's because I'm lonely or sad about my mum. Elena and I work quietly, with me helping her.

We enjoy the silence together. She doesn't pressure me to talk, and I appreciate it. Instead of me getting lost in my negative thoughts, I focus on the task at hand.

Eventually, Elena calls it for the day because she wants to take a nap. I return to my seat and play my music through my headphones. After twenty minutes, I turn toward her, taking in her sleeping profile.

I'd never say it to her face, but she's one of the prettiest women I've been around. Natural with the best kind of curves, full cheeks, and skin with a healthy glow. All while radiating positivity and a sassiness I've come to enjoy despite our spats.

As I drift out of consciousness, I realize I didn't take a Xanax to calm down before the long flight. I can't tell if it was the relaxing activity of the puzzle or being around Elena.

The last thought concerns me. Elena is the one thing I couldn't anticipate this year. She threatens everything I thought I could accept about my life.

I don't want to hope. I don't want to be better. And most of all, I don't want to be reminded how empty my life is now that I've been around someone who makes the bad days bearable.

CHAPTER SIXTEEN

Elena

J ax surpassed my expectations. I predicted for him to test my limits since Monaco is known for its crazy parties during the Grand Prix weekend. Besides the mandatory events Jax needs to attend for McCoy, he stays in his suite at night, minus the alcohol. I welcome how calm it's been without him stirring up trouble. It gives me hope that he learned from his Barcelona slipup and plans on controlling himself better.

To pass the time, Elías hangs out with me in the suite.

"Let's play a game." Elías dangles a black box above my head.

I somehow muster up my most bored expression.

He shakes his head and rolls his eyes. "Tough crowd tonight. Seriously, I won't survive another episode of *Buffy the Vampire Slayer*. I'm sorry, but you need to get your head checked if you're Team Spike. Angel is irresistible and caring while Spike has no soul."

"I'll pretend you didn't say that. Spike sacrifices everything for her in the end. Even his own life! Angel runs away once things get hard. Way to be a hero."

Elías whispers *psychopath* under his breath. "Anyway...I invited a few people over to play because we need to make more friends."

"Why do your ideas always make me suspicious?"

"Probably because I'm going to ask you to go knock on Jax's door, seeing as his buddies are coming over."

"No! Why do you want to interfere?"

"Because playing Cupid is fun. Your sexual tension is hot. Like hotter than *Spike screwing Buffy despite being enemies* hot." He smiles.

"No." I stick my tongue out at him.

"We can do this the easy way or the hard way."

I shake my head and cross my arms, refusing to move from the couch.

"Hard way it is. You asked for it." With little effort, Elías pulls me up and pushes me toward Jax's bedroom. He knocks his fist against the door and passes me the box before running into my room.

"Lovely. He doesn't even bother to help me out," I huff under my breath.

Jax's bedroom door creaks open. His eyes scan me from head to toe, making my skin feel hot underneath my leggings and T-shirt. "What do you want?"

"So... Elías has this crazy idea."

"All his ideas are crazy."

I swallow back the lump in my throat. "I agree. But seeing as it's already a plan in progress, do you want to play a game with us?"

"I'm not a kid. I don't play games." His jaw clenches.

"Okay…" I stare down at the Cards Against Humanity box. "Well, I think Elías invited some of your friends, so we'll be out in the living room if you want to join us."

"I won't. I was in the middle of a phone call when you interrupted. If you're done now, I've got to go call my dad back." His eyes close, but not soon enough.

I catch the redness in them, the sheen he attempted to hide with his bad attitude.

I can't believe I'm considering this but has Jax been crying? I'd almost think I made it up, except when he opens his eyes again, they have a puffiness to them I've never seen before.

Holy shit.

Guilt consumes me for interrupting him when he is clearly having a rough time. "I'm sorry if I bothered you during something important. I was trying to see if you wanted to hang with us, but I can tell it's not a good time for you."

"Even if my friends are coming over, I want to be left alone right now."

His avoidance of his friends tells me everything. A year ago, Jax was all smiles and known for being *most likely to close a club down.* The male in front of me is a ghost of that person. He's become a man who seals himself off from the world instead of sharing his burden. And a small voice in my head wants to be the person for him. The same insane voice finding him attractive in the first place.

"Okay then. If you need to talk later, you know where I live." I point a thumb over my shoulder toward my bedroom.

He offers me a tight smile before closing his door. I turn on my heel. The image of Jax, upset and sad, pulls at my heartstrings from all different directions.

I step into my room to find Elías lying on top of my bed.

He offers me a weak smile. "I'm guessing that didn't go as planned based on your frown."

"I don't understand him."

"Did he have a reason for his mood this time?"

"Something about me disrupting a call with his dad."

Elías gazes at the ceiling and lets out a grunt. "I don't know why something feels off."

"Probably because he is off."

"Well, sucks for him. His friends are going to have fun with us while he pouts in his bedroom."

An hour later, our living room is filled with laughter. Liam, Noah, Maya, Sophie, Elías, Santi, and I sit around a coffee table centered in the living room.

Everyone seems like they are having a good time, even without Jax. Besides Liam asking about him thirty minutes ago, no one mentions his absence. Maya and Sophie spent the better part of the hour including Elías and me in every conversation, never making us feel like outsiders.

"'This is the prime of my life. I'm hot, young, and full of poor life choices.' Damn, who knew I was such a catch." Santiago reads off his winning card set.

"When you describe yourself as a catch, that's usually a bad sign." Noah takes a swig of his beer.

"I think he's been learning a thing or two about cockiness from Noah. Save him from a life of eternal damnation, Maya.

Don't let him fall into the same trap as your boyfriend." Liam dumps the unchosen cards in the box.

"I've tried. My mother has tried. Even our local priest gave him a speech about being humble." Maya jokingly grimaces at me.

Noah tugs Maya into his side. "I even talked to him. No one likes a cocky asshole unless you're Maya. She loves me despite all my assholery."

Santi presses a palm against his chest and flutters his lashes exaggeratedly. "There's hope for us all."

The door to Jax's bedroom opens. He makes his way toward the couch, nearly tripping over his feet. "So, everyone's out here having a good time." Jax slurs his words. He drops onto the couch and shuts his eyes.

Liam narrows his eyes at his friend. "Why don't we get you to bed? You don't look too good."

"I'm tired of being in my room. You all get to be out here, having fun and laughing. I hate hearing it."

Liam rises from the floor. "You were invited, but you decided to act like an asshole instead. Don't be mad at us."

"I'm always mad lately." Jax sighs. His dilated eyes find mine across the small space, and my breath hitches. I thought he was improving and laying off the Xanax.

"And whose fault is that? You can talk to us if you want." Noah's eyes reflect the concern I feel.

"There's no point. You will all move on, and I'll be alone."

"You'll never be by yourself because you're stuck with us." Sophie shoots Jax a genuine smile.

"And what about them?" Jax points a shaky finger at Elías and me. "You're going to ditch me to hang with this new couple?"

"It's not like that and you know it." I somehow find my voice despite my throat clogging up.

Jax's eyes slide from Elías to me. "If Elías fucks her, I'm going to get angry."

Elías sighs. "Focus on yourself. Seriously, you have nothing to worry about."

"I'm not worrying. She might be with you, but based on the way she looks at me, she'd rather be with me. You must be a sucky lay if your girlfriend is lusting after another bloke." Jax attempts to swat Liam's helping hands away, but Liam doesn't let up.

"That's it. You're done for the night." Liam grabs onto Jax and helps him back into his room. Everyone remains wide-eyed and silent as Liam shuts the door to the bedroom after pushing Jax inside.

The joking mood from earlier is gone, replaced with worry and unease. No one protests when we end up calling it a night. Everyone leaves, including Sophie and Maya, claiming they need some girl time.

Minutes pass without any sign of Liam. Growing anxious, I pace the small living room. Why is Liam taking this long? My head snaps toward Jax's door once it opens.

Liam puts a finger toward his lips. He tilts his head toward the main hotel door, and I follow him.

"I don't know what's happening to him this season. He won't open up, and fuck, I've tried my hardest."

"Of all people I would've expected to know about what's going on with him, it would've been you."

"We're best friends, but I can't even get him to admit what's been eating away at him for the past few months. I feel like

I'm failing him in some way. He always had these random bouts of sadness and anxiety, but it's increased ever since winter break last year. Keep an eye on him and these." Liam passes me an orange bottle of pills. "I don't think he's abusing them or anything because they wouldn't let him drive if that were the case. But I'm worried he might start, especially after tonight. Xanax is clearly not helping him cope with whatever the hell is bothering him. He should consider better options."

"Options?"

"Xanax is known to be highly addictive, to the point that the UK avoids prescribing it. I'm going to have a talk with him and offer to help find a better alternative. Pills aren't bad, but those aren't the best for an athlete like him."

Shit. I stare at the bottle, wishing I could help more than just with Jax's image. Maybe the therapy sessions aren't enough for whatever is happening inside of his head. Our help can only go so far if he continues down this road of numbing his pain.

"I better get going. Maybe you can get through to him. He acts differently around you, both in a good and bad way." Liam leaves with a goodbye.

My heart settles down after a few minutes of eyeing Jax's pill bottle. An idea hits me, and I scramble to my room for some paper and a pen.

I sneak into Jax's room an hour later to place the pill bottle on his nightstand. Hopefully, my idea has some impact, however small.

I take a moment to peek at him. He looks peaceful as he sleeps, clutching onto a pillow. Something stirs within me. I want to help Jax get out of his dark place. Not for a contract and definitely not for money. He acts lost and defeated, hiding behind pills and secrets.

Instead of following my intuition warning me to give up and run away, I give in to the devil on my shoulder telling me to help him at any expense.

But that's the thing about costs. None of us knows the price we're willing to pay to be someone's redemption.

CHAPTER SEVENTEEN

Jax

When I first started karting, I loved the pre-race jitters. I lived for the adrenaline high before a race, the buzz of the crowd fueling me. The chemical rush coursing through my body fed my addiction to adrenaline.

Now, I look at my shaky hands with fear and hesitation. Not wanting to freak out during a random interview, I grab my bottle of pills from my race day bag. After last night's episode in front of my friends, I need to be more careful with the amount I take at one time. But after yesterday's call with my dad, I felt the urge to make everything in my head turn off for the night.

Good fucking work that did. Guilt already consumed me this morning after reading Liam's text offering to listen if I needed someone to talk to. As appreciative as I am for Liam, I talk enough to Tom as it is.

I unscrew the cap and pour the pills out in my hand. My body stiffens at the sight of multiple folded pieces of purple paper mixed with the pills.

I pour the rest of the bottle's contents on the coffee table of my suite. After staring at the square papers for a few moments, I pluck one from the group, curious about what it says. Delicate cursive writing I recognize as Elena's covers the paper.

Save a Xanax, buy a puppy. It'll make you happier in the long run.

I don't know why the ridiculous statement draws a laugh from me. Interested in seeing what else Elena wrote, I grab another.

If I swap your Xans for Tic-Tacs, would you notice?

I grab the rest, barely hiding my shit-eating grin as I unfold each one.

Hugs, not drugs. Seriously, this is your free hugs voucher.
If you skip the pills, I'll offer you one activity of your choice.
One 'get out of a gala free' coupon if you skip the pill.
Pills are so 80s. You are way too cool to be doing something so out of style.
Free movie night on me, dinner included, if you throw the pill away.
One free lesson of Spanish dirty talk if you don't take the pill.

I never expected something simple like this to put me at ease. Elena, not even present in the room, fills my chest with something warm.

Elena didn't have to do this. She could've let me take my pills, as long as I'm on my best behavior. I thought that was all she cared about, but maybe I was wrong. Maybe her wanting to help me is more than a quick way to make money.

I place the pills and pieces of paper back in the bottle. Some switch inside of me flips as I save the one I want to use once the race is over.

I want to change. Not because McCoy wants me to or

because everyone keeps judging me. I want to change because someone who has every reason to walk away refuses to leave my side.

And this is how I come to the realization that I need to save myself.

"This is what you want to use your activity on? Really?" Elena eyes the purple piece of paper she wrote. I start the engine of my McCoy Z-Wagon SUV and pull out of the hotel's parking lot.

"Yup. Type in your address." I hand her my phone.

Turns out saving myself includes facing some of my fears about Elena. The first step in my plan is to spend more time with her while actively trying harder to not be a dick. She deserves better from me after everything she helps me with.

"I won't lie, I thought you'd choose a more fun thing to do on your day off before practice rounds tomorrow."

"And miss out on seeing your exclusive snow globes? Never." I keep my eyes forward, ignoring the pull I have to look at Elena.

Okay, I want to see snow globes and get Elena away from the F1 scene for an hour or two. I never pretended I wasn't a selfish shit.

"I'm totally going to regret showing you these. I know it." She hands me back my phone with her address typed in the GPS application.

I drive us to her small flat located on the outskirts of Monaco. The older apartment building looks much different than my lavish penthouse located by the coast.

"This is your flat?" I stare at the run-down building looking about one wind gust away from toppling over.

"Yes. I know it may not be what you're used to, but not all of us can afford a high-rise apartment with personal valet service."

"I'm sorry. I didn't mean to insult you." Fuck, I didn't realize how vastly different our lives were until now. She makes little comments here and there, but it didn't fully hit me until this moment.

She grabs her keys from her purse. "It's fine. I think it's homey."

It's shit, that's what it is.

Elena and I walk up the stairs to the entrance of her building. I follow her as she makes a sharp turn down a small hallway with too many miscellaneous stains for comfort. "You live on the first floor? Isn't that kind of dangerous?"

"Dangerous?" She looks back at me with her brows raised.

"Yes. You know, not safe from burglars and stuff." I struggle to deny the concern laced in my voice.

Elena's back straightens as she fiddles with her keys. "Please, I grew up in Mexico. A staircase isn't going to protect me from the bad people out there." She opens the door to her flat.

I check out the rusty deadbolt lock before following her inside. "But you live alone. That's different."

What is wrong with me, getting all concerned and shit?

Elena seems to share the same thought, with her eyebrows pinching together as she looks at me with wide eyes. "I've lived on my own here for two years. I think I can handle it."

"Do you go back home often? To Mexico, that is?"

She clears her throat. "That's not home anymore."

Okay, way to fuck this up, Jax. "So, show me the goods."

Smooth. Ten out of ten transition.

I'm screwed. This plan is taking a turn for the worst.

Elena gives me the quickest tour known to man, seeing as her flat is the size of my walk-in closet back in London. She leads me toward the shelf near the window housing her snow globes.

"Whoa." I stand eye to eye with a snow globe of two sugar skulls. It's not exactly what I'd expect from someone like her.

"Sugar skulls represent departed souls." She grabs the snow globe.

"If they're departed, why is it colorful?"

"Because in my culture, death shouldn't be gloomy and gray. It's supposed to be a time of celebration. I think it's easier said than done, though, because it's hard as hell to celebrate something that causes pain." Elena shakes the snow globe. Colorful glitter falls down over the set of skulls. Her eyes become cloudy as she places it back on the shelf.

"Does that one play music?"

"No." She moves onto another. "This one I bought after Elías got me a job with F1. It was one of the best days ever. I was so excited, I ended up buying the first snow globe I saw, which wasn't for Elías's team." Her smile reaches her eyes.

"I'll look past the fact that you bought a Bandini snow globe because it's pretty cool." I check out the red Bandini car centered in the middle of a fake F1 track, surrounded by fallen glitter.

Elena laughs as she picks it up and shakes it. "Well, I think you'll appreciate this part." Her small fingers twist the metal knob on the bottom of the globe, and the F1 theme song plays. It's a light melody compared to the usual dramatic one sports channels play on the telly.

Elena held true to her fact, with each snow globe serving a unique purpose. There are a variety of snow globes, ranging from different sizes to themes. She even has one she bought after she graduated from university, with a fake diploma and a small photo of Elena inside of it. Her beaming smile shows her pride.

"I never graduated from uni. Hell, I never even went." I brush my thumb across the glass sphere.

"There's nothing wrong with that. You were driving in what, like Formula 3?"

"F2, but who's checking." I flash her a cocky grin.

"That's why I believe you can win another Championship again. You have a natural talent for racing; you only need to get out of your mental fog to do it."

"Your optimism is cute."

"Today, you did it. You didn't take your pill. Instead, you're out here with me." Elena places the snow globe back on the shelf.

She shows me a couple of others. Her passion and happiness about her greatest moments spreads to me. Hanging around her fills me with a warmth equivalent of laying out in the sun.

Gratitude about her vulnerability makes me stupid. "Thanks for sharing this part of you."

Her eyes wander, not landing anywhere in particular. "I thought you'd choose to go somewhere for your activity. Like I don't know, do something guyish. I'm surprised you asked to see this collection. It's tiny."

"I couldn't resist the temptation to learn more about your secret."

"Why?"

My hands tremble at the urge to be honest with her. "Because even though I tell myself daily you don't need someone as fucked up as me around you, I can't resist wanting more from you than I should." Something pushes me to cup her cheek. The same something in me that wants to pull her close and press my lips against hers.

She looks at me with her eyes wide and captivating. "What are you doing?"

"I don't know." I lean in closer, taking in a deep breath of her shampoo. I'm addicted to the way her eyes darken as they scan my face before lingering on my lips.

She shuts her eyes as my thumb grazes her cheek. "What happened to no touching? It's a rule."

Touching her sparks a gush of possessiveness inside of me.

"Be a rule-breaker with me." I close the gap between us as one hand goes around her neck, pulling her in. She gasps as our lips touch.

I keep it soft and innocent, unsure how she'll react. Instead of pushing me away, her fingers grip the fabric of my shirt, tugging me closer.

Our kiss is nothing I'm used to—all sweet and soft. I want to apologize for forgetting our first kiss because I was a drunk arsehole. To apologize for putting her through shit in an effort to keep her far away. It's a shock to my system when her tongue traces the seam of my mouth before she bites down on my bottom lip. My body reacts like never before, a tingle creeping up my spine.

A growling noise makes its way up my throat. I break away. "So that's how it's going to be? I'm trying to be nice here."

Her eyes have a rare lightness toward me I've never seen before. "Who would've thought the guy famous for so many naughty things would try to be nice?"

"You're fucking around with someone who won't take your taunts lightly."

"If it's as light as your kisses, I think I'll survive." She presses a palm to her chest and smiles at me.

I shut her up with a punishing kiss. My tongue lashes out against hers, not letting her off easy, wanting to own her. To show her our connection and to make her imagine my tongue in other places. Licking, teasing, taunting. Elena melts into my body, giving into me.

It's intoxicating, the feel of her against me. She gives as good as she takes. My skin heats with awareness from her running her hands across my straining arms. I must have drunk my weight in alcohol at the club to not remember kissing her. I'd kick myself all over again for making such a stupid decision because this shit is memorable.

Kissing her tastes like the sweetest kind of destruction. She brings my body to life by her touch, a jolt of energy shooting down my body. My dick throbs in my jeans as she runs her tongue along my lower lip. I press my hips into hers, showing her how much I want her. Desire makes my head cloudy.

She breaks away from the kiss before stepping away. Her fingers brush across her swollen lips, drawing my attention toward the damage I caused. "I don't think that should happen again."

"Why not?" I step toward her.

She steps back again. "We work together. There's no need to complicate things."

"Trust me when I say that kissing you is the least complicated thing about my life right now."

Her eyes flash with something I recognize as pity. "You're not in a good place."

"I'm tired of living like that." And I'm tired of letting every single day get bogged down by my anxiety.

"I think that's a great first step, but that doesn't mean we should do what we just did again."

"Are you going to act like it never happened?" I fist my hands together.

"Sure, seeing as we did so well with the first one." She turns to grab her purse off the kitchen counter.

Anger bubbles inside of me at her nonchalance. I'd be insulted and questioning my skills if it weren't for the way she pressed her body against mine, practically begging for more. "What if I don't want to pretend it didn't happen?" I blurt out.

Her shoulders drop as she sighs. "I'm not going to ruin your recovery over something like lust. You need stability, and something between us would be anything but."

Even I know that's true. I'm trying to get better and fight with the anxiety holding me back while she wants to build her business through helping me. And if I learned anything from my friends, it's how wherever there's lust like this, love is a risky side effect.

I hate how Elena is right. I hate it so much that I stay silent for the entire drive back to the hotel.

My anxiety wins again, fucking up my chance at something good. Elena and I wouldn't be steady, but not for the reasons she thinks. Relationships—even the physical kind—need a basic level of trust.

While some people have solid foundations built to withstand life's hardships, mine is the equivalent of a house of cards—susceptible to collapsing from the slightest change.

CHAPTER EIGHTEEN

Jax

"**I** want to get off the Xanax," I say after counting tiles for what feels like thirty minutes. Elena's words in her apartment have followed me the entire week. She's right, which makes me angry. If I were a normal man, I wouldn't have to worry about a connection to someone threatening to throw me over the edge. Her reluctance to even kiss me again shows how deep I've fallen into a hole of self-resentment and isolation.

Tom crosses his leg over his knee. "Would you like some referrals for psychiatrists?"

"Yes. I want to go about it the right way, so whatever you think is best."

"I'm wondering what changed your mind regarding the medication?"

"I still think medication is necessary, but I don't think Xanax is the right choice for me personally anymore. I want to try something different that fits my lifestyle better."

"I'm proud of you for wanting to change this, Jax."

He should be thanking Elena, but I don't want to bring her into these conversations. "Thanks."

"I can put together a list of referrals if that works for you."

"Sure. The sooner the better. Do you think the change will affect my racing or anything?"

"I think a psychiatrist can help determine what's the best course of action. But they know how to work with an athlete like you."

"That's good then." I nod, pleased with myself for taking this first step.

"I know you can beat this, Jax. Anxiety doesn't define you." Tom smiles at me.

"That's easy to say when you don't know my fears."

"If you're willing to share, I'd like to help you.'"

"Let's save that battle for another week."

I pace the living room, staring at Elena's bedroom door. Ever since she texted me to let me know she wasn't feeling well, I've been on alert.

Over the past few months, she's never taken an hour off, let alone a day. While I'd rather feel wounded about Elena avoiding our kiss, something tells me she wouldn't back down from helping me, least of all because of a kiss.

A kiss she wants to forget ever happened.

A kiss I couldn't forget even if I tried. And fuck I've tried. I've tried so damn hard, I nearly bashed my head into the wall of the shower yesterday after jacking off to the idea of her.

I've stooped to new lows, and that says something coming from the guy who lives at rock bottom.

Her evading me has left me on edge. Not because I care about her well-being but more so because I don't want to get sick with whatever virus she is incubating within her body.

Liar.

I've resisted the urge to knock on her door. I attended the press conference without her, making sure to review the email she sent me this morning with answers to potential questions. That's the type of workaholic she is, sending me shit to stay on top of everything.

Agitated with myself and my stupid pacing, I knock on her door. My heart threatens to escape my chest as I wait for her. Minutes pass and the ache in my chest fails to lessen.

I knock again, wanting to make sure Elena is alive and not choking on her vomit or something. For some reason, *PR rep dying by her own throw up while her roommate waits outside* sounds like a terrible headline. She'd want me to check on her for that potential reputation killer alone.

After another minute of silence, I place my forehead against the door. "Elena, are you alive in there? I'm not exactly concerned, but your radio silence is unusual." Okay, I'm slightly concerned, but what the fucking ever.

"I'm not feeling well. Can you not go out or do anything that can get you in trouble today? I know the parties are crazy fun and everything, but I don't want to deal with any repercussions tomorrow."

A cold feeling spreads through my chest at her off-sounding voice. "Do you need medicine or some shit?" I can't believe I'm talking to a door at the moment, practically begging for Elena to open up.

This is unbelievable of me. I should leave, but my feet stay planted to the carpet.

"No."

"Is this because of lady problems?" God, I'm turning into a fucking pussy today.

"No. God no. Go hang with your friends without getting drunk please." Her hoarse laugh doesn't ease my budding worry.

I hate her forced laugh. It's not her usual. Fuck it's not even her sarcastic one she saves for when I'm a total arse.

I step away from her door, heeding her advice. Liam answers my texts and tells me to come on over to his hotel.

In the car, I can't stop fidgeting in my seat, wondering if Elena needs something to feel better. I ask the driver to turn around and stop at the nearest pharmacy.

I reason with myself while standing like an idiot in the women's hygiene aisle. I'm purely doing this because I need Elena to help me with my reputation. Nothing more, nothing less. Emphasis on the *nothing more*.

I'm lost as I stare at the different products, all advertising shit about heavy flows and anti-pesticide products. Bloody hell. I thank God for not being a woman at this moment. Who the fuck wants to worry about chemicals shoved up their vag?

I dial my mum. "Hey, quick question. What do women prefer for their time of the month? There's a bunch of shit labeled pads or tampons and I can't fathom why a woman wants to insert something looking like a cardboard bullet into her body."

My mum laughs for a solid thirty seconds into her phone. "Please tell me why my son is shopping for sanitary wipes on a Wednesday."

I groan as I lean against a shelf. "I don't know what I'm doing. Elena's acting weird as fuck and I thought it might be her period."

"So, you went to the local drugstore for her?"

"Yes."

"Did she ask for anything in particular?"

"No. She told me to go hang out with my friends."

"Yet you're calling me from the store? That doesn't sound like your usual type of hanging out."

"Do you want me to spell it out for you?"

Mum chuckles. "Nope. I'll have fun reaching my own conclusions! I'm impressed with how she's worked quite some magic on you in such a short amount of time. I thought she'd take half a year, at least."

"This is nothing but a kind roommate thing to do."

"Because you're an advocate for kindness all of a sudden?" My mum's snort makes me smile.

"Okay, fine. She helps me with a bunch of shit so I feel bad. I've been going slightly crazy since she's been holed up in her room all day."

"Interesting indeed. Are you worried about her well-being?"

"Let's not get into this right now. Are you going to help me or not?"

"Of course. Anything for my son who clearly doesn't like Elena." My mum rattles off a list of items I should grab.

Twenty minutes later, I enter our suite with two bags packed with shit women apparently need to make it through their time of the month. It didn't take a genius to guess Elena's favorite candy, seeing as she munches on it every week while working on that damn puzzle. I bought everything Mum recommended from top-notch organic sanitary wipes to some heating pad that apparently helps with cramps.

If I thought I was fucked with Elena before, today seals the deal.

I hesitate as I near her closed door. Mustering up the courage, I knock, hoping she finally opens.

Her muffled sigh carries through the door. "Jax. I'm not in the mood today."

"Okay, well I bought you shit to make it through your bad day, so hopefully you're in the mood for Reese's Pieces." If she doesn't come out for that, then she needs to be rushed to the nearest hospital because she has to be dying.

Her silence chokes me. I never thought I'd be intimidated by the sound, but damn Elena fucks things up inside for me.

After a solid minute of standing by the door acting like a wanker, I consider giving up. As I move to place the bag on the floor, Elena's door cracks open.

Elena's puffy eyes feel like a blow to my chest. She traded her usual work attire for leggings and a huge sweater with Ed Sheeran's tour dates on it. Her hair resembles something straight out of a porno, ruffled and unlike her. The whole ensemble is concerning, especially when her face flashes with shock as she checks out the bags I clutch onto.

I can't describe the feeling inside of me. A mix of relief and pain, both at her clearly suffering and at her showing me she is at least breathing. "I bought you stuff." I pass her the bags like a bloody idiot.

She stares at the items with bulging eyes. "You went to the store for me?"

"Not for you. I had to grab a new toothbrush and thought

you might need a few emergency items. Can't have you getting sick and shit before the Grand Prix because I need you in tip-top shape to keep up with me." *Way to not come off like a dick, Jax.*

"Oh, right." Her eyes close. "Well, thank you. This is kind of you." She grips the handle of the door and moves to shut it.

Without thinking, I block it with my booted foot. "Wait."

She rears back. "What?"

I rub the back of my neck. "Is something bothering you?"

"No."

"The way you look begs to differ."

"Wow, you really know how to make a girl feel special." She attempts to push my foot out of the way. Her tiny purple-painted toes are no match for me.

"Well, if something is wrong, you can talk to me." *Because you've done a good job of that yourself. Moron.*

"We might have kissed before, but we're not friends. We don't talk about feelings and personal stuff. You've made it pretty clear."

Her shutting me out sucks more than I care to admit. I didn't expect it to burn like a bitch, but I get it's warranted. Being on the receiving end of a cold shoulder doesn't feel too great. Lesson learned. Is this how others feel when I brush them off?

"Well, I'll be here tonight if you want to talk or anything. Feel better." I remove my foot. She shuts the door with a soft goodbye.

I park myself on the couch and text Liam that I need to cancel our plans. I tell myself I'm not in the mood to go out—that I'd rather watch the latest action movie than meet up with my friend. It's not because I want to be around in case Elena needs me.

Right.

A knock on the hotel door an hour later stuns me. I open it to find Elías standing there, looking a little worse for wear. "What the hell are you doing here?"

Is Elena's shitty mood because of this idiot?

"I brought dinner for Elena." He lifts a brown bag marked takeout.

"She's not feeling well, so I doubt she wants to eat with you." I can't escape this fucker no matter how hard I try.

"I know that. We text. Are you going to let me in or keep staring at me like I want to steal your favorite toy?"

I open the door wider, giving Elías room to enter. The fact that Elena texted Elías pisses me off. The notion makes me feel stupid, buying her supplies to feel better when she has him to count on.

I stare at his bag of food with contempt. "Good luck with her. She's all yours."

Elías looks at her closed door before staring back at me. "This isn't what you think it is. Don't get mad at her because I'm here to help."

"I never said I was mad."

"The way your jaw ticks tells me differently. I've told you that she and I are friends. That's it. She's having a bad day, and I want to make sure she eats something."

My stomach sinks. Fuck me. "What's going on? Why is she acting the way she is?"

He shakes his head, lowering his voice. "It's not my story to tell."

"Fantastic." It looks like I'll never get answers because based on my attitude, I doubt Elena wants to delve into her feelings with me.

"If you expect others to open up, you should do the same."

"I didn't ask you for advice."

He shakes his head. "Fine. Don't be pissed because I'm here when I'm the one person she can count on."

"Do whatever the fuck you want. Hope you get your cock sucked real good for bringing her dinner." A perfect storm of anger enters my bloodstream, fucking everything up even more.

"Fuck you. I almost feel bad for how pathetically jealous you are." Elías doesn't bother looking back at me as he enters Elena's room, closing the door quietly behind him.

I go to my room, desperate to escape Elías's words. Screw him being all connected with Elena. This is the perfect reminder of why dicks like me don't get close to other people. We're better suited for breaking things beyond repair, surely ruining everything we touch.

Someone knocks on my bedroom door. I expect Elena, but instead, Elías is on the other side. Somehow, I resist the temptation to close the door on his face after his little stint with bringing Elena food a few hours ago.

"Do you mind if I come inside for a second? I don't want Elena to hear me." He glances behind him toward Elena's closed door.

"I mind, but it's not like you're giving me much of a choice." I give him space to come inside.

"Some things need to be cleared up."

I close the door behind him. "Can't wait."

"Well, I've tried my hardest to be your friend and a decent teammate." Elías focuses on everything but me as he walks back and forth.

"You have." I lean against the dresser and tuck my hands in my pockets.

"And all you've done is be a dick to Elena and me."

"No use denying it." I shoot him a tight smile.

"This is the issue I want to address with you. I can't ignore how part of you is angry at us because you think I'm into Elena, but I can assure you I'm not."

A loud laugh bursts out of me. "Do you think I'm stupid? You both have this thing with each other."

"As much as it pleases me to know you at least like her enough to be envious of my relationship with her, it's not right. You shouldn't be acting like a dick to her because you're intimidated by me."

"Can you quit your fucking pacing?" I bark out.

Elías stops in place. He stares at his hands, still not looking at me. "I don't like Elena like that because I'm gay."

Of all the things I expected Elías to say, his confession wouldn't have made the list. If what he says is true, then I'm the biggest idiot on this planet.

Scratch that. Biggest arsehole on this side of the universe.

"Shit. For real?"

He sighs. "Yeah, dumbass. You've been jealous of a gay dude hanging with his best friend."

"Wow...I mean, you're...well, you. I didn't expect that." I find my ability to produce words mind-boggling.

"Why? Because I race cars and like manly shit, that means I'm not gay? Everyone's perceptions and stigmas are the very reason I keep it a secret in the first place," he snaps back, staring into my eyes for the first time.

"I'm sorry, I didn't mean it that way. It's just, you never hinted at it."

"Your reaction is exactly the reason why. It's my secret. One that only Elena, and now you, know."

I try to wipe my face of surprise. "Why are you telling me this then?"

"Elena doesn't deserve your bullshit anymore about us—especially since she helps you all the damn time and you act like a child. The least I can do is make her life a little easier. You want to be a dick to her because of other reasons? Fine. But I'm not going to let you sit and be a jealous idiot over someone who'd rather fuck *People Magazine's Sexiest Man of the Year.*"

I laugh. "Well, at least I don't need to give her a hard time about you anymore."

"You need to stop giving her a hard time. Period. You'll regret it."

"If only life were that easy."

Elías nods. "Life is never easy. Coming in here and telling you my secret to help my friend? Hardest shit I've had to do in a while. Trusting you despite barely knowing you? Even worse. From what I hear, you tend to have loose lips when you get intoxicated, so I'm not exactly thrilled to confide in you."

Shit. I'm floored he trusts me enough to tell me this in the first place. And his reasoning behind it is something I not only respect, but slightly envy because I don't have his kind of balls. Him willing to sacrifice himself to protect his friend is a personality trait I can't exactly ignore.

Elías is a bloody good mate. No wonder Elena is drawn to him.

"I'll keep your secret. I swear it." I mean every word. "I may be a dick, but I'd never betray your confidence like that. What you did for Elena is admirable."

Damn, Elías. He's becoming more likable in my eyes every day.

"But you're still going to be distant with her? Despite knowing I'm not going to make a move?"

I guess Elena didn't confess how we were anything but distant yesterday. Little does he know that I pushed for less distance but was met with her resistance. "We have too many obstacles in our way."

And fuck, I'm the biggest one of them all.

CHAPTER NINETEEN

Elena

Time doesn't heal heartbreak. It's a stupid phrase meant to instill hope. In reality, moving on has yet to heal my heart. And God knows I've tried.

Every year it's the same feeling. The despair overrides everything else in my life on the anniversary of my parents' death. Responsibilities get put on the backburner while I spend the day mourning the life they should've had.

Elías left hours ago, making sure I was fed despite my resistance to his offerings all day.

I step out onto the balcony of the hotel. The Monaco racetrack is so close, I can see the lights from here.

I look up at the star-filled sky, tears pricking my eyes as I think of my parents. "When will it get easier? Every year I try to pretend it's okay, but instead I end up avoiding everyone. I feel guilty I'm here while you both aren't. Spending time with others on the anniversary…it reminds me of everything you both lost."

I whisper the words up to the sky. "I wish *Papi* was here to see me use English every day. I think he'd be proud of how little of an accent I have now. And sometimes I pretend Mami is here singing into my ear, telling me everything will turn out all right. I'd like to think she'd be fussing with *Abuela* about the lack of grandkids by now, too."

I sound crazy, talking to myself. "God, sometimes I feel so lonely, even with Elías and *Abuela*. It's not the same without you two."

I sniffle as more tears fall. It's stupid yet cathartic to get these words off my chest. I sob silently while staring up at the sky, thinking of my parents watching me from above.

Time escapes me. The sun slowly rises, basking the Monaco racetrack in a golden glow.

The sliding door to Jax's room squeaks opens. I rush to return back to my suite, but Jax's voice stops me.

"You don't have to go inside because of me. If you want, you can pretend I'm not even here."

I wipe my cheeks with my sweater, willing away any impending tears. "That's impossible. Trust me, I've tried." I keep my back toward him as I stare at my sliding door, wondering what to do.

"Are you openly flirting with me? Now I'm concerned you're sick."

The weakest smile known to humankind graces my lips. I turn around and take up a spot leaning against the handrail, facing the rising sun. "I'm fine."

"Mum taught me whenever a woman says that she is fine, then she is definitely, under no circumstances, fine."

I let out a soft laugh. "Your mom sounds great." My chest

burns at the idea of not having mine.

We stand in silence for minutes. I gather control of my raging emotions while Jax stares ahead. The sun continues its slow climb.

Jax remains facing forward. "Yesterday an interviewer asked me what makes me feel alive."

I turn my head toward him. "What happened to you keeping silent so I can pretend you're not here?"

"I thought you hated how much I kept to myself. Here I am being nice and offering you a few breadcrumbs." His lip twitches.

"I was raised on rice being an essential part of my food pyramid. Breadcrumbs are for women on terrible diets." I hide my smile behind the sleeve of my sweater.

His laugh fills me with a surge of warmth, replacing the cold dread I've felt for the past twenty-four hours. "Well, be happy with what I'm willing to offer you. So...anyway... The reporter asked me what makes me feel alive, and I answered racing."

"Okay, I don't know if I'm struggling to follow you because I haven't had coffee yet or because that's not surprising."

"Maybe a little of both. Well, I lied. Kind of—about the racing at least. Sunrises make me feel alive."

Does Jax sound nervous or is it me overanalyzing things? "Why?"

Jax stays silent for a solid minute. He has me hooked, waiting for his response. "Because it reminds me of how I get to live another day."

"That's shockingly deep of you."

"Your turn. You tell me, Elena Gonzalez, what makes you feel alive?"

I pause. "My job?"

He imitates a buzzer sound, and a rush of laughter escapes me. It feels good to laugh carelessly, to ease the ache in my chest. "Try again. No way that's what makes you feel alive. If so, we need to find you some hobbies."

"Fine. Okay." I chew on my lip as I think up my response. "It's going to sound so stupid."

"You're speaking to the man who makes more stupid decisions in one week than you could during your entire existence. Try me."

"Rain," I blurt out.

"Rain?" His voice matches the disbelief on his face.

"I knew it sounded stupid," I mumble under my breath.

He closes the distance between us. His hand softly grasps my chin as he forces me to look at him. "I didn't say that. You're doing a shitty job explaining yourself, no offense. And that says something, coming from me."

My body becomes attuned to his presence. It feels like touching an electric socket, with a spark causing a jolt to my heart. "The rain makes me feel alive because it reminds me that life's a cycle. Water falls from above to be sucked back up again by the clouds eventually—round and round. I love the storm clouds before the first drops fall. Love how the rain feels against my skin, and I love the way it smells. It's so weird, but my favorite days are the gloomiest. And it teaches us how even the ugliest storms can lead to a rainbow at the end."

Jax's eyes stay glued to mine. The look in them—mystified and something else—scares me. I step away from his embrace, giving us both some distance.

"That was rather poetic." He runs a hand through his curls.

"You made my answer pale in comparison."

My eyes watch the sun slowly creeping up into the sky. I don't want our moment to end, a rare occasion with Jax sharing a part of himself. "Why did you come out here?"

"Truth?"

"No, tell me the lie." The poor lighting hides my eye roll.

"I try my best to see every sunrise."

My heart sinks. For some reason, I thought he came out here to see me. In reality, I encroached on his territory. "I didn't know that. Thanks for letting me barge in on your morning ritual then."

"The fact that you're thanking me for sharing a space with you for ten minutes speaks to how much of a dick I really am."

"Then why not change? Why have you made it your mission to keep everyone emotionally distant from you?"

He sighs as he faces the handrail again. "Do you believe in fate?"

"Are you actually going to change the subject like that? You didn't even answer my question."

"Humor me."

"Okay…" I think back to my parent's death. To how fate played a part in taking them away while keeping me alive. But I also think back to other positive moments like Elías getting me a job in F1 or moving away from Mexico for university. "I mean, I wish I didn't. It seems cruel to think some events are destined to happen like dying young, or sickness, or even trauma. But how else can we explain things that happen? I think people wouldn't be able to cope with life if they didn't believe things were meant to happen exactly how they were."

"Yeah, I believe in fate too. How unfortunately everything

happens for a reason, despite some people being too stubborn to accept it. Like you said, sickness, death, life. All of it is a part of the grand scheme of things whether we like it or not."

"How does this connect to why you can't be different with me, though?"

"It does." He looks at me. His eyes darken as emotion floods his eyes, revealing sadness and regret. "Some people see their future in others. Someone they want to spend their life with because they can't imagine going a day without them. But with you, I see nothing good. You wonder why I struggle to be around you, and that's valid. It's because while some are fated to become something great, we're different. We're fated from the start to fail. When I look at you, I'm reminded why God is a joke and life is one big 'fuck you' moment after another."

Wow. The heaviness of his words presses against the already building ache inside of my chest. His words hint at a lot more than wanting a friendship, and I'm not sure how to cope with that.

"We can never be friends, can we?"

"No. Spending time around you, wanting more from you than a quick fuck—that's the reason fate is cruel."

I'm hit with another wave of sadness. My mouth opens to say something, anything really, but Jax's hand cupping my face shocks me.

He turns my head gently, hitting me with a look of despair. "You're the biggest 'fuck you' from fate. But it's not because I dislike you. It's because I'm terrified of what would happen if I stopped trying to avoid you."

Mierda. "And what would happen if you do?" I don't want to give up on asking him questions, not when he is finally opening up to me.

"Something tragic from the start."

"That's your perspective. What about mine?"

"Go ahead. Tell me what you think would happen if I stopped avoiding you."

"Well, if you were able to control yourself more, I think you'd finally feel something in your life other than anger and sadness. Whether it's from a friendship or a relationship, everyone deserves happiness, including you."

Jax frowns, pulling his hand away from my face and placing it on the handrail. He turns his head toward the skyline. "Looks like our time has ended."

"Jax, I mean it. Happiness isn't something to fear." I place my hand over his, heating the palm of my hand.

"I don't fear happiness. It's more like I fear the despair that comes afterward."

Before I have the chance to ask him anything more, he places the softest kiss by the corner of my mouth. My skin hums with awareness as his lips linger on the spot.

I hate myself for leaning into him. Jax is addictive, proving to me how much I crave his lips against mine. The kiss in my apartment didn't satisfy a craving—it created one. One I have no place experiencing in the first place, seeing as I asked him to focus on himself rather than something between us.

Jax steps away from me. "Learn to let go of whatever's haunting you. You don't want to become like me, ruining anything good in your life. Unfortunately, people like me don't get a big happy ending. But you deserve it all. The *dancing in the rain* finale with some lovesick twat who can give you the best of him for the rest of your long lives."

He walks back to his room, leaving me in a mess of my own emotions.

Jax Kingston stole a piece of my heart, and I'm not sure if I'll ever get it back. And worse, I don't know if I want it.

CHAPTER TWENTY

Jax

"So, how have you been this week?" Tom interrupts my usual counting. We've fallen into a comfortable pattern, with me answering a few of his questions every week. I won't tell Connor but having someone to vent to has helped me manage my anxiety more effectively. I still get the usual trembles and what not, but it's unavoidable while transitioning to a new medication.

"It's been all right. I've been prepping for the Canadian Grand Prix and keeping busy."

"Busy is good. And how's your family?"

"Mum's doing a bit better this week. For the first time in a while, Dad was able to travel for work. People think he sits around all day, but he actually sponsors some up-and-coming MMA fighters. He says sadly boxing is a dying sport."

"MMA is pretty entertaining. And it's good to hear your mom's having a better week. I'm sure that helps with your stress."

"Yeah, thank fuck. They actually asked me to stay with them

during the summer break before the British Grand Prix."

"How do you feel about that?"

"Good, except Elena is stuck babysitting me in London, too. That means she would spend a month with me and my parents." I run my hand across my stubbled jaw.

"A month is a long time."

"No shit."

"Do you want Elena to meet them?"

"Not really. For multiple reasons, and the biggest issue is how she doesn't know my mum is sick."

"Is that something you want to share with her?"

"I know I can trust Elena not to say anything, but it doesn't make the process any easier. But I honestly don't have much of a choice."

"What about her knowing makes it hard for you?"

"It feels like I'm knocking down the last barrier between us. She'd know everything there is to know about me."

"And what about it makes you afraid?"

I take the deepest breath as I consider backing out of telling Tom. Instead, I power through, knowing I need to talk to someone about it. A bloody anomaly. "My mum has Huntington's Disease."

Tom remains quiet. His silence feeds my fear, causing me to sit up and look at him.

I hate the sadness in his eyes. I've grown accustomed to that look throughout my life. "You don't need to look at me like that."

"Shit, Jax. I'm sorry to hear that." He shakes his head.

"This changes nothing I've said and the decisions I've made." I fist my hands in front of me.

He taps his pen against his leg. "Have you been tested?"

"No. And I don't want to."

"The trembling you have and the anxiety…you've been worried about it, haven't you?"

"No shit. I'm guessing you're familiar with the disease then."

Tom lets out a sigh. "I knew someone who was diagnosed. I would have given you other recommendations had I known this might've been part of the anxiety you experience."

"Like what?"

"I'd start by asking you to consider the genetic testing rather than trying a different med to manage your symptoms. One of the very first things psychologists consider when diagnosing is any pre-existing medical condition."

"Fuck no. That's not an option. Plus, I've always been anxious, ever since I was younger. This has only made it worse."

"Options change. You're talking about a 50/50 chance of having Huntington's Disease yourself. That can't be an easy thing to sit with every day, especially if you might have a younger onset compared to your mom. It depends on the test results."

I drop my head into my hands. Hearing it from someone who isn't my parents doesn't make the fact any easier to swallow. "You think I don't know that? And I've already met with a genetic counselor in the past. I went through the whole process before the testing yet couldn't go through with it. I've been there, done that."

"That was an extremely brave first step."

A cruel laugh releases from me. "Brave? I had a panic attack before entering the facility for my test. I quit before it even mattered."

"Believe it or not, I find you attempting to take a test that could define your life forever as something incredibly courageous of you. Not everyone would sit through months of genetic counseling in the first place." Tom's praise has my cheeks uncharacteristically flushing.

"Yet I'm not strong enough to follow through with it," I mutter.

"You sitting here and opening up about your fear is strong. You switching new medicines because you realize the other one wasn't helping you is brave, especially during the middle of a season. I, for one, think you're a lot stronger than you give yourself credit for."

I retreat back into myself, staring up at the ceiling.

Tom breaks the silence after a few minutes. "My job isn't to push you to get tested. I can only recommend for you to think of the pros and cons. We can do that together, and see what solution is best."

Why bother, when my life has a fifty percent chance of a shitty expiration date?

I toss and turn all night, struggling to fall asleep for hours after my P3 win for the Montreal Grand Prix. Switching over to new medication has been rougher than expected, especially with curbing the instant relief a Xan offers at bedtime.

I roll out of bed, craving a cool glass of water. Keeping quiet, I make my way toward the kitchen. The lights shining under Elena's door have me making a detour.

She usually falls asleep after me, but 2 a.m. is a new level of sleep deprivation for her.

I open her door. "What are you doing awake past your

bed—" My voice cuts off when I find her curled up under the covers fast asleep. She looks bloody peaceful and youthful, her brown hair covering the pillow while her hands clutch the white comforter.

"How the hell do you fall asleep with all the lights on?" I whisper as I brush aside some loose locks of hair from her face.

Good God, I'm becoming a creeper, watching her sleep. I take a moment to assess her room. Living on the road means we don't have many personal mementos, so the photograph on her nightstand sticks out to me. A young Elena hangs on the back of a young man I assume is her dad. A woman stands next to him, looking like a slightly older version of Elena. They look happy and carefree.

I step away, shutting off the lamp on her nightstand before making my way toward her bathroom to turn off the light in there.

She must've been dead tired to fall asleep like this. Maybe she works too hard following me around all the time, including the late-night galas and traveling.

After shutting off all the lights in Elena's room, I close her door. I grab a glass of water in the kitchen and head back toward my room, ready for a good night's rest.

CHAPTER TWENTY-ONE

Elena

A raw scream escapes my lips as I wake to a dark room. I press a shaky hand against my chest as if I can calm my racing heart. My door slams against the wall as Jax rushes in.

"Jesus fucking Christ, Elena?" He comes to my side of the bed.

I stare at my hands, failing to manage any words. Images return of the worst night of my life. So much blood. Sticky, dark blood.

Jax's fingers press into my shoulders. "Tell me what the bloody hell is wrong with you?"

Bloody.

I tumble out of bed and rush to the bathroom, switching on the lights before making it to the toilet. Acid coats my tongue as my dinner fights its way back up. My fingers tremble as I clutch onto the side of the ceramic seat.

"Fuck. Are you sick? Should I call a doctor?" Jax kneels down next to me, lifting my hair away from my face.

"Lights," I hiss. "Why did you shut off the lights?" My voice sounds broken. Weak. Defeated.

His wild eyes roam over my face as he clutches onto my hair tighter. "This is because of the dark? You scared the shit out of me. I thought something was seriously wrong with you."

Another round of sickness rolls through me, but I fight it. I stand, my wobbly legs nearly buckling as I walk toward the sink.

More unwanted images flood my mind. Shattered glass. Blood, dark and thick, sticking to my body. I take a few deep breaths as I turn on the water, pump soap into my hands, and start washing.

"Elena, talk to me. You look like you're about to pass out."

My hands tremble as I rid myself of the soap. I switch tasks, deciding to vigorously brush my teeth to the point of pain before turning off the water. My eyes linger on my hands, looking clean despite the feeling of disgust sitting heavy inside of me. I turn the water back on to wash them again.

Jax grabs me and lifts me up, throwing me over his shoulder. "No more weird handwashing. Stop freaking the fuck out and talk to me."

I scream as he carries me back into the pitch-black room. "No!" I claw at his back.

"Fucking hell. Cut it out."

"I want the lights!" My body shakes as I battle the tears begging for release.

He places me on the bed and turns on the lamp. "Shit, Elena. You're afraid of the dark?"

I shake my head and tuck my knees into my chest. My eyes linger on the photo of my parents before I close them. Pain, blindingly hot, shoots through my chest. A wounded cry comes out of me. I place my forehead against my knees and sob, curling into myself to save me from the embarrassment of Jax watching me lose it. Shame fills me at letting someone see me like this, but I haven't had a nightmare this vivid in a long time. So long I forgot what they feel like.

"What in the bloody hell happened to you?" Jax whispers. He surprises me when he slowly gets on the bed and pulls my curled body down onto the mattress. His body molds into mine. My skin prickles with awareness, craving his closeness, especially after what I experienced.

I don't want to be alone, and somehow, he knows this.

Jax drags the comforter up our bodies, cocooning us.

"Don't turn off the lights again. Never ever again. Promise me," I rasp.

"Shit. I'm sorry. I had no idea you were afraid of the dark when I shut them off. I thought you fell asleep and forgot."

"I'm not afraid of the dark."

"Your screaming begs to differ."

"I'm afraid of my memories," I speak softly, unsure if he heard me.

I jolt when he runs his hand through my hair. My eyes shut and my head tingles from his slow caress through my waves. I'm painfully aware of Jax's body. His heat surrounds me, offering a sense of protection.

"Go to sleep. I'll keep watch for any bad guys."

A new tight feeling in my chest replaces the one left behind from the nightmare. I don't think I've ever been as grateful for Jax's presence than in this moment. "Are you counting yourself?"

"Always. But I'll protect your virtue, don't worry."

"This isn't a good idea."

His hand finds mine and gives it a squeeze. "Nope. Not at all."

Even amidst my sadness, my heart rate picks back up. "Then why are you here?"

"You always ask me questions I don't have answers to." He sounds confused.

Minutes pass. Jax's hand encases mine, calming me despite everything.

"What's happening to us?" I whisper to myself.

"I wish I knew the answer to that too. But to be honest, I'm scared shitless to find out."

My eyes grow heavy as I listen to the rhythmic sound of Jax's breathing. I battle unconsciousness and lose the fight. Jax's hand returns to my hair, running through the strands for what feels like an hour.

Jax leaves behind the softest kiss near the base of my neck. "I wish I hated you. But instead, you're making me like you more. You pretend to be this put-together person, but you're broken— damaged like me. And the absolute fucking worst is that I want to know your messed-up parts too. I want to put them together with mine and see what we create. So, I don't know whether to run in the opposite direction or beg you for a chance despite how much of an arse I've been," he whispers.

Oh, God. He thinks I'm sleeping.

"But most of all, I wish I wasn't a coward. I'm not brave. Fuck that. If I were, then I'd face my future for you. And bloody hell, if that doesn't worry me more than anything else. You have the power to change it all."

I don't know what he says next. Even though I try to stay awake, exhaustion wins, with my eyes drifting shut again.

Jax watches me from his seat on the couch as I exit my room. "I need to talk to you about last night."

I'm afraid of what he wants to say, but I gather the courage to sit on the couch opposite him like a mature adult. My eyes try to find a spot in the room to stare at, but he stands and sits next to me.

I become acutely aware of his body, like crackling electricity coming off him in waves, leaving behind goosebumps on my skin.

Those hands were on me last night, holding me, making me feel safe.

"How often do you get nightmares?"

"Not often anymore." I avoid his gaze.

"And it was because of me turning off the lights?" His voice draws my eyes back to him like a ship seeking a lighthouse on a stormy night.

"I don't like the dark."

His eyebrows pull together. "I had no idea."

"We aren't exactly best friends."

"I don't want to be," he grumbles under his breath.

"Yeah well you have the personality of a cactus, so I'm not exactly interested either."

The corner of his lips lift. "I can't say I've heard that one before."

"Does dick sound more familiar?"

"Did you call me a dick?" He mockingly gasps as he clutches onto an invisible pearl necklace.

"Dick. Asshole. *Pinche pendejo.*"

Jax covers my mouth with his palm, his eyes reflecting a lightness I wish to see more of. "Stop. My virgin ears can't handle this!"

I open my mouth and nip at his finger. *Who am I, and why did I do that?*

Jax moves his hand away from my mouth. His thumb caresses my bottom lip as he stares at me, with desire and something else, pulling me in.

I'm so screwed beyond reason.

Jax pulls away before I have a chance to process how good his touch feels. "You ask me to pretend we never kissed, but I'm finding it pretty damn hard at the moment."

"Because I bit your hand?"

"Because you're looking at me like that's exactly what you want." His knuckles brush across my cheek.

My body comes alive like I touched an electric fence. "You need to stop."

"The problem is I don't want to anymore. Avoiding you is exhausting." He tugs me into his firm body while his eyes search mine for permission.

My eyes flutter closed the moment his hand palms my cheek. His lips brush against mine, tentative and testing. The soft kiss isn't what I'd expect from him; it's shocking yet invigorating, making it impossible to resist. So much so, I forget about who we are and give in to the moment.

I sigh, offering him access to my mouth. His tongue teases mine. Our kiss intensifies and grows more passionate. Jax pulls me onto his lap, encouraging me to straddle him. His erection grows as I grind into him, failing to ease the ache inside of me. His kiss becomes more dominant. He fights back for control with his tongue while his hands grip my hips to the point of pain. Everything about the kiss begs me to submit to him. I groan as he nips at my bottom lip, tugging and sucking on the sensitive skin.

My mind becomes cloudy as we kiss. His hands grip my ass and tug me closer. A groan escapes his lips as he palms my ass, eliciting a shiver from me.

Our kiss is erotic and toxic, with a hint of chaos.

Jax moves onto my neck, leaving my lips swollen and throbbing from his assault. A ringing phone sounds over our heavy breathing, reminding me of everything wrong with this scenario.

I still, no longer rubbing into him like I want to give his dick a ride. My cheeks flush as I climb off him and stand on shaky legs, pressing my hand to my lips.

"Shit!" He leans his head against the couch.

"What is happening to us?" I whisper to myself.

"The worst thing."

A sharp pain echoes through my chest. "It'll never happen again. It *can't* happen again."

His hands tug at his hair. "Fuck. That's not what I meant."

"Then why is it the worst thing?" I throw my arms in the air. "One second I think you like me, the next I'm wondering what's going on with you."

He shuts his eyes. "Liking you isn't the problem."

"Then what *is* the problem? Because ever since I met you, you're always snippy with me. Even when I was helping Liam, you barely looked at me, barely spoke to me. And now you're acting nicer, and I have no clue what to do with that either."

"You don't get it. Being normal with you threatens everything I've set up for myself."

"There's nothing wrong with normal."

"For people like me, it is. I can't have that kind of lifestyle."

"Because of your job?"

"No. Because I'm an arsehole who doesn't deserve hope. It's cruel for both of us."

"Everyone deserves hope." My heart cracks as Jax looks at me with the most pained face.

"Not those without a future." Jax rises from the couch and enters my personal bubble again. He places a soft kiss on the top of my head before stepping away. "You deserve moments worthy of buying a snow globe, not ones tainted with sadness and regret."

He steps away, but I clutch onto his hand, not letting him go. "No. You stay right here and tell me what you mean. I'm done with the doom and gloom attitude and half-cloaked statements."

He looks down at our hands as if he can sense our weird bond too. "My mum has Huntington's Disease. It's genetic and shitty as fuck, which means there's a fifty-fifty chance I'm going to end up with the same disease. That diagnosis would ruin any chance at a normal life. No forever and always. No happy ending. Nothing except a future riddled with pain for me and whatever family I have. I refuse to drag anyone down with me, watching me fade into a person they don't recognize."

Tears pool in my eye ducts. "God, Jax, I'm so sorry."

"You don't need to apologize. It's nothing I haven't accepted."

"But have you? You act like a fifty-fifty chance is the end. Aren't there tests to check if you have this disease in the first place?"

"I'm not one of your damn puzzles. There's no way to solve the problems in my life because I don't want the test results. I can't imagine going through life if I test positive, knowing the outcome of that kind of disease. I already met with a genetic counselor last year and decided against testing, so there's no use trying to convince me."

"But you're assuming knowing you have it is worse than not knowing. It can't be healthy either way."

His jaw ticks. "Stop psychoanalyzing me."

"I'm not trying to. I only want to help you see other options."

"You need to accept my choice. Your job is to keep an eye on me and help me with my reputation. That's it. We can be attracted to one another—hell, we can kiss and fuck and do every dirty thought I've played in my head over and over, but this can never turn into anything more."

Can I deal with something like that? If my work reputation wasn't at risk, would I want to try for more with Jax?

Jax softly tugs his hand out of my grasp. "Shit. Don't bother thinking about that offer. You deserve more than that. You deserve more than *me.*" His back is the last thing I see before he enters his suite and shuts the door.

I drop onto the couch, attempting to wrap my mind around Jax's revelation.

After an hour of thinking and researching, I come to a conclusion. Jax needs to believe in his future. He needs to want something more in life than succeeding with Formula 1. But most of all, he needs me to show him there's more to life than the things we fear.

If we let the nightmares define us, then we lose sight of our dreams.

CHAPTER TWENTY-TWO

Elena

While Jax completes his qualifier for the Hungarian Grand Prix, I meet with Connor to check in on Jax's progress. We sit in his office, mulling over the positives of Jax's career and where he can still use improvement.

"You've truly done an amazing job. I didn't think he'd keep it together for this long."

"I have a few more things planned for him. Some extra one-on-one activities with a few hard-core fans."

"He'd like that. He's not one for meeting with too many people at one time."

"Yeah, anxiety tends to do that to people."

"Even that's improved for him. Thank you for suggesting the therapist, by the way. That was a great idea and even some of the crew members have been benefiting from the help."

I blush. "It's the least I could do. I've read the research on athletes and I had only hoped it would work for these guys."

"Not to change the subject, but I've been meaning to ask you about something I've noticed."

Are people talking about Jax and me? *God, please don't ask what I think you're going to ask.*

He laughs to himself. "I don't mean to cause you any alarm, but it's hard for me not to say something."

I bob my head up and down, unsure if I could say anything at the moment. *Dios, dame paciencia.* My heart can't catch a break this week. It beats rapidly in my chest, and my knee shakes as I bounce my leg up and down.

"I notice Jax fancies you. The other day I caught him staring at you for a long period of time at a McCoy debriefing. I wanted to ensure you don't feel uncomfortable or think that your job is in jeopardy if you deny his advances."

Seeing as Jax has shoved his tongue down my throat on three separate occasions, I'd definitely say it's a little too late for this conversation.

I fake a laugh. "Oh, no, Jax has been nothing but polite."

The dry look Connor sends my way calls me out on my bullshit. "Please, save your lies for the media. I know Jax is a difficult person to work with. I only want you to feel secure."

"It's not like that between us."

"Well, if you ever told him to fuck off, you won't lose your job because of it. I promise you that."

I gather the courage to ask the question that's bothered me for weeks. "Why is there no rule against this sort of thing? Don't you want to eliminate any unnecessary workplace drama?"

Connor shrugs. "My dad fell in love with his family maid's

daughter. They spent way too many years being told they shouldn't be together by everyone who should've supported them. I don't want to be the person to get in the way of someone's shot at true happiness, especially after hearing how much it affected my parents."

"That's a much deeper reason than I anticipated."

He laughs. "I only mentioned the thing about Jax to make sure you felt secure since you'll be visiting his family for the summer break. I appreciate you keeping an eye on him."

"You don't need to thank me. It's part of my contract." I brush my shaky hands down my dress.

"Contract or not, the guys are lucky to have you working for them. You truly are one of a kind. Plus, it doesn't hurt that Jax has a crush on you. Makes him much more compliant."

Well, that settles it. Too bad everyone knows Jax Kingston has a crush on me except for the man himself.

I'm convinced I'm currently living in an alternate dimension. That would be the only explanation for everything happening now, including my crazy conversation with Connor earlier.

With Jax busy with a late-night McCoy debriefing, I expected to come back to an empty hotel room.

And I did.

But I also didn't.

I walk in to find a pitch-black room, with a lit nightlight by the front door. It's a plastic F1-themed blue race car looking exactly like something a parent would buy at the gift shop.

"No way." I leave the nightlight on, allowing the small light to guide me. Another nightlight is lit in a dark corner of the living room near my bedroom door.

I open my room to find another race car next to my bed. "Oh my God." Multiple nightlights offer me guidance toward my bathroom, where I find the final lit nightlight.

Unexpected tears flood my eyes. Why would Jax do something like this? And why does he have to slowly destroy the wall I have protecting myself from him?

I head back to my bed. Somehow, I missed the note next to my pillow. Jax's familiar scrawl marks the page.

> Because someone has to help you fix your terrible sleep cycle. No more bullshit about sleeping with all the lights on. All self-respecting adults use cool TJ nightlights nowadays.
>
> P.S. If some paparazzi posts a photo of me buying this crap and says I'm afraid of the dark, I might lose my shit.
>
> P.P.S It was totally worth the risk to my manhood.

I clutch onto Jax's note as I lie down on my bed. Everything feels like it's shifting between us, with him changing in the smallest ways.

I thought I'd be the one to figure him out. It looks like during my mission, I lost sight of his power over me.

I gave someone who destroys everything in his life something I can't take back.

The possibility of earning my love.

CHAPTER TWENTY-THREE

Jax

Having Elena fix up my reputation despite the urge to push her away? Risky.

Having Elena come into my home, meet my parents, and join us like the British Brady Bunch for the summer break? Downright stupid.

To be fair, I didn't have a choice. Connor made it clear Elena needed to join me wherever I vacationed, but I didn't think through the cons of having her spend the month-long break with my family.

One look at Mum embracing Elena in a hug the moment they meet is enough to sound the alarm.

"Elena, it's great to have you here. I'm thrilled to meet the woman who puts my son in his place."

"Oh. Hello." Elena's arms remain at her sides as Mum uses what little strength she has to tighten the embrace.

Elena's reaction has me laughing to myself. Her glare fails

to achieve the desired effect. Instead, my smile expands.

"We've heard you're the one to thank for the detox of Jax's liver." Dad pulls Mum back, letting her lean on him instead of using a cane.

"Are you all going to keep talking about me like I'm not standing here in the same room? Way to make me feel welcome." I cross my arms.

Two members of the staff grab Elena's and my belongings off the floor and carry them upstairs.

"Oh my, how big you've gotten! Come closer so I can get a good look at you." Mum jokingly gasps.

I walk up to her and place a kiss on her cheek. "McCoy feeds me well."

"Looks like the new gym routine we made is working out." Dad pinches my arm muscles.

Jackie comes into the room, greeting Elena and me before announcing that dinner is ready.

"You're in for the best meal of your life." I wink at Elena.

"Can't wait." Her wide eyes look around, lingering on the crystal chandeliers and expensive furnishings.

We all walk into my parents' formal dining room. It's fit for a TV set, with a large table that can seat twenty people at a minimum. Large windows show off our lush backyard with a pool and garden.

"Whoa. I feel grossly underdressed and underprepared," Elena whispers to me before she stares down at her clothes. Her cheeks redden as her runners squeak against the floor.

"I happen to like what you're wearing." I tug on the sleeve of her Rolling Stones jumper.

Dad helps Mum into her chair at the table. "I hope this

isn't too fancy. By the time I realized it, Jackie had already set up dinner here. We usually eat in the kitchen."

Elena and I take up a seat next to each other, sitting across from my parents.

Dad pours himself a glass of wine after offering some to Elena and me. "It's good to have you back home, even if it's for a little bit."

"I'm happy to be back. I hate living out of a suitcase."

He gives his glass a swirl. "Anything special you have planned during your time here?"

"Not exactly. Nothing besides the extra stuff planned with McCoy before my home race. You know how wild the British GP is here."

"Well there are a few things I have planned for him. The first one is this weekend," Elena speaks up.

I tilt my head at her. "And what's that?"

"The Make-A-Wish Foundation contacted me to set up a day or two where a fan follows you around and spends time with you."

My parents look at Elena with endearment. Shit. I'm tempted to cover Elena's mouth with duct tape to prevent my parents from falling in love with her.

...And now I'm thinking of tape wrapped around Elena's wrists while I fuck her. *Way to go, Jax.* I shift in my chair, attempting to rein my thoughts in despite the blood rushing to my cock.

Dad smiles at me. "A kid's wish is to hang out with Jax? Wow. You should be honored, son."

Right. Please think of the more important topic at hand.

"I was surprised when they contacted me." Elena blushes as

she looks at me. "Not because you're not good at what you do. I was nervous to plan something that is clearly important to this kid."

"Why's that?" Mum tilts her head.

"The first time I called him and told him who I was, he screamed into the phone. I could barely make out anything he said, but I did understand him screaming about how meeting Jax will be the best day of his life. I don't want to plan anything boring for him or not meet his expectations."

"The kid is lucky to have you planning everything. Trust me on that." I squeeze her hand, shooting her a soft smile.

Dad eyes our hands while Mum clamps her lips together to hide her smile.

"We'll have to invite him over for dinner or something. Give him the whole Kingston experience!" Mum claps her hands together. "This is delightful. We haven't had a kid around here since…well…Jax was a kid!"

Elena grins. "To be fair, he's a teenager."

Mum can't contain her excitement. "Oh, I love some good teenage angst. Keeps me on my toes. You must tell us what you have planned for him."

Elena and Mum hit it off, sharing details about Caleb, who is rumored to be my greatest fan. I spend the dinner listening intently without offering much. For the first time around Elena, I want to filter the words coming out of my mouth.

It's hard seeing as now instead of being a total douche, I'd rather do other types of things. The naughty kind. The reckless kind. The kind that ends with nothing but orgasms and failed promises.

CHAPTER TWENTY-FOUR

Elena

When Connor made me agree to spend the summer break with Jax's family in London, I thought it was a perfect setup. It was supposed to give me the opportunity to keep an eye on him while planning a few more activities to restore the public's faith in him.

In all the craziness of planning fun outings for Caleb, I completely neglected the idea of spending that much time with Jax and his family. I expected it to be similar to us sharing a hotel.

I was wrong. So wrong in many ways.

The real wild card is Jax's mom. I don't know how Jax came out the way he did, all rough edges, because his mom is an absolute gem. Vera's sweet and caring—exactly what I wish I had in my life lately.

"So, I was thinking about going shopping downtown. Do you want to join me?" Vera sips her morning tea. Jax lucked out with inheriting some of his mom's good looks. She has pale blonde hair that matches her light skin, and gray eyes with a permanent gleam to them.

"I don't know about that. I'm supposed to meet with Jax and discuss some plans for the break."

"I think Jax can take care of himself for a day. Zack wants to spend time with him while we have a little fun anyway. Come on, take a day off." She bats her dirty blonde lashes at me.

"Let me check in with him first."

"If you must." She waves me off with a smile.

I make my way up toward Jax's wing of the house. I wasn't aware of how well-off his family was until they disclosed how they have enough rooms in their house to name areas after compass directions. Wealth isn't something I've grown up with and being surrounded by it reminds me of how I don't belong. I'm pretty sure the sheets in my guest room are more expensive than my monthly loan payment.

I knock on Jax's door. He opens a few seconds later in nothing but a towel around his waist. Water trickles down his face from his wet hair, landing on his chest before dripping down his abs.

I count the ridges of muscle before meeting his eyes.

He leans his head against the door frame. "Morning. Did you knock on my door to stare at me or did you have something else in mind?"

"Uhm." My eyes flit from his face to his abs. "Your mom asked me to go out with her. I told her I couldn't agree until I checked in with you. I know we planned on discussing your schedule and going over Caleb's visit, but she seems pretty set on spending time together."

His lips press into a thin line. "You can have a day off for fuck's sake. I'm not going to rat you out to Connor."

"Well, I didn't exactly say that…" I rock back on my heels.

"No, but I know you." His eyes rake over me, taking in my yellow summer dress. "Anything that makes Mum happy is always a good idea."

Sigh. If only he treated other women in his life with the same respect. "Okay, sounds good. See you later." I make a move to turn away. Jax's hand grips mine softly, stopping me. My body instantly reacts to his touch like static sparking.

"Do you mind coming in for a second? I wanted to ask you a question about Caleb's visit. The kid has been texting me ever since you gave him my number." Jax opens the door wider for me to enter.

"Sure." I take a few hesitant steps into his room.

"Let me get dressed."

I check him out again. *By all means, please don't.*

His beaming smile threatens to knock me out. He disappears into his bathroom, ending my perusal of his defined body. The very one covered in tattoos I want to explore in greater detail.

I take the opportunity to check out his childhood bedroom. Band posters cover one of the walls, showing off tour dates for Coldplay, Fleetwood Mac, and Stormzy. He has an old-school turntable with a box of vinyl records on his dresser. I flip through a few of them before pulling out Ed Sheeran's *Multiply* album.

Jax comes out of his bathroom in jeans and a T-shirt. I hold back my sigh at the loss of his abs.

"Having you in here is like handing over my diary." He comes up behind me. His body heats my back, making my skin pebble. His finger toys with the strap of my sundress.

"Didn't you want to show me something?"

"Right." His voice comes out rough.

I move to put the vinyl back, but Jax's hand stops me. He plucks the record from my grasp and pulls it out.

"Big Ed Sheeran fan?" His breath heats my neck.

I attempt to suppress a shiver and fail. "The biggest." I turn around. My chest brushes against his, eliciting the slightest inhale of breath from him.

"Maybe I'll introduce you two." Jax looks over my shoulder as he fiddles with the player. Ed Sheeran's "I'm a Mess" begins playing.

"No way," I squeal.

"I shouldn't be jealous of the ginger fucker, but now I am." His smile should send me running. It's unusual for him, untroubled and tempting.

I want more of his smiles and more of this side of him, carefree and happy.

He makes a move to pull me in, but I sidestep him, hitting him with a mischievous smile of my own.

"You can't take back that type of offer because of jealousy."

"No take backs?" He lets out a low chuckle.

"No take backs," I repeat as I walk toward the other side of his room where he has trophies and photographs lining the shelves. A picture stands out to me and I grab it. A teenage Jax smiles at the camera, ignoring the tattoo artist behind him while Vera sits next to him and pouts.

"Mum is pretending there. She's the one who signed the release for me to get my first tattoo before eighteen."

"Really?"

"Oh, yeah. She even picked out my first tattoo." Jax tugs the frame from my hands, his fingers brushing against mine. The touch sends a current of energy up my arm.

"No way."

"Yup. At the time, I thought it was embarrassing, but I love it because it reminds me of her."

My heart threatens to melt into a puddle at Jax's feet. "Which one?" I grab onto the same arm from the photograph, searching the countless tattoos he has.

"Bet you can't guess which one," he teases.

"You're on." I meticulously search the tattoos on his arm. By the end of my investigation, I'm stuck between two options. I go with my gut, stopping my finger on the one I think his mom picked. "This one. Definitely."

His body shudders as my finger trails across the ink, pulling a smile from me. This tattoo doesn't fit the grim themes of his other ones. A beautiful flower stands out compared to his other hauntingly beautiful designs, ranging from a grim reaper to a tombstone. Safe to say he's got creepy covered.

"Too bad you didn't specify what happens if you chose right."

"What?" I screech. "I guessed right?" I break out into a victory dance, twirling in a circle, making my dress swirl around me.

Jax grins. "Yeah." He runs his index finger across a tattoo of a paper rose made out of music sheets. "How'd you know?"

"Honestly, your other tattoos are a bit..."

"Depressing?"

"I wouldn't say that... You do have a butterfly one after all."

He laughs to himself. "I choose my tattoos based on my mood."

"Typical Gemini."

He knocks his head back and lets out a roar of laughter. When Jax looks as untroubled as he does now, it throws me for a loop. The smiling teen in the photograph is a far cry from the man I've gotten to know over the past few months.

"When did you find out about your mom's diagnosis?" I blurt out.

His eyes dart toward the photo in his hands. "Twenty-one. They knew before, but they held off on telling me until they felt I could handle the news."

My hand grips his bicep. I rub my thumb in circles, wanting to soothe him. "I'm sorry. I can imagine it's hard for you, with her being one of the coolest people I've ever met."

"She's the best. Hands down my favorite person out there."

I can't stop my eyes from watering.

"Why are you looking at me like that?" He lifts a brow.

"Because beneath all the tattoos and grumpiness, you're not a bad guy."

"Elena…" He sighs, avoiding my gaze.

"Hear me out. You may have made bad decisions. Actually, wait—terrible decisions. But that doesn't make you a bad person. You can choose to be better. No one's stopping you."

"No one but me."

"Exactly. Which is kind of dumb if you really think about it."

"You don't say. Tell me why." The corner of his mouth lifts into a smirk.

"Yes. You're a grown man so you're the only one who can decide to be better. If I were you, I would find it exhausting to keep up such a rough exterior all the time."

"As opposed to your version of shitting rainbows?"

"At least there's a pot of gold at the end of it." I grin at him.

"Don't start wishing for things that can't happen."

He lets out a breath as I run a hand down his chest, letting my finger drag across his muscles.

My sanity has temporarily left the ten-thousand-square-foot mansion. "It's already happening. You're changing."

"Don't make me prove you wrong."

I laugh. "If you have to make an effort to be worse, then you're proving my point."

"I tried to warn you."

"Well, you buying me nightlights doesn't scream wanting to avoid me anymore, now does it?"

His eyes flash with something unreadable. "I didn't want to wake up to your screaming again."

"Right." I roll my eyes. Before I have a chance to consider the consequences, I stand on the tips of my toes, leaving behind the faintest kiss on his lips. "Choose to be better."

I step back, but Jax tugs me into him. His fingers run through my hair and hold my head in place as he kisses me.

Screw that. Kissing is too simple to describe what he does. Jax devours me, licking and nipping at my lips before his tongue owns me. The trophies rattle above our heads as he pushes me against the wall.

He presses his body into mine. The contact has my head spinning from lust. His tongue fights mine as his hand moves from my head to my thigh, lifting my dress up. I'm committed to making one of the most reckless decisions of my life, but I can't stop it.

No. More like I don't *want* to stop it. Not with my heart pounding in my chest and my clit throbbing to the point of aching. I want Jax, and I can't help denying myself this small reprieve. He makes my body buzz like never before.

"Shit. I want to kiss you everywhere and check if you taste as good as I think." He runs his tongue down the column of my neck.

It's a thrill, kissing him, touching him. Like a shot of adrenaline coursing through me.

My body trembles as his hand traces the inside of my thigh. "This is so wrong."

"But it feels so damn right." He shuts me up as his lips return to mine. His fingers tug at my underwear, pulling my thong down.

His fingers run against my slit, eliciting a gasp from me. The palm of his hand pushes against my most sensitive place. The pressure inside of my body builds as he teases me, pushing his thumb against my clit. Jax captures my moan as he pumps one finger into me.

I shouldn't like his touch as much as I do. If I had any common sense, I'd push him away and end this thing growing between us. Instead, I give in to our attraction, not willing to end it.

How can I when he makes my body feverish from want?

He pumps his finger into me before adding another, filling me up and teasing me. "Look at the way your cheeks flush from my fingers alone. I wonder how red you'll look with my cock rammed to the hilt inside of you."

His other hand pulls down the strap of my dress and the cup of my bra in one go, revealing my breast to him. The cold air hits my skin before Jax's mouth wraps around my nipple.

I groan as his fingers increase their tempo. My head rolls

back as his teeth brush against me. I shouldn't like the bite of pain. Any sane person shouldn't. But I can't deny the deranged push inside of me that wants to take anything Jax has to offer.

"Come for me. I know you want to. And fuck, I've been delirious wondering how you look as you fall apart for me."

My legs shake to the point of giving out, but Jax holds me up. With a few more pumps and his fingers brushing against my most sensitive spot, I give in to pleasure, letting it invade my mind and body.

Jax stares at me with heat in his gaze. Once my breathing slows, he pulls his fingers out of me and traces my slit once more, showing me how desperate I am for him. He doesn't bother going to the bathroom to clean his hands.

No. He continues the show, licking his two tattooed fingers clean. I nearly collapse at the sight of him.

"Jax, have you seen Elena? She told me she needed to ask you something quick, but she never showed up again." His mom's voice crackles.

Oh, shit! My body stands straight as fear chases away my lust-induced high. Jax smiles at me and winks, before walking to a wall speaker.

Oh my God. My heart rate fails to slow down. I can't believe I thought Jax's mom was in the room.

Jax winks at me as he presses a button. "She left a few minutes ago. Said something about grabbing her bag before going out with you."

Who is this version of him and how do I keep him?

"All right. I'll buzz her room then."

I place a hand against my chest, checking on my poor heart. "Oh God. I thought she was here."

"Clearly not. They don't come over to my side of the house. At least not since I was a teen and they caught me jacking off."

As much as I want to ask a follow-up question to that story, I need to focus. "We can't do this in your parents' house."

"I prefer words of affirmation. Like 'Oh God, we *can* do this, especially in your parents' house.' Come on, live a little." Jax laughs.

I move to grab my thong off the floor, but he beats me to it. "Give that back."

"I've grown rather fond of them. Get another pair."

"What? Who grows attached to underwear?"

"Me. I'll take it as a white flag of your surrender."

"To what? Your insanity?"

His wide smile makes my chest tighten. "I love the way you verbally spar with me." He tugs me into another kiss despite my innate need to escape the room.

"Jax, stop." I breathlessly protest after he kisses me for another minute.

"You better get going because it looks like Mum wants to give you a day to remember."

"So, we're going to act like this never happened?" I point at the scene of our crime.

"Oh, no. It definitely happened. And it'll happen again. And again."

"What about fate's big fuck you?" I tease.

"While fate's fucking me over, I might as well fuck you."

CHAPTER TWENTY-FIVE

Elena

"I've been dying to get you alone before Caleb comes over tomorrow, but Jax kept saying you were busy. Does anyone tell you that you work a lot?" Vera clutches onto her cane as we stroll through a small park in the heart of London. When I asked earlier if she wanted me to call the car after walking through multiple shops, she brushed me off and claimed she wanted to take a walk.

After Vera stumbles again, I steer us toward a bench. "Do you mind if we sit? My shoes are killing me."

She offers me a knowing smile. "Oh yeah, those sandals look beyond uncomfortable."

I laugh as we sit under a tree. "You don't let people off easy, do you?"

"Where's the fun in that? And to be fair, I've heard a thing or two about you, which tells me you're the same way."

"I guess it takes one to know one."

"Indeed. Anyone who can manage my son for months on

end definitely deserves a Nobel Peace Prize. Tell me, why did you sign up for the job to help him?"

I keep my eyes focused on a family playing tag on the grassy quad across from us. "I needed the kind of money they were offering."

"To help your grandma, right? Jax mentioned to us that she is sick."

I nod my head up and down.

"Ah, that's such a sweet gesture of you. And a sacrifice too for someone as young as yourself."

"She was always there for me while I grew up. I owe everything to her, so the least I can do is make sure she's well taken care of." I don't realize my mistake until it's too late.

"What about your parents? Do they live in Europe?" She speaks soothingly.

I swallow back the lump in my throat as I turn my head away from her. "No. My parents passed away when I was younger."

"Oh, dear. I'm so sorry to hear that. Jax never told me." Her shaky hand clutches onto mine in a motherly way.

"He doesn't know. It's not a fact I share with many people."

"I appreciate you trusting me, especially when pain has a way of making us retreat into ourselves."

We sit and people watch for a few minutes. I don't know what to say, and Vera's silence tells me she might not either.

Vera laughs to herself. "You know, my parents are total arseholes. To be honest, my whole family is a rotten bunch."

I turn my head toward her. "What happened?"

"They threatened to cut me off from the family once I started dating Jax's father. At first, they thought I was rebelling, choosing to date a Black man from a poor family. My mum's

British and my dad's Swedish, as if that can justify their mentality. Once things became more serious with me and Zack, they couldn't handle their daughter not dating a white man. It went against everything their racist hearts believed in."

"Really? So, what did you do?"

"I told my sisters to keep in touch with me before telling my parents to rot in hell."

"No." I cover my mouth.

"With my middle fingers in the air, too, I should add." She winks at me.

A giggle explodes out of me. "You're iconic."

"Like vintage Chanel, darling."

"How do you keep this positive? Tell me your secret."

"Rather than what? Wallow in my diagnosis and hate my life?"

"Whoa, I didn't mean it that way. Please don't take offense." I lift my hands in submission.

"I know, I'm only teasing you." She knocks her shoulder into mine. "I've always been this way. Mind over matter is my way of life. I can't change the cards I've been dealt, but I can change the way I approach my hand."

Okay, Jax's mom used a poker reference. She instantly gains cool points in my eyes. "That's admirable."

"I wish parts of me rubbed off on my son." Vera's lips press together in a thin line. "He's changed along with my lifestyle, and it breaks my heart. I keep extra positive for him because I don't think he could handle it any other way."

"I don't think he could either." Based on the way Jax handles everything with his mom now, I can't imagine what it would be like for him if she revealed how much she suffers privately.

"He's such a fragile person, despite the front he puts on. That boy is all marshmallow fluff on the inside no matter what the media says about him. But he's changed for the better over the past few weeks. He's less agitated when I call him, and of course we all know he's not getting into much trouble this season—if any. Thanks to you, I reckon."

I smile at her. "It's my job."

She shakes her head from side to side. "It's more than that. A job makes it sound much less significant than it is."

My eyebrows raise. "What do you mean by that?"

"It was destiny for you to work with him. People are put into our lives for special reasons, and I think you need to explore that."

I keep quiet as I think of what she said.

Vera's shaky hands clasp together. "All I want is for my son to be happy. Truly, deeply happy. More than what he feels when he races. I want him to heal and grow, and you are part of that equation."

What does someone say to that? Nothing. Absolutely nothing.

Vera moves onto another subject, saving me from my reeling mind. We spend an hour in the park talking about anything and everything.

At some point, we end up both crying as I share my story from start to now. She's the first person outside of *Abuela* and Elías who knows my history. Vera has this calming mother's sense about her that I didn't realize I was desperately wanting, however temporary.

Vera pulls me in for a hug once we stand up from the bench. "Thank you for being brave and sharing a part of your life with me. When I heard about everything you were doing for Jax, I expected you to be strong, but you're so much more. Thank you for being everything my son needs. For someone who lost so much at a young age, you truly have lots to give to the world."

After my day with Vera, Jax's dad planned his version of a family dinner. He barbecues with Jax standing by his side, both of them chatting while Vera and I sit at a table near the pool, sipping wine together. It's nothing I'd expect from a family with enough money to have their own staff working all hours of the day.

"I could use some more wine. Do you want another glass?" Vera points at my empty glass.

"Sure. But I can get it." I rise from my seat, but Vera places a trembling hand on my shoulder.

"Nonsense. You're our guest. It will only take me a moment." She uses her cane to get out of her chair. Jax's dad offers to help, but she tells him to bug off.

Jax strides toward me and leans against the glass table. "Surviving the whole day with my mum?"

"More like thriving. She's incredible." I crane my neck and smile at him.

He grins back at me, his eyes lighting up in a way I've come to enjoy. "Good response. I'm kind of surprised you're relaxed about all of this since a normal girl would be afraid of meeting a guy's parents."

I scoff, pretending I wasn't scared meeting Zack and Vera for the first time. "That only applies to meeting the parents of a guy you like."

AKA Jax, but it's not like I need to confess this information to him.

Jax rubs the spot near his heart. "Here I was thinking you liked me. You're wounding me."

"Well—"

Glass shatters in the distance. Zack rushes inside the house with Jax and me on his heels. Another sound of glass exploding pushes us toward the bar area. Vera stares at the ground, her flushed cheeks stained from fresh tears. The sweet smell of wine hangs in the air.

"Shit, sweetheart, are you hurt?" Glass crunches under Zack's sneakers as he goes to grab Vera.

"No. What a fucking mess! Just another day of me screwing up a fun time for everyone. I don't know why the bloody hell you stay with me," she snaps.

Zack lifts Vera and places her on a barstool on the opposite side of the mess. "Because I couldn't imagine a day without you."

"Cut the shit. This is hell for everyone." Vera's eyes darken, a stark contrast to the warmth they usually reflect.

Shock ripples through me at her sudden change of mood. Is this what the medical journals meant when they described mood changes with Huntington's Disease?

"No. It's a rough moment during a good day. That's different." Zack pats her thigh.

I shift my attention toward Jax. His eyes match the frown on his face as Zack assesses Vera for any injuries.

"Shit, you were cut. Let me go grab the first aid kit." Zack rushes off after checking out the gash on Vera's foot.

"What happened, Mum?" Jax walks up to her and grabs onto her trembling hand.

"What do you think? Put two and two together."

Jax looks over at me with a pained expression I feel deep within my own chest. I open my mouth to offer reassurance but shut it again once he shakes his head.

Jax faces his mom again. "Accidents happen. It's just a wine bottle."

"The only accident is me thinking I could live a normal life. Instead, I cause messes and annoy everyone around me."

Jax sucks in a breath. "Mum, this isn't you."

"This is me. That's the worst part." Her eyes water.

My heart clenches at her vulnerability. Jax and Vera don't need an outsider looking in on their tense moment. I step away from them, slowly inching back until I'm in a separate hallway.

I turn, running into a hard body. Zack's hands wrap around my arms to steady me. A single tear runs down his face. The silent pain these two men experience daily fills me with despair.

"I'm sorry," I whisper.

"Please ignore what happened. Vera has mood swings from time to time. She's not proud of them so I'm asking you to pretend you didn't see her break down like this."

"Of course. Is there anything I can do to help?"

He swallows and nods. "Will you please check on the food? I'm sure it's burnt by now and the last thing we need is a fire."

I agree, and Zack walks back toward the bar. My footsteps echo through the empty halls. Mindlessly, I keep an eye on the food on the grill while working through my thoughts.

In my research of Vera's disease, a lot of doctors talked about mood swings and irritability. And there's one thing reading about it, but it's a whole other experience seeing it with my own eyes. No wonder Jax has anxiety and stress about his mom. If I were in his position, I doubt I'd be any better off, feeling helpless to her deterioration.

The click of the grill shutting off surprises me. I turn to find Jax's eyes looking down at me. He doesn't hide the pain in his gaze as he takes a few deep breaths. Without second-guessing myself, I wrap my arms around his waist and give him a squeeze. "I'm sorry about your mom. God, I'm so freaking sorry you have to experience that and pretend everything is okay. No one in your family deserves this, most of all your mom."

His arms copy mine, holding me closer to his body and resting his chin against my head. "I wish she wasn't sick."

"Me too."

"I wish she didn't have these mood swings. Not because it bothers me, but more because it breaks her heart. She hates herself afterward for the things she says. I know it's not her, but I still take her words personally sometimes."

"No one would blame you for feeling that way. Does this happen often?" I move to step out of Jax's embrace, but his arms tighten around me.

"Enough times that they recently changed her medicine. It's the only part of her disease she can't hide with a smile. When she gets in that headspace, it's a battle with herself."

"How do you feel about it?"

"I feel like donating every single euro I've made to finding a cure."

"Do you think doctors will find it?"

"Probably not in my mother's lifetime."

I hope, if Jax has the same disease, a cure would be discovered before any symptoms kick in. I mentally hit myself for thinking the very thought in the first place.

Jax releases me from the hug, giving me room to take a few breaths of fresh air.

My hands have a mind of their own, pressing against his cheeks and forcing him to look at me. "You can always talk to me. I'm here to help you."

"What happens when you have to go away at the end of the season?"

"What happens if I want to stay?"

CHAPTER TWENTY-SIX

Jax

"This is Caleb? He looks so…"

Elena lifts her brow, taunting me to finish my sentence.

"Pure," I force out. During my back-and-forth exchanges with Caleb, he never sounded innocent. But one look at him has my preconceived notions going up in flames.

It blows my mind that a skinny guy wearing a bowtie, pastel shorts, and boat shoes is supposedly one of my biggest fans. Caleb's bald head shines as he says goodbye to his cab driver.

"Don't judge a book by its cover," Elena rasps.

"With the kind of porn books you read, I definitely do."

"They're called romance." She throws her head back and laughs.

I wish I could kiss the curve of her exposed neck. Ever since our hookup yesterday in my room, I can't get her out of my head. Kissing Elena is erotic as fuck. It's something I want to repeat again, under different circumstances, preferably with little to no clothes on.

One taste wasn't enough. I want to have her to myself, chanting my name as I thrust into her, solidifying the need I have to claim her in every way.

I shove my lust aside as Caleb walks up the steps to my house. "Welcome, Caleb. My parents can't wait to meet you."

"Fuckin' mega. This house is amazing! And you! Bloody hell, Jax Kingston." Caleb pushes the bridge of his horn-rimmed glasses up his nose.

"He looks innocent and then he drops the word *fuck*. Boys," Elena whispers under her breath.

"Now that's my kind of fan." I wink at her before I grab Caleb's weekend bag from him.

We walk inside and I introduce our new guest to my parents.

"Get out. They never told me I'd get to meet the King Cobra too!" Caleb's voice bounces off the walls of our entryway.

My dad laughs as he offers his hand for Caleb to shake. "I can't say I've heard that nickname in a while."

"Please. You're one of the sickest boxers to ever live. I've watched some of your old fights that my dad has on VHS."

"Well, kid, you aged me about twenty years from that sentence alone." My dad gives Mum some space to greet my little fan.

"We're happy to have you in our home. When Elena told us about you wanting to spend time with Jax, we *had* to invite you over. Anything for Jax's biggest fan."

"Best bloody choice ever." Caleb high-fives Elena.

The way her nose scrunches has me laughing. "Wait for tomorrow. Elena planned some cool activities for you."

"Yes!" Caleb throws his fist in the air.

My parents spend the entire dinner getting to know Caleb. Turns out the guy is a bit of a rebel with a couple attempts of breaking out of his hospital room.

It seems like we will get along fine.

Caleb has many qualities I deem suitable.

He cracks jokes and he speaks fluent sarcasm. His pastimes include watching my races, scouring the web for new music, and flirting with hospital nurses. In other words, he's my kind of mate.

The kid has endless energy. He still wants to do more after I let him sit by my side during a debriefing meeting and took him to a sponsor event.

Elena says he is energetic because he's excited to spend time with his idol.

Me. An idol. God help us all.

"Here's your helmet." I pass the safety gear to Caleb as he stares slack-jawed at the older F1 car. The crew abandoned us on the grid, returning to the pit to give us directions through the team radio once we are ready to race.

"We're actually going to be driving these? Oh my God."

I chuckle. "That's what Elena scheduled for us."

"Bloody hell, I might have to kiss her."

I raise a brow. "Want to amend that statement?"

His cheeks flush. Looks like my new mate has a crush. "So, what's up with you two? Are you dating?"

"No."

"Banging?"

"No." I roll my eyes.

"Snogging?"

"Is there a reason for the round of twenty questions?" I tuck my hands in my race suit's pockets and lean against my car.

Caleb grins. "Oh, yeah. Definitely snogging. Nice." He offers me his fist to pound. I let him have his moment, hoping he leaves the conversation about Elena alone.

"So, when are you going to upgrade from kisses to more?"

And there goes my attempt to satisfy his curiosity. "You know, maybe we should head to the press room instead of the racetrack. With the questions you're asking, I feel like you might enjoy that more."

Caleb snorts as he shoves the helmet over his head. "No need to get your knickers in a twist. I'm only curious."

"Less curiosity, more adrenaline, please."

"Trust me, my heart is pounding in my chest at a rate my doctor would consider alarming."

My smile drops. "Is that bad? Maybe we shouldn't do this."

Caleb waves me off with a gloved hand. "Oh, please. I've been waiting for this day for years!"

"You have?"

"For sure. Cancer sucks, but at least the Make-A-Wish Foundation makes it worth the journey."

"I'm sorry, mate. I can tell you're a good guy who doesn't deserve this."

The best ones usually don't. It's a lesson I've learned time and time again.

"Thanks. But I don't exactly hate my life because I'm meeting you after all. Cancer can suck my pale arse."

I shoot him a small smile. "What's your secret to staying upbeat?"

"Tomorrow isn't guaranteed so I might as well make today my bitch."

I can't help the obnoxious laugh that leaves me. It's hard not to admire someone like Caleb who doesn't let his illness define him. I want to learn all his secrets and apply them to my own life. Maybe if I had his kind of courage, I wouldn't be such an anxious wreck who runs away from the unknown. "I admire people like my mum and you who keep a smile on your face despite everything."

"Your mum? She has cancer too?" Caleb's jaw drops open.

Shit. What a fuckup. "No. We better get going." I point to Caleb's car in a silent demand to get going.

He ignores me. "Is something wrong with your mum? You know you can trust me because I'd rather go through another round of chemo than reveal any of your secrets."

"My hesitation isn't because of trust."

No. It's about being judged for not getting tested by someone who has gone through his own medical hell and smiles anyway. I can't look at Caleb without questioning my own cowardness.

"No, but I want you to know that either way. Is your mum okay, at least?"

I sigh. The way Caleb's lips purse and his eyes narrow tell me he won't drop this topic, no matter how much I wish it. "My mum has Huntington's Disease. It's not the same as cancer, but it has a terrible prognosis as well."

"I'm sorry to hear that, mate." Caleb places his thin hand on my shoulder. "It might not be cancer, but it's your own hell. All terminal illnesses carry the same weight inside of us."

If Caleb has any idea about the hereditary risk Mum's illness poses for me, he doesn't reveal it. And for that I'm grateful.

Sharing this small part of myself with Caleb feels like progress. Hell, spending a weekend with Caleb has challenged some of my own thoughts and beliefs about living with a terminal illness. The way he views life despite knowing he has cancer makes my anxiety seem unjustified. I want to be fearless like him. What if I was always meant to spend time with someone like Caleb and see life from a different perspective?

Maybe fate isn't always a ruthless fucker after all.

"So, Elena. Tell me what it would take for you to go on a date with me?" Caleb sits down next to Elena on my living room couch.

A wave of possessiveness hits me out of nowhere. "Besides you needing to be the legal age limit?"

"Ouch, mate. Age is only a number."

I cock a brow at him. "That's what they all say before jail."

Elena hides her laugh behind her palm.

"Come on, what do you say about dinner?" Caleb waggles his brows at her.

Elena shakes her head.

"We'll both take you out to dinner," I blurt out.

Caleb squints at me, clearly unhappy. "We?"

"*We* will invite Elena to dinner."

"Dude, really? Way to steal my thunder."

"Better than getting rejected."

Caleb shrugs, giving in. "Okay, I'm sold. Elena, put on your nicest dress and jewelry."

"Dates usually have to say yes first." I look at Elena, daring her to say no.

Caleb kneels down in front of her. "Please, Elena Gonzalez of Mexico City, will you offer me the luxury of taking you out on a date. Preferably on Kingston's dime because I'm capped out on my monthly allowance after buying a new pair of Yeezys."

Elena laughs as Caleb clutches onto her hand and kisses it. "Sure. Anything for you."

I wish Caleb could go screw off somewhere while I take Elena out by myself. Seeing as the likelihood of her saying yes to a date with me is zero to none, I push aside the desire.

I'm good at denying myself what I want. And with Elena, I want more. And fuck if that isn't the most troubling thought of all.

Caleb wasn't joking when he asked us to get dressed up. He shows up an hour later dressed in a suit and a bowtie.

I stare at him incredulously. "Did you seriously pack that in your bag?"

"Of course. A gentleman never knows when he needs a suit."

"Are you sure you're from this century?"

The clicking of heels draws our attention toward the top of the stairs.

Elena grabs onto the hem of her green dress. She makes her way down the stairs, material clinging to her curves in the best kind of way. The mouth-watering, dick-pulsing, *I'd do anything to fuck her* kind of way.

I cough and elbow Caleb. "Tell her how pretty she looks."

He rolls his eyes at me. "Amateur. I'll do you one better." He steps behind the couch and pulls out a set of a dozen long-stemmed roses.

The little shit is trying to outdo me. Although slightly irritated at the way Elena's eyes light up at the flowers, I'm impressed by Caleb's thoughtfulness. Clearly, I need to step up my game.

"Aw, this is sweet." Elena takes a deep breath of the bouquet before flashing Caleb a dazzling smile.

Okay, I'll give the kid some points, he knows how to make a woman happy.

Her soft brown eyes find mine. Bright and beautiful, with a hint of mischief. My kind of girl.

Caleb pulls out a vintage pocket watch. "We better get going. The reservation is at eight." He offers his elbow to Elena and she laughs to the ceiling.

Her happiness has my stomach clenching like a pussy. Bit by bit, Elena slips past my carefully placed barriers, and this time, I can't say I'm sorry about it.

The rental car drops us off at an expensive restaurant that would make a grown man cry after seeing the bill. It's nothing I'd expect Elena to like, but Caleb claimed he'd never had a fifty-dollar steak. I refused to let the wanker leave my care without the best of the best at least one time in his life.

A hostess sits us in a corner, offering us privacy. Caleb helps

Elena into her seat before excusing himself to use the loo.

"This is a bit much, don't you think?" Elena looks up at me from her menu.

Like a wanker, I focus on the way the candle makes her eyes glow. "I reckon so, but it'll make him happy. Don't rat us out to his mom, but I plan on slipping him some wine, too."

She lets out a soft laugh. "You're too much."

"Says the girl who went above and beyond to plan the weekend of a lifetime for him. I'm trying to compete here."

"You planned a prom for him and his friends in a couple of weeks since they can't attend a real one. *I'm* the one who can't compete."

"Yet he'll probably rank this date as his favorite thing. He totally milked you for it."

Her cheeks flush the best shade of pink. "If it makes him happy, then I'm all for it."

"Too damn selfless for your own good."

Her head tilts in question, but Caleb interrupts us. "So, what does it take to get a drink around here?"

Elena laughs. We order our entrees and I keep true to my promise, asking for an extra wine glass for Caleb to sneak a few sips out of occasionally. Our food comes out soon after and we all dig in.

"Is the steak as good as you hoped?"

"I don't know how I'll ever eat hospital food again." Caleb closes his eyes as he sticks another forkful of food into his mouth.

"And you?" I probe for Elena's attention. I'm becoming a needy arsehole and I don't know how to make it stop. Someone— anyone—*please* make it stop.

"I'm not one for fancy restaurants, but this definitely lives up to the hype." Her lips wrap around her fork as her lashes flutter closed.

I imagine she would look the same with her lips wrapped around my cock. Reverent and seductive while she takes me to the point of gagging.

I force my eyes away and adjust my pants. "That's what I like to hear. I can cook a mean steak on the grill though, so at least I have that going for me if racing doesn't pan out."

"You cook?" Caleb rears back in his seat.

"Of course. While growing up, I liked spending time with Jackie. She taught me to cook everything I know."

"Wow." Elena stares at me.

"What fine cuisines can you cook? Don't let Jax show you up." Caleb points at her with his fork.

"Mainly Mexican dishes you won't know."

"If you say guacamole, I might never let you go."

Elena chuckles. "And homemade tortilla chips."

"You're the perfect girl. Marry me tonight. You cook, I'll clean. Match made in heaven." He smiles at her.

She shakes her head as a loud laugh erupts from her. "As sweet as you are, I'm not interested in a life behind bars. Sorry."

"So, I have one last request before my time is over with you both." Caleb fidgets with his bowtie.

I glance at him. "Strip clubs are off the table."

Elena chokes on air. "Oh my God, Jax, stop it. You're embarrassing him."

Caleb holds his chin higher. "I want to get a tattoo."

I eye him. "For real? But you're only sixteen."

"This is priceless coming from the guy who got his first tattoo at the same age."

"That's different. I had approval."

Caleb rubs his bald head. "My mum will agree."

My eyes land on Elena's. "What do you say? Let's grant his last wish from me?"

"I'd like nothing better." The smile she shoots my way makes my heart constrict oddly in my chest.

Shit.

I don't want to fall in love, but damn if her smile doesn't make the crash landing worth it.

CHAPTER TWENTY-SEVEN

Elena

Caleb is absolutely enamored by Jax. I expected Jax to be involved and nice to Caleb, but he goes above and beyond to make his fan experience the best aspects of F1. The tattooed man who invades my thoughts showed me a sweet side of himself that he keeps hidden from the world.

While I planned a fake race with old F1 cars for Caleb, Jax went out of his way to plan other outings. He introduced Caleb to Liam and Noah during a surprise lunch. Even our dinner, while under the guise of taking me out, was really to make Caleb's last night with Jax memorable.

Basically, Jax is so swoon worthy, I'm susceptible to falling over from a light breeze.

After dinner, Jax calls his tattoo artist to open up his shop while I call Caleb's mom to check if she approves of his decision. She emails me a scanned copy of a signed consent form, supporting the plan.

I spend most of the car ride listening to the two of them discuss F1 gossip and statistics. Something about Jax this week is different. I'm not even talking about the recent incident of shoving his tongue down my throat and making me come.

He seems...happy. True happiness unlike anything I've seen from him before. I don't know if spending time in London makes him feel more at ease or if it's the break away from the F1 pressures.

Part of me is waiting for everything to go wrong. But a bigger part—a stupidly hopeful part—is wondering if he will stay like this for the rest of the season.

God, I hope so. This version of Jax is one I like more and more by the day.

Our car stops in front of a modern storefront, ending my thoughts.

"Ready?" Caleb offers me his hand as he exits the car.

"This is a crazy idea." I grab onto his extended hand.

"The best ones start out that way." He gives my hand a kiss before letting it go.

Seriously, I don't know where this guy learned his moves, but he amps up the charm by the hour. I find the whole display hilarious.

We enter a chic office I'd never associate with tattoos. A modern chandelier hangs above us, highlighting the welcoming waiting room.

"This place is awesome," I whisper to Jax. My eyes linger on the way his black button-down shirt clings to his arms, emphasizing muscles I was clutching onto the other day. Ones I want to trace my tongue across.

Jax's fingers lift my chin up before he winks. *Busted.*

My cheeks flush before I scan the accent wall to our left.

"The wallpaper is made up of designs Alan did. Maybe if you look long enough, you'll find one or two of mine." Jax shrugs.

"No way! That's amazing." I check out the different patterns as Caleb and Jax review the paperwork.

I get lost in the designs, loving the mix of colors and art the owner created. My fingers hover over a snake that looks familiar. "Found one!"

"It looks creepier when it's staring at me like that." Jax walks up to my side, heat emanating from his body.

I tug at his hand without thinking. An electric rush surges through me, like someone is holding a sparkler to my skin. "The snake slithering through the skeleton bones is what makes it creepy."

He stares at my hand touching his. "Why?"

"It's morbid."

His lips turn down. "I got it in honor of my dad."

And now I feel like shit. "I didn't mean to—"

A small smile tugs at his lips. "I'm teasing you. Like Caleb said, the King Cobra used to kick ass back in the day. This is my tribute to him."

"And the bones?"

Jax's fingers intertwine with mine. "Well, that's more of a badassery thing. You wouldn't get it."

"You're the last person who needs tattoos to prove how badass you are."

He tilts his head at me. "Was that a compliment?"

I roll my eyes while grinning. "Don't get used to them."

"Jax, stop hitting on my date. Let's go!" Caleb waves at us from the hallway.

Jax looks like he wants to say something, but I tug on his hand. We follow Caleb to the back room where Jax's tattoo artist, Alan, sets up his supplies.

Caleb settles onto the main chair while Alan preps his skin. Jax and I sit next to each other in the cramped corner. My body becomes aware of his proximity, with his legs brushing against mine.

Desire tugs at my stomach when Jax laces his fingers together with mine again. His thumb rubs over the thin bones of my hand, evoking goosebumps across my skin.

"That's really what you want, mate?" Jax eyes the sketch of Caleb's tattoo.

"Yup."

Jax nods at Alan, fighting a smile. "Give the kid what he wants."

Caleb sits through the pain, making jokes as Alan inks the letters. The process is rather short. Our new friend shows off his tattoo located on the inside of his arm where I usually get blood taken out.

I trace around the red skin to avoid hurting him. "'No rain, no flowers.' Interesting choice for someone your age."

"It's my mom's favorite quote."

"And the location?" I tap a vein.

"I thought it would be nice to have something strong to look at during my next round of chemo." Caleb's response causes my vision to blur.

He shoots me a wobbly smile. "Don't cry over me, love. That's the way the cookie crumbles."

"Hey, don't steal my nickname for her." Jax wraps an arm around my shoulder, tugging me into his side.

Jax's simple possessiveness has my heart working overtime to keep up.

"I'm guessing that's all." Alan begins to pack up his supplies.

"Wait," I blurt out. "I want a tattoo."

"You want a tattoo? *You*?" Jax's head jerks back.

"Is it that hard to believe?"

"To be honest, yes," Caleb chimes in.

I scoff before turning toward Alan. "I want a small one."

Jax raises a brow at me. "You sure about this?"

"Yes."

Jax shrugs before taking a seat with Caleb across the room. I'm grateful he doesn't ask me any more questions because I'm afraid I'll lose my nerve.

I show Alan the design I want and where I want it. It may seem childish and stupid to anyone else, but to me it symbolizes everything I want to become while embracing the broken parts of myself.

Alan cocks a brow at me. He pulls out his iPad and sketches the design, making it identical to the photo I showed him.

"Perfect."

"And to double-check, you want it here?" He taps the side of my middle finger where a jagged scar remains from many years ago.

"That's right." I offer Alan my hand and he gets to work with the transfer paper.

He prepares the skin. The buzzing sound echoes off the walls. I flinch when the needle touches my skin, hissing at the unexpected pain.

Alan frowns. "Sorry. It's going to hurt."

"Caleb didn't even wince. How's that possible?" My eyes

bounce between all the men in the room.

"I get stabbed all the time with needles." Caleb shrugs.

Jax squeezes Caleb's shoulder in the sweetest gesture. The way Jax looks at Caleb has me forgetting the pain for a second. "That's what makes you the toughest guy I've met."

Caleb laughs as if Jax said the funniest thing ever. When Jax doesn't laugh in return, Caleb's eyebrows pinch together. "Oh, you're serious?" His voice echoes his confusion.

"Of course. Any person who has dealt with the shit you have and still wears a smile every day is a badass in my book." Jax lets go of Caleb's shoulder.

"Whoa. You're giving me all the feels." Caleb readjusts his glasses.

Jax shakes his head. "I'm serious. In some ways, I look up to you."

My heart threatens to explode from my chest. I didn't expect Caleb's visit to impact Jax as much as it has, but I'm grateful Jax connected with someone who battles his own struggles day after day. Caleb carries himself with strength and positivity, and it's something I think Jax can learn from with time.

"Well, uhm, thanks." Caleb's cheeks flush as he looks down at his new tattoo.

Jax drags his chair to the side of the bench, and grabs onto my unoccupied hand. "Finger tattoos hurt more than some other ones. Squeeze my hand whenever you're in pain. It'll be over sooner than you know it."

My mind focuses on his touch rather than the burning sensation. "Wow. How did you cover your entire body in these?"

"Pain is only temporary." Jax offers a tight smile.

Alan gets back to work. I clutch onto Jax's hand like a

lifeline, concentrating on his thumb rubbing against my skin soothingly. Caleb chats with Alan while I remain entranced by Jax.

I look into his eyes, catching him staring at me. Fighting the urge to turn away, I allow myself to give in to the moment. His eyes darken as they roam over my body, lingering on my chest before meeting mine again.

Go me for picking the green dress tonight. The look he sends my way makes the strapless bra all the more worth it.

"Fuck. You're really something else. Beautiful, inside and out, which is painfully cheesy to say." He brings my hand up to his face and presses his lips against the fragile bones. My body burns with want as I focus on my reaction toward him rather than the needle prodding my skin.

I scrunch my nose in mock disgust. "Who knew you lacked any flirting skills?"

"That's because he usually doesn't have to work for it since women fall into his lap. Give him a run for his money," Caleb says over the buzzing of the needle.

"Does the kid ever know when to shut up?" Jax mumbles under his breath.

"Nope. I started talking at a year old and never stopped. My mum threatened to buy me a muzzle."

Alan gives me the all-clear to move off the bench, ending my moment with Jax. "I haven't had a request from that movie before."

My vision becomes fuzzy as I assess the mocking jay pin covering the scar from the night of my parents' deaths. I attempt to hide my emotions, but Jax grabs my hand and assesses the dainty tattoo.

"Interesting choice for a first tattoo."

"Big Katniss Everdeen fan, I take it?" Caleb bumps his shoulder against mine.

"Hmm." Quite the opposite. But I can't ignore the connection I have to the story, seeing as it's one of the last memories I have of my dad.

Jax helps me up from the bench.

"Anything for you, mate?" Alan points the needle at Jax.

He shakes his head. "No. I'm good today."

Jax ignores my request to pay for the tattoo. He covers the costs of everything and leads us to the exit. We all stop, staring at the pouring rain, not finding our town car in sight.

"Shit. Let me check on the driver." Jax pulls out his cellphone and walks back inside, leaving us under the awning.

"Hey, Caleb, have you ever danced in the rain?"

He shakes his head. "Nope."

"Is it okay for you to be in the rain for a few minutes?"

"I like the way you think. Plus, I never say no to a lady." He beams.

I grab onto his hand and drag him into the storm. The rain beats against our skin as I play a random song on my phone. Caleb grabs my hand and spins me around.

Is it reckless for Caleb to expose himself like this? Yes.

Is it worthy of his own snow-globe moment? Absolutely.

CHAPTER TWENTY-EIGHT

Jax

I can't take my eyes off Elena, smiling despite her wet hair clinging to her face. She shouldn't be attractive to me at that moment since she resembles more of a drowned cat than a human. Caleb and Elena dance in the rain, laughing despite the thunder rattling the window next to me.

Her smile snatches away my oxygen. I want to steal her for myself while owning her lips, her smiles, and everything in between.

Elena laughs into the dark sky as Caleb twirls her in a circle. They ignore everything around them as they both dance terribly together in the middle of the storm.

Something in me snaps. I want more time with Elena. More stolen moments and intense kisses. More of her struggling to finish puzzles and me silently helping her.

Staying away from her is impossible, no matter how hard I try. Not only because of our undeniable chemistry. It's stupid to deny the pull I have toward her, this endless tug of war between my sanity and my desire. I want to be different—to change my life path for her.

Most of all, I want to be normal with her.

It's not about our attraction to one another, but rather something deeper. Something I can no longer turn a blind eye to.

I want Elena and I'm done pretending otherwise.

After an hour of tossing and turning in bed, I make my way toward the kitchen, wanting a glass of water.

The light sound of the piano playing steers me toward the living room. Mum rarely plays the piano nowadays, and I'd love to catch her tinkering away next to Dad like when I was a kid. Instead, I'm surprised to find Elena in the dimly lit living room.

Elena sits at the piano bench by herself with her back facing me. I recognize Yiruma's "River Flows in You," but the sound is off.

Elena swipes her sleeve across her face, sniffling over the music.

I take a hesitant step toward her. "I didn't know you played the piano."

She jolts. I close the gap between us, finding her phone resting on the music rack, playing the melody from YouTube.

"Why sit at a piano and not play?" I wave my hand for her to scoot over.

She offers me a weak smile. "I don't know how to."

I'm tempted to find out the reason for her tears, but I choose against it after she looks away to wipe her face with the sleeve of her jumper. "Why this song?"

"My mom loved it. She played but couldn't convince me to try because I wanted to focus on ballet instead of her afternoon lessons. I wish I had, though."

I don't miss her usage of past tense. Instead of pulling more information from her, I pause the video. I run my fingers across the keys before starting the song over again.

Her eyes expand. "You play the piano?"

I nod. "You're lucky I know this one. It's a classic."

Elena adjusts her body enough to get a view of me playing. I take a moment to gaze over her tear-stricken face. Her sadness makes me scowl. When a few tears fall down her cheeks, I turn back toward the keys, offering her privacy.

The melody wraps around us as I play the song for her again. When I get to the second chorus, I amp it up, adding more notes. My fingers dance across the keys as Elena watches me.

I only ever perform in front of Mum, but playing for Elena is invigorating. A moment I want to keep, unwilling to part ways with cheering her up. To erase the pain in her face even if it's only for a few minutes.

When the song ends, she moves to get up, but I grip her wrist. "Wait. One more."

She sits down again, looking stunned. A thrill shoots through me as I begin playing the first notes of a song that I think is perfect for her.

Her face brightens once she recognizes Ed Sheeran's "Photograph."

"I'm honestly not sure if I'm dreaming right now. Pinch me?"

I pause the song and tug on her hair instead. "Do I usually appear in your dreams?"

"Nope. Not dreaming." Her back shakes as she attempts to hide her laughter.

I focus on the keys, playing her a song reminding me of the hope she gives me. The crazy drive she stirs up in me to be better—to be more.

More for her. More for me.

The combination of us is deadly yet unstoppable. My self-restraint has hit its maximum, like a rubber band about to snap.

Elena places her hand over mine after I finish playing the song. "Thank you." A new tear trickles down her cheek.

I hate them. Before she has a chance to leave, I brush the droplets away with my other hand. "Why are you crying, and how do I get you to stop?"

Elena looks at me with misty eyes. "Hearing you play the song she loved, it stirs up a lot inside of me. The second one was an added bonus."

"Like what?" my voice rasps.

"Everything. Happiness, pain, appreciation. So much is happening in my head I can't make sense of it. But most of all, I miss her."

"I reckon you lost your mum?"

She sniffles. "Yes. When I was twelve."

"Shit. I'm sorry to hear that." The thought of going through life without my mum now makes me anxious. I can't imagine growing up without one, to begin with.

"I lost her and my dad on the same day." She pauses, staring down at the keys. "They were murdered." She exhales a shaky breath.

I grip her trembling hand, clutching onto her fingers like the lifeline she needs. "Fuck."

"I was there. When it happened."

Holy shit. I don't know what to say. Everything in me hurts at the thought of a child having to experience that type of trauma.

"It was the worst night of my life. I was reading in my closet, hiding in case my parents checked on me before bed. But then my parents were screaming, and the gunshots happened. And then there was silence."

"You don't have to say any more."

"No. I need to." She takes a deep breath. "The men tried to find me, but I was hidden behind clothes and boxes. Once I was sure they left, I went downstairs, and I found them." She pulls her hand away from mine and covers her face to hide her distress. The sob she lets out wrecks my heart, with me helpless as she falls apart. Nothing I will say can take away that kind of pain.

"That's why I don't sleep in the dark. I get nightmares. In some, the men find me and kill me after my parents die. In others, my parents are shot in front of my eyes, with me not being able to stop the men."

I stand and pull Elena up with me, holding her to my chest, needing to keep her close. "We'll eliminate those nightmares one at a time. Fuck it all and fuck anyone who tries to mess with you again."

Elena deserves someone in her corner, willing to protect her. The way she looks at me tempts me to be that for her. Except I'm no hero.

And that's what makes me devastating.

CHAPTER TWENTY-NINE

Elena

I press my hands against Jax's chest, wanting to process his words.

He tugs my hands into his and holds them to his chest. His heart races beneath my palms. "I'm sorry I've been an arse to you. Fuck, I'm sorry for treating you the way I have. All of it. The partying, the pushing your buttons, the mean things I've said. You deserve better than what I've given you."

"I don't want someone to care about me because of my life story." I attempt to pull away from him, but he holds on.

"It's not because of your story. It's because of who you are despite that story."

His words grip onto my heart and hold me in place. I don't know what to say or how to feel about the shift in his personality. Sharing my story wasn't meant to make him pity me. In all honesty, I have no idea what possessed me to share that dark part of myself with him in the first place.

But I did. I wanted him to see the real me. Not the put-together version of myself everyone sees, but who I am when everything insignificant and temporary is stripped away.

"Give me a chance to make it right." His calloused fingers brush across my cheek.

I can only nod in agreement.

He leans his head, brushing his lips across mine.

My lips tingle where his tentatively touch. A burst of energy spreads through my lower stomach, but I pull my head away to look into his eyes. "You want to risk everything? For real?"

"I'm risking nothing for everything. It's different."

Well, how can I reply to that?

Jax saves me, pressing his lips to mine. The warmth from my stomach spreads across my body as he traces the seam of my mouth with his tongue. The very tongue that takes ownership of me, consuming all my doubts about our connection.

One of his hands loops around my waist while the other grips the back of my head. Our breathing becomes erratic as our kissing grows desperate, with teeth grazing one another in our haste.

His hand dips to my butt before he tugs me flush against him. I moan into his mouth when his erection presses into my stomach. He nips at my lower lip before he pulls away. "I want you so bloody much, I don't know where to begin."

My fingers trail up his chest, eliciting the slightest rumble from his chest. "I have an idea," I whisper before I grip the back of his neck and tug him toward my lips. Our lips collide as I tear down the last mental barrier between us.

Desire grows within me as we kiss to the point of oxygen deprivation. Jax groans as he tears his lips away, darting his tongue across the swollen flesh. He clutches onto my hand

and grabs my phone from the piano stand before dragging me through the halls and up the stairs toward his bedroom.

I remain silent until he closes his bedroom door. "So, this is it."

He flashes me a wicked smile that liquifies my insides. "No. *This* has only just begun."

I back into the bed as he places my phone on the dresser. He slowly walks toward me, prowling like a predator, with his gaze burning me from the inside out. The dim lighting peeking through his window offers us some guidance.

He grips the hem of my sweater before tugging it off, revealing my cotton bra. Cue Justin Timberlake's "SexyBack."

Jax's eyes remain on my chest. I attempt to cross my arms, but he swats them out of the way. He unclips the bra and chucks it over his shoulder.

"Fuck that shyness. You're beautiful." His fingers grip the waistband of my leggings and drag them down slowly, making me shiver as his warm fingers trail across my skin.

I'm left in nothing but my underwear with little polka dots. Before I have a chance to comment, Jax lifts me and places my ass on the bed. He parts my legs and stands between them.

Jax kisses me lazily as his fingers skim the inside of my thighs. He cups the area begging for his attention.

I grip onto his shoulders as he pushes the cotton to the side. His finger traces my slit before pressing against my clit, my body jolting at his touch. A moan escapes me as he spreads my arousal. "You're a responsive little thing for me, aren't you?" His eyes brighten as he continues his slow torture on my bundle of nerves.

He inserts a finger into me as his lips find the hollow of my neck. "I wonder what noises you'll make when I fuck you with my tongue. Are you a moaner? Screamer? Or the silent type who has yet to experience an earth-shattering orgasm?"

"Earth-shattering?" I giggle into his chest.

My taunt isn't taken nicely. He pushes me down to the mattress, the heat from his body warming me everywhere. "That better be the last time you laugh when I'm finger-fucking you." His thumb applies more pressure on my clit as he steals my gasp with his lips.

His lips make a journey from my lips to my nipple. He tugs sharply. Pain radiates before pleasure takes hold, with Jax licking the area he grazed. His fingers pump into me in unison.

My back arches off the mattress as he sucks on the sensitive skin around my breast. He takes his time on a spot before moving on, his skill and attention bringing about another surge of pleasure.

Red marks bloom wherever his lips linger. I grow more impatient as Jax slowly pumps into me, not pushing me over the edge.

"Are you going to hold true to your promise or are you going to continue to torture us both?" My breathless words fill the silence.

"Torturing you is my favorite pastime." He smiles at me.

"Not funny."

"But I promise, in the bedroom, it'll only be the best kind of torture."

My heart soars at the notion, beating faster as Jax moves away from my chest. He leaves a path of kisses down my stomach. The sound of his knees hitting the hardwood floor excites me.

He pulls down my underwear before replacing his fingers with his tongue.

His fucking tongue. The very thing that makes my toes curl into the side of the bed. His mouth devours my most private place, leaving me breathless and needy with anticipation. A few desperate moans escape my mouth. It's an unfamiliar sound to my own ears.

Jax thrusts two fingers into me at the same time as he sucks on my clit. The galaxy bursts behind my eyelids. A blinding heat rushes down my spine before spreading throughout my lower stomach.

His tongue traces a line from my center to the inside of my thigh as I come down from my orgasm. My body trembles before his lips suck on the skin there, leaving behind hickeys where no one can see. Branding me for his eyes only. As if he needs to prove to no one but himself that he had me.

Jax takes everything from me. Every gasp, every moan, every damn nerve firing off at his torment. He rises from his spot on the floor while he licks his lips. It's erotic, with his eyes capturing mine.

I sit, grab the hem of his T-shirt, and drag it over his head. My fingers trace over the array of tattoos covering his chest, wishing I could see them better. His eyes shut as my fingers hover over a king of hearts card near his shoulder. Instead of a lively king, a skeleton takes its place next to a broken heart. Something inside of me cracks at my interpretation of his tattoo.

He's a lost man who gave himself a life sentence of solitary confinement. Someone with little hope for his future, despite how successful he has been so far in his life. Someone who needs to be shown what he would be missing out on if he continues down his destructive path.

I want to show Jax how I care about him. He may feel undeserving of affection and someone in his life, but I plan on making it my mission to prove him differently.

I pull him into my body and our lips crash together. My fingers find his hair, tugging at the soft strands. He pushes into me and I fall back, taking him with me without us losing the kiss.

I press into his erection with my hips, initiating him to roll over, giving me the power position. He lets out a huff as I pull away.

"Scoot toward the headboard and hold onto the frame." I point at the gap in the iron headboard.

"You're not supposed to be ordering me around."

I roll my eyes. "That's all I've done this season so far."

"Things are going to change." His eyes burn with excitement.

"I sure hope so." I smile at him timidly, hoping his words apply to all areas of his life.

He follows my lead, sitting up against the headboard and clutching onto the bed frame. The sight of his tattooed body at my mercy has me bursting with excitement.

His teeth tug on his lower lip as I crawl up to him. I clutch into the band of his joggers, and with him lifting his body, I pull them off. "Shit."

Jax laughs. "That better be a good shit."

I swallow back my concern at the size of him. "Yes." I run a hesitant finger down his length. His dick pulses as I trail a vein before I swipe at the bead of precum at his tip.

"Fuck." He drops his head back.

I smile before sinking my body into the mattress between

his spread legs. My tongue replaces my fingers, tracing lines down his shaft.

Jax's breathing grows heavier, encouraging me to continue. My lips wrap around the head of his cock. He lets out a groan as I switch between sucking and playing with my tongue. His body becomes rigid as I continue to tease him to the brink of pleasure, before returning to slow licks down his shaft.

"The longer you play, the longer I'll delay your orgasm when I'm balls-deep inside of your greedy cunt."

Liquid heat bursts in my lower belly. I squeeze my legs together to ease the ache but fail miserably. My lips wrap around his tip again before I'm ripped away and thrown on my back.

A whoosh of air escapes my lungs as I brush my hair out of my face. "Really?"

"That's it for tonight. If I'm going to come, it better be from your pussy fisting me." Jax gets off the bed and grabs a foil packet from his nightstand.

"A condom in your nightstand? What are you, a pre-teen hoping to score in his parents' house?"

"More like a lusty twenty-six-year-old who knew I'd land you in my bed." Jax makes quick work of the condom.

Who knew I'd have a thing for cocky men?

He grabs onto my thighs and drags me toward the edge of the mattress.

My spine tingles in anticipation. "What happened to doggy style being your favorite position?"

He rubs his tip across my slit, preparing me. "There's always next time."

Next time. Because he wants to do this again. Such a simple statement has my heart clenching in my chest.

He lifts both my legs and places them over his shoulders. In one swift motion, he enters me. A hiss escapes my mouth at the sudden intrusion. No warning. No sweet kisses. Nothing but pure dominance as his fingers clutch onto my hips, leaving behind indentations.

Damn, I like it. I like the way his eyes shut—an image of bliss and something else I can't translate. He opens his eyes, staying rooted in his spot as he looks deeply into mine as if he can read me.

A wave of emotion takes over. I lift myself up on my elbows to plant a soft kiss on his lips. "Are you okay?"

"Yes. I'm a bit overwhelmed."

I don't ask why, and he doesn't explain himself. Jax leans over to leave a trail of kisses from my jawline to my neck. He moves again. His pumps grow more erratic as I match his thrusts.

I love the feel of him. The fullness, the strength, the growing buzz inside of my body.

His fingers lift my ass off the bed as he adjusts his angle, hitting me in a way that steals my breath away one thrust at a time. The warmth spreading across my spine grows stronger as my orgasm takes over my mind and body.

My explosion encourages Jax, who becomes desperate as his fingers grip my ass cheeks to the point of pain. I clutch onto the comforter to hold my position as he continues to slam into me.

His cock brushes against my G-spot once more, eliciting another out-of-body experience for me.

"Fuck!" Jax's body shudders while his hips continue pumping into me. His pace slows as he collects himself. He removes my legs from his shoulders before his body collapses on top of mine, tucking his head into my neck.

"Elena...what the bloody hell am I going to do with you?" He leaves behind the softest kiss at my racing pulse point.

"I'm sure we can get creative."

He lets out a rough laugh—one that fills my heart with a warmth I want to trap there. One I want to bring out of him every day until he grows comfortable with happiness and optimism.

One I wouldn't mind being the reason for every single day.

CHAPTER THIRTY

Jax

Everything changed yesterday. I didn't expect to destroy any last boundaries between Elena and me. But with her sad eyes and traumatizing past, I couldn't help the desire to make things right between us. To be someone she can count on in a world that took almost everything from her, and to make amends for the shit I've done.

Sometime in the middle of the night, she escaped my room, leaving me to wake up in an empty bed smelling of her and us.

Uncertainty takes hold of me, making me anxious to find her. The thought of her holding back again and avoiding me doesn't sit well with me after what we shared.

And fuck did we share. Addicted doesn't begin to cover how I feel about her. If last night was any indication about how it can be between us, I want to punch the old me for holding back this long.

I walk to the center of the house where her guest suite is

located and knock on the door. "Elena, open up."

The door opens to a groggy Elena with her wavy hair resembling something out of an eighties' music video. I stare at her thighs, poorly hidden by her large T-shirt. Purplish bruises peek out, drawing a smile from me. I'd love to turn her around, lift the hem of her shirt, and see if her ass bears my fingerprint marks. I may have been a bit rough, but I couldn't hold back. After ignoring my attraction to her for months, it was hard to rein in my desire, and her body took the brunt of it.

She rubs at her eyes. "What's up? I'm napping."

"At 9 a.m.? Who are you and what have you done with the real Elena?"

"You kept me up most of the night. What do you expect?" She yawns, scrunching her face in a cute way.

"For you to actually stay until morning, for starters." My voice carries more bite than intended.

"I didn't want your parents to catch me in your room."

"They haven't visited my bedroom since I was a teen, remember? They use the intercom instead."

She squints. "Oh."

"Right. *Oh*. So, your room or mine?"

"What?" She crosses her arms, poorly concealing her hardening nipples. What a shame.

"Time is running out. Decide."

She opens the door wider, giving me room to enter.

"Good choice." I lift her up and throw her on the mattress. The squeal she lets out puts a smile on my face.

"What are you doing?" She laughs.

I crawl onto the bed, tucking us both under the covers. "Hush. You kept me up most of the night. I need my beauty sleep." I pull her body into mine, and she places her head on my chest.

"Jax…"

"Yes." I wrap her hair around my fist to hold her head in place. The smell of strawberries calms me as I ignore my growing erection at Elena's closeness.

"What happens now?"

"We try."

It's the only answer I can provide her with, but it's good enough for me.

She needs to ask herself if she can handle something with me. I'm not a selfless fucker. I take and take until there is nothing left to offer.

But with Elena, I'm willing to share. The good, the bad, and the hopeless.

"To what do I owe the pleasure of your phone call?" Connor answers his phone after two rings.

I lay on my bed, staring up at the vaulted ceiling. "Besides wanting to congratulate the man who successfully secured a one-hundred-million-dollar sponsorship yesterday? You've been busy this summer break."

Connor laughs. "While you've been busy doing nothing, I've been putting in the work."

"Hey, taking a break every now and then is worth it."

"I know. You sound better. More relaxed."

I cough. "Right. I wanted to share something with you."

"Go ahead." Some papers rustle in the background.

"So, you didn't outright say Elena couldn't be in a relationship with me, but I—"

"You're dating now?"

"Well, we're…exploring our options. But I wanted to tell you before a reporter takes a picture of us or something."

"You don't need my blessing. But I should warn you to—"

"Not break her heart?"

He scoffs. "No. I'm not that predictable. I was going to warn you to take care of yourself. You're in a vulnerable place, and I worry you'll struggle with a relationship after recently finding your footing."

"I can take care of myself."

"I'm sorry I don't entirely believe you. I don't want you to lose the one person who has been supportive of you throughout this whole process."

"I'm not going to lose her because I want to try things out with her."

"Anal isn't the way to a girl's heart no matter what they tell you."

I clench my teeth together to suppress my frustration. "I'm serious. I want to try to be better than I've been—for her and for myself. And not because of sex."

Connor pauses. "Serious relationships take work. You can't give up at a moment's notice when things get hard."

"Gee. You don't say. I get enough love advice from my mum, mate."

"If you're looking for my blessing—"

"I'm not. I want to make sure nothing bad will happen to her if we come out to the public."

He chuckles. "If you're asking for me to not fire Elena,

I won't. As long as you both act like professional adults with everything related to McCoy, I will turn a blind eye."

"And I'll keep work and play separate."

"Why do I have a feeling I'll regret this?" Connor sighs.

You and me both. But damn if the path to hell isn't paved from the greatest adventures.

CHAPTER THIRTY-ONE

Jax

"So, Jax. Tell me how you've been." Tom gives me his full attention despite us talking through a laptop.

Tom gave me a week off from our sessions before we scheduled weekly telehealth check-ins throughout the summer break. He offered to rent a temporary office here, but I refused after he mentioned his family back in the states wanted to see him. I may be a selfish wanker, but I'm not that greedy.

"Fine. How's your family?"

"Good. They're happy I could sneak a visit in. How about yours?" Tom's eyes reflect the kindness he constantly exudes.

"Better now that I've had a chance to visit. Seeing Mum happy makes my weeks better."

"You look happier too. Is it a relief to see how she's doing with your own eyes rather than to hear about it over the phone?"

"Yes." And it doesn't hurt to have Elena in my bed too.

"How are you handling all the changes? I know F1 means a lot to you, so I wonder how the break impacts your day-to-day life?"

"I haven't given it much thought. Besides Caleb coming to visit last week and wanting to learn everything related to McCoy, I've been okay. I've been pretty happy actually and not really stressed at all."

I'm not too sure if the change is because of the positivity radiating off Elena, my visit home, or my transition to a more reliable anxiety med.

Tom's eyebrows shoot up. "That's great. Shit, fantastic, honestly."

I run a hand through my hair. "Yeah. I'm actually taking Elena out today to visit London and see some touristy stuff. The last week was kind of busy for us and we haven't explored much."

"I take it things are working out better than you expected with her visiting your family?"

"Well, I could do without my mum becoming attached to her. But besides that, things have been…" I pause, wondering how much I should tell Tom.

He sits in silence, giving me the choice.

I beat back my fear of opening up and go for it. "Things have been great. We found a rhythm with each other." Both in and out of the bedroom, but Tom doesn't need to know those kinds of details.

"Does she know about your mother's condition?"

"Yeah."

"And does she know about your side of the story?"

"Unfortunately, yes. I might as well be honest, seeing as she can google information about it and find out anyway."

If Tom is surprised, he hides it well. "You've opened up to her. That's a big deal coming from you. You should be proud of how far you've come over the past several months."

"I'm sure she's a big reason for that."

"Have you given any thought about the testing?"

Yes. "No."

"Do you think not knowing could impact the development of anything serious with Elena?"

Yes. "No."

Tom nods his head. "Well, if you want to get tested, I'm here to guide you through that process."

And like it never came up in the first place, Tom continues asking other questions, including what I planned for Elena today.

I'm thankful for the transition. I have thought about genetic testing more times this week than I ever have in the past few years. With Mum struggling and Elena challenging my beliefs, I'm tempted to potentially blow my sanity to shit. The idea of learning about my future has the same allure as Elena— unavoidably destructive.

"No one should be this excited to see the Houses of Parliament." I nudge Elena's ribs with my elbow.

She shoots me a dazzling smile as she snaps a photo. "It's Big Ben."

"I can show you what else is big."

She covers her mouth to muffle her laugh. *"Ay Dios. Ayúdame y dame paciencia."*

"Weird. You confused me with God last night too."

Elena bends over, laughter bubbling out of her uncontrollably. "Stop." She smacks my hands away as I pinch her sides. "I can't handle this version of you."

"The nice kind? You want me to go back to being naughty?"

She stands straight and smiles at me. "Happiness looks good on you."

"You know what else looks good?"

Her eyes roll effortlessly.

"*You.* You look good." I kiss the top of her head.

Elena runs a hand down her light pink dress. A natural blush creeps into her cheeks, contrasting against her golden skin.

I place a kiss on each of her cheeks, eliciting a sigh from her.

"I thought you being mean was going to be the death of me, but I've changed my mind. You being caring and sweet is absolutely frightening."

"Oh, love. If only people's nightmares looked this good." I twirl on the heels of my boots.

Her laugh shoots straight through my heart, hitting me with the best feeling. One I know I'll grow addicted to, despite fearing if it's only temporary.

We spend the better part of the late afternoon visiting every touristy part of London. Elena invites me to a teatime, and I let her pay because gratitude seems important to her.

I realize I enjoy time away from the F1 circuit. The anxiety that usually eats away at me isn't making a presence over the summer break. I find the experience rather refreshing. For the first time, I'm hesitant about returning back to race. This unusual uncertainty makes me wonder if I'm enjoying myself enough with racing to sacrifice the good years my mum has left.

Elena thrusts her phone in my hand, prompting me to table my inner dilemma for another time.

She walks away, leaving me behind as she enters a telephone booth. "Could you take a picture of me? I want to send it to Elías."

Elena poses like an influencer. I snap a few pictures of her like that before I crack a joke. The photo I take of her laughing is my favorite, and like a wanker, I send it to myself before she has a chance to take her phone back.

"Any other wishes before we go back to my parents' house?"

"Can we go in that?" She points to the London Eye: the ultimate tourist attraction and an eyesore.

I think up a plan quicker than the blood in my brain can relocate itself to my dick. See, I may be acting like more of a gentleman, but I'm not *that* much of a gentleman.

"Sure. Let's wait for nighttime. It'll be better—I swear." I steer us toward a local pub. We sit in the corner, away from prying eyes, with my back facing the bar.

These moments make me hate being a celebrity. Today alone, twenty people have asked for my autograph. The attention stifles me at times, especially when I want to blend in like a normal arsehole taking his girl out in the city.

Shit. My girl? Damn.

Our waitress's eyes rake over me before they flare with recognition. She pretends otherwise as she asks for our drink orders. Thank fuck.

Elena's nose scrunches as her eyes scan the menu. "What do I get?"

The simple trust she offers me fills me with a sense of pride I'm unaccustomed to.

"Two pints of Guinness, please." I smile at the waitress. She takes off before returning with the drinks.

Elena gives me free rein to order our food too, so I ask for two orders of fish and chips. Her reaction to the first sip of her drink has me nearly spitting out my own.

"This is disgusting." She coughs before chugging from her water glass.

"You said the same thing about swallowing my cum the first time. Look how far you've come."

The look she sends my way has me dropping my head back and laughing.

"Can you go back to being less likeable?"

"You like me? You really, really like me?" I bat my lashes.

She throws a wadded-up napkin at me. "Nope. Not at all."

"Bet you liked me last night when I was between—"

"Two orders of fish and chips!" Our waitress blushes as she drops off the food.

"That's totally going to end up on Twitter. Thanks a lot." Elena pops a chip into her mouth.

"Would that bother you?"

"What?"

"If we somehow ended up on a social media website?"

She eats a few more chips, no doubt buying herself time to think. "I don't know, to be honest. The thought scares me because I'm a pretty private person."

"And I'm not." I say it with more venom than intended. It's not directed at her, but rather my situation. Fame is nothing it's cracked up to be. Unlike Liam and Noah, I wouldn't mind disappearing from it all.

"It's not entirely your fault, but you can't help the fame

attached to your name and job. I prefer to be behind the scenes."

"I don't like it either. The fame and constant disappointment following me if I cock up."

Elena frowns. "I'm sure you don't. And also, I'm afraid of what others in PR would think of me. They could assume I'm sleeping around to get ahead and land more clients."

"Fuck them. Who cares what random people have to say about us?"

She raises a brow. "Is there an us?"

Yeah, Jax, way to fucking go. Good luck navigating this one. "I know there shouldn't be."

Her eyes drop to her lap. "Right."

The way my chest aches at the sight of her pain is fucking unsettling.

I grip her hand, holding it hostage. "But I want more with you. To spend more time together and for us to get to know each other on a deeper level."

"We've spent months together already. Honestly, I could've lived without knowing you drink orange juice after brushing your teeth. That's basically the eighth deadly sin."

I smile while shaking my head. "I want to know everything about you."

"You really don't."

"I'll never be satisfied until I know every dark secret that goes on inside of your pretty little mind."

"I thought I was vacant like my dolls?"

"Please, love. The only vacant thing about our entire exchange was my words. And I regret them."

She rolls her eyes.

I squeeze her hand tighter. "But…I'm sorry. Seriously, I'm

sorry for every shitty thing I said. I'll make it up to you in time. With my words, with my actions, and most definitely with my tong—"

"Stop! Okay, you're forgiven." A blush creeps up from her neck to her cheeks.

I pop a chip into my mouth and smile.

After dinner and a couple of drinks, Elena and I make our way toward the lit-up London Eye. I skip past the line with Elena in tow. She raises a brow at me as the security guard lets us through without an issue, not even asking for any identification.

The attendant at the loading area looks at me with wide eyes. "Shit! Jax Kingston!"

Another worker smiles at me and asks for my autograph.

"Sure. Hand over whatever you want signed. I assume you have a Sharpie or something?"

The two guys nod and pass me their work hats. They ask me about this season, and they tell me how they're rooting for me to win the British Grand Prix in a couple of weeks.

The reminder fills me with dread. I don't want my break with Elena to be cut short. Things between us are starting to feel right. Banishing those thoughts, I whisper something to the worker, grab Elena's hand, and walk into the next capsule. A conveniently empty capsule as per my last-minute request to the fan.

She giggles to herself as she walks to the safety bars.

"What?" I walk up to her, pressing her body into metal.

"The guy tripped over his own feet to secure you a private ride."

"All the more fun for us."

She raises a brow at me before she leans on the glass. I press my front against her back as I run a hand up her thigh. Her wearing a dress is an added bonus, giving me access to what I've been craving all day.

"What are you doing?" she whispers even though no one else is in the capsule with us.

"What do you think?" I push her hair to the other side of her neck, allowing room for my kisses. I trace yesterday's hickey with my tongue before sucking on the sensitive skin again.

Elena moans, pushing her ass into my cock. "Stop. People can see."

"Who?"

Elena looks around at the other capsules in our eyeline. The guys who asked for my autograph set us up with an empty capsule behind us. The people who loaded before us are all watching the London skyline with little interest in what we're up to.

"There are people right there." Elena points to the occupied capsule.

I lift the hem of her dress so her bare ass presses against my jeans. "Who gives a shit? Sucks for them because I got the better view."

One of my hands snakes around her to hold her in place. I make quick work of removing her knickers and pocketing them in my jeans. "Turn around."

"But what about the camera?" She points to the corner of the pod.

"Remember my new favorite fan down there? I emphasized the need for privacy, cameras included."

"Do you always get what you want?"

I chuckle. "Basically. Now turn around."

She hesitantly turns toward me.

"Sit on the rail."

Her head snaps toward the people in the other pod. "Oh my God. I can't believe you."

"I won't ask you again. Sit on the rail like the good girl we both know you like to be."

She blushes as she sits on the cool metal. Her back faces our neighbors, and the long hem of her dress blocks them from seeing me sink to my knees in front of her.

Elena follows my silent command and places her legs over my shoulders, giving me full access to her. Her eyes shut when I part her folds and sink my tongue into her.

Fuck. I love the way she tastes as much as the way she reacts to my touch. The moan she releases makes my cock throb in my jeans. I fuck her with my tongue, teasing her to the brink of pleasure.

Her needy fingers grip my hair and tug me closer. I suck on her clit, pulling a soft sigh from her I wouldn't mind hearing every day.

Every day.

Damn.

Anxiety creeps up my spine before I have a chance to shut it down. I don't want to worry and feel guilty about the future. But it's hard to ignore how Elena makes me think about the what-ifs, and that alone is risky.

I take my confusion out on her body, fucking her relentlessly with my tongue before her orgasm rips through her. Her legs tremble against my shoulders as she attempts to gather herself.

But like me, I don't want her to pull herself together. I want her desperate for more. For her to silently understand my need to dominate her—to have some semblance of control over the spiral our lives are becoming together.

I stand. Elena moves to get off the railing, but I shake my head. "Stay." I unfasten my jeans and push them down enough to release my cock. I pump it a few times, loving how her eyes focus on me. All of me.

Elena turns her head to check on our neighbors. The group of tourists is enamored by Big Ben and all the London goodies.

"They give zero shits about what's happening here." I grab a condom from my wallet and sheath myself. Elena sighs when I rub the head of my cock against her opening.

"This is what you do to me." I nudge her legs apart, having her spread more for me. "You make me desperate for more."

We both groan when I enter her with one thrust. I rock back to slam into her again, slapping my palm against the glass next to her head.

"Oh, wow." Elena sighs as she grips my shoulders for leverage.

My tempo increases as our capsule continues its ascent to the top. By the time we are at the highest point, a trickle of sweat drips down my back. The connection I have with Elena continues to grow as I pump into her like a man who is a moment from losing control.

Elena holds my head between her hands and kisses me. I still inside of her, feeling the energy shifting around us. It's charging, growing into something unfathomable. Her kisses say everything words can't. She demands my attention as her teeth sink into my bottom lip.

I kiss her while I fuck her, moving faster and sloppier. Elena banishes my negative thoughts with her erotic kisses, shrouded in trust and salvation.

A craving builds within me to be everything Elena needs despite my growing anxiety.

To be everything she didn't know she wanted but couldn't live without.

And with that thought, we explode together in more ways than one.

CHAPTER THIRTY-TWO

Elena

The sounds of Jax and his dad's grunts fill the at-home boxing gym. Vera and I took up a spot on a bench that seems custom-made to offer her the best comfort.

"You know, something is different about you." Vera taps my sneaker with her cane.

"I'm testing out a new hairdo." I brush a hand across my braided halo crown.

She shakes her head. "I call bullshit. Mothers know best. You've got a glow to your skin I'm not used to seeing, and my son has been smiling a lot more than usual. That was the dead giveaway."

My cheeks flush. "Maybe it's something Jackie feeds us. I had a feeling there was something off about her brownies."

Vera lets out a cackle. "Whatever you're doing for Jax, thank you." Her words surprise me more than her arms wrapping around my body. "I've wanted nothing more than for him to find someone who makes him happy. To make him want more in life besides trophies and contracts. These last few weeks with you have been amazing for him."

"I don't know what to say."

She pulls away. "Don't worry about that. There's nothing a mother wants more in life than to see her children happy. You're that for him."

"We've only been getting along for a month—two months tops."

"The heart doesn't care about time. It cares about feelings." She taps her chest.

"What if it's wrong?"

"The question you should be asking yourself is what if it's right." She turns her body back toward the ring.

"Do you plan on staring at me all day or are you finally going to get in the ring?" Jax yells at me from across the room.

"I think that's my cue to go." I rise from the bench.

"Show him how it's done."

I throw a smile over my shoulder as I stride toward the sparring ring. Zack nods at me before he exits and strolls toward Vera.

"I want to test a theory." Jax parts the ropes for me to enter.

"Oh, do tell."

"How many seconds until you surrender?"

"Fifteen." I plaster on a fake nervous smile.

He offers me a cocky grin. "Five."

I shrug. "Game on."

"When you're slamming your hand against the floor begging for this to be over, remember not to deny me again."

"You make it sound like I denied your offer for sex rather than self-defense classes." Last week when he asked, I politely declined, telling him I didn't need them. I guess Jax still holds a grudge about it.

Zack yells from across the gym, counting down from three. The moment he shouts *go*, Jax makes a clever move I didn't see coming.

He swings his foot out, knocking me on my back. Zack laughs while Vera yells at me to get up and show him how girls run the world. My legs remain planted on either side of his thick frame, giving me a good vantage point.

Jax's body sits on top of mine as he pretends to choke me with a smile. He's sure to take a majority of his weight off me which works to my benefit. "You look pretty with my hands around your throat."

A rush of laughter escapes me. "You're sick."

"But you like me anyway." He plants a soft kiss on my cheek before sitting and applying a little more pressure to my neck.

He hesitates when I shoot him a smirk similar to his. I use his stance against him, with my legs wrapping around his waist as I press my right arm on the inside of his left elbow and my left arm on his right shoulder blade. I push my foot into his hip bone before turning my body. Both my legs move out from under his before pressing his head into the mat.

My legs grip his trapped arms between them before I grab his wrist and make the sound of a bone breaking. "You were saying?"

Vera hoots while Zack claps.

Jax mouth parts as he stares up at me. "That was hot as fuck."

I push his wrist a little more, not wanting to hurt him. He slaps his hand against the mat.

I stand before offering him my hand. "I denied your request because I already took self-defense classes. If you'd quit your moping after I said no, I would've told you."

He grabs onto my palm and lifts himself up, barely hiding his smile. "I like you more and more by the day. You might be my dream girl, Gonzalez."

The warmth radiating throughout my body at his words tells me how much I want that to be true.

I'm going to be Jax's date to the benefit gala raising money for foster children. The event is to support a foundation he donates lots of money to every year in honor of his father. That means walking a red carpet while clinging to Jax's arm, coming out officially as a couple.

To put it lightly, I'm freaking the fuck out.

I pace my makeshift bedroom, my heels clicking against the hardwood as I walk back and forth. A wave of nausea rolls through me as I think of my name being splashed across tabloids and social media accounts.

A knock on my door has my spine straightening. I take a few deep breaths before opening. Jax leans against the door frame, looking attractive in his tux. The shiny material glistens and grips to his form in the best ways.

"I thought we should talk before tonight." He enters my room without an invitation. Not that he needs one, seeing as he comes to visit me daily now.

"About?" I move toward the dresser, fumbling with my clutch.

"It's not too late to back out of this before it turns into something we can't control."

"It is too late for that. We definitely can't control this," I grumble to myself.

"It's not. I don't want you to regret having your name connected to mine. We can show up separately and no one would know the difference." He walks up behind me, heating my back. His sincere eyes looking at me through the mirror tug at my heart.

"Give me a good reason why I should go with you."

"Isn't that the million-dollar question?" He turns me to face him. "I can give you countless reasons why you shouldn't. That would be the easy part. But there's no turning back from showing you off to the world and claiming you as mine."

"You're not selling yourself here."

His fingers clutch onto my chin, forcing me to look at him. "I don't want to disappoint you. And fuck, I know I will. But I unapologetically want you tied to me. To show you off in this dress and prove to everyone that you're mine and no arsehole can have you."

"But?"

"But the good part of me—albeit a small part—wants to tell you to run in the other direction. That I'm not worth the risk. That my unknown future could tie you down."

"You're worth the risk," I say with confidence even though we are talking about two different risks. Him of his future, and me of my heart. It's only a matter of what will blow up first.

"Even with Connor potentially disapproving?" He raises a brow.

"He won't."

His brows scrunch together. "How do you know?"

"I talked to him the other day."

"Good. So did I." Jax flashes a telling smile.

I smack his shoulder. "Asshole. You were testing me!"

"I know how much you care about your job. I don't want to have you unhappy with me because of something going wrong with that."

"I love my job, but…"

"But?" Jax leans in closer, leaving behind a phantom kiss on my lips. I yearn for more.

"But having a job isn't my life goal."

"Then what is?"

I shrug, not interested in pushing him further than what he can handle. "That's for me to find out."

The goal I have in mind doesn't scare me like it should. And that in itself is proof of how possible it would be to fall for someone like Jax.

Let's hope he's willing to fall with me.

"Ready, love?" Jax scoots toward the door of the limo.

I cling to the seat, my nails digging into the leather. "Not really."

Expectations swamp me with self-conscious thoughts. Jax doesn't ever bring dates to these kinds of functions, let alone someone like me. Someone not connected to a rich family or a fancy company. One who has loan payments and drinks BOGO bottles of cheap wine. What was I thinking agreeing to this?

I steal a glance in Jax's direction, drinking in how he looks in his tux.

Oh, right. That's why.

A few cameras flash behind the glass, reporters anticipating our entry. My breath comes out faster as panic sets in.

"Hey. Take a few deep breaths." Jax tucks a piece of my hair behind my ear. He takes deep breaths in unison, making me feel less stupid about freaking out. "You'll answer one of their questions and they'll end up loving you. I can promise you that. You've got this way with people."

His compliment warms me in a way few words do. "I'm sorry. I don't usually freak out like this. Like ever."

A ghost of a smile crosses his lips. "It's a nice change of pace for me to be the calm one for once. I'm the one who tends to be a bit of a mess."

I laugh. "That's one way to look at it. I thought I'd be okay after we left the house."

His hand lingers, cupping my cheek. "If you want to get out of here, say the words. We can crash a pub and drink until we can't walk straight."

My breath hitches at his idea. I can't believe Jax is willing to ditch an event that clearly is important to him for me.

I raise my chin, hiding my distress. "No. We are doing this."

"That's the spirit, love."

Somehow that one word makes my insides all warm and mushy. Jax exits the limo and offers me his hand. I step out on wobbly legs, praying I don't trip in my high heels.

Cameras flash and I fight the urge to shield my eyes.

"Deep breath," Jax whispers in my ear.

"A part of my introvert self is dying. I can feel it."

Jax laughs, gaining even more attention. I clutch onto the

sleeve of Jax's tux like he's the last lifeboat on the *Titanic*.

Jax walks the carpet with a swagger I'm accustomed to seeing from him. He grips onto my hand, throwing me a smile from over his shoulder. My heart threatens to burst at his look of uncontained happiness.

A reporter calls Jax over. He stops, tugging me into his side.

The blonde speaks into her microphone. "Jax. It's a shame your father couldn't make it tonight."

His smile slips but he recovers. "He sends his regrets. But he is proud of how much the organization has grown since he first donated ten years ago."

She nods with enthusiasm. "Most definitely. And I must say, it's not too often we see you with a woman on your arm. Who is your date for tonight?"

Jax's eyes remain on me the entire time he addresses the reporter. "I'm lucky to have Elena Gonzalez accompanying me tonight."

The reporter's brows knit together. "Gonzalez? The same ones who dominate the Latin-American pharmacy market?"

I cover my smile with my free hand. Jax's eyes lighten up at my reaction. He turns toward the reporter, giving her his full attention. "No. Elena Gonzalez as in the fantastic public relations rep who keeps me and other F1 athletes in check. I'm lucky to have her working with me this year." He flashes a dazzling smile at the camera and gives my hand a squeeze.

I love that smile. I love it so freaking much, I don't process his words for a few seconds. Everything inside of me threatens to burst with happiness at his praise.

The reporter blinks, clearly disarmed by the enigma that is Jax Kingston.

You and me both, sister.

The reporter turns to me. "Well, it's nice to meet you Miss Gonzalez. You must have some special powers if you were able to control this one. I can imagine he's a tough one." Her voice hints at her admiration. "And who are you wearing tonight? I want to guess Valentino's new summer collection, but I'd hate to be wrong."

"Uhh…Zara's sale rack?" I shrug, regretting my statement instantly. My cheeks warm and I consider retracting my statement, but both the reporter and Jax laugh, easing my distress.

Jax leans into me. His lips kiss my temple before they brush over my ear. "I fancy you so fucking much, you have no idea."

I lose myself in his words, willing away the sense of imposter syndrome I have. Jax has a way of making me feel like I belong by his side. No reporter or question can take that away from me.

I raise my chin and look straight into the reporter's eyes, allowing my confidence to grow. While I might not own any Valentino or have a trust fund, I still belong here. I've worked my ass off year after year to assist the elite, and it's time I enjoy myself a bit.

The pawn doesn't become a queen through sheer luck. It takes grit, work, and confidence.

And I'm so damn ready to make my way across the board.

"Welcome to the *Oh shit, I'm famous* club." The bed sheets rustle as Jax rolls on top of me.

I shove my crazy bedhead out of my face. "What? There's a club for that?"

He laughs as he tugs his phone out from under the comforter and hands it over to me. I scan the article, ignoring the way Jax's lips find his favorite spot on my neck.

"Oh my God. My anonymity lasted less than twenty-four hours." The nervousness I expected to feel once the press connected me to Jax doesn't happen. Instead, I can't help the warmth that fills me at the article's mention of Jax and me together.

"They praise you in the article and mention your company's success with Elías, Liam, and me. See?" He taps the screen. "They didn't say anything bad. And thank fuck for that because I really don't want you to have to clean up a fight I have with a newspaper."

"Hmm." I chew on my lip.

"Say you'll never doubt me again and that I'm always right." He stares me down.

He tickles me when I remain silent for too long. I laugh to the point of tears, admitting he was right about the whole thing.

I pick up the dropped phone. "Did they really just say how JaxAttack is now tamed and out of commission? One: that nickname is awful. And two: we look pretty damn good in this photo." I zoom in, checking out how incredible we look together. I'm surprised to say I glow under the limelight despite all my hesitation in the limo.

Jax's stubble scrapes across my upper body as he continues his exploration downwards. "I can assure you that JaxAttack is tame with everyone but you."

My scoff becomes a moan as he lifts the hem of my shirt and flicks his tongue across my nipple. "Seriously. Don't talk about yourself in the third person. It's very Julius Caesar of you."

"Or very caveman of me. It fits, seeing as I want to keep you all to myself and fuck you every hour of every day, marking you so no fucker comes near what's mine."

My cheeks heat. "You're not for sweet words, are you?"

"Naughty words make the heart grow fonder."

I giggle. "That's so not how the saying goes."

He moves down my body, his lips finding my clit in no time. And with a few swipes of his tongue, I'm screaming naughty words up to the ceiling too.

"You can turn around now," Jax says with excitement.

"What are we doing here?" I look around at an empty rooftop bar.

"I'd rather show you." Jax tugs on my hand, leading us toward the edge of the balcony.

My jaw drops as I lean against the glass railing. "No way."

"Surprise," he whispers in my ear as he presses behind my back. His hot breath pulls the slightest shiver from me. One he notices based on the way he laughs into my ear before nipping at it.

Hundreds of hot-air balloons float through the sky, an array of colors matching a kaleidoscope.

"Wow. It's almost exactly like the puzzle."

"All you're missing is a good trip on ecstasy."

I lean my head against his chest and laugh. "It's a pretty ugly puzzle, right?"

"The ugliest. You need to get your eyes checked."

"Says the man who my eyes are attracted to in the first place."

"Okay, you're right. You need to get your eyes *and* head checked."

A giggle escapes me. A loud, *no holding back* laugh.

Jax's arms wrap around me. "I like it when you laugh like that. But more so, I like being the reason behind it."

"Your narcissism has no bounds."

He laughs, holding me to his chest. "I like my ego stroked."

"Among other things."

The shaking of his chest pulls a smile from me. "So, is this everything you dreamed of?"

I'm not sure which dream he refers to. The one of him finally opening up to me and giving us a chance or my dream of attending a hot-air balloon festival. To be safe, I go with the latter option.

"I told myself I would go to one of these when I was older."

"Why older? Why not now?" His fingers interlace with mine against the railing. A trail of heat snakes up my arm straight to my chest.

"I wanted to go when I felt like I had moved on from everything in my past. I wanted it to be this big moment of letting go."

"That's a lot of pressure to put on yourself."

"How so?"

"I don't think anyone ever truly moves on. You can heal, sure, but letting go insinuates you don't want to remember anymore. And the memories aren't the problem. The mistake people make in life is that they assume pain is bad. But really, pain means you feel something. It means you're alive. It's about using it as a weapon rather than a weakness. So, heal yourself, but don't let go of the memories. They're what make you so very you."

I sit with his words. "That was...well, wow." No other words come to me. All I know is that I want to soak up this new version of Jax until there's nothing left of him. When Jax was an asshole to me, I struggled between wanting him and disliking him. But this version of him is intoxicating.

Jax turns me around, pushing my back against the glass. He cups my face before planting a soft kiss on my lips. "I want your pain. I want the demons who linger in the darkest part of your brain. Share the scary thoughts with me and share the happy ones. I wouldn't trade them for anything. I'm done resisting what I should've taken a long time ago."

"And that is?"

"You. It's always been you. I was screwed ever since you walked into that McCoy conference room when Liam needed help. Even when I made it my mission to have you stay the fuck away from me. Especially when you were vulnerable with me. I want to be broken with you."

"That's not usually how it works."

He leans in, his lips brushing mine. "Fuck the usual. I don't want to be picture-perfect with you. I want to be a fucking mosaic, made up of broken pieces so damn colorful, you can't help finding them beautiful."

CHAPTER THIRTY-THREE

Elena

"**H**appy birthday, sweet child of mine!" Vera rises from the breakfast table to give Jax a hug.

Today is Jax's birthday? Obviously, he mentioned being a Gemini, but I didn't put two and two together. "It's your birthday?"

He grins. "Yeah. I don't usually make a big deal of it, though."

"I'll never understand why he prefers to spend them with his old parents. Every summer it's the same with him." Vera rolls her eyes.

Jax sits next to me. Jackie places Jax's cup of tea and breakfast in front of him.

He steals a piece of bacon off my plate. "Nothing I like more than spending the day with the most important people in my life."

"I'll take it, seeing as the only other option is hanging out with those party people you always get in trouble with," Vera says.

"What do you like to do?" I scan Jax's face, taking in his easygoing smile. Day by day he grows more relaxed.

"I have some traditions."

"Like?"

"Oh, it's much better if we show you," Vera chimes in.

I offer her a small smile. "Whatever the birthday boy wants…"

"The birthday boy gets." He flashes me a mischievous grin.

"This is tame compared to what I imagined. A movie marathon is the last thing I expected of you," I whisper to Jax as I eye his parents, cuddled together a few seats away. A large screen hangs in front of us to create a movie theater ambiance.

"And what did you expect? Me throwing some rager at my parents' house?" Jax grabs a fistful of popcorn from the bowl in my lap. The movie's opening credits disappear, and my heart hammers in my chest as *The Hunger Games* begins.

Nausea hits me out of nowhere. I clutch onto the bowl of popcorn with sweaty palms, desperately trying to keep calm.

The first scene plays, and it reminds me of my childhood—of my parents and everything I've lost. I place the popcorn in the seat next to me and rush to exit the home movie theater.

Hot tears trickle down my face as I walk through the hall. The tattoo on my finger burns, mocking me, calling me out on my bullshit of wanting to be brave. I curse the tears and wipe them away with the sleeve of my sweater.

"Elena, stop," Jax calls out.

I keep walking, ignoring him.

"Elena." His voice sounds closer.

I turn a corner, desperate for some distance while also craving his comfort. *Great, even my thoughts are a jumbled mess.*

Jax's hand wraps around my arm and turns me around. "What's wrong? I thought you would like *The Hunger Games.*" He grimaces.

I avoid his gaze. "No."

"Then why get a tattoo of it? I didn't mean to upset you, I swear. I thought you'd be happy."

It takes everything in me to ignore his stare. "I got the tattoo for my dad."

"Shit. I keep fucking up."

I shake my head trying to force the tears away. "No. It's not your fault. You couldn't know. The book—" I let out a ragged breath. "The book I was reading the night they were killed…"

"Was *The Hunger Games.* Fuck." He finishes for me. His hand wraps around the back of my neck, forcing me to look up at him. "We can choose something else. I don't give a shit what movie, as long as you're okay with it."

I stare at him. His sincerity mends the tattered remains of my heart. He chose something on his birthday thinking it would make me happy. That kind of selflessness allows for a new sense of warmth to replace the cold inside of me.

His presence gives me courage to do something stupid yet brave. To banish some of the last bad memories plaguing me.

"I think I want to watch it."

Jax's thumb presses against my thrumming pulse, awareness flooding my body. "Even if it scares you?"

"Especially because it scares me." I lift my chin.

"I'll be there for you. You have me."

I believe his every word. We walk back to the movie room hand in hand. Someone presses play, and the movie starts up again. Jax doesn't let go of my hand the entire time. He softly brushes over my new tattoo as I silently sob to myself at the part I remember reading on the worst night of my life. His actions tell me everything words can't.

I'm here for you. I'll fight the memories with you. We'll beat this together.

And I can't prevent falling a bit more for him that night.

"I can't believe I get to hang out in the pit on a race day. Holy fucking shit!" Caleb bounces up and down.

"Hey, language. There are kids visiting." I'm tempted to smack him with the side of my clipboard.

"But come on, this is the coolest thing ever. Look at Jax in his race gear. Hold up." Caleb pulls out his cellphone and snaps a photo of Jax.

Trust me, I don't think I can look anywhere *but* at Jax in his race gear.

I snap out of my daze. "Here, let the camera crew take a photo of you two."

"Of course, *mi princesa Mexicana.* Good idea." Caleb grins.

Jax laughs as he wraps an arm around Caleb's shoulder. The press snaps some photos of the two of them, with Caleb beaming at Jax.

Caleb's mother makes her way over. I assume if Caleb had hair, it would be similar to his mother's blonde color. They have the same light eyes and freckles covering their noses.

She gives me a hug. "Thank you for everything you've done for my son. It's all he could talk about this month. It kept his spirits up even after another round of chemo." Her smile wobbles once she lets me go.

"Of course. It was no trouble at all. You did such an amazing job raising him because he's one of a kind."

"In every sense of the phrase. I have two younger children, and neither of them has his kind of personality." She points out her two other kids, both small and blonde, mesmerized by the mechanics working on the race cars.

"I don't know how you do it. Three kids are a lot."

"You don't have any?"

"Oh, no. Not yet at least." I nearly choke at the thought.

"Just wait. I grew up as an only child, and I didn't want that for my kids. Three might seem like a lot, but I had to convince myself not to have a fourth if you can believe that." She laughs to herself.

"I'm sure three is sufficient."

"Most definitely. You'll see. One day, you'll realize what I'm talking about. These three couldn't be any more different, but they love each other. And they would do anything for one another, too." She smiles at her children.

A yearning I've never had before takes up a spot in my heart. One I shouldn't have but can't deny.

I don't want something temporary with someone. I want everything. The relationship. A family. The moments I want to hold on to for the rest of my life.

And most of all, I think I could want that all with Jax.

CHAPTER THIRTY-FOUR

Jax

I embed my earpiece into my ears, tuning out the rest of the world. Mechanics roll my car toward my second-place position on the grid. The engine rumbles behind me as it heats up, reminding me of the race day reality.

Grueling heat. Intense pressure. And worst of all, my very own devil on my shoulder in the form of performance anxiety.

"Oh my God. So fucking cool, mate. Elena got the engineer to let me speak to you on the radio! Do you think they can hear me on TV?" Caleb yells into the mic.

The mic picks up on Elena telling him to talk lower as if she can read my mind.

"Enjoy it, kid."

"Who are you calling a kid? I'm only like ten years younger than you."

"A decade goes a long way when you get to my age." I grip my steering wheel tighter with my gloved hands.

"Stop being such a depressing twat before your race."

I snicker. "Any last words before they kick you off the mic?"

"Kick ass, Kingston. Show those fuckers what it's like to be part of a DNA dynasty. Your dad may be a legend in the ring, but you're the king of the track."

I laugh at his comment. Little does he know my DNA sucks arse once my dad is taken out of the equation. But I promise myself to give Caleb a good show, wanting him to enjoy every last second of his experience with me.

The mechanics run the last checks before the start of the race.

"Gotta go, mate. See you at the winner's podium."

The crew pulls off my tire warmers and rushes off the track. One at a time, five lights flash above my helmet before shutting off.

I push against the throttle while hitting buttons on my steering wheel. My car propels forward, screeching as I hold my spot behind Noah, the race leader. Tension courses through my body as my heart works to pump blood faster. The sound of engines roaring adds to my rush, feeding the demon inside of me that craves adrenaline.

"Good job getting out of turn one unscathed. Can't say the same about a Sauvage driver. Mind turn two—that tends to be where you lost time during the qually round," Chris speaks into my radio.

I keep focused, rushing up to Noah's side on the straight, only to have him push me back into second. The blurring red car in my side mirrors tells me Santiago is too close to my rear bumper for comfort.

"Monitor Santiago behind me. I don't like how he

performed yesterday." I tune into what the other engineer has to say. Santiago tends to take riskier moves that usually pay off, but I'm not up for him cocking up my home race because of an accident.

A swarm of people cheer from one of the stands as I pass them in a blur. Pride makes me push harder to overtake Noah at the next turn. It feels good to represent my home race with a front-of-the-grid spot. The British GP has always been one of my favorite races, with fans from all over Britain coming to cheer me on.

At the next turn, I drive on the outside of Noah's car. Pushing against the brake a second later than suggested gives me the edge against him. I pull ahead of his car, securing the first-place spot.

I drive past one of the Grandstands with the roar of my engine. F1 fans cheering me on invigorates me, feeding my ego and the adrenaline rush coursing through me. The waves of blue, red, and white give me a sense of nostalgia and pride.

Lap after lap, Noah and I compete with one another. We both pit our cars, only to come back and compete for first place again. I take the lead once more and keep him in my side-view mirror.

My eyes slide from the mirror to the road a second too late. A piece of debris on the road catches on my tire.

"Shit!" I switch gears, hoping there wasn't any damage.

Another lap goes by before I get the disastrous news.

"You're losing tire pressure. We're going to need you to pit," Chris speaks up.

I clutch onto the steering wheel harder, anger replacing the rush of energy from earlier. Me pitting again means Noah gains his first-place spot back with little likelihood of giving it up to me again.

Fuck.

I pit, and the crew rushes to replace my tires. My car exits the pit lane and enters back into the race.

I race through the track, hitting speeds risky of collisions, attempting to regain my position in second place. There are only a handful of laps left for me to secure a home-race win. Santiago leaves a small opening on the inside of the next turn, which gives me the chance to drive past him.

Sweat trickles down my face into my protective mask as I secure the second place.

"Good work, Jax!" Chris's voice booms.

The car rattles as I press my foot against the accelerator. Noah keeps in the center of the road, not giving me room to surpass him.

"Fuck. He won't let up."

"You have two laps left to try," an engineer offers.

You don't fucking say. Passing the next Grandstand fills me with dread rather than excitement. Fear of failing my fans eats away at my confidence to pull off a first-place win.

No matter what I try, I'm met with resistance from Noah. Being stuck between him and Santiago isn't ideal, with the latter riding my rear bumper like he wants to fuck me from behind.

Noah seals my fate during the final lap. Both of us pass the checkered line seconds apart from one another, with him winning the Prix.

A flicker of disappointment runs through me at not achieving P1 at my home race. But unlike the past times, where anxiety reared its ugly head to bask in my frustration, I remain calm. While I'm bummed about not winning, I'm not bothered much by it. I have Elena and Caleb to hang out with when the festivities are all said and done, which excites me more than a trophy.

When Noah, Santiago, and I stand on the podium, I keep a smile on my face. I turn toward the side of the stage, finding Elena and Caleb cheering me on.

I may not have won first place, but the reward is just as great. My eyes find the woman who has kept me sane during this entire season. Elena looks at me with happiness instead of a burning dislike. And Caleb...well, Caleb looks like he might pass out from screaming and jumping around.

My top fan barrels into me once I step off the stage. He wraps his arms around me and squeezes with impressive strength for someone who appears weak. "Thank you for the best memories. I will never ever forget this for as long as I live."

I give him a hug back. "You're one of the coolest guys I've ever met. You inspire me."

Caleb lets go of me and looks up at me in disbelief. "How?"

My eyes slide from his to Elena's, catching her beautiful smile as she faces us. "To be stronger than the demons holding me back."

"Do you have to leave?" Mum wraps her arms around me, making it impossible to move.

"The season is halfway over. Then I'll be back home, spending time with you all over again."

"Okay, fine, if you must go. But what do you say about

leaving Elena behind? We will feed her well, we promise." Mum bobs her head while Dad hides his laugh with a cough.

"I need Elena to help me out. Maybe she'll come back and visit one day." I wink at Elena.

Mum walks up to Elena, using her cane for help. She wraps her arms around the latest object of my affection. The sight of Mum whispering to her hits me hard.

I don't know where the fuck the sudden emotion came from, but it chokes me. Mum never had a daughter or even a girlfriend of mine she could speak to. Elena hugging Mum back stirs a longing inside of me. Longing for Elena to stay longer. Longing for her to spend more time with my family like our movie nights or post-tea piano sessions.

Longing for her to become something more stable in my life.

And greatest of all, longing to face my biggest fear for the biggest reward.

CHAPTER THIRTY-FIVE

Elena

Austin, Texas is filled with American fans who are decked out in Bandini gear, cowboy hats, and boots straight out of a country western movie. They play honky-tonk music from the radio and fans tailgate in their pickup trucks. I soak it up, enjoying the Southern food and action of the race week.

Jax and I choose to eat dinner at a restaurant located close to the track. We decide on a table outside, enjoying the tourists walking past us.

I eye him curiously, taking in his rigid posture. "You can take off your sunglasses, you know. The sun is setting."

"I'm trying to blend in." He lowers his Ray-Bans before adjusting them again.

Shockingly, he's right. No one has come up to him so far during our dinner, which I call a win. "Is that how you plan on living the rest of your life? Hiding in plain sight?"

He tilts his head at me. "No. If I had it my way, I'd live close to my parents while still remaining secluded. When I retire, I plan on buying a big property and making it so cool, I rarely have to leave."

"Like what?"

"A bowling alley, a small movie theater, a pool with a water slide. Maybe even a lazy river."

I clap my hands together. "Don't forget about a mini-golf course."

"And a mini-golf course." He smiles.

"And a treehouse!"

Jax lets out a deep laugh. "Anything else?"

"You forgot about a fire pit with hanging string lights. You know, the circular ones they have in movies and on Pinterest?"

"This project is turning out to be rather costly if you have it your way."

I roll my eyes. "Hey, you said you wanted a property that you'll never want to leave. I'm helping make the dream come true. You should be thanking me."

"I'll have to leave eventually. But rarely is preferable."

"Like for groceries?" I grin.

"Precisely. Fuck the paparazzi always bothering me. I wouldn't want that for me or my—" His voice trails off.

I fill in the blank based on the way Jax's hands clench in front of him. The weight of his slipup, along with the way he shuts down, shows how much his unspoken words rattled him. It's been a month since we first got together, and he still struggles with the idea of a future. I try to not take offense, but my chest tightens at his apprehension. I'm not asking for forever, but a little faith would be nice.

I attempt to lighten the conversation again. "When do you plan on executing this grand plan of yours?"

"I'm not sure. I only got myself a girlfriend a month ago. She needs to give me time and whatnot, but who knows what will happen one day."

Girlfriend.

Girlfriend?!

Internally I'm screaming at myself while I'm playing it cool as a freaking igloo on the outside.

"So, your girlfriend, huh? Who is she?" I lean across the small cafe table and poke his chest.

"Someone I think about all the fucking time."

"Oh, tell me more." I bat my lashes.

"She's got a wicked mouth that's good for multiple things."

I snort. "Nothing like being multi-talented."

"You're telling me. Plus, no one can compare to this girl. She's hands down the most beautiful woman I've ever met." Jax laughs, hitting me with the best version of himself—carefree and all sorts of handsome.

"Hmm. You better be careful because looks only go so far."

"I wasn't talking about her exterior."

My heart melts as Jax's intense words leave me speechless.

"Did I mention she also makes my morning tea the way I like it? Or that I love how she somehow moved into my bedroom without asking. And how she sucks like—"

"Okay! *She* gets the point!"

A few other restaurant patrons look at us, frowning before I wave them off.

"You forgot one important part." I keep my face neutral, not wanting to smile.

"What?" He goes from smirking to scowling.

"You never asked this girl to be your girlfriend in the first place, Kingston. I can imagine it's a foreign concept, seeing as you rarely ask for anything." I sip my water as I stare off in the distance, pretending I'm not dying to hear what he says next.

"Weird. I thought us spending all this time together made that pretty clear." Jax closes the distance between us, leaning across the table. The noise around us lessens. His lips linger close to mine, hovering near the place I crave him the most.

"There's a difference between asking and assuming."

Jax's lips press against mine, and I let out a sigh. "Elena Gonzalez—" kiss "—will you do me the honor—" his tongue traces the seam of my lips, making me shiver despite the summer heat "—of being my girlfriend? Officially." His teeth scrape my bottom lip before his tongue darts out apologetically, soothing the sore area.

"Yes," I offer breathlessly.

He smacks one last peck before grinning down at me. "See? I knew you'd say yes. I don't like asking stupid questions that I already know the answer to."

And like that, Jax wins another part of my heart, with a few kisses and a smile.

CHAPTER THIRTY-SIX

Jax

L iam pulls me away from our group of friends, leaving Sophie and Maya to chat Elena's ear off while we wait for our Escape Room appointment.

"I wanted to tell you that it makes me happy to see you no longer flipping your shit every week. Love looks good on you." Liam passes his debit card to the employee.

Instead of coming back with a snappy comment, I place my hand on Liam's shoulder and give it a squeeze. "Thanks. I'm sorry I haven't been the easiest person to get along with this year."

The employee leaves us alone, mumbling something about checking if our room is ready.

"That's an understatement. But with you taking the human equivalent of animal tranquilizers, I can't blame you. Speaking of those pills, are you still using them?"

I cross my arms. "No."

Liam's eyebrow raises. "No like 'No, I'm not taking them,'

or 'No, I enjoy them from time to time like indulging in ice cream'?"

I chuckle. "No. I'm done with that shit. Permanently."

He lets out a loud breath. "Thank fuck."

"I still keep them around for any out-of-control panic attacks, but I switched medications." I ignore the urge to tell Liam about Tom and my therapy sessions.

"Will you promise me one thing?"

I lean against the counter, needing something to support me for whatever Liam is about to throw my way. "What?"

"I'm happy for you and your relationship. I really am. But I want you to reassure me that even if it doesn't turn out well, you won't fall back into the cycle of pills and partying."

I frown. "Not good how?"

"Relationships take work. They're not easy."

"And?"

"And for someone like you, I worry that you might return to self-destructive ways to cope with the negatives in your life."

"I promise you that I won't, even if my relationship doesn't work out or shit gets hard. I'm done with Xanax. And partying isn't as fun anyway without you and Noah."

Liam pulls me in for a hug, surprising me. "Good. Now let's go kick ass and show Noah we're the smarter ones. He's all high and mighty, thinking he will win."

The employee shows up a few minutes later to usher us into a hallway.

"Okay everyone, you're going to put on these blindfolds, and we will help guide you into two dark prison cells. Split up into two groups with who you want to be locked up with. An alarm will sound, and the lights will turn on, indicating you can take off your blindfolds. Do not take them off until then. Search for clues to help get you and your friends out of the cells. You'll have one hour. If you need a clue, use the walkie talkie your group leader has." He passes us each a black blindfold.

"Reminds me of good times, right, Sophie?" Liam winks as he waves the blindfold in front of her face.

"You're embarrassing me!" Sophie blushes and stomps to my side. "I'm joining Jax's team now."

"We're all on the same team." Noah scowls at the orange jumpsuit we were asked to put on.

Elena holds on to her blindfold with trembling hands.

"Are you okay?" I tap her hand.

She looks around before whispering, "I didn't know we were going to be in the dark."

"Do you want to not do it?"

"I can't quit. That's embarrassing." Her cheeks turn pink at the thought.

"No one will give a shit. We can go do something else and explore Austin."

Her eyes slide from her blindfold to mine, betraying her fear. "You'll be in my group?"

"Sure."

Elena sighs as she places the blindfold over her eyes. She clutches onto my hand, seeking comfort. Before Elena, I've never been that for someone. More importantly, I've never *wanted* to be that for someone. But with Elena, these moments fill me with a sensation I've never experienced before. It should frighten me, yet I feel invigorated to have her trust. Our relationship has been growing slowly and I can't say I'm sorry about it.

I give her hand a squeeze as the attendants guide us into our

324

prison cells. They ask us to place our hands on the cell bars, but I clutch onto Elena's hand instead. It shakes and her breathing becomes more audible as Liam, Maya, Santiago, and Elías are set up in the other cell.

"You've got this," I whisper in the general direction I assume is her ear.

The sound of the other cell door closing gives me hope this will all end soon for Elena. Once the alarm rings, I rip off my blindfold. Elena does the same.

"I did it." She offers me a timid smile.

"I knew you could. Now go put your skills to the test. You're our saving grace." I tug on the sleeve of her orange jumpsuit.

We spend the better part of ten minutes scouring the small cell for clues.

My jaw drops as Elena kneels on the cement floor. "You did not stick your hand in a toilet."

Elena glares at me, her arm half immersed in the empty bowl. "There might be something in there."

"I'm disgusted yet slightly impressed by your commitment."

"Care to stop flirting with your girlfriend and search for clues? You've barely helped." Noah paces the five-by-eight prison cell, searching for anything to help us escape. Sophie attempts to lift the mattress off the bed but fails. I move to help her, lifting it with one arm while she searches the seams.

This is who I've become, hanging out with my friends, doing normal shit without a pending panic attack holding me back. The group didn't have a problem accepting Elena and Elías. Albeit, they already hit it off during their Cards Against Humanity night that I ruined after one too many pills. But we all choose to ignore that night.

"Earth to Jax, can you pass me the spoon?" Elena snaps at me from her spot in front of the toilet.

"I don't want your dirty hands on our only clue."

She waves her clean hand in front of me before offering me a vulgar gesture.

"You've been hanging around Jax too much." Noah laughs.

"More like I've been hanging out in her too much."

"Jax! *Cállate*." Elena's eyes narrow at me.

"Yes, please, Elena is like a sister to me and I could do without hearing those details." Elías groans from the other cell.

Laughter fills the two cell blocks. I don't resent it. Instead, I welcome it, knowing I'm on a path to healing, one day at a time. With Elena by my side, I have hope I can recover from the mistakes I've made and the people I've pushed away.

I want to be different, but there's still one thing holding me back. And for the first time in a long time, I'm considering the impossible. The one thing Mum has begged me year after year to do.

And damn, it's scary as fuck.

"The party bus picked us up from the hospital and drove us around for an hour before dropping us off at the club you rented out. It was dope, looking like something straight out of the roaring twenties," Caleb yells into the phone.

"Did you ask Francesca to dance?" I place him on speaker while I tie the laces of my race sneakers. After our Make-A-Wish week, Caleb wanted to start a tradition of calling me before qually rounds, claiming he can be my good luck charm.

Have you ever tried denying an adolescent? They're tenacious and fucking stubborn. So, naturally to avoid his whining and nonstop messages, I obliged and accepted my new tradition.

"Of course. With the dance moves Elena taught me, I was the most popular guy there."

"You're probably the most popular guy, period."

Caleb laughs. "Thanks for the compliment but I'm for sure the nerdiest. The coolest guy award goes to Dylan. He's done with treatment, which is basically a badge of honor around these parts of the hospital."

"And how is your recent round going?"

"Burns like a bitch."

My heart dips at the thought of Caleb in pain. I've grown fond of the kid. He texts me memes every day after I gave him permission to contact me whenever he wanted.

"You're taking care of yourself?"

"Reckon so. As much as I can, at least. But I'm dying of boredom here. They blocked access to HBO so I'm fresh out of luck."

I let out a roar of laughter. "Why don't you go sneak off somewhere and make out with Francesca?"

"Do you know that you act like a weird older brother?"

Well, crap, I guess I kind of am acting that way with him. "You'd be lucky to have me as a sibling."

"No shit. That would get me so much street cred around here. My visit with you already won me over with Francesca and her friends. Getting my first tattoo with Jax Kingston dimmed Dylan's spotlight for a solid week."

Who knew hospitals have a social hierarchy like high school? I sure as shit didn't.

"How's my Mexican princess?" Caleb purrs.

"She's good."

"Just good? You must be a terrible boyfriend then."

I release a deep laugh. "Why's that?"

"Because she said the same thing about you when I called her last week."

"You talk to Elena?"

"Duh. Someone has to make sure you're kept in line."

"And she said things are good?" Curiosity makes me sound like a damn wanker.

"Good God, you'd think the two of you don't speak to one another. She said things are good and that she's happy. Is that good enough for you?"

That's better than good. For some reason, hearing it from Elena is one thing, but hearing it from Caleb is a whole other situation. A bigger thing because she wants to share part of our relationship with others.

Yup. I'm turning into a bloody wanker. "Yeah, that's good news, mate."

"Please don't break her heart. At least not until I turn eighteen and can be there to pick up all her broken pieces and put her back together."

I laugh at his joke, hoping I don't break her heart. Not because I don't want Caleb to have her. But rather, I want to keep her longer than originally anticipated.

Hate to break it to Caleb, but there's nothing longer than forever.

"I'm calling in on my favor." I lean against the doorway, breaking Elena's attention away from packing her luggage.

She pushes her glasses up the bridge of her nose. I'm a bloody wanker who loves how she gives off sexy disheveled vibes. I like Elena in dresses and heels, but I like her just as much in sweats and a hoodie she stole from my bag. My fingers twitch, craving to rip it off her.

"Aren't we past favors?" She tilts her head.

"I won mine fair and square, which means you're taking a week off."

Both her brows jump. "What? A week off from what exactly?"

"Work."

She shakes her head. "I can't do that—"

"Of course you can. I already asked Connor. And before you ask, I promised to be on my best behavior so you can enjoy yourself like Sophie and Maya do."

"You can't call in and use my sick days."

"I can and I did." I shrug. "You'll thank me for it. We can't have you working yourself into a shallow grave." The idea hit me after Elena confessed to me during lunch one day how she has never taken a sick day off of work. Not even when she was seventeen and had to work during her birthday. That's a bloody tragedy no one should experience in their lifetime.

I'm working to rectify her addiction to working. At least a little bit, so she can have enough free time to actually enjoy the life she works hard to provide for.

Look at me, all thoughtful and shit. Mum would be proud.

"I'm not seeing how this is a favor for you?" She scrunches her nose in the cutest way.

Cute. Adorable. Beautiful. Elena brings out the hopeless romantic in me that can't help wanting to make her smile again. I'm tempted to grip my balls to make sure they're still attached to my body, but I ignore the urge.

"I want you to enjoy a week by my side as my *girlfriend*. Galas, press conferences, race-day podiums. You know, actually enjoying the Mexican Grand Prix like a local, rather than an employee."

She lets out a laugh that settles me. "You know, people would be surprised to know what a soft teddy bear you are underneath all those tattoos, muscles, and grumbly words."

"It's a good thing you're good at your job, love, because I can't let that secret get out."

Elena hits me with a stunning smile that makes my skin grow hot. She walks away from the bed and tugs my shirt, pulling me toward her. "This is one secret I'll guard with my life."

"Oh, and why is that?" my voice rasps, my need for her becoming obvious.

"You're famous, which means the world knows more about you than both you and I would like. But the man you are when the cameras shut off is someone I want to keep all to myself. It's selfish...but I never claimed to be an angel." Her smile changes to something devious, the sparkle in her eyes hinting at more.

"Be as selfish as you want. I never asked for an angel."

Elena wraps a hand around the back of my neck and pulls my lips toward her. She shows me exactly why angels are overhyped and lust is the deadliest sin of them all.

CHAPTER THIRTY-SEVEN

Elena

My phone beeps, and I move to grab it off the nightstand of our hotel bedroom. Jax's hand swoops in and steals it away from my grasp before I have a second to check it.

He stands over me like a shadow, shaking his head. "Nope. I'm holding this baby hostage for a week."

"That's pointless. I have an iPad."

He smirks. "Confiscated as well, love."

My smile drops. "What? Why?"

"No working means *no working*. And since you're you, I couldn't chance the favor with you breaking the rules. It's only Monday, after all."

"Says the guy who asked me to be a rule-breaker," I mumble under my breath.

"Ahh. But that's different. I reap the benefits of those broken rules. Anyway, you can smile instead because we're going out."

"Out?" Last time I checked, Jax had a gala tonight. A look at the hotel's clock tells me he is running out of time to get ready.

He grabs my hand and lifts me out of the bed. "You're going to a gala."

"I've been to a gala."

"Yes. But have you ever gotten drunk at a gala on two-hundred-dollar bottles of champagne?" He smiles wickedly.

I see where this train wreck is going. I'd say no, except the smile on Jax's face tells me a favor is a favor, and unless I'm willing to owe more, I better suck it up.

"I'm going to regret this, aren't I?" I rasp.

"Only in the morning, love. For now, let's let loose and have some fun."

For people like Jax, fun is synonymous with trouble. But when you date the ultimate troublemaker, you're bound to join in eventually.

I decline the champagne after a glass because if I plan on getting drunk, that's the last hangover I want tomorrow. Jax asks the bartender for a bottle of top-shelf tequila. A whole bottle. One-hundred percent blue agave and one-hundred percent likely to get us all fucked up sooner rather than later. I clutch onto the tray carrying the *sangrita* chasers, lime wedges, salt, and eight *Caballito* glasses for us and all our friends.

Elías and I teach everyone the proper way to drink tequila. We weren't raised to knock back shot glass after shot glass. Our grandparents taught us to cherish the flavors and enjoy the glass sip by sip.

Jax helps me get settled into my seat at our table. Sophie and Maya eye the tequila bottle with a smile while Noah rubs his eyes.

"We love tequila." Sophie grabs the long glass.

"So does the toilet after you puke up your guts." Liam pinches his nose.

"That happened a while ago." Maya laughs.

"That was last month," Noah offers dryly with a smirk.

"Okay, remember to sip rather than shoot," Elías calls out to the group as he pours the glasses.

Everyone holds out their full glasses in the center.

"A toast…" Santiago calls out.

"To friends…" Elías starts.

"…who become family." Noah smiles in Maya and Santi's direction.

Elías and my eyes meet. He started this connection with everyone by hosting his game night, but Jax and everyone else solidified it. I can't help the feeling of vulnerability settling in my stomach at gaining new friends.

Awareness washes over me as I move my attention toward Jax. Damn him. He's working his way into every single crevice of my soul. He makes me want to be accepted by him and his friends, who act like a family I've always craved but couldn't have. No one wants to be friends with the person who keeps cancelling because of work and other obligations like helping *Abuela*. Well, everyone except Elías, who doesn't take "I'm busy" as an excuse.

Jax must sense my mood changing because he squeezes the area above my knee reassuringly.

"And to sad wankers like Liam who will never win another Championship in their lifetime." Jax breaks the silence by clinking his glass against the rest.

The group laughs, washing away my darker thoughts.

"And to assholes who made history by falling in love faster

than anticipated." Liam raises a brow in Jax's direction.

I pretend not to notice Jax shaking his head, fighting a smile. I pretend my heart didn't squeeze at the idea of Jax falling in love. I pretend so well, I end up drinking quicker than intended.

A few glasses of tequila later, I gain new friends, along with securing myself one killer hangover.

And it was most definitely worth the pounding headache.

"So, I have a question I've been dying to ask you…" Sophie rocks back on the heel of her sneaker.

"Oh God. *No.*" Maya groans at her best friend.

Reporters and camera crews move around the room, concentrating on setting up their gear before the press conference with Noah, Jax, Santiago, and Elías. The four of them sit side by side at a long table, waiting for the start of the event. No one pays us much attention.

So far, I'm loving my vacation. I've honestly enjoyed myself, including the girl time I've spent with Maya and Sophie getting massages and binging on ice cream while watching a new TV series. It's normal…yet everything I didn't realize I needed.

"So, Jax clearly is a bit of a wild card, if you catch my drift." Sophie starts anyway, ignoring Maya's protests. "I've been dying to know if he has a kink we don't know about. Everyone knows he gets off on public shit, but you know…does he have a daddy kink?" Sophie waggles his brows.

If I had a glass of water, now would be the time I choke while drinking from it. Jax definitely has a public sex kink. I don't think I'll ever look at pictures of the London Eye and not think about our time in there. But instead of confessing the dirty details, I remain composed like I train athletes to do. "I'm sorry? A daddy kink?"

Sophie looks around before whispering, "Yes. Daddy. Spanking. The works. Come on. Share with the girls."

I try my best not to break out into a fit of hysterical laughter. Reporters continue asking questions, focusing on the racers instead of our gossip session in the back of the room.

Deflect. Always deflect. "Is that something he's known for?"

Please say it's nothing he's known for. I don't think my heart could handle that news.

Sophie shrugs. "That's why I'm asking you. You're the girlfriend here."

Maya rubs her eyes and tries to step away from Sophie. "Ignore her. She's been convinced about this idea since last year."

"Is this some kind of friend initiation test?" I tilt my head.

Sophie and Maya laugh in unison. Okay, that was kind of freaky. I'm not ready for that cellular level of friendship from anyone.

Maya smiles at me. "You've been a friend for quite a while. Getting drunk on tequila the other day sealed the deal."

"But dishing some gossip wouldn't hurt to test your loyalty." Sophie winks.

I laugh with them. Hanging out with Sophie and Maya without worrying about the next item on my to-do list is refreshing.

Jax looks over at us and smiles wide. His eyes remain on me as Noah answers a question. I don't bother looking away, loving every second of his attention.

Jax finishes his conference and whisks me away from his

friends, claiming he needs to take a nap. We enter a waiting town car and head back toward the hotel.

I sit with Sophie's words for five whole minutes of silence before I let curiosity get the best of me. "So…I have a question."

He lifts one brow. "Okay?"

"Do you like to be called 'Daddy' while you're having sex?"

The roar of laughter that escapes him answers the ridiculous question. "I'm going to tell Liam to buy Sophie a gag so she can learn when to speak."

My jaw drops open. "So, it's true! A gag is totally something a Daddy would use."

Jax laughs to the point of coughing. "Fuck no. If you call me Daddy, I think my dick would attempt to break off my body and run away."

"Thank God," I whisper up to the ceiling of the car.

"But I do have other…quirks." He smirks.

Jax shows me just how much he enjoys public displays of affection. He kisses me the entire car ride to the radio our driver blasts at eardrum-shattering levels.

Jax leads me toward a new section of the McCoy paddock, clutching my hand in his as we walk through the narrow halls.

I concentrate on the way his race suit accentuates his butt, enjoying the view. "Don't you have to get ready for the race?"

"I'll go to the pit once I set you up." He smiles over his shoulder as the doors to a large room open.

"Where is everyone?" I scan the unoccupied space.

"This private place is meant for my family and friends." He

leads me toward an area with a couch and televisions showing the pre-race footage.

That explains the emptiness. Jax keeps his family life private from the public. He doesn't let them attend any races, including his home race. The thing about Jax is he loves too much, which makes him worry about what the media will say about his mum's disease. So instead, Jax chooses a life of isolation from the press. Seeing his race day spent by himself makes my heart ache for him in a new way. I now understand how, while his favor helped me relax, it also benefits him to have someone appreciate him.

He places a headset on my head and checks all the cords with a huge smile plastered on his face. "This lets you hear everything from my team radio." He explains different buttons and how to mute his voice, as if I could do that. This is like an all-access pass to Jax's head on a race day and I'm taking it.

I look up at him, smiling. "This is so cool! I'm so excited."

"Enjoy it. I've been dying to have you in here, but you always find some way to work during the races." He tugs me into him and places a kiss on my lips.

My heart threatens to become a puddle beneath my feet. From the top of my head to the tips of my toes, my body hums with approval.

"There's water in the fridge, and you can press the button next to the TV if you want food and champagne brought to you."

"Wow. Talk about five-star service. Be careful, Kingston. A girl can get used to this kind of treatment." I raise a brow.

Jax chuckles to himself. "You're simple to please." He walks over to a drawer and plucks a bag of Reese's Pieces from it.

If I wasn't questioning my affection toward him already,

LAUREN ASHER

now would be the time. The way he wants to make sure I'm provided for has my eyes stinging. "I don't think I've ever had someone take care of me like this. Not since *Abuela*—"

"I know. And I want to be the one to take care of you for a bit—if you don't mind, that is." He smiles sheepishly.

Dios, ayúdame. A sweet Jax is irresistible. But a shy Jax makes me want to spin in a circle and laugh up to the ceiling like a giddy cartoon character with hearts floating around me.

I walk to him, rise on my toes, and kiss him with every ounce of appreciation I feel. For the first time in a long time, I allow myself to rely on someone else.

CHAPTER THIRTY-EIGHT

Jax

Things between Elena and I have evolved over the months. From avoiding her to liking her, everything is shifting after our summer break together in London. Ever since we left my parents' house, we've fallen into a comfortable pattern together. A pattern so easygoing, I try to make her happy all the time.

After all the events she planned for me, I couldn't help wanting to return the favor. Under the guise of fixing my reputation, I put together an event to raise money for a charity of my choice. Except, unlike my other PR events, Elena has no clue about this one.

Yup. I planned it all on my own after a week of research, Maya's help, and begging my friends to participate.

"You owe me big time for this," Noah grumbles under his breath.

I look around the McCoy conference room I reserved for today's activity. Bright lights shine on Noah, Liam, and me as we sit in three chairs side by side. Maya spread out all kinds of makeup and supplies on a table in front of us. Her camera sits on a tripod in the center of the room, waiting on standby to film us.

"I bet Sophie will win." Liam shoots us a cocky grin.

"I wouldn't be too sure about that. I've seen Maya do this with Santi and he looked like the belle of the ball after she was done with him." Noah grins.

"Okay, Sophie's bringing her over now." Maya jumps from her chair.

Footsteps echo through the hall. The door creaks as Sophie and Elena enter the room.

Elena checks us all out before looking over at me in confusion. "What's going on?"

"Surprise!" Sophie claps. "We're doing a makeup challenge!"

"Makeup challenge?" Elena's mouth drops open and her eyes snap toward me. "You remembered?"

Oh, hell did I remember. After making fun of her on the plane months ago, here I am doing exactly what I accused my friends of participating in one day. A makeup challenge for charity.

That's me—romancer extraordinaire. Noah's sappiness and my dad's life lessons have rubbed off on me in more ways than one.

"Your boyfriend here wants to fundraise in a different kind of way using Maya's vlog." Liam shoots me a telling look.

Yeah, I get it. After all the shit I've given them about their girlfriends, I've fallen into the same trap. *Pot, meet kettle.*

"No way." Elena can't help smiling at me.

Okay, maybe this is worth all the shit my mates will give me based on her smile.

"Yes! And he chose such a wonderful charity. He wants to raise money for Alzheimer's Disease using the ad money on my video." Maya checks on her camera.

Elena's eyes soften. She walks up to me and stands between my legs. "You planned this for me?"

I tug her onto my lap. "Well, I did think my reputation could use a little help."

She raises a brow. "And you thought a makeup challenge was the right idea?"

"Someone once told me committed wankers did this kind of thing, so I thought I'd give it a try and see what the hype is all about." *Okay, that someone was me, but screw it.*

"Your mom was right." She grins.

"What do you mean?"

"She told me you were all marshmallow fluff, and I have to agree with her."

"Marshmallow fluff? Now I'm *very* curious to see how Jax acts with you when no one else is around," Liam calls out from the other side of Noah.

I flip him off. "Call me that again and I'll ram my boot so far up your arse, you won't walk straight for a week."

"Fuck marshmallow fluff. Jax is more of a Vegemite kind of guy," Noah chimes in.

"Okay, moving onto the more important part of our programming. Makeup time!" Sophie checks out the supplies on the table. She plucks a clamping tool that looks like a small torture device and waves it at Liam. "Your lashes are going to look so pretty, I'll be jealous."

"Jax, you owe me a weekend stay in Ibiza after this." Liam groans.

"Deal."

Elena kisses my cheek. "Thank you for this. It means a lot to me that you chose a charity to honor *Abuela*."

Everything inside of me warms at her approval. I'm glad I decided to do something to support people like her grandma while giving Elena her very own version of something she enjoys watching every day on her phone.

"Ladies, get to your battle stations," Maya calls out.

Elena hops off my lap. "That's my cue."

"Make me look the best, love. Please show these boys who's the sexiest of them all."

Something within *me* is changing, and it's not only because of a new medication. It's more than that. It's because of time with Elena, sessions with Tom, and a growing feeling of hope within me.

Hope my life will turn out differently.

Hope that I might not have Huntington's Disease.

Hope that I can end up happy with Elena, living without worry and sadness.

"Are you ready for the Prix this week?" Tom welcomes me into his office before taking a seat in the chair opposite of me.

"As ready as I can be." I get comfortable on the couch. "So, I've been thinking."

"Thinking is good."

I let out a loud laugh. "Well, actually I've been thinking about a few things. The first is that I didn't realize I like being in a relationship."

"And how's that going for you?"

I tap my fingers against the hole in my ripped jeans. "Good. Surprisingly good." So fucking good I hope I don't cock it up.

"You sound surprised by that."

"I am. I've never made the time for anything serious like this before."

"How long have you been dating Elena? Has it been two months already?"

"Close. And trust me, I'm equally shocked."

Tom laces his fingers together. "What about being in a relationship shocks you?"

"Do you need more besides the fact that I'm me, and Elena's Elena?"

He tilts his head. "Tell me what that means to you."

Oh, Tom. As we've grown more comfortable around one another, he becomes bolder with his questions. I'm not exactly opposed to it, but it does challenge me to be more open with him.

"Elena has her life pretty put together besides a few hiccups. Even her messed-up parts are tame compared to mine. She wants to achieve the highest standards, and has no problem facing her issues. And fuck me, she trusts me to help her through her fears."

"Does that scare you? Someone relying on you to be their rock?"

"It's fucking terrifying."

Tom chuckles. "I can attest to that."

"You're married. Talk about reaching the highest level of reliance." I point at his ring.

"Of course. But I wouldn't have it any other way."

I fight to roll my eyes. "Of course, you would say that. You're married and a therapist, so you're bound to preach about good vibes and Motivation Monday quotes."

Tom lets out a roar of laughter. "Tell me something. How does it feel to know Elena trusts you enough to count on you when she is scared?"

"Good. Really fucking good. Like I'll do whatever I can to banish all the shit holding her back, one way or another."

"Then there you have it. I feel similarly about having someone rely on me, too."

Shit. Talking to Tom gives me a new perspective.

"I have another problem."

"Let's hear it."

I swallow back my nerves. "I want to do the predictive test. I need to know if I have Huntington's or not so I can move on. I'm going to ask my mum to set up the genetic counseling and the actual test."

Tom's eyebrows raise—his only tell of surprise. He leans in closer. "That's very brave of you. What changed?"

Everything. Every fucking thing and there's nothing I can do about it. Not when Elena has infiltrated my carefully erected walls, blowing through them like they were made of paper.

"I've decided maybe I've been going about this situation the wrong way. With the new medication, some of the tremors have been better, and I'd hate to think I'll keep worrying over nothing."

"I'm glad to hear the medication change has been helping you. I can tell you've made some big improvements in your life so far, and I'm really proud of you."

I nod my head. "I don't want the worries to take over my life anymore. It's exhausting."

"You know I will always play devil's advocate. While I'm impressed by the progress you've made, I worry what would happen if you don't receive the news you want to hear. Especially if you find out bad news before the season is over. What then?"

My eyes slide from Tom's eyes to my hands. "Then I do what I do best."

"And what's that?"

"Self-destruct."

CHAPTER THIRTY-NINE

Jax

I dial my mum's number with shaky fingers.

She picks up on the first ring, not giving me much time to prepare myself. "Hey! What a surprise treat!"

I take a deep breath. "Hey, Mum. I have a question."

"I'll do my best to answer it."

"You've said the same thing since I was a kid."

"Because you were too curious for your own good, and you'd ask a million questions. Have sympathy for raising a child without a smartphone."

"Wow, I forgot how old you were."

She giggles. "What did you want to ask?"

"You told me you would have someone do the predictive testing if I wanted it?"

Her lack of a response adds to my nervousness.

I continue, wanting to fill the silence. "I can always wait for the end of the race season. But—" Maybe that's a better plan in case things don't go the way I want them and I'm slapped with the life sentence I didn't want.

"No! It's fine. I can have a genetic counselor meet with you through telehealth sessions before you can see them in person when you land in Italy. They can get the results expedited."

"Will you come to Italy? I don't know if I—"

"Of course," she says without hesitation. "Dad and I can fly there and meet with you before we all go to the counselor. That gives us about two weeks to make arrangements."

"Thank you."

"You don't need to thank me. It's my job as your mother. And I'm so proud of you for wanting to do this—for being brave enough to try."

"I've been watching someone else face their fears, and it's time I did the same."

CHAPTER FORTY

Elena

A scream rushes out of me as I jump from the bed. Darkness makes me shiver as a wave of nausea hits. I take in big gulps of air to ease my rolling stomach, wanting to fight the distress.

It's not real. It's only a nightmare. I'm in Italy, not Mexico. I'm an adult, not a kid anymore.

"Fuck, I'm sorry. I forgot to leave a light on." Jax's sleepy voice is barely audible over my heavy breathing. He hurries to find the nightlight switch.

Low light illuminates his groggy face. I attempt to rise out of bed but Jax tugs on my arm, making my head land on his chest.

"Don't go. You don't need to run from the nightmares anymore," he whispers into my hair.

A few tears trickle down my face and land on his bare chest.

"Do you want to talk about it?" He runs his hand through

my hair in a gesture I've come to love.

I shake my head. "It's embarrassing that I can't sleep in the dark. What kind of life is that?"

"One where you're still healing. Things like this take time."

"How would you know?"

"Because I'm learning to heal, too. It's not as easy as the movies make it look."

I let out a hoarse laugh. "You're secretly a dork."

"Why do you think Liam and I get along? He has his books and I have my movies." He wraps his arms around me, squeezing me into his chest. His spicy scent calms me.

Silence wraps around us. With Jax holding me, the darkness doesn't seem as intimidating. The mental prison I've created over the years loosens its hold as Jax runs his hand soothingly through my hair.

I take a deep breath, centering myself before I chicken out. "Jax?"

"Mm." His chest rumbles beneath me.

"I think I'm falling in love with you." The words leave my lips in the faintest whisper.

He keeps quiet for a solid minute. I second-guess myself, but he squeezes me tighter into him. "Elena?"

"Mm." I copy him.

"I already know I am."

CHAPTER FORTY-ONE

Jax

My mum held true to her promise, scheduling me a coveted spot with an Italian genetic counselor who could expedite my tests. Mum isn't one to throw money at people, but she'd do about anything to get me tested quickly before I chickened out. I had the blood withdrawal done on Monday. By Thursday, I had the results.

My parents and I sit together in the doctor's office. I scan the doctor's facial features, hoping for a smile or a sigh of relief. His face reveals nothing as he reads the document in front of him.

Mum and Dad each grab one of my trembling hands. I let them care for me, anxiety making it difficult for me to breathe right.

The doctor looks up at us, and he opens his mouth.

It takes one word to change someone's life.

Only one word to destroy all the hope I've built with Elena.

Eight letters. Three syllables. One meaning.

Positive.

CHAPTER FORTY-TWO

Elena

I look for Liam's number in my phone and give him a call. "Hey, is Jax with you?"

"No. I'm hanging with Sophie. I thought he was with you?"

I frown, double-checking the rooms of our suite again. Ever since London, we started sharing a room. His Docs are thrown in a corner beside my favorite pair of heels, and my makeup is lined up on the bathroom counter next to his razor. It's domestic and unlike anything I would've imagined.

My search comes up empty. "No. He hasn't answered my calls. Earlier, he texted me, saying he was spending time with you today."

"He'll turn up. Maybe he went out with some friends after practice rounds. Give Noah a call because maybe he's heard from him."

"Okay. Thanks." I hang up and have a similar conversation with Noah after I interrupted his early dinner with Maya and

Santi. I text everyone who hangs out with Jax, including Connor, but no one has any idea where he is.

I send another text asking Jax to call me. My gut tells me something isn't right, but I can't figure out why. Instead of worrying myself sick, I take a long bubble bath, hoping a bath bomb can calm me down.

My phone beeps while I'm in the tub. I rush out, dripping water everywhere as I grab a towel and wrap it around my body.

Jax's name lights up my screen and I answer. "Hey, where have you been? I've been worried and thought something happened." I let out a sigh of relief.

"My bad. My parents flew in as a surprise and I've been with them all day. I'm sorry I didn't call sooner." His voice sounds strained and out of the ordinary.

"Oh." Disappointment fills me at the lack of an invite.

"Yeah. They're staying at one of my dad's rentals, so I decided to spend the night with them. Will you be good by yourself tonight?"

Giddiness consumes me at his concern. "I've slept alone for twenty-five years. I think I can survive one night without my personal bodyguard. Plus, I always have my super cool, totally adult nightlights someone got me."

He doesn't laugh, replacing my happiness with worry. "I want to make sure you'll be okay. If I'm not there…" His voice trails off.

"It's one night so no big deal. You can make it up to me with extra cuddles tomorrow."

"Right."

A gnawing sensation inside of me tells me something is wrong, but Jax doesn't seem open to sharing right now. I don't want to be an annoying girlfriend or anything when we're new. "I guess I'll meet you at the track tomorrow if you're staying with your parents tonight."

"Sure." He lets out a resigned sigh.

"Is everything okay?"

He doesn't respond right away. "Not really. But it will be eventually."

"Do you want to talk about it?"

"No." Jax pauses. "I'm sorry." He doesn't say anything else.

"I'll let you go then so you can spend time with your parents." I hide the hurt in my voice at his distance.

"Take care." Jax hangs up, not giving me a chance to ask what he means.

After watching an episode on TV and turning on my nightlights, I shut my eyes, drifting into unconsciousness.

CHAPTER FORTY-THREE

Jax

Mum begs me not to leave the apartment. Even Dad asks me to stay and talk to them—to not ruin everything good that has happened to me this season. I don't listen to their pleas. I'm committed to fucking myself over in the worst way possible to save the best thing in my life.

Earlier, it took everything in me to lie to Elena and not confess the disastrous news I found out. To ask her to love me anyway, disease and all. But I can't do that to her.

After everything with her grandma, I refuse to be another burden in her life. I can't drag her down with me, hoping she'll be okay with never having children of her own. I definitely can't ask her to choose a relationship with someone who will wither away like a starved plant as he grows older. Bloody hell, I won't fuck like I used to, let alone worship her like she deserves.

Every painful decision I make tonight is for her.

The fake partying in Milan's most exclusive club.

The angry outburst I have, resulting in flipping a table and breaking bottles everywhere.

The bouncers escorting me out of the club and throwing me on my arse outside.

The paparazzi called by yours truly to be there at the same time, filming my demise. My fake drunkenness will be plastered across every social media platform by tomorrow morning.

I allow the rage to consume me as I mourn the life I wanted. I'm sober for every damn second of my downfall, wanting to remember the pain. I deserve it, knowing exactly how much it will hurt Elena when she wakes up to realize I betrayed her in the worst way.

She might not believe I love her after everything I did, but I feel it seeping out from every nerve in my body. Love isn't about the mushy feelings someone gives you. Screw the butterflies and shit. Fuck movies promoting unrealistic endings where the guy gets the girl, no matter the drama and obstacles in their way.

Love is dangerous and lethal. It's about sacrifices and a willingness to protect the people you care for at all costs. Elena may not see it that way, but I want to save her.

Elena's nightmares have nothing on the one I'll become one day. To save her, I fuck my relationship to hell, with me along with it.

CHAPTER FORTY-FOUR

Elena

I wake up to my phone falling off my nightstand after vibrating over and over again. Forcing myself out of bed, I bend over to grab it, hoping whoever is calling me at 5 a.m. has a good reason.

I have four missed calls from Connor, eight texts from Elías, and multiple Twitter notifications. Before I have a chance to check, my phone rings again, flashing with Connor's name. I answer without a second thought.

"Hey, Connor. I just woke up and saw you called me?"

"Where the fuck were you last night?" Connor's irritable voice hits me like a shot of caffeine.

My heart rate escalates. "Sleeping in my hotel room?"

"Why weren't you watching Jax?" he snaps.

"Jax? He's with his parents."

"Check your messages."

I put Connor on speaker so I can open the texts he sent me. Each message gets progressively worse, from Jax partying with a group of strangers to him flipping out and going on a rampage. I battle to get oxygen in my lungs.

"Why would he do this?" The words come out in a wheeze.

"I don't know, but you have to understand why I need to hire someone else to finish this job. I need someone who is objective about the situation. It was a mistake, thinking you could work together after you both started developing feelings. I'll own up to that."

"Wait. Please don't tell me you're firing me?"

"It's nothing personal. You know I think you're exceptional at your job, but Jax...you're too emotionally invested and I need someone to fix this ASAP."

"Let me be the one to fix this. *Please*." I hate begging. It goes against everything in me, but I'm willing to do it for Jax and *Abuela*.

Connor sighs. "I'm sorry but I don't think it's a good idea."

"But…" My strained voice makes me cringe.

"I truly am sorry to terminate your contract early. I absolutely hate to do this, especially since I've enjoyed having you around."

"I understand." Which makes this whole experience all the more painful. I failed. Plain and simple. I failed so horribly that I hope my career can recover from this. "Thank you for the opportunity. I'm the one who is sorry about what happened."

"Elena, please don't let this termination or Jax knock down your confidence. You truly are incredible at your job."

Who cares about being incredible when I won't have enough money to help *Abuela* long-term?

"Thank you," I manage to say.

"Please don't hesitate to ask me for any recommendation letter or referral. While Jax didn't work out, I'm sure there are others who will be a better fit for your kind of services."

"I appreciate that." The fallout of Jax's decision wreaks havoc on my emotions; my body shakes as I attempt to keep myself put together on the phone.

"I'll have the company send over your last payment. Feel free to reach out if you need anything."

A shaky breath slips past my lips as I consider the loss of my bonus. "Goodbye. Thank you for everything, Connor. I'm sorry I let you down."

"Take care, Elena. Bye."

The click of the phone adds to the emptiness in my chest. Everything spins around me. I lay back on the bed and close my eyes, willing the tears to go away. The darkness I'm all too familiar with begs to take over. I try to fight it back the best I can, but the betrayal makes the sadness wrap around my broken heart.

Jax ruined more than my trust in him. It took him one reckless decision to throw away my chance at providing *Abuela* with the best care. I press my face into a pillow to muffle my cries. The one person I let into my life more than anyone else ruined it in a matter of twenty-four hours.

I cry for my grandma and my now tainted work reputation. My tears of sadness become those of frustration as I blame myself for growing close to someone like Jax. He warned me nothing good could come from us getting together and he was right.

I thought I was Jax's salvation, but it turns out he was my damnation.

Nothing good could come from him. No matter what I do, I can't save someone intent on drowning themselves in alcohol, self-loathing, and self-pity. Especially not when he's desperate to push everyone away at the expense of his own depression and anxiety. And most importantly, I don't want to.

I deserve better than that. Fuck. I deserve better than *him*.

I spend the next hour packing my luggage to pass time. Jax needs to come back eventually to grab his racing bag before his practice rounds, and I need something to occupy my mind. If not, I'll end up crying, and I don't want to let the dark thoughts win today.

By 7 a.m., Jax strolls into the hotel room like he owns the goddamn place. His eyes slide from my luggage by the door to meet my gaze.

"Why?" I scowl at his red-rimmed eyes, hating how it reminds me of how much alcohol he drank last night.

His indifferent gaze makes my heart ache. "I wanted to have fun."

"Why lie? Why not ask me to go with you?" *Why smash my heart with an emotional sledgehammer?*

"Because I didn't want you there, obviously. I wasn't in the mood for your disappointment and judgment."

"Did something happen with your mom? Is that why they came to Italy? If so, it's okay if you made a mistake in the heat of the moment. I'd understand." It would be hard, but I'm willing to forgive him because I care.

"No. Not at all. I've got a lot of shit going on and I needed a night without you. I wanted a night of sleep without you waking up and screaming."

My mangled heart shreds a bit more at his words. "That's how you feel about us? A couple of months ago, you were all about wanting to be different. People don't change that fast.

What happened?" My voice croaks.

"I don't want to be around you anymore. Things are changing too fast, and I can't keep up with you and the demands of the season. I'm sorry for how things are ending between us."

"I don't want your apologies. I want to be with someone stronger than the fear holding them back." I somehow hold back the hurt in my voice, shielding my pain behind a wall of ice.

"That's rich coming from the person who is afraid of the fucking dark."

I suck in a sharp breath, failing to ease the burning in my chest and eyes. "This isn't you."

He turns his head away from me. "I get that I'm too fucked up to handle someone as equally fucked up. Everything happening right now in my life proves how I can't be that kind of hero for you. And I don't need to date someone plagued with nightmares and bad memories, or who ruins my birthday because they can't even handle watching a movie meant for teenagers. I might be a mess, but you're the same. You only hide it better. Go home and fix yourself. Heal. Find someone who is better for you than me." His voice cracks.

A single tear escapes my eye and trails down my cheek. "I didn't know you felt that way about me."

His chest shakes, revealing his pent-up irritation. "I realized yesterday after everything with my mum, I need someone who can support me, rather than me support them. Life's too short to spend it with the wrong kind of person."

The ragged breath I let out hurts so damn much. "The only person who is wrong here is you. Enjoy your life, Jax. I hope it's a long one so you can stew in your resentment and self-loathing. Thanks for fucking over my job, and thanks for smashing my heart into nothing to match yours." I grab onto my luggage and pass him without a backward glance. "And I might be afraid of the dark, but maybe it's for a good reason seeing as there's monsters like you out there." I walk away with my chin held high despite my heart cracking.

I spend the entire journey toward a cab chanting to myself that I can make it. How I can keep my emotions neutral until I'm out of eyesight. The moment I enter the car, a sob tears through my throat. I shut my phone off and give in to the sadness and betrayal, allowing myself this one moment of weakness.

I promise myself when I get home, I won't cry anymore. Not for my career. Not for my past. And most definitely not for people who don't appreciate the good in their life.

I'm done saving people at the expense of myself. I'm done holding on to a past of hurt, hoping it gets better without putting in the work. And most of all, I'm done with Jax Kingston, and nothing anyone can say or do will convince me otherwise.

CHAPTER FORTY-FIVE

Jax

"**I** hope you're fucking happy, you piece of shit." Elías shoves me.

Sweat runs down my face after an intense practice session. My parents thought it would be a good idea to skip the rest of the race weekend, but I couldn't do that to my team. Plus, missing would set off too many of Elena's alarms. I couldn't give a shit about winning the Championship anymore, not when I lost so much already. Even being a few points behind Noah is lackluster. How could I be happy about possibly winning a Championship in a couple of months when I have nothing to look forward to afterwards?

Somehow, Elías kept his anger at bay for a few hours while we finished interviews and practiced around the track. It was no secret he resented me for what I did to Elena this morning, but he kept it professional in front of reporters and the crew. My moment of peace comes to an end as he stares at me with his nostrils flaring and his eyes wild and out for my blood.

Elías pushes me again, causing mechanics to stare at us.

I snap. "Keep your hands to yourself before I show you how nice mine feel when they rearrange your face."

Elías snarls. "You're the worst teammate. The worst boyfriend. Just the absolute fucking worst."

"Do you plan on sharing some new information with me?" I pocket my hands to hide their trembling.

"I shouldn't have told her to try anything with you. You ruined everything. Now her grandma has to move to a new facility after getting used to her new home. All because you're an asshole who couldn't keep your cool for one year. One fucking year! Elena and I grew up with barely anything, and you're here ruining her job because you want to. I'm going to make it my personal mission to make your life miserable here. I promise you."

My body stiffens. "What do you mean her gran will have to move homes?"

Elías's fists tighten. "Your contract was based on a monthly pay. Now that the season is cut short for her, she can't afford that new place. And Elena doesn't accept shit from people without her working for it, so she'll never take my money if I offer to pay for her *abuela's* stay. Trust me, I've tried. Your little stunt not only made it hard for others to hire her but now she doesn't get the bonus she was relying on to pay off her bills. So, fuck you, Kingston. I hope getting drunk was worth ruining your reputation and hers." Elías flips me off and leaves the garage.

Shit. I didn't think through the issue about Elena's contract. How could I when I was battling my own news.

Fuck. Motherfucking shit. This is why I overanalyze decisions. Irrational ones like the one I did lead to shit like this. I ignore the anxiety creeping into my brain because I don't have the luxury of freaking out right now. Elena needs my help whether she wants it or not. It's the least I can do.

I hurry to Connor's office and barge in without knocking.

"It was only a matter of time before I saw you again. Come back for more berating? I'm surprised this morning's lecture wasn't painful enough for you."

Trust me, his lecture was the least painful thing of my entire week.

"I'm not here for me. I need to talk to you about Elena."

Connor shakes his head. "Why do you care? You're the one who didn't want her around."

I sit in the empty chair across from his desk. "I don't want her around but that doesn't mean I think she shouldn't be paid for all the harm I've caused. I'll cover the rest of Elena's contract, so don't withhold her pay because of my mistake. Consider it hazard pay."

"I should say no so you learn your lesson and live with the consequences of your actions."

My hope takes a skydive. "Punish me however you want. I don't give a shit as long as she gets the money she always planned on receiving." My voice hints at the desperation I feel.

Connor sits back in his chair and stares at me. "Tell me why you did it and I'll see if I feel up to your demand."

"No."

"You're not in the position to bargain. If you don't share, then it's not my problem what happens to her." He shrugs, dismissing me.

I weigh my decision carefully. A few deep breaths do nothing to ease the heaviness in my stomach. "I didn't plan on ruining her chance at a job and her paychecks."

"Yet you did." He taps his pen against the desk.

One deep breath. Two deep breaths. Three—oh fuck this shit.

"I took the genetic test."

Connor's face shifts from anger to compassion. "Fuck."

"I didn't get the results I was hoping." I look away from Connor's gaze, afraid to see his pity. Accepting others' sympathy feels like a way of accepting my disease, and I'm not ready for that.

"Shit, I'm sorry, Jax, even though my apology can never be enough for you. How can I help?"

I swallow, fighting the thoughts threatening to consume me. I've avoided talking to everyone about it, including my parents because denial seems safer than accepting the bleak outcome of my life.

The first thought I had yesterday was how I needed to push Elena away. Not because of my own selfish reasons, but because I couldn't be selfish enough. And let's face it—a lot of decisions in my life have been centered around myself. But ending things with Elena? That was 100% the most difficult thing I did to myself.

"I want things to be normal. I don't need anyone else knowing before the season ends. If I even decide to say anything."

"But is the pressure good for you? I don't want F1 to put your body through more stress."

"This is all I have going for me. I've survived my whole life behind the wheel so I think I can handle the rest of the season."

Connor nods his head. "I'll help Elena out. Don't worry about it."

"Don't tell her it's because of me, please."

"You're really letting her go?"

I look away. "She was never mine to keep. Life with me would be like living in a gilded cage—pretty to look at, but a cage nonetheless."

I've never experienced a pain quite like breaking Elena's heart. Learning about my diagnosis and ruining any chance of me having a future with the person I love all in twenty-four hours drained me. I fight everything in me to not call her and beg for a chance. To not fight for her and us because I can't imagine not having her around.

It takes a gross amount of strength to enter our bedroom after this morning's fight.

My bedroom.

I take a shower to give myself something to do. Something in the trash bin catches my eye when I'm about to exit the bathroom. I grab the bin and tip it upside down. Every nightlight I bought Elena falls into the sink. The dull pain in my chest becomes a full-blown wound as I find her little purple notes she must've taken out of my bottle of pills.

I struggle between wanting to smash my fist into the mirror and grabbing a mini bottle of alcohol from the fridge to drown my emotions. Fighting the urge, I vote against the two options, hoping I can control myself enough to get past this rough patch.

I pluck the notes from the sink. Instead of returning them to the bin, I put them in my carry-on bag. My hands shake as I throw each nightlight back in the bin because I have no use for them.

I lay in the dark, struggling to fall asleep for the first time without Elena. To avoid the temptation of calling her, I head to the bathroom to grab a drink of water. The bin filled with the lights taunts me once again. On a whim, I grab one and plug it into the outlet on Elena's side of the bed.

I stare at the F1 car and hope she can find it in her heart one day to love someone else. Causing her pain now rather than later seemed like the better option, but the reasoning behind my actions doesn't ease the pain in my chest.

I can't imagine her pushing me around in a wheelchair or giving up her choice of having her own child. Her life has been plagued with sacrifice after sacrifice, and I can't find it in me to be selfish enough to add to her misery.

I close my eyes, accepting the heartbreak, knowing I made the right choice for her.

Mum knocks on my door before coming into the hotel bedroom. "Your dad wanted me to ask if you were interested in grabbing dinner with us? We don't want you going to bed hungry before your qualifier tomorrow."

I don't bother getting up from the bed. After putting on a fake face during practice rounds, all I wanted to do was wallow in my feelings. "No thanks. I'm fine calling for a meal in a bit."

Mum moves to the other side of the bed and climbs onto it. She lies down and grabs my hand like I'm a little kid again. "Tell me how I can make this better. How can I fix it?"

"There's nothing to fix. It's done because I destroyed everything."

She squeezes my hand tighter. "You can always apologize. If you regret it, it's never too late to make things right with Elena. You're in a vulnerable place right now. She would understand more than anyone how things can spiral out of control."

"No, she won't. I made sure she wouldn't want to be with me ever again, let alone speak to me. I used every secret and vulnerable moment she's ever shared with me against her."

"Why?" Mum can't help the sadness in her voice.

"Because I'm not her knight in shining armor. I'm the grim fucking reaper, stealing away her goddamn future."

"I feel so guilty. It breaks my heart to hear you talk like this." She turns her head. A few tears stream down her face onto my pillow.

A cold sensation spreads through my body at my mum's distress. "Please don't cry. I'm sorry."

"I can't help it. You're my child, and I brought this upon you. It's my fault."

"It was a fifty-fifty chance. The odds were stacked against me from the start."

"But you were happy." She wipes away a few tears. "You were finally finding happiness. I should've discouraged you from taking the test. Instead I helped you, thinking it would be different. And now…"

"Now I saved Elena from a life of pain. Not knowing would've eaten away at me eventually. Better to know now than later, after marriage and…"

"Kids." Mum nods her head in understanding.

"I wouldn't have been able to deny Elena that experience. If we ever got serious like that."

"Shouldn't you let her decide that?"

"She would decide to stand by me."

"Then that's someone you want in your corner from the get-go." Mum offers me a wobbly smile.

"You don't get it. I can't carry that weight of her being unhappy with me. I would never have a child of my own, knowing I could pass on the gene. That and I wouldn't want my girlfriend, or maybe wife one day, to take care of me while I waste away."

She recoils, her body tensing. "Is that how you think your dad feels about me?"

"Shit. No. Dad loves you more than anything. But I'm not blind to the pain it causes him to see you upset and hurting."

Her lip trembles. "I beg you to reconsider your relationship with Elena. You don't want to be making a serious decision when you're emotional and lost. You received news that would turn anyone's world upside down, and that's not the time to make a life-changing decision."

"I ruined any chance of us getting back together either way. I had to do it. I honestly didn't expect the test to be positive." My voice chokes. "I thought I had a real chance because the tremors were better after switching medications and my anxiety was more controlled."

I did my job well, demolishing all of Elena's hope toward having any kind of life with me. I embraced her hurt like it was my own, with each pained word escaping her mouth hitting me like a dagger to the chest.

I had hope, for once. And like everything in my life, it was useless and temporary.

Mum squeezes my hand harder. "I know. I was hoping it wasn't. God, I prayed day and night after we booked the appointment."

One tear leaks out of my eye. I'm not used to crying, but

everything feels like it's crashing down around me. Every single damn thing. "Where do I go from here?"

"You'll rise above this and take advantage of all those years you have left. I can't answer what you want from life. Only you can."

"Everything I wanted or thought I wanted, seems impossible." I stare up at the ceiling.

"Only to you." Mum remains quiet, keeping me company amidst my misery.

Mum doesn't say anything else. She holds my hand while I teeter on the edge of breaking, not wanting to push me over the edge.

My sadness recedes, replaced by emptiness.

Black, numbing emptiness.

CHAPTER FORTY-SIX

Jax

I take a deep breath as I walk up the steps of my private jet.

"Hey jackass, are you planning on going inside or do you want to keep us waiting out here?" Liam calls out behind me.

Sophie laughs.

"Why did I invite you both again?" Clenching my fists, I enter the cabin. Memories flood my head as I check out the seat Elena always preferred. The emptiness in my chest shifts to longing as I assess the completed puzzle.

"Because you're a good friend and my jet needs a maintenance check," Liam calls out behind me as he walks inside.

"You should fly commercial."

Liam mockingly gasps. "You hate me that much?"

I flop into a chair across from Elena's old one.

Sophie eyes the puzzle, tracing her finger along the edge. "Wow. This is impressive. I didn't peg you as a puzzle person."

"He's not." Liam slides into the chair across from me.

"Oh." Sophie's eyes flare with recognition.

"The things we do for the ones we love." Liam pats the chair next to him for Sophie to sit.

"Why did you end things with Elena?" Sophie bites down on her bottom lip.

"I'm not talking about this with you both. It's not too late for you two to catch a flight." Guilt destroys my mental clarity as I think up the real reason I ended things with Elena. I hate the unsolicited image infiltrating my head of her upset at me, holding back her tears as she lifts her chin in defiance.

Most of all, I hate wondering if I will regret pushing Elena away for the rest of my life. It turns out inviting my friends on a flight is anything but helpful, instead making me frustrated while giving them an all-access pass to my hell.

Liam frowns. "Don't be a dick to us because you fucked up."

"Stop." Sophie pinches Liam's side.

"No. What's the use of pussy-footing around this?"

"Because you don't know other people's reasons for what they do."

Yeah, Liam, listen to your girlfriend. I fumble with my headphones, pretending to ignore their conversation.

"Based on how miserable he looks, I don't think he made the right decision. Someone has to be the voice of reason around here."

Oh, fuck off. "You don't know what the bloody hell you're talking about," I snap. "There's a difference between making the right decision and making the easy one. Don't cast judgments about shit you don't understand." Anger feels good. Anger feels so fucking good I want to hold on to the feeling rather than the anxiety pulling me under time and time again.

Liam's mouth drops open. "I'm sorry. I only want to help you."

"I don't want anyone's help, especially for shit you can't begin to comprehend, let alone help with."

Hurt flashes across Liam's face. "Listen, I can't understand you if you don't share what's going on in the first place. We're friends, and friends help one another."

"This isn't something you can undo with a smile and a big *take me back because I'm a total wanker without you* speech. Not all of us can be Liam freaking Zander, king of fucking up and still getting what he wants in the end." My skin becomes hot and irritated, and I rush to stand.

My eyes land on the puzzle. Every emotion rushes through me, making my chest ache as I assess the hot-air balloons. The memory of taking Elena to the festival plagues my thoughts. An image of her—radiant as she smiles at the sky above with the same reverence she saves for me. Of how she kissed me until both our lips were swollen, whispering sweet words into the sky.

The balloons remind me of that stupid, hopeful fool who agreed to a test because of love. Anger and sadness fuse together, replacing the memory with despair.

Before anyone has a chance to stop me, I swipe my arm across the table. Hundreds of puzzle pieces fly through the air, scattering across the black carpet like snowflakes.

Snow-fucking-flakes.

Another memory of Elena's snow globes assaults me like bullets from an automatic rifle. I clutch onto my shirt as if it can dull the pain echoing through my chest.

I stomp across the puzzle pieces as I walk toward the bedroom at the rear of the cabin, snapping some unintentionally with my boots. The door slamming behind me matches the throb in my chest before I'm met with silence.

Silence isn't for the faint of heart. That's where the demons come out and play.

Welcome back, motherfucker.

A soft knock wakes me up. I rise from the bed and open the door to find Sophie staring up at me.

"Hey, can we talk?"

"Do I have a choice?"

Liam calls out from the front of the cabin. "No, you bet you don't, you fucking asshole. And you better treat my girlfriend with respect or else I'll smash that cocky-ass grin off your face."

Sophie mouths *sorry*.

I pop my head out from the bedroom and meet Liam's gaze. "I'm sorry for being a dick earlier."

His eyes soften. "Yeah, yeah, whatever. Don't go getting all teary-eyed on me." He smiles back as he wipes under his eyes with his middle finger.

I let out a laugh as I open the door wider for Sophie to enter. "Come on in."

"And keep the door open, Sophie Marie Mitchell! You know the rule about other boys." Liam's voice echoes.

She bites down on her lip to hide her laugh. I ignore Liam's protest as I shut the door behind me.

"I'm sorry for freaking out earlier." I sit in a chair across from the bed.

"And I'm sorry you're hurting right now." Sophie copies me, sitting on the edge of the mattress.

"I still shouldn't react like that. I'm better than letting an angry outburst control me."

"We all have emotions. Honestly, I'm grateful you expressed yourself, anger and all, because I think you've spent too long hiding how you feel."

I tilt my head at her. "Why do you say that?"

"Because I've been around you for almost two years. Everyone knows what lingers behind the playboy facade is never pretty."

"And what made you come to this conclusion?"

"I compared how happy you seemed with Elena to how you are now without her."

I take a deep breath in an attempt to ease my growing worry about Sophie poking into my head. "And?"

"And it's obvious you love her enough to feel miserable in her absence."

"Can we not talk abou—"

Sophie stands and walks up to me. She bends down to wrap her arms around my body and tug me into her. "I don't know why you broke up with her, but you don't have to face your sadness or anxiety alone. Don't take the pills. Let us be there for you, and please don't push us away. Especially Liam. He cares a lot about you and only wants to support you if you let him."

"I don't know how to start explaining myself."

She pulls away and smiles. "That's the beauty of friendship. We'll stick around, with or without a full understanding of what's going on."

For the first time in a few days, I feel relief. I have friends who care enough about me to not let me fall back into a vicious cycle of pills and drinking to combat overwhelming feelings.

And with relief comes the tiniest flame of hope that I will get through this.

I've made it my personal mission to make sure my mistake doesn't cause Elena any more harm. After fixing her finances with Connor, I need to make connections for her. I start with the team I know best and plan to work my way from there.

Liam set me up to meet with James Mitchell, Bandini's team principal, and the man who basically runs the show there. He may have graying hair and a few wrinkles, but the man is an absolute beast. I reckon he can out bench press me any day of the week.

James looks at me with stern green eyes before they drop to the paper in front of him. He crosses his legs and leans back in his office chair, hitting me with a scowl. "Why her?"

"Noah told me he doesn't like the Bandini PR reps. I thought I might as well solve your problem while fixing mine."

Okay, more like Noah gave in after I explained Elena's situation because of my mistake, but James doesn't need to know that.

He raises a dark brow. "Let me get this straight: you fucked up and got her fired, yet you want another company to hire her. I wonder why that is."

On the outside, I'm the usual Jax, cold and uncaring. But on the inside, I cringe at how far my mess up went that even James knows about it. "She's a hard worker and knows her shit. My actions don't reflect her work ethic. Quite the opposite seeing as she lasted almost a whole season around me."

"Yet you're the one with a high-paying job while she's out of one. Funny how the world works."

"It's not funny. If you don't want to hire her, fine. I'll take her references to Sauvage."

"I didn't say that. But tell me, why do you care if I hire her?" He remains stoic except for the smallest twitch in his lips.

"Do I have to spell it out for you?"

"Please and say it slowly to make sure I hear it all. I'm getting old."

I'm tempted to flip him off but refrain because Elena being hired is more important than my twitchy middle finger. "Liam told me about you."

"Anything he says is probably a watered-down version of the truth. You best remember that." James hits me with a full-blown grin this time.

I tap my knee with my shaky hand. "I want her to be taken care of. She doesn't deserve to lose everything she worked for because of me. I made mistakes—big ones—but it wasn't my intention for her to lose what she cares about most."

"From what I'm gathering during this conversation, I don't know if that's what she cares about most."

I frown. "How do you know?"

"If you being here is any inclination of how much you care about her, I have a feeling she feels similarly. Not that I'm out here offering free advice, but if I were you, I'd consider fixing things. I can take a look at her resume and consider her for a job, but it doesn't change the damage you've caused."

"Consider?"

"Don't push your luck. Tell her that you love her. Grand gestures like this are sweet and all, but—"

"She can't know," I blurt out.

James tilts his head at me. "Now that's interesting. Why?"

"I don't want her to know I recommended her for the job—if you decide to hire her, that is." And I fucking hope he does.

"I'm going to cut it to you straight, similar to how I did with Liam."

"Fuck," I whisper under my breath.

"Ah, you're familiar with my unsolicited advice. Well, allow me to be your surrogate parent for ten minutes, seeing as you're my daughter's friend and all. Consider this situation carefully. People are lucky to find someone they love—I mean truly love—once in their life." He taps Elena's resume for emphasis. "If Elena is that person for you, put your shit aside and fix it. Shelve the pride, pull out your best apology, and win her back. Mistakes can be forgotten but wasted time can never be earned back."

His statement hits me hard, and not because of his original intention.

Elena can't waste her time on someone like me.

Someone who is meant to live a life shrouded in hard moments.

Someone who is never going to have their own kids, let alone be alive for grandkids.

Someone who will never be worthy of her, no matter how much I wish it weren't the case.

And the last statement is the truest one of all.

CHAPTER FORTY-SEVEN

Elena

The moment I saw my bank account, I called Connor. "You made a mistake." I skip the pleasantries and cut to the point.

"I can assure you I didn't."

I pace the small hallway of my flat. "You told me last week I was only being paid for the months I completed. This is definitely not the price we agreed upon." I check the bank statement one more time to make sure I'm seeing things right. "Hell, this isn't even the bonus price we signed about."

He sighs. "I shouldn't have said something like that when I was angry. You worked hard to help Jax and I shouldn't hold his mistake against you. As for the bonus, consider it hazard pay."

"Hazard pay?"

"You know, for Jax being an arsehole and messing with your reputation. For keeping to your NDA and not sharing anything Jax might have said or done during your time together."

"I can't accept this kind of money for that." Even I have values and accepting two-hundred thousand euros for a failed job feels like I'm taking advantage of the situation.

Does Jax breaking my heart hurt? Yes.

Does it deserve a price tag of an extra year's worth of pay? Definitely not.

"I don't know what to say." I sigh.

"Say you'll accept it and move on. I've got a meeting to run to and I don't have time to chat and gossip about boys together."

I let out a soft laugh. "Yet you're the first one to gossip."

"Fine. You caught me. Seriously, it was nice talking to you, but I need to go. Good luck with your grandmother and I wish you the best of luck out there."

Grandmother? I don't remember mentioning her to Connor. I say thank you and hang up, chalking up the situation to Elías's big mouth. I lean my head against the back of the couch and whisper my thanks to God.

There are good people out there, I only need to search for them in the right places.

"You look exhausted." Caleb brings the FaceTime camera closer to his face.

To put it nicely, I look like shit because my sleep has never been worse. I refuse to sleep with lights anymore, not after everything Jax said. The fear and bad memories have always been my weakness and maybe Jax is right. Not everything he said, but a small part. I need to face my fear to let go of the nightmares trapping me. But things like this take time, seeing as I've had nightmares six out of seven nights.

He taps on the screen, getting my attention. "Come on, turn

that frown upside down."

"How about now?" I offer him a tight smile.

"Hideous and fake. Cut the crap, Elena. It's been a week already and you've barely left your apartment."

"I barely left my apartment *before* I had a job traveling around the world."

"Har, har. Hilarious. Don't make me fly out there and kick your arse."

My eyes narrow. "I'd like to see you try. Let me see those arms again."

"Put away the puzzle, get some clothes on that don't look like they belong in a Goodwill fashion show, and go outside after I hang up."

"Wow, thank you. With your charm, you should call me more often. It's doing wonders for my self-esteem."

"Oh, please. You had Jax Kingston lusting after you, so I can't say you're hard on the eyes." Caleb laughs until he coughs.

"Are you okay?"

He waves me off. "I'm fine. You're the one I'm worried about. I wasn't sure if you were in the same bad mood as Jax, and from the looks of it, you're almost as bad as he is."

My heart dips at the mention of Jax. "Caleb, as much as I want to talk to you, I don't want to talk about Jax."

"You don't even want to hear how he's been?"

"No."

"Or how miserable he is without you? He looks like a mess during his interviews. Guy's got the darkest under-eye circles even Sephora can't fix."

Now that's interesting. My eyebrow raises, but my lips remain in a neutral line. "Not even that."

"Okay, well too bad, I'm going to tell you anyway. He looks like week-old trash without you. I've never seen a man look as down and depressed about dumping someone. Isn't that weird to you?"

I expected Jax to be better off without me. After everything he said, I thought he wanted to be done with me.

Of course, he does. No one says the stuff he did to someone they want to be with.

"I think you're reading into things too much." I pull at the loose strand of a throw blanket. "You're young and haven't been in a relationship. Words he said can't be taken back with an apology."

"I may be young, but I've been through shit. And I'm not stupid or blind. I don't know what he said to you, but by the looks of him, it's eating him up inside."

"Great, he's human after all," I mumble under my breath.

"Look, something about this isn't right. He obviously isn't happy without you. He got seventh place last race. Seventh! Racers like him don't go from podium finishes to mid-tier. Not when he's a couple of races away from beating Noah for the title! Hello, he hasn't won a Championship in years."

"That's a shame." My flat voice doesn't match the concern worming its way into my brain. I shouldn't care about Jax's performance risking his chance at the World Championship, but I find it hard to not empathize.

Here I am, experiencing the same empathy that got me into this mess to begin with.

"Oh, shut up." Caleb sighs. "Maybe he's sick."

I roll my eyes. "Sick from what? Breaking his own heart?"

"Now she finally gets it," Caleb whispers up to the ceiling.

I let out a laugh. "And what, oh wise one, do you suggest I do?"

Caleb smiles. It would look rather sinister except his horn-rimmed glasses take away from the look. "You? Nothing. Him? Everything."

I remain quiet because I'm afraid to ask. I'm grateful for Caleb. He and Elías have kept me sane over the past week as I processed my breakup with Jax. Without them, I'd be knee-deep in takeout food and cheap wine to numb the ache.

Caleb looks off to the side. "Ugh, Elena, someone came in to check my vitals. I'll message you later?"

"Sure thing. Bye."

I hang up and go back to preparing dinner. The entire time, I struggle to get my mind off what Caleb said. The only question running through my head is why.

Why does Jax struggle after ending everything with us?

Why do I care what happens to him?

Why do I feel the urge to call and check on him despite how awful he treated me?

I erase the last question from my mind, not allowing myself to care for another second. I eat a sad dinner for one before crawling into my bed. Darkness floods the room as I shut off the last light and pull the covers up to my chin.

My heart races for a few minutes before settling down. I drift to sleep, hoping for no more nightmares.

I run from my bed to my kitchen after smelling my burnt dinner. Smoke billows from the oven as I open the door, cursing to myself for forgetting to set a timer.

"Great. Pasta it is." I put on my oven mitts and grab the pan out of the oven. A cough escapes me as I fan the air around me.

They say talking to oneself is a sign of insanity, but I happen to find it rather comforting lately. I'm always used to being busy. I've been a hard worker since university, and I find it hard to wind down like I have lately.

Hence the recent attempt to try new recipes.

My phone rings in the other room. I ignore it as I fill up a pot of water. The ringing starts back up again. Leaving behind the half-filled pot in the sink, I exit the kitchen and find my phone hidden somewhere within the covers of my bed. My phone stops ringing before I have a chance to answer.

It beeps with a new voicemail. I unlock it and press play, curious about the new number.

"Hi, Ms. Gonzalez. This is James Mitchell, the team principal of Bandini. I didn't have the chance to meet you while you were working with McCoy, but I've heard good things from Connor and Noah about your work. I'm in need of a PR agent who can help my team with press conferences and managing their image. We need someone who works remotely from Monaco but can be on standby for last-minute flights and conferences. If this is something you're interested in, please get back to me no later than this Friday to discuss the logistics. If not, I will take your silence as a rejection and move onto someone else. Have a great day."

Oh my God. No way.

First Connor's news a few days ago, and now this. I can't be this lucky.

Can I?

I mean I pray and all, but I didn't think God worked in this many mysterious ways. Clutching my phone to my chest, I flop onto my bed, thanking whomever is up there helping me.

Despite everything that happened to me in the past week, I smile and thank God for the little blessings.

Peace only lasts a few hours before I wake up alone and in the dark, crying out for my lost parents. Fear paralyzes me as I catch my breath. The nightmare reminds me of how truly alone I am, and I cry myself to sleep.

Darkness wins tonight, stealing away my happiness.

The ringing of my phone wakes me. My eyesight is half blurry as I grab it off my nightstand.

"Hello?" my voice rasps.

Silence on the other end of the phone prompts me to check out who called. Hindsight: should have done that before I answered. *Mierda.*

"Jax?"

Heavy breathing and rustling of sheets tell me he's still on the line.

"Why the hell are you calling me at 4 a.m.? Actually, why the hell are you calling me at all?"

"I don't know," he slurs.

Great. Mark *getting a drunk booty call from an ex* off my bucket list.

"So, you called me because you're drinking again."

"No." He answers too quickly.

"I don't want to talk to you. And I especially don't want to talk to you when you are drunk."

"I didn't mean to drink tonight."

"Yet you somehow are slurring your words."

"I drank by myself—" he hiccups "—in my hotel room to celebrate my win."

"Congratulations, you won *most likely to be an asshole for the rest of your life* and the Singapore Grand Prix in one weekend. You must be so proud."

He sighs. "I'm not proud. I'm surviving."

"Why did you call me?" I enunciate my words with a hint of bitterness.

"You want the truth?"

"With you, maybe the lie is better this time. Your version of the truth is a bit brutal for my taste."

"Okay. Lies it is. I don't miss you."

My heart clenches in my chest. "I'm hanging up now." Yet I can't find the will to press the red button on the screen.

"Lie. I'm happy without you." He sighs. "I don't think of you at all. I don't wake up every morning, dreaming you're there, only to realize none of it is real. Lies, lies, lies."

My frustration grows as he toys with me. "You don't get to call me, drunk and alone, saying you miss me when you pushed me away. I'm not here to console you. You ruined everything for me." *You ruined us.*

"I know," he says somberly. "I only wanted to hear your voice. It was selfish of me."

"Why do it then?"

"To remind me why this is all worth it. The pain, the loneliness—all of it. To not give in and beg you to take me back."

"Jax… I don't know what you want me to say." My heart aches in my chest, dull and throbbing at his admission. I can't begin to understand the complexity of his mind.

"Nothing. This was enough, so thank you for answering. Sorry I called. It won't happen again." He hangs up before I can respond.

My confusion turns into anger before devolving into sadness. I don't understand Jax's true reason for calling me, but I do know he left a hole in my heart the size of his fist.

CHAPTER FORTY-EIGHT

Jax

Shit. I fucked up.

Drinking was a terrible idea. But getting pissed and calling Elena is exactly the reason I have trust issues with alcohol.

I type out an apology text to her the minute I wake up in the morning. As my finger hovers above the send button, I stop and call Sophie instead.

"Hi. I need help." My hoarse voice sets the desperate tone I feel at the moment.

Sophie groans. "At 7 a.m.?"

"Can you please explain why the fuck you're calling my girlfriend at the ass-crack of dawn?" Liam's irritated speech is cut off by his yawn.

"I wanted to ask her for advice."

"Fine. You owe me Starbucks after waking me up this early," he replies. Sophie mumbles something I can only imagine dulls Liam's annoyance. I'd gag if I wasn't jealous.

"Okay, forget the Starbucks. Bother us every morning for all I care." Liam laughs.

Sheets rustle as Sophie asks me to hold on a second. A door shuts on her end of the phone before she answers again. "So, what's up?"

"Sorry to bug you this early."

She laughs. "Don't worry about it."

"So, I made a mistake last night."

"Like?" Sophie's concerned voice adds to my guilt.

"I caved and called Elena after drinking."

She lets out a deep sigh. "Okay, it's not as bad as I thought. What did you say?"

"Things I shouldn't have. I admitted how I feel."

"I'm having trouble following you on why this is a bad thing. You told her you miss her?"

"Yes," I hiss. "It's not good because I don't want to give her false hope. And now I'm worried if I should send her an apology text or pretend it never happened."

"Why are you wanting to apologize for telling her the truth?"

I battle between telling Sophie the real reason I pushed Elena away or pretending I don't need her help anymore. Desperation about hurting Elena again has me shelving my pride. "I haven't been fully honest with you about why I ended it with Elena. It's more complicated than you think."

About as complicated as the wires in my brain telling me to chase after Elena despite everything up to this point.

"Give me a second," Sophie mumbles into the phone. I listen intently to her footsteps as she opens a door again. "Liam, make sure my coffee has a shot of Baileys in it."

"This early?" The phone's microphone picks up his voice.

"Jax, do you think I need alcohol for this conversation?"

My confirmatory mumble has her following up with shooing Liam out the door of their hotel room.

"So, tell me what's going on."

After swearing Sophie to secrecy, I share everything that has happened up until this point. By the end of the conversation, she sobs into the phone, her sadness matching the way I feel.

"Why me? Why am I the first friend you told?"

"Because I'm desperate for a woman's advice about how to go about apologizing for something careless."

"But that's not the advice I want to give you." She sniffs.

"As much as I appreciate your advice, I can't give Elena more than this. So please help me think of what to say," I whisper, resigned about the situation.

"Okay, first you need to apologize for your drunk confessional." Sophie rambles on, giving me a list of instructions.

After I type out what Sophie deems the most perfect message, I hit send without second-guessing myself.

> **Jax:** Saying I'm sorry will never be good enough but I want to say it anyway. I'm sorry for calling you because I'm too weak to stay away from you for longer than two weeks. I'm sorry for earning your trust and ruining it with my decisions. I'm sorry for breaking your heart when you trusted me to protect you and it. I'm sorry for being selfish in the first place, hoping we would fall in love, only to rip it away when things got hard. And most of all, I'm sorry for not being the man you deserve, yet wishing I was anyway.

Sophie hangs up after she assures me she won't tell Liam about my secret.

Minutes go by without a response. I attempt to busy myself with working out and watching pre-race footage, my uncertainty and concern growing as more time passes.

My phone beeps and I rush to pick it up, knocking over my laptop in the process. "Shit."

The one person I didn't expect a message from lights up my phone.

> **Elías:** If you value your fingers, don't text Elena again. Chinga tu madre, pendejo.

Realization I didn't want to accept hits me, shredding any last hope that Elena will ever forgive me.

"Hey, arsehole. Good luck with your qually today. I'm still mad at you, but I hope you place P1." Caleb rolls his eyes at the FaceTime camera.

The pit crew ignores me as I lean against my race car, tapping my trainer. "Thanks for the sweet words. Love you too, mate."

"If your love is anything close to what you had for Elena, I'll have to pass." Caleb turns his words into bullets, piercing my carefully erected armor.

"What do you know about love?"

"Enough to know you fucked up."

"Are you going to tell me the same thing before every qualifier?"

"If that's what it takes for you to pull your head out of your arse, then I'm all for it."

My eyes dart from the screen to Elías, who scowls at me from the other side of the garage. "Good thing I only have a couple qualifiers left then. I can't imagine my life without your cheerful attitude."

"That's what you get for breaking Elena's heart. What did I tell you?"

"I didn't answer your call so you could lecture me," I snap, exhaustion sucking up my patience. Guilt already makes it difficult for me to function every day, so the last thing I need is a sixteen-year-old kid schooling me on what little he knows about love.

"No, you answered to ease your guilt. I'm not like the paid help you have around you. I'm going to call you out on your bullshit."

"By all means, call me out."

"You need to go chase after your girl. It's been three weeks already. What are you waiting for?"

A miracle sounds a bit religious for my taste, so I keep it fake. "Sometimes people don't work out."

"Well those people are idiots like you who destroyed their relationship with a mistake."

"I've done what I can to correct my mistakes and make sure she is taken care of."

"Wait, what?" Caleb eyes me suspiciously.

Shit.

"I've made sure to amend my mistakes with McCoy."

"How did you make sure she is taken care of?"

"What are you talking about?" *Smooth, Jax.*

"Okay, mate, chemo might suck, but it doesn't kill off my brain cells. You said you did what you could to make sure she is taken care of."

A crew member waves at me. "I've got to go. They're calling me to get ready."

"Don't make me go all 007 on you and dig into what you're hiding."

My laugh comes off forced. "Okay, James Bond. I don't know what medicine they give you, but your delusions are trippy as fuck."

Caleb narrows his eyes at me. "Good luck today, bye." He hangs up without letting me say goodbye back.

Shit. For his sake and mine, I hope he doesn't go digging around.

I can't have news get back to Elena that I've been behind her recent opportunities.

Elías scares the shit out of me as I exit the pit lane.

"Fuck. Do you have a thing for lurking in corners?"

His scowl twitches. "You caught me. I've been waiting for the right moment to jump you."

"If you're trying to bitch me out about Elena some more, save it. I've had a shit day." My qually went to hell after my conversation with Caleb. I somehow managed my panicking before it became anything dangerous, but it impaired my performance.

"I wanted to thank you, actually."

I pause. "What do you mean?"

Elías leans against the wall. "Elena told me how Connor offered her a ridiculous sum of money for all the damage you caused."

I shrug. "That's great. At least she got rewarded for my arseholeness." My body goes on high alert as Elías assesses me.

"Yeah, thank God Connor is nicer than you, right?"

"Right," I offer in the driest voice.

"Imagine my shock when Elena then called me the next week saying how James Mitchell from Bandini offered her a PR job."

I raise my eyebrows in surprise. "You don't say? Maybe my bad press made the enemy interested in her."

Elías shakes his head. "You're telling me. How crazy is it for these two coincidences to happen within the same month for someone like Elena?"

"About as crazy as you thinking I care about us having a conversation about my ex-girlfriend." My words have a bite to them. I don't want to talk about Elena, especially to someone like Elías. I think about her enough on my own without her personal bodyguard and best friend snooping around.

Elías's smirk turns into a full-blown grin. "And then I got a call from Caleb who wanted to quote 'check in on Elena and give me updates' unquote. But before he hung up, he mentioned how you've been mending your mistakes with Elena. What do you make of that?"

Dammit Caleb, I trusted you. "That you are shit at connecting the dots."

"I think you're hiding something. There's no way Connor happened to offer Elena a hundred-thousand euros to stay quiet about working with you. Even he's not that generous."

Well, fuck, Connor must have felt terrible for Elena. "That's a shit ton of money. I didn't know I was worth that kind of hazard pay."

Elías's eyes narrow. "Weird. I didn't mention anything about hazard pay, yet Elena used the same statement."

Fuck, fuck, fuck. Abort the mission.

"We did date after all. We're bound to have the same humor."

"*Right*. Either way, I might hate you for breaking her heart, but I can't hate you for setting her up to make sure she would be taken care of. I admire that, even if you won't admit it." He stands to his full height, making us eye level.

"I don't know what you're talking about."

"Your secret is safe with me. I wanted to thank you." Elías holds his hand out to me.

I grab onto it and shake. "You never planned on telling her, did you?"

He smirks. "No. I wanted to confirm it for myself. I think you've caused her enough pain as it is, so I want to let her keep her dignity about her job."

"You're an all right guy, Elías. I respect that."

"It's about time you noticed it after working with me for a whole season."

I let out my first genuine laugh for the day. At least I can survive another day knowing my sacrifice means something to Elena, even if she doesn't know.

"I've been meaning to talk to you." Dad's voice rumbles through the speakerphone.

I take a seat on the couch of my hotel suite, preparing for a long-overdue conversation. Ever since my diagnosis, I've kept my conversations with my parents neutral, not wanting to upset them more. Mum can't look at me for extended periods of time without getting teary-eyed. Dad, on the other hand, has kept relaxed and never probes.

I should have guessed he was biding his time. "I guess the time has come for you to give it to me."

"I'd ask you how you are, but I'm guessing based on the press videos, you're barely hanging in there."

I clutch onto my phone and press the speakerphone button, wanting to give my hands something to do. "I'm excited for the season to be over."

"I can imagine. You've been through a lot in the last year."

"Understatement of the century."

"How has everything been since you pushed Elena away?"

"Shitty doesn't begin to cover how I feel about it all."

He sighs. "Well, you know that I'm not one to dance around an issue."

I pinch the bridge of my nose. "Hit me with it."

"I've been patient, trying to wait this out and see how you handle the situation with Elena. But it's gone on too long and I'm afraid what will happen if you continue down this path."

"I've been keeping straight. No partying or drugs to feel better, no matter how much I wish it could dull the pain."

"That's not my concern, although I'm happy you've been staying clean and focused. I'm talking about a different kind of path."

"Elena and I are on two separate ones."

"It's not too late to amend that. I want to talk to you and plead her case."

I grunt. "That's not how this works."

"It does when you're not giving her a fair chance at trying things with you, diagnosis and all."

"You and she aren't the same. She has a choice to walk away, you didn't."

"That's where you're wrong. We all have choices. I chose to stay with your mum even though I knew she would get sick and need help because I love both of you more than anything else in the world. No disease could keep me away."

My lungs burn from the deep inhale of breath I take. "You were married. You had vows not to abandon her. I only sped up the inevitable with Elena."

"Which is what?"

"That I'm going to get sick one day and I don't want to bring her down with me."

"Your mother doesn't bring me down. That's my point, and why I wanted to talk to you. She's the best part of my days and I couldn't imagine it any other way. Even when she is at her worst, I feel grateful she's there to begin with. *That's* why I stuck by her when she was diagnosed. It wasn't about a vow. It's about a feeling I have toward her that nothing can compare to."

"And that's why you'll be devastated when she dies," I rasp. "You're bound to die along with her in every way that counts."

I love my dad. The last thing I want to see is the light fade from his eyes little by little as Mum gets worse.

"I'm not going to die." He lets out a long sigh. "I'll be the same man who promised her I'd fight for her and you. No matter what happens to your mum, I'll always have you. And you are the greatest gift she could have given me. Which is why I'm here to tell you to get your head out of your arse and chase Elena because we Kingstons don't give up on the people we care about."

My chest tightens. "I love you, Dad. I respect you for

everything you've given me, including help when I needed it the most."

"But…"

I let out a resigned sigh. "But I can't follow your advice this time."

His sigh sounds similar to mine. "At least give it a thought and consider what I said. And think about what life would be like if you allowed yourself to enjoy all the good moments with Elena before life gets hard. That's a lot of good memories to counteract the tough ones."

"For you, I'll think about it."

His deep chuckle echoes through the phone. "Don't lie to me. Actually do it."

"All I've done is think about my decisions."

"Yet you're still miserable. Sounds like a bad decision to me."

"Dad?"

"Mm."

"How do you feel when Mum has a bad day?"

"Like I want to rip apart the world and find a solution for her. I want to scream about how life isn't fair and what was the point of making all this money if I can't buy the one thing I want."

"My point exactly."

"That might be yours. But my point? The bad days will never outweigh the good ones. Nothing can replace all the memories I have and all the ones I'll continue to make with Mum. So, no, son, your point is null and void. I could scream life isn't fair. But life gave me her, so it's a sacrifice I'm willing to make. You need to ask yourself, will you let Elena do the same?"

CHAPTER FORTY-NINE

Elena

I wake up and get dressed so I can visit *Abuela*. The new facility I put her in when I started working with Jax is only a few minutes' walk away. Everything about the place is convenient, and I'll miss it when my funds run out and I have to move her. Consistency is essential for people like *Abuela*, and it kills me to disrupt her life yet again.

I walk into the building and greet the staff. One of the managers calls my name, asking me to come to his office.

A bunch of scenarios run through my head as to what he wants from me. Year after year I received disappointing news about *Abuela*, and I'm afraid this is no different. He points me in the direction of an empty chair as he takes a seat across from me.

"So, Ms. Gonzalez, I'm sorry to call you in before you could see your grandmother, but I didn't want to miss you."

"Is she okay?"

"Oh, yes. I didn't mean to cause you any alarm. She is doing fine and is rather happy here. That's what I wanted to talk to you about."

I relax in my seat as my heart rate slows down. "Oh, good. I was worried something happened."

"If anything were to happen, we would give you a call and have you come down here right away."

Right. Way to jump to conclusions. I nod.

"I know we discussed the breakdown of fees before you had to travel. I wanted to let you know that the remainder of your grandmother's stay has been covered."

My jaw drops open. "The remainder? But I don't know how long that is."

I do the math in my head, wondering who would donate that much money. The only person I deem sneaky enough to do this plan is one of London's richest non-royal citizens.

The very one who broke my heart only a few weeks ago.

I run a shaky hand over my mouth, processing the breakdown of fees the manager shows me. When I ask who donated the funds, he replies that he can't say.

Why would Jax do this? Why would he want to help me after he said he wants nothing to do with me? This type of donation is not what someone does when they don't want to see someone again.

The only type of question that keeps popping up in my head is *why*.

Why this?

Why does he still care?

Why did he let me go?

Why didn't he love me enough to share his burden with me?

I say goodbye to the manager and walk up the steps to visit my grandma. Her frail body sinks into the bed. It pains me to see her shallow cheeks and sunken eyes as she looks over at me with glossy pupils.

I take my usual seat next to her and tug her hand into mine. *"Hola, como te andas?"*

"Marisol, no me gusta la ultima doctora. She poked me with a needle. I want to go home."

I shake my head and sigh, wishing *Abuela* would remember me once. Tears fill my eyes as I take on the role of my mother. Every painstaking minute drains my energy, but I hold true to my promise to visit her.

Even when she doesn't remember me.

Even when she gets angry because of her situation and yells that I'm leaving her to rot in some nursing home.

Even when my heart breaks day after day when I visit, hoping she might remember me, even for a second.

I do my family duty, carrying the burden. My parents would have done the same and tenfold. Shelving my sadness, I enjoy the time I have with *Abuela* until the nurses tell me visiting hours are over.

I rise from my chair and stretch my aching legs.

"Marisol, are you coming tomorrow?"

"Si, como no." I lean over and kiss the top of her head before exiting her room.

My heart stops. My feet stop. Everything around me stops.

Vera leans against the wall, tapping her cane to the beat of the clock above her. She offers me a tight smile. "Elena." The skin around her eyes wrinkles, reflecting the sadness etched in her gaze.

"Vera?"

"You look like you've seen a ghost."

I look over her glossy blonde hair and porcelain skin. "You're pale and all, but no. I'm shocked you're here. How did you even know I was here?"

"I have my sources."

"Are you the one who paid for my grandma to stay here indefinitely?"

Vera smiles. "I prefer my donations to remain anonymous. Showing off is so passe."

"Are you behind my new job and bonus check, too?"

She shakes her head in disagreement. "I can only assume that was because of another Kingston. I may be fabulous, but even my power has its limits."

An unrestrained laugh escapes me.

"Come, let's take a walk." She offers me her elbow.

I interlock my arm with hers as I fist my sweaty palm. "As nice as this surprise is, what are you doing here?"

"I'm doing my motherly duty."

"For Jax?" My words reflect the confusion no doubt etched in my face.

"For you." She remains silent after that.

I process her words as we exit *Abuela*'s facility. The late October sun shines down on us as we stroll toward the coast. Vera picks a spot near the jagged shore, giving us a good view of the Mediterranean Sea.

We both sit together on a bench, similar to our chat in London all those months ago.

"I'm here both for my own selfish reasons and because I think you could use some motherly advice. Your mum was taken from you at such a young age. I can't imagine the kind of pain you've dealt with, and the struggles you have now with your grandma. To be young yet carry such a big responsibility on your shoulders must be exhausting."

I nod. "The selfish part of me is so tired of it."

"It's not the selfish part, it's the human part. And that's what makes you genuine."

I drop my head and focus on my hands fisted in my lap. "Some days it's hard to visit her."

"Because she thinks you're her daughter?"

I swallow to combat the dryness in my throat. "You heard?"

Vera grabs onto my hand in a motherly gesture I crave, reminding me of her trembles. "I didn't know her condition was this severe."

"It is what it is." I shrug.

"Oh, cut that toxic positivity out. You don't need to be strong all the time. Tell me how you honestly feel."

"Lonely. So freaking lonely I cry myself to sleep some nights." With Elías traveling and *Abuela* in the state she is in, I feel deprived of affection to the point that it suffocates me like the dark I despise with everything in me.

She shakes her head and pats my hand. "My son is an idiot. A selfless idiot, but an idiot nonetheless."

The mere mention of Jax has me bristling.

"I want to tell you a story, but you have to promise to listen until the end. Don't interrupt until I'm finished."

My brows pinch together as I consider what kind of story she wants to share. Probably something about Jax that will tempt me to break down in front of his mom. But Vera deserves my respect and time, so I nod in agreement despite my brewing emotions.

"I found out about my condition a few months after I

gave birth to Jax. When my grandfather was diagnosed with Huntington's Disease, my parents sent me a courtesy letter about it. No phone call, no greeting, no congratulations on giving birth to a child. Only a basic letter wishing me well and suggesting that I should get tested in case I carry the gene." Vera's voice cracks.

She continues, clutching onto my hand harder. "I couldn't wrap my head around that kind of diagnosis. I was newly married and just had a child. But when I found out about my grandfather, it was as if my world paused. Zack was my only support system as I navigated through the process of meeting with a genetic counselor. The only reason I went through the testing in the first place was because of my son. I could have lived a happy life not knowing about something I wouldn't encounter until an older age, but I knew my son deserved to know. That he deserved to enjoy every moment I could offer him before my disease started taking its toll."

She lets out a ragged breath. "It was the hardest decision I ever had to make. When I found out I carried the gene, I got angry and then I got depressed. Zack was there for me every step of the way, ensuring I had someone on my side. And oh God, Zack was barely an adult himself. His career was starting to pick up in the boxing scene, and here I was, a new wife and a new burden for him. The news of my diagnosis and the post-labor hormones caused me to fall into depression. A deep, dark, lonely place filled with self-doubt and hatred. For myself, for my situation, for the odds I stacked against my newborn son without knowing it.

"I was barely living. Barely even breathing, but I made sure to carry out my basic motherly duties. One day Zack held our son out to me and, dear God, I still remember his speech to this day. I swear his words wrote themselves on my heart and never left. Zack said, 'The sun might seem as if it stops shining from time to time because of a cloud or a rainstorm or the nighttime, but it's still there. It endures everything to nurture the lives that depend on it. You're my sun. I don't care if you're hidden because of a storm or the end of the fucking world. I can't live without you, and I can't imagine a world where my son would want to either.'" A couple of tears escape Vera's eyes. I wrap my arms around her and give her a hug, still not speaking like she asked because she needs to get this out.

"I stopped shining. I stopped living. I allowed a diagnosis that wouldn't affect me for years to suck up my happiness like a vacuum. But Zack's kindness and my love for Jax got me out of it, along with therapy. And you might be wondering why I'm telling you any of this, but I swear it is important."

She lets out a deep sigh. "I understand my son more than anyone else. He might be built like his father, but he has every ounce of my heart. He pushed you away rather than keep you to himself. It took him years to agree to a genetic counselor the first time, but after less than a season with you, he was willing to do the process all over again. A light I hadn't seen in him since he was younger was finally lit again. He wanted a future that was different than the one he made up in his head about him living by himself for the rest of his life."

Everything in my body tightens. I'm afraid of what she will say next, but I wait with bated breath for her to continue.

Her voice cracks. "As his mother, I was worried when he asked about testing again. How could I not be? I prayed day after day he would receive the news he so desperately needed and craved. Except he didn't get the news we were all hoping for." The few tears Vera shed turn into a waterfall down her cheeks. My face mimics hers, and I don't try to brush them away. "It kills me to know my son has Huntington's Disease because of me. Him destroying his future with you stole a bit of my soul because of the pain he experienced doing it. I hate seeing my son devastated over not being with the person he loves. I don't want that for him."

Jax has Huntington's Disease? My heart doesn't ache, it explodes in my chest like a bomb. Everything around me drains of color as I stare at his mother, desperate for this to all be a joke.

"He was diagnosed?" The words leave my lips in a whisper.

She bobs her head up and down. "God, I wish it weren't the case."

We cry together, hugging one another. Tears run down my cheeks as I think of everything Jax did to push me away. I cry for him and for his future he desperately wanted to escape from.

She pulls out of my arms, only to clutch my hands in hers. "I love my son with everything in me, so I came here to ask you to forgive him. He wasn't in a good place when he said those things to you, and he only said them to make you hate him. I can't sit back and watch him become a shell of someone I barely recognize because he denied himself his chance at love. He deserves the sun, no matter how much he hides from it and lives in the shadows. Be that for him. Get him out. Have it in your heart to fight for him even when he believes whole-heartedly, he doesn't deserve it. Love isn't easy, and I'm not here to tell you that your love story will be like that. But I can promise you that my son is single-handedly one of the best men I know, and it's not because I raised him. The actions he took to protect you after pushing you away speak more about his character than anything I could say. He's loyal to you, even when apart."

"I don't even know what to say." I brush the tears off my cheeks.

Pain grips onto my chest like rusty claws. The fact that Jax will shoulder another burden in addition to his anxiety...I can't bear the thought of him being in agony.

"My son did the hardest thing I think anyone can do. He broke the heart of the woman he loves to protect her—to give her a chance at her own happiness, no matter how much it deprived him of his. And while I feel guilty he upset you, I won't deny how I'm proud of him. I raised him to care more about other people than himself, and that to me is a win. So, please, have it in your heart to forgive him. Fight for him like my husband fought for me. Show him that the sun doesn't stop shining, even on the worst of days." She squeezes my hand before letting go.

"What if he rejects me again?"

"He might." Her lips press together in a thin line. "But I think the second question you should ask yourself is, 'What if he accepts you, screwed up future and all, because he couldn't imagine a world without you in it?'"

And like that, Vera and I stare out into the ocean, both in our own worlds.

I come to the realization that not every love story is written the same way. From the start, Jax and I were never meant for any basic ending with the boy chasing the girl into the sunset. In our story, I'm the one who needs to embrace the dark to pull him out and save him. From our past. For our future. And most of all, for the love I know is stronger than any shitty diagnosis or anxiety.

I don't need a happy ending. I need *our* ending. The one that might be messy and imperfect, but exclusively ours.

And it's about damn time I go and fight for what I know is rightfully mine.

CHAPTER FIFTY

Jax

I always thought I was a miserable, insufferable bastard before Elena. But life without Elena? It's like living in the eye of a hurricane. It's calm, quiet, but you're painfully aware of destruction looming nearby.

Liam frowns at me from across my suite. "You look like shit. I wouldn't have guessed you placed P1 for tomorrow's race based on how depressed you've been."

"I might not look it, but I'm thrilled for the season to be over tomorrow. I'm ready for a break."

"For a break or for a binger?"

Besides my one moment of weakness the night of the Singapore Grand Prix, I haven't touched a lick of alcohol since I broke up with Elena. Not even Jack can cure the Elena-sized hole in my chest, no matter how much I wish it did.

And you bet your arse I wish it did.

"A break. I want to spend time with my parents." And I want to heal. I can't do that when I'm living under Connor's microscope and F1's excessive demands.

"Will your new babysitter join you?"

Sam, my latest ankle monitor and constant reminder of how much I ruined my life, hangs out on the couches outside of my suite, giving me privacy for once all day.

"No. Connor trusts me to behave this time." Probably because I won't be a burden anymore.

"That's shocking. I thought he'd be the first one to want you supervised after last time."

"He doesn't have a reason to worry anymore. I'm done with F1 after tomorrow."

Liam stares at me with wide eyes. "What? Not a funny joke, asshole."

"I'm not joking."

"You're quitting? What the fuck has gotten into you?" He scowls.

"I haven't been fully honest with you." I look away.

"No shit."

I take the deepest breath, hoping it gives me additional courage. These are the moments I wish I had a Xan. I let it all out, telling Liam about everything since my parents told me Mum had Huntington's. The pills, the alcohol, the constant anxiety crippling me to the point of barely living. By the end of my story, we're both silent and processing. Liam gets up from the other couch and sits next to me. He looks stunned.

"I'm all for our bromance, but I don't need your tears." I elbow him in the ribs.

Liam wraps his arm around my shoulder and tugs me into him in the manliest hug I've experienced. "You're a stupid asshole for keeping this all to yourself. I would've been there for you if you had only asked."

"I didn't want to be a bother to anyone. Plus, you have Sophie now, and Noah has Maya."

"We'd be the shittiest friends if we ignored you for our girlfriends when you needed us the most. And let's be real, if there's anything about me and Noah you'd expect, it's that we never half-ass anything, friendships included." He smacks me on the back and lets go. "You don't need to face any of this alone. If you want to quit racing, we'll stand by you the whole time. You deserve to do what makes you happy."

"I don't know if I'll ever truly be happy." A life without Elena, even if I live by myself near my parents' house, sounds lonely as fuck.

"Bullshit. You only need to find what makes you feel that way. If it's not racing, so be it. If it means moving back to London and moving on with life, then have at it. You have a big enough bank account to not work another day in your life."

"The biggest." I wink at him.

Liam laughs up to the ceiling. "All I know is I'm going to miss you. Please beat Noah's ass tomorrow so you can leave F1 in style. I won't accept anything less."

Sweat drenches my back as my engine rumbles against my spine. The lights shut off in front of me. I press my foot to the pedal and take off, the sounds of screeching tires echoing behind me. My car makes it through the first corner before my earpiece buzzes with activity.

"Hey. Keep up the pace and mind your tires. And watch out

for Noah because he wants to ride your ass."

I monitor Noah the entire time I race, making sure not to give him many opportunities to pass me. Turn after turn we battle for the first-place spot. He takes the lead once, but I beat him back after a successful pit stop.

"You're turning too wide at corner three," an engineer speaks through the team radio.

My breathing grows heavier as I continue to push toward the finish line. Blurs of crowds pass me, screaming as the rushing cars fly by.

Noah inches up toward my rear wing, but I smash the accelerator, flying through another lap. With one last go around the track, I need to push my car to the limit.

Chris makes his presence known again. "Steady. Don't screw this up in the last lap."

I concentrate on the track in front of me while minding my mirrors as I push the race car to its breaking point. Turn after turn, I keep my lead, not giving Noah much space to pass me. With one last turn, I surge down the final straight of the Prix.

Fireworks go off as I pass the checkered flag. The sounds of roaring crowds pull a smile from me as I run through the track for a cool down lap.

"You fucking did it. Damn, you're a two-time World Champion. Good work, Kingston!" Chris yells.

I throw my fist in the air, enjoying the last lap of my career.

My eyes are deceiving me. There's no other explanation for the apparition standing to the side of the podium, watching me.

Elena motherfucking Gonzalez, in the flesh. She smiles at me and waves, rocking a McCoy T-shirt with my number on it. Liam, Sophie, Maya, and Elías stand next her, cheering us on.

What the hell is she doing here? But more importantly, why is she smiling at me like I hung the fucking moon for her?

I attempt to ignore her as Noah pours champagne all over me, but my eyes find hers every time. When they hand me my trophy, I smile at her before lifting it in the air. The crowd goes wild as Noah and Santiago spray champagne on screaming fans.

The announcers call for the end of the celebration, and I exit the stage. I take a look at her. A good long look, wondering how the hell I deserved her visiting my final Prix despite everything I've done. I stroll toward her, soaking her in like the earth in the middle of a rainstorm after a year-long drought.

"Hey." She offers me a small, nervous smile.

"What are you doing here?" I fight my smile and fail.

"I wanted to see what a World Champion looked like up close and personal. Figured it was worth checking out if the final podium meets the hype."

"Did it meet your standards?"

"Not really. I expected better fireworks to be honest."

I shake my head at her. *What the fuck is she doing here?*

She grabs my hand and tugs me away from my friends. A zing of energy courses up my arm at our contact. I'm tempted to pull away, but I allow myself the moment of torture.

Although I'm happy she came—elated even—I can't exactly express it. I'm on standby as she pulls me through the crowds before leading me toward a dark motorhome.

"You don't have to look conflicted about having me here." She places her palm against my cheek.

I lean into it, craving her touch like the fucked-up man I am. What's the harm in a few minutes of her attention, even though I know it will devastate me once she leaves? "I'm happy you're here. Honest fucking truth."

"Well, that's a relief. I wasn't sure if you'd ignore me or kiss me."

I remain silent because I'm afraid my words will betray how I truly feel about her. As much as I wished for her to be here, it's not what should happen.

Elena sighs. "I might as well get this over with." She rubs her thumb across my stubble before pulling away. "First off, you're the most frustrating man I have ever met. You pushed me away on purpose and if you ever do that to me again, I will threaten bodily harm."

"I don't know wha—"

She presses a finger against my lips, shutting me up. "Save the bullshit for anyone but me. I know, Jax. I know about it *all*." Her voice becomes somber as she stares at me with tears reflecting off her eyes.

"What do you mean?" my voice croaks.

"I know you didn't get the news you wanted. I know you said every terrible thing to get me to run away. That you somehow got Connor to pay my entire year salary despite being fired, and how Bandini hired me because of your connection. You tried your best to make sure I was okay without you, even though I most definitely wasn't. You don't need to pretend anymore that you're okay. I don't want you to. I want the good and the bad, and everything in between with you."

I lean my forehead against hers and let out a deep breath. "Who told you?"

"Does it matter who? That's not the point."

"No, but is that the reason you came here? Because of me helping you?"

"No." She lets out an agitated breath. "I came here because you deserve the whole goddamn world and every snow-globe moment. And I'm selfish because I want all those moments to be with me."

I shut my eyes, shielding the yearning. "I should walk away. Permanently."

She scoffs. "I'd like to see you try. I don't care about any of it. Nothing about your diagnosis scares me. You could start having symptoms tomorrow, and I'd want to be there for you every single day after. I've been through drastic losses in my life and the last thing I want is to lose the person I love because he would rather be alone than with me." Her voice breaks.

I grip her neck and force her to look up at me. "You don't know what you're asking for."

"Who said anything about asking? I'm taking our future into my own hands."

"What about kids?"

"What about them? There are other ways to have children. Sperm donors, adoption—the options are endless. I don't care about the details as long as I can have you."

"Elena…" I look away, nervous to meet her gaze. "Are you sure about this? Because if you claim you want it all, then I get to do the same."

Her small fingers clutch my chin and force me to face her. "I wouldn't want it any other way. Live a messy life with me, Jax Kingston. I want chaos. I want darkness. I want sunshine and rainstorms with you. But most of all, I want you any way I can have you because I love you."

Her words sink into my skin, etching themselves like the ink that covers my body. I didn't realize how much I needed her until I let her go.

"I love you too. Even when I tried my hardest not to." My hand tightens around the back of her neck and I tug her lips to mine. I kiss her with every ounce of love I feel, hoping I can express every apology I wanted to say to her. To remind her of every moment I missed her, craved her, wanted to crawl back to her.

She sighs and I take advantage, running my tongue along the seam of her lips before having a taste. With Elena, one kiss is never enough. It'll never be enough, in all the days of my life, from here on out. Despite my desire to continue, I pull away.

She protests with a groan. I chuckle as I clutch onto her hand and drag her toward McCoy's motorhome. Fans call my name out and I nod, barely paying attention because I'm on a mission.

My dick throbs in anticipation as we make it back to my private suite. I pull her in for another kiss, making quick work of removing her clothes. She tugs on the zipper of my race suit, and I help, ridding myself of the sweaty, champagne-soaked clothes.

"Fuck. I've missed you." I take her in, loving every curve on her body.

"Me too." She sighs as my lips find her neck and suck.

"If I were a good guy, I'd take you back to my hotel and give you a reunion you deserve."

"I'm not here to date the good guy." She cups my erection and rubs her thumb across the slit.

I drop my head back and groan. "Then be prepared for all the bad."

She laughs. "I look forward to it."

I push her toward the couch. Elena lies down, taking up the entire length of it. She looks up at me like a present I don't fucking deserve but can't help keeping.

"It's okay to be happy." She smiles.

I grab her legs and pull her toward the side of the couch, lifting her ass up over the armrest. My knees hit the floor as my mouth ravages her. The taste of her is fucking addictive, reminding me of everything I was stupid to let go of.

I kiss, lick, and appreciate her with each stroke of my tongue. Her moans are a symphony to my ears. She gasps when my lips wrap around her clit. I pump a finger, and then another into her, prepping her for me.

She moans my name before she detonates around me. I can't pull away, wanting to consume everything she has to offer me.

"Shit." She sighs. "I've missed you so much."

"Move back."

She follows my command, moving so her entire body covers the couch again. I grab a condom from my gym bag and put it on before crawling over her body.

"I've missed you more than I can begin to explain. I'm sorry for everything, Elena. I'm sorry for hurting you and for making you feel like you weren't good enough for me. The truth is you'll always be too good for me. But damn, I can't give you up ever again."

"Keep me forever." She pushes onto her elbows and kisses me. Her hands go to my dick, touching me before guiding me toward her entrance.

I push into her, groaning as she tugs on my hair. "Fuck."

She gasps when I move. I keep a slow pace, wanting to

enjoy the moment with her. Steady, tantalizing strokes prompt her to tug on my hair harder.

"As much as I love slow sex, this is torture."

"The best kind. Always the best with you." I kiss her neck as I increase my tempo and strength, hitting the spot that makes her scratch at my back. The moan leaving her mouth excites me. My pace grows erratic as she clutches onto my back, chanting my name in my ear.

With a few more pumps, she explodes around my dick. My movements grow relentless and desperate as I chase the high only Elena provides. A warmth trails down my spine as my release closes in. I come, pounding into her, devouring her sighs with my lips.

I collapse on top of her, hugging her close to my body. "I love you."

"I love you too." Her voice cracks.

I lift my head from her neck, brushing away a tear from her cheek with the pad of my thumb. "Sex that good?"

"The greatest. But I'm scared you'll change your mind if things get hard."

"For all the days of my life, I promise you I won't push you away. When life gets hard, I'll lean on you. When you need me, you can count on me to do the same. I want our kind of love story." I kiss her softly.

"No take backs?"

I smile at her with every ounce of love I feel. "No take backs."

CHAPTER FIFTY-ONE

THREE MONTHS LATER

Jax

E lena might have been the one to fight for me, but I can't deny the creeping anxiety that everything is only temporary. Whenever I fall into a negative thinking cycle, Elena pulls me out. And to be real, I lock myself into my mental prison all too much after the World Championship.

Moving on from F1 was easier than I thought. It's the doctor's visits and adjusting to my new life that isn't. I try my best to make positive strides forward. Tom is my permanent therapist now, and I've been spending time making amends with Elena.

All kinds of amends. The good, the sexual, and the downright swoony kind.

Which leads me to my next dilemma. Logistically speaking, Elena and I are currently in a long-distance relationship.

Ha. fucking. ha.

Me, the one with an allergy to anything more permanent than last week's leftovers, is committed to something other than my career and my family. But despite my patience and loyalty to Elena, I can't keep living with her far away. A flight from London to Monaco is too long for my liking. Even Caleb gives me shit about Elena living far away from me.

Neither one of us has mentioned where we want to go from here. After I finished my press events and wind-down from my last season, I flew to Monaco, wanting to surprise Elena.

I made plans. Big plans that make me drunk on excitement rather than nervousness. Unlike my last big life change, I thought everything out. Every single detail and all the possible scenarios. I know it's crazy. I know the whole damn thing will make my friends question whether I've completely lost it. But if this year has taught me anything, it's that I can't spend my life waiting anymore.

I don't want to spend another year of my life biding my time because of societal norms. Well, I don't want to waste another month, let alone another day without Elena next to me. And most of all, I want to live every day to the fullest now that I know my life will change drastically as I get older. Hence my plan.

The first step was prepping.

The second step involved breaking and entering.

And the final step is about to occur, based on the rattling of Elena's doorknob to her flat.

I take a deep breath, tucking my fidgeting fingers into the pocket of my ripped jeans. Elena opens the door and drops her keys on the side table. She shuts and locks her front door before hanging up her purse, all without giving me a second glance.

Her awareness is shit. Combine that with her crappy flat and you have the latest inspiration for a *Criminal Minds* episode. Bleak but honest.

"Well, love, I'll tell you one thing, you've proven exactly why you shouldn't live alone anymore."

Elena screams, jumping a foot back before hitting the door. "What the fuck, Jax!"

I lean against the wall, smiling at her. "I've been waiting for you."

She pushes her hand against her chest. "And you couldn't have texted me that? How did you even get my key?"

"Your landlord was easily bought."

"*¡No mames!*" She hits the light next to her, basking us in a glow.

After a year of being around her, I've picked up on her slang words. "Okay, fine, I'm joking. I borrowed your spare key last week."

"By *borrowed* you mean 'took it off my keyring'?"

"Precisely. You've always had a way with words."

She walks up to me, abandoning her spot by the door. Her eyes slide from me to the newly built shelf hidden behind a bedsheet. "What's this?"

Spoiler alert for all the sad saps out there: building Ikea furniture is like assembling a *Millennium Falcon* Lego set without any instructions. Fucking terrible.

"A gift."

"Trying to buy my love already after a few months together?"

I grin at her before placing a soft kiss against her lips. "Why buy something I already have?"

Elena shakes her head, hiding her smile. "So, what is it?"

I tug on the sheet, revealing my creation.

Elena doesn't move, let alone speak, as her eyes land on the rows of snow globes.

"You kept all the notes?" She traces the glass of one snow globe as if she can touch her lavender piece of paper secured inside of it.

"I couldn't let you throw them away. I haven't cashed in on all of them yet."

"What do you mean?"

"Check them out yourself and you tell me."

Elena reads off each of her vouchers to me. I laugh at the mention of Xanax, shaking my head at how much of a dependent, irritable arsehole I was. She pushed me to want to save myself with a few notes scribbled and hidden inside of my pill bottle.

I grab one of the snow globes and shake it, before twisting the knob at the bottom. The soft melody of Ed Sheeran's "Thinking Out Loud" plays as I pass her the snow globe.

"No way! Ed Sheeran?"

We remain quiet as the melody plays. Tears run down her face as she reads my note. I try to brush them away, but I miss a few.

Her eyes slide from the snow globe to my face. "I didn't write that note."

A soft laugh escapes me. "Obviously not." My messy *Will you marry me?* sticks out, unlike her elegant cursive.

"This is crazy."

"But so real." I place the snow globe on the shelf and tuck her into my body. Her warmth seeps into me, hitting me with a new wave of happiness.

"It's way too soon."

"Nothing in my life is 'too soon' anymore."

"I have a life here."

I chuckle to myself, loving the rational part of her that needs to question all the possible issues before agreeing. "If you want to stay here, I'll live here, too. I can travel to and from London more often."

"You'd do that for me?" She looks up at me with tear-stained cheeks.

"Of course."

"But what about your mom?"

"I'll visit her often."

Elena shakes her head.

My chest becomes tight at her potential rejection. "There's no point for me to wait for something I know will happen either way. I don't want to spend another day without you—not anymore with my diagnosis. Whether we start a life in Monaco or London, I only need you. And your grandma because she's part of the package."

More tears fall from Elena's eyes. "Yes."

I freeze. "Yes, you'll marry me?"

"Yes. Yes. Yes!" She cups my face with her hands and pulls me down for a kiss. A kiss meant to consume me from the inside out, solidifying my need to keep her forever.

She pulls away. "Yes. Let's get married!"

"You don't even want to see the ring first before you agree?"

She drops her head back and laughs. "No. You could offer me a rock from outside and I'd still say yes."

"I can assure you, it's a gigantic...rock."

Her giggle turns into a snort. "Please stop. You're killing the moment."

I tug the small box out of my jeans, get down on one knee, and pop open the lid. My hand grips hers in a stronghold. "Elena Gonzalez, I can't wait to spend the rest of my life with you, no matter the place, the time, the issues. You're the hero in our story, willing to stand by my side, no matter how dark the future looks. All I want to do is make you mine, forever and always. No take backs."

The same three words are inscribed on the inside of the ring because I'm a sappier motherfucker than my two friends. What can I say? She has a way of bringing that out in me.

She smiles at me with unconditional affection. "No take backs, not even a single moment. Not in your darkest time or your hardest day. I'll love you through it all."

I slide the ring on her finger. My chest expands at the sight of the solitaire diamond branding her as mine. I stand and tug her hand up to my lips, kissing her ring finger.

I pull my fiancée in for a real kiss, possessively marking her in all the ways I can. To thank her for her love, forgiveness, and acceptance. To kiss away her doubts and show her I want it all.

Hope is for men with their futures ahead of them.

Hope is for those who wish under stars, or in a church, or in a desperate moment of need.

And most of all, hope is for people like me.

EPILOGUE

ONE MONTH LATER

Elena

"**N**o peeking." Jax readjusts the blindfold covering my eyes. He grabs onto my hand and pulls me out of the car carefully. Somehow, I lasted the whole ride from his parents' house without getting nauseous or scared, seeing as my eyes have been covered the entire time. Darkness doesn't make me afraid anymore. Not after a month's worth of therapy sessions and exposures to what I feared the most.

"Where are we?"

"Do you need an answer for everything?"

"Yes. Especially when you've stolen me away before I could take a bath."

Jax laughs. He didn't give me a chance to ask questions or shower after our sparring match at his parents' house. My skin hums with anticipation as Jax leads me toward the unknown.

I attempt to use my other senses to get an idea of our

location. Grass crunches beneath my sneakers and birds chirp nearby, giving away nothing. What in the world does he want to do with me at night in the middle of nowhere? He lifts me into his arms as he walks up something I assume is a short set of stairs. A door creaks open and plastic rustles under our feet. "Murdering me already after one month of living together?"

"I want to murder myself for agreeing to live with my parents while we figured out our living situation. End of story."

I snort. "I thought you were happy I chose to move to London?" The moment I told Jax about my idea, he requested a refund for *Abuela*'s care and set her up to live in the best facility in the city while we temporarily moved into his parents' house.

"Oh, love, I'm ecstatic. But I think my parents are cramping our style." Jax halts.

I run into his back, and he steadies me. He helps me sit on some kind of bench before he settles right next to me, his nearness bringing a smile to my face. My heart rate increases as he leaves a lingering kiss on my cheek.

His fingers brush across my lips before tracing a path of heat to the blindfold. I'm met with a vision of Jax smiling at me as he pockets the eye covering.

I blink in confusion at the piano in front of us. A few lit candles provide some light, hinting at a house under construction. "What are we doing in a random deserted house?" My voice echoes through the empty area.

"Let me explain with a song instead." He runs his hands down the row of keys before the sweet melody of "All of Me" by John Legend fills the air around us.

I smile at him. "I love when you get all romantic on me, even though the location screams more creepy than cute."

Jax throws his head back and laughs. He misses a beat before picking up the song again. I love when he plays for me, the peace of him getting lost in the music making my eyes cloud from happy tears. Longing grows inside of me as an image of him teaching our kids to play the piano one day hits me. I want to enjoy every memory with this man before his illness steals bits and pieces from him. Every kiss, every tender moment, every fight we have.

A large piece of blue paper spread across the music rack catches my eye.

I lean in closer. "What's this?" I grab my phone from my pocket and turn on the flashlight.

"Keep looking."

I flip past the first page of a basic sketch of land. A note at the bottom mentions how the architect needs to include a bowling alley, a movie theater, and a closet with extra space for heels and shoes.

The next page makes me smile. It's a sketch of the exterior with a patio, firepit, hanging string lights, a pool with a slide and a lazy river, and the layout for a mini-golf course.

The final sketch has water pooling in my eyes. I trace a finger over the colorful drawing of the coolest tree house, with a sign hanging in front labeled *The Kingston Kiddos*.

I can't hide the happy tears falling down my face as I remember Jax and me discussing what a future house would look like. He listened to every single idea and had someone draw it up to match our vision.

I wrap my arms and legs around Jax, forcing him to stop playing the song.

His arms squeeze me into him. "I take it you like the plans

then?"

"Like them? I *love* them!" I pull his lips to mine, leaving behind a searing kiss. My toes curl into my sneakers as he kisses me senseless, his hands leaving behind a path of warmth wherever they linger.

He points to a massive window across the room. "The tree house can go over there." He forces us to face another window, facing the vast forest. "And the pool and firepit over there, next to the course."

"Are we going to live here? For real?"

"Not only us."

I tilt my head at him. "Oh really."

"No treehouse is complete without kids." He smirks.

I kiss him again. The way his eyes brighten at the idea of kids fills my heart to capacity. There's not a doubt in my mind that this man will go above and beyond to make his kids feel every ounce of love he has in him. I should know, seeing as I've been on the receiving end of it for months.

Jax leans his forehead against mine. "I love you. I love you so much that I want to keep you all to myself. But the bigger part of my heart wants to spread your love to kids who need it. To *our* kids one day. It definitely doesn't have to be now, but I want you to know my intentions. You deserve it all and I want to be the one to make it come true."

A wave of adoration rushes through me. "I love you. Every single thing about you."

"Great. Now for the second part of tonight."

I lift a brow. "There's more?"

"Of course. Now that the romancing is over, I'm here to show you the second reason for the piano." Jax leaves a soft kiss by the corner of my lips.

"Hmm. Tell me more."

"I've been dreaming of fucking you against one for months. Now's my chance."

I laugh into the night sky.

"Well, Jax Kingston, what have you been waiting for?"

"You. Always you."

A warmth spreads through my body as Jax shows me exactly how much he loves me. Our story won't be easy, but it's real. Jax wasn't the only one who needed rescuing. While he was fighting his future, I was battling my past. But together, we don't need to fight alone.

We are stronger than a diagnosis or fear itself.

But most of all, we are stronger together than we are apart.

EXTENDED EPILOGUE

THREE YEARS LATER

Elena

"**H**ow long does a C-section usually last?" I brush my sweaty palms down my dress.

"Fuck if I know. Maybe we should google it?" Jax bounces his knee up and down. The German hospital's waiting room is filled with Liam's family, our friends, and Sophie's dad who happens to be my boss.

"About 45 minutes." Lukas, Liam's lookalike and older brother, replies as he paces the small space.

Jax looks down at his watch. "We still have thirty minutes."

I can tell he's anxious, but I don't know why. "Want to take a walk?"

Jax nods. We both exit the waiting room and walk down the halls together. He remains silent for a few minutes until he freezes.

"Are you sure about not wanting to have kids of your own?" he blurts out.

I take a step back. "Why are you asking me that?"

"Because both Maya and Sophie have already gotten pregnant, and you never bring it up." He runs a shaky hand through his hair.

"I haven't thought about it much." Lie. I can't stop thinking about it lately, especially after Sophie's baby shower.

"Be honest with me."

I ignore him and keep walking, not wanting to meet his eyes.

He grunts. "Don't treat me like I'm some fragile china set." His assumption can't be further from the truth.

We turn around the next corner, and I stop again. A glass window reveals a few babies in small plastic containers, wrapped in blue or pink blankets.

I place my hand against the glass and take a deep breath. "I know you're not fragile."

"Then what's stopping you from wanting a baby?"

"It's not about you. It's me." My words hang between us.

"What do you mean?" He stands next to me, staring at the babies as well.

The truth escapes me before I have a chance to stop myself. "I'm afraid of not being enough for them."

Jax wraps his arms around me and tucks my head under his chin. "You'll always be enough. Any child would be lucky to have you as their mum."

"I'm afraid of doing it on my own. I miss my parents, and I don't have any family to help me. And I'm afraid if something happens. What if I lose them, too?" My voice cracks.

"I can't bring your parents back, but I can share mine with you. And I'll be there to protect you and any child we have. You'll never be alone a day in your whole fucking life, as long as I live. I'll be by your side, raising them to say proper British curse words and teaching them that their mum is the best thing in this world."

My chest shakes from laughing. His arms give me another squeeze before letting me go. My eyes stray back toward the babies in their beds. One child sticks out to me, with only his weight and height written on the card. He sucks his tiny thumb and stares at us with big brown eyes.

"Why do you think he doesn't have a name?"

"The poor baby was abandoned at a local church. No one has named him yet." A new voice sounds from behind us. A nurse smiles and wheels a cart of baby supplies through the hall.

"He doesn't have any parents?" I can't take my eyes off the child, snuggled in his blanket, his tan, pudgy face looking sinfully cute.

"Not that we know of. And I honestly doubt they'll find them. Based on the condition they found the child, he's better off being adopted anyway."

Abandoned. Alone. Better off adopted.

It's like the light bulb shines between Jax and me.

"Are you thinking what I'm thinking?" I whisper, tracing the outline of the baby's face with my finger.

"That's our fucking child and we won't have it any other way."

Jax places his palm over mine, trapping it against the glass. Our child looks at us with the sweetest brown eyes I want to get lost in. His entrance into the world was anything but loving, but with Jax by my side, we plan on loving that baby with everything in us.

And together, the three of us create our very first snow-globe moment as a family.

THANK YOU!

If you enjoyed WRECKED, please consider leaving a review! Support from readers like you means so much to me and helps other readers find books.

Join my Bandini Babes Facebook group for all the grid gossip about the Bandini and McCoy racers.

SCAN THE CODE TO JOIN THE GROUP

ALSO BY LAUREN ASHER

Throttled

Read Noah and Maya's forbidden romance.

Collided

The Dirty Air series continues with
Sophie and Liam's story.

Redeemed

if you like fake relationship romances with a grumpy hero,
check out Santi's story.

SCAN THE CODE TO READ THE BOOKS

ACKNOWLEDGMENTS

To my mom—You might call me your sunshine, but you're mine, too.

To Julie—Thank you for always helping me make every book better. Whether it's the content, the promo before release, or listening to my rambles, you are the best support, and I'm lucky to have you as a friend!

To Mary and Val at Books and Moods – I love you guys and all the content you create! Thank you, Mary, for teaching me how to pull my social media aesthetic together while also supplying me with endless laughs. You're such a fun friend, and I appreciate you. Val, I'll get to that book one day, don't you worry.

To Erica—You're the best editor! I couldn't make these projects come to life without you. Somehow you always have a way of knowing what needs to be done or fixed. Please teach me how to remember tiny details like you do because it is a talent.

To my beta readers—Thank you! Without your individual talents, Wrecked wouldn't be what it is today. You are all so special to me, and I can't express with enough words how much I appreciate you taking the time to push me to do better. Each of you gave me feedback that helped make this book come to life!

To the real F1 drivers—You don't know I exist, but I will thank you anyways. Your endurance, fearlessness, and dedication to the sport inspire me to continue writing about characters I think would compete against you.

CPSIA information can be obtained
at www.ICGtesting.com
Printed in the USA
LVHW081420200822
726395LV00015B/350